CITY OF THE IRON FISH

CITY OF THE IRON FISH

SIMON INGS

The right of Simon Ings to be identified as the author
of this work has been asserted by him in accordance with
the Copyright, Designs and Patents Act 1988.

This edition first published in Great Britain in 2014
by Gollancz
An imprint of the Orion Publishing Group
Orion House, 5 Upper St Martin's Lane, London WC2H 9EA
An Hachette UK Company

1 3 5 7 9 10 8 6 4 2

A CIP catalogue record for this book
is available from the British Library

ISBN 978 0 575 13089 0

Typeset by Deltatype Ltd, Birkenhead, Merseyside

Printed in Great Britain by Clays Ltd, St Ives plc

The Orion Publishing Group's policy is to use papers that
are natural, renewable and recyclable products and made
from wood grown in sustainable forests. The logging and
manufacturing processes are expected to conform to the
environmental regulations of the country of origin.

www.simonings.com
www.orionbooks.co.uk
www.gollancz.co.uk

For my mother

By words, this is it seems the idea, we are handed over to the tender mercies of the Past. That is that parasitic no-longer-with-us class of has-beens, he cleverly calls it. In other words the dead.

Wyndham Lewis *The Apes of God*

PART ONE

1

'Why must we feed the gulls?'

'Put your coat on, child,' said my mother, from the shadows of the hall. It was not yet dawn. The morning was damp and chill and uninviting. I belonged in bed. I moved away from the door, and slipped further into my father's study. He was bent over his desk, a book open before him. He had little need of sleep. I wondered if he had been to bed at all.

'But why must we feed them?' I insisted. 'Why do they need us?'

My father turned to me, amused by my naïve attempt to disguise reluctance with such a burst of curiosity. He said, 'There are a great many inventions in the world. The gulls are but one invention.'

'Why—?'

'They cannot feed themselves. They are an invention. They have no native wit.'

I shrugged. 'So?'

'If we did not feed them,' said my father, 'they would die.'

I scowled: would that be so great a loss? Nasty, ugly grey birds …

My father read my expression. 'They are our invention, and we have a responsibility towards them.'

I shuddered. It seemed an abomination: how could any living thing lack wit enough to feed itself? 'Why did we make them like that? Why didn't we make them better?'

My father sighed. 'The process by which they were made – I mean, we couldn't …'

From the hall my mother shouted: 'Get your coat on!'

'I'll explain it to you later,' he promised me. 'These are complicated matters. Now go with your mother.'

'Come on, child,' my mother echoed. Her boots clacked on the hall parquet.

The City, our home, lay far inland, at the centre of a great desert. It was built on two hills. A sheer cleft divided these hills from east to west, and along its bottom ran a contiguous band of black stone, polished to a high sheen – a river of marble. The City was old, and people said that its magic had faded. Nonetheless, it fascinated me: it seemed capable of anything.

Our walk took us over the road bridge joining the two hills of the City. At its mid-point it arched several hundreds of feet above the marble river: here we stood, unmoving, with baited breath, facing east, scant minutes before the break of dawn.

Such an hour! Cool. Moonless: starlight edged my mother's coat with silver and turned her breath to ectoplasm. My reluctance evaporated, as we stood and took in all the lights of the City: the gas lamps of the upper slopes and the firebrands of the lower terraces. I searched for patterns, and my mother pointed, marking out for me with her delicate gloved hand the boroughs of the City—

That dark swathe on the flank of the Southern Hill? A cliff face, and above it lie the vertiginous streets of the Baixa, famed for their whores and their seafood! That luminescent smudge, pulsing softly at the foot of the Northern Hill? 'The Circus of Birds: the feathers of a thousand grey gulls reflect the gas-light there.'

So many patterns: firebrands and gas lamps, grids and curlicues, thoroughfares real and imagined. We gave up our game at last and stared at the reflection of all this richness in the polished marble below. The reflections gave a sense of dazzling immensity to the view. 'As if there were no bottom to this place—' my mother whispered; her poetry was a secret gift she shared with me alone

2

'—and this fine city were floating in space, an isle of humanity cast by an unseen hand upon the void …'

Her beautiful, half-understood words echoed in my mind like the fall of distant waters.

At length the stars went out. The horizon took on an indeterminate colour, somewhere between black and blue and green. The light swelled rapidly. In it a structure formed, a black lattice silhouetted against the dawn: the rail bridge. Twin to the bridge on which we stood, it too spanned the crevasse between the Northern and Southern Hills. Below and beyond it, the roofs of docks and warehouses coagulated from out the morning mist. The temperature fell. There was a moment of unutterable stillness – I smelled the breeze before I felt it: salt and kelp. Rotten and refreshing and delicate, it weaved up mistily from the City's lower terraces.

Mother led me across the bridge to the Northern Hill. From here we ascended winding brick-paved streets, to the gardens which lie at the summit of the Baixa. There was an artificial lake here: Quiet Lake, frequented by strange birds.

My mother stroked my neck. Her woollen gloves scratched my skin; I shivered.

'Don't be afraid,' my mother said. 'Feed them. They're hungry.'

The gulls looked at me with big round greedy eyes. They walked very slowly back and forth over the dusty gravel, as if they were thinking of something strange and huge, something that escaped definition.

When we had fed them, we walked hand in hand up to a high point: a promontory from which we could look across the great rift between the North and South hills and watch the trams trundle this way and that over the road bridge. 'Look!' said my mother. 'Do you see the flower cart? Do you see it? Look, it's scattering flowers on the road.' I squinted at the bridge, and noticed a tiny figure, naked, perching on the parapet at its middle point. I gasped. My mother spotted the figure too late to shield my eyes—

The man dived from the bridge.

I gripped my mother's hand so tight she gasped with pain. The man's descent was surprisingly swift and soon he was lost to sight.

3

Mother and I returned home. Father was in his study still, poring over a book. My mother, pressing her finger to her lips for silence, motioned for me to stand outside: she went in and closed the door after her. I heard a murmured conversation. Footsteps. My father opened the door. He looked pale, and stared at me abstractedly, as if he did not know who I was. He said, 'You have seen a strange sight.'

I said, 'He will be all right, won't he?'

My father was silent.

'Won't he?'

My mother came up and nudged my father in the back. 'Ah,' he said. 'Ah yes. Indeed.' He gave me a big, false smile. 'Come into the kitchen,' he said. He led us into the back of the house.

A bright patch of late morning sunlight shone upon the brick floor of the kitchen. Flecks of mica in the peach-coloured brick danced in my eyes. I crossed to the patch of light, and looked out the window. Josey, our maid, had climbed a few feet up the trellis where the sweet peas grew and was leaning over the garden wall: flirting, no doubt, with next door's chauffeur.

Mother came up behind me, reached past me and swung the window open. 'Mrs Hugg!'

Josey swung around wildly and fell from the trellis into a bed of petunias. 'Silly tart,' my mother muttered; she took my shoulder and turned me to face the room. My father sat at the head of the kitchen table, his hands splayed upon the bare wood. 'Be seated,' he said, with gentle authority.

Mother and I sat beside him on opposite sides of the table. He said, 'In view of the things Tom has seen, and interpreting them as we must, I believe it will be necessary for us to perform certain observances.'

My mother stirred uneasily. She disliked arcane procedures; she felt that they undermined the modern comforts of her life. I, on the other hand, leaned forward towards my father, eager to hear what these exciting observances might be.

'First,' said my father, 'we shall wear nothing but blue for the next six days.'

My mother sighed. Blue was her least favourite colour, and yet so many of these observances were associated with it – the symbolic colour of the absent yet ubiquitous sea.

'For the six days following,' my father went on, 'we shall wear nothing but yellow.'

It was my heart's turn to sink: I knew from afternoons at the wash-tub listening to Josey's prattling that yellow dyes take most easily, and were therefore used on the cheapest, roughest cloth.

'Throughout this time,' my father continued, 'we shall refrain from eating plaice.' He smiled, then – a self-satisfied sort of smile – made the sign of the circle over his breast, and stood up from the table.

Even then, such rituals had been largely forgotten; people looked askance at us when we performed them.

Far from being embarrassed, however, I took snobbish pride in my father's strictures: and though that month I was much teased for my yellow sack-cloths, I was priggishly pleased that they marked me out from my schoolfellows: indeed, I promised myself that when I was older I would continue to obey such observances.

The next day, my father tried to explain to me about the gulls, and about the other strange and contradictory inventions upon which the City was founded.

He began by taking me by tram across the road bridge to the Northern Hill. We descended from the tram at Central Station and walked under glowering rain-clouds towards that triangle of waste ground which slopes up to the Sé. The downpour began the moment we reached the foot of the hill. My father swung a fold of his blue cloak around me so that I might be protected from the rain, and led me up the right-hand side of the triangle, where a steep lane wound round the bluffs and spurs, shielded by a terrace of dingy and defeated properties. The rain had begun to ease by the time we reached the Sé. We waited in the shadows of the Southern portico, and watched the clouds dissipate at last, under the fierce glare of a mid-morning sun.

'This,' my father explained, 'is where the Ceremonies begin. The procession winds down Green Monkey Street, gathering subsidiary processions from east and west, and comes to rest at last, after many ritual stops and starts, at the Circus of Birds.'

He was speaking of the Ceremonies of Stuffing and Hanging; they were the central ritual of our city, and took place once every twenty years. The next festival was only six months away.

We set off down Green Monkey Street, with mincing steps, lest we slip on the rain-silvered pavement. 'Of course,' my father confided, 'the coming festival will be only the third one I've attended. The Ceremonies of Hanging and Stuffing take place so rarely, it is unheard of for people to witness more than four in their lifetime, though of course, people tell tales ...'

It was a commonplace exaggeration when describing an aged person to say that they had 'seen five fish'.

'It's now, when the preparations for the Ceremonies are once more under way, that those tatty old books I've been collecting demonstrate their true value,' my father explained, with pride. 'Without such works, no-one would remember what form the Ceremonies should take; and without the correct observances—' he shuddered '—heaven knows what would become of us.'

I waited for some explanation, but none came. 'Really?' I said, to prompt him: but he only nodded, and frowned ominously, lost in some private rumination.

'What would happen?' I insisted.

'Depends,' he muttered, still off in some place of his own.

'On what?'

He shook himself. 'Beg pardon?'

I shrugged: my face, mask-like, hid a sudden flood of resentment. As usual, my father was talking more to himself than to me.

I was immature still: I did not know how to deflect my hurt onto others: instead I stored it up inside, charged it up like a corroded battery, labelled the battery: 'Father'. I was young, and I loved him. I admired his powers of concentration, his upright frame, the precision of his movements, his clockwork habits. Boys adore machines; so I adored him. I wanted to be like him. I wanted to read his books, and perform his observances; these, I knew, were the keys to his heart. It never occurred to me that he had bolted his heart from the inside, that he didn't want to teach me; that, though I wished to follow, he did not care to lead.

As we walked, he drew my attention to the street's various furnishings: insignificant objects, which only came into their own during the Ceremonies. 'You see those large brass hooks, above the lintels of the houses, either side of us? Close to, you can see that they have grotesque faces moulded into them. They are very old, very carefully tended. All the bunting is attached to them. It is very bad luck to secure it to anything else. You see how there are little ledges mounted on the window sills here? That is so the fruit and flowers and rag dolls placed here for the ceremony do not plummet onto the revellers beneath. Those poles mounted in the street? When the parade begins, barrels of raw wine are set beside them and a flag of gold cloth is run up the pole. And there …'

I covered my mouth with my hand and yawned. The street was long, my father lost in a world of his own: my eagerness to learn notwithstanding, I was bored.

This was of course a special time for him. As the son of bargee, he had been refused admittance to the Academy. Now, many years later, the Academicians were having to consult with him. In their search for details about the forthcoming Ceremonies, they were having to peruse with him – and in a more or less comradely spirit – all those various manuals he had rescued from depositories and junk shops. Such gentle vengeance gave him great pleasure—

'And here,' he exclaimed, 'lies the Circus of Birds!'

I reawoke, and looked around me. The wide road down which we had come had opened out like a funnel into a roughly circular space surrounded on all sides by spare and dirty tenements, six or seven storeys high. At the centre of the Circus stood a huge pig-iron gantry, all lattices and chains and pipes. The stone beneath this gantry was scooped into a shallow and rainwater-filled basin, stained brown with rust.

My father made a wide gesture, taking in the whole draughty space. 'This is where the Ceremonies take place.'

I looked around me. 'Father,' I said, 'why are all the buildings boarded up?'

He looked around at the decrepit tenements, the boards in the windows scribbled over with sooty graffiti by a desperate hand, the gutters everywhere stuffed with sodden papers and vegetable matter. 'It is unsettling to live here,' he replied at last, subdued by our surroundings. 'This is the epicentre of our City's mutability.'

I blinked up at him.

'I mean,' he said, conscious that his enthusiasm had run away with his vocabulary, 'that this square is a ghostly place: the mutagenic forces released here during the Ceremonies linger, trapped in the very fabric of the buildings: shadows, strange sounds, inexplicable occurrences, small but unnerving ...' He looked at me: his mouth twitched in irritation. He did not know how to talk to children.

He took me by the arm and led me up to the scaffold. It looked as though it had been constructed by a party of madmen let loose in a railway yard. It towered above me, terrible and absurd in its purposeless complexity – chains, funnels, valves and curlicues of ribboned metal. The structure rested upon three massive iron legs, arranged in a tripod. I reached out and touched the leg nearest me. The whole structure seemed to vibrate under my fingers. I snatched my hand away. Droplets of rain water fell from the higher parts of the structure: a light drizzle, filling the shallow stone basin beneath the scaffold. With a start, I realized that the basin was no deliberate structure; rather, it had been chiselled by the water itself, caught and funnelled and concentrated upon this patch of stone by the many strange spigots and gutters and dishes welded to the scaffold.

How long would it have taken, I wondered, for these few drops of water to carve out the basin? It chilled me, to think how old this place – this very scaffold – must be.

'And this,' my father said, pointing to the top of the scaffold, 'is where we hang the Fish!'

2

Father had explained much to me that day, but he was a half-hearted teacher, and none of what he said really added up. Though I knew he might think me ungrateful for saying so, I explained my confusion to him. Out of the blue he said, 'If you want to know more, it's time you began reading my books.'

My heart leapt: I was to be initiated.

Father's study was not one of those mahogany-lined talking-pieces – those confections ill-learned men furnish in baize and brass to impress their equally ill-learned friends – but a study in truth: a workshop of the intellect. Books and papers lay stacked about his desk in orderly rows. Wire trays held abstracts and borrowed manuscripts, lists of enquiries, bookshops's bills and learned correspondence. There was something fetishistic about this clutter and business with which my father surrounded himself: it was not, I think, altogether necessary to his studies; rather, the show of it pleased him. But I am not inclined to blame him for his vanity: he worked alone, without the approbation of colleague or mentor; and he was entitled to his foibles if they lent meaning to his life.

From a high shelf, he took down a heavy volume and set it before me on the hearth rug.

'Go on,' he said, seeing me hesitate. 'It won't bite.'

I opened it up—

'Mind the spine.'

I winced, closed the book; then opened it again, more gently, and held the cover at an angle so as not to strain the binding.

'Better,' he muttered.

I reached the title page:

A Companion to Mutagenic Poesy

'Father,' I said, 'what does "mutagenic" mean?' He was sat at his desk already, working. 'Father?'

He glanced away from his book. 'Eh?'

'What does—'

'What? Does what?'

I took a deep breath. 'There's a word I don't understand.'

'In the corner: dictionary.' He turned back to his book, leaned forward, grew still again.

I stood up, went to the shelf he had pointed to, took up the dictionary, opened it. The marks on the page were incomprehensible. 'Father?'

He sat staring at the papers on his desk, but I could see he was not reading them. He was waiting – quite still, with the patience of a cornered mouse – waiting for me to be quiet. To give up. To go away.

'Please—'

'*What?*'

I felt helpless, and stupid: I don't understand the script.'

'Oh, that,' he muttered. He paused a moment, summoning up the strength to speak to me: 'It's how our forefathers wrote: clear enough if you practice it.'

'Can you—'

'For God's sake,' my father exclaimed, with sudden fury, 'I'm in the middle of a translation. Can't you at least make a stab at it on your own?'

I murmured an apology. He waved it away and turned back to his books and papers.

Unable to decipher the dictionary, I went back to *Mutagenic Poesy* and contented myself with the illustrations: drawings and water-colours behind translucent protective papers, cataloguing with skill and rigour the thousands of elements which go to make up the Iron Fish. When I was done, I turned back to the text and did my best to understand …

The *Fesh* is bigged according to strict & arcane Principles, by a Woman taken up at Puberty by the *College* of *Makers* – it being a secretive Sect of talented *Females* – and inducted to the Mysteries of *Smith & Engraver*.

Two Years before the *Ceremonies of Stuffing & Hanging*, the *Fesh* is begun with the carving of a fine Skeleton of fire-hardened Mahogany. The Initiate rivets to the Frame a Latticework of Burnished Copper, plated with Lead to forestall Corrosion. To the Frame she applies molten Scales of Iron and when the *Fesh* is cool she engraves upon each Scale the *intricate swirling Details* required of her by the Foremothers.

Each Scale – & some Nine Hundred & Forty-Seven Scales

make up the *Feshes* Skin – is designed in accordance with an unique Rule, each Rule possessing its own *History,* its own unique Matrix of *Stricture & Expectation* – its own '*Meter*'.

(Indeed, it is often said that in the Fashioning of the *Fesh,* the Engraver's Art approaches the condition of *Poetry.* Some observers – both Poets & Smiths – have suggested that – *au contraire* – the City's fine Tradition of Poetry has been drawn from the Techniques of *Engraving,* which seems to this author a very *pretentious* Assertion.)

This, then, is the *Iron Fesh:* intricate, elegant, eccentric – &, for the present moment, powerless: a firing mechanism without powder. For the *Fesh,* it will be minded, is *nothing of itself,* but rather it is the *Vessel* or *Womb* which potentiates the Contents placed inside it during the *Ceremonies of Stuffing & Hanging—*

'But they were only details, Father,' I complained, as he wished me goodnight. 'I want to know why things happen.'

He sighed, tucked me into bed, pressed his lips to my forehead, then sat with me for a while, rattling his brains for some reply a young boy might understand.

'There is, you know, no end to the number of times one can ask "why" something is the way it is.'

'I'm sorry,' I said.

But he went on: 'Our city is a place of invention. It is reinvented every twenty years, by our Iron Fish. That is how things are. True, not everyone is satisfied by that. It seems to some people that the arrangement is somehow insufficient: that the world should not need to be reinvented; that it should be given to us whole. They point to the legends which say the world was once a given thing, a thing that sustained itself and did not need us to reinvent it. They resent the fact that now we do have to keep reinventing it, moment by moment, ritual after cumbersome ritual. They search the City for signs of their "given world" and if by these means they find nothing—'

'Then,' I said, intuiting a new link between the lessons of that day and the incident which had inspired them, 'they do what that gentleman did – on the bridge?'

11

'Yes,' my father replied, thinly. 'They do as you saw that man do. They jump – from the bridge.' He looked away from me. 'It's traditional.'

I nodded, sagely. I did not see – I did not see at all – but I was content to know that the man I had seen plummet from the bridge was, after all, simply performing one of my father's prized 'observances'. This was enough to make the incident seem less frightening. 'So he's all right, then.'

'What?' my father exclaimed.

'So he's all right – the man who jumped.'

'Oh.' He sucked his upper lip, searching for the right words. 'Quite. He – I am sure he's happier now than he was.'

'Good!' I exclaimed, my mind put to rest.

'Now, try to sleep,' said my father, brusquely, 'or you'll be late for school tomorrow.'

That night I dreamed romantic dreams – heady fantasies in which I spent my time probing the secrets of the City. With each pronouncement of the word 'why?', one gauzy veil after another was lifted from my sight, revealing a world ever brighter and more magical. I imagined myself standing naked on the parapet of the bridge, laughing and joking with the man I had seen jump the day before, readying myself for my own leap. I dreamed that we were adventurers in that land of the final 'why', leaping with pride into the unknown mysteries of our time … I awoke with a start, exhilarated and happy. I dressed and waited impatiently for breakfast time. I wanted to tell my friends at school what I had seen and learned; most of all I wanted to tell them about the man on the bridge, the brave diver, and how one day I would follow him on his ambitious descent.

Circumstances, however, conspired to upstage me: I arrived at school to learn that my 'brave diver' was the father of a new boy, one Boris Stock. He was not, furthermore, in any sense 'all right' after his jump: upon contact with the impermeable black river his head had shattered like an eggshell, spraying brain matter all over the marble.

Gruesome details of Stock *père*'s messy suicide flew about the school for days. Such bloody and horrible reports confused me: I, who knew so much about ritual, as yet knew nothing about life.

One evening, about a fortnight before the Ceremonies of Stuffing and Hanging, my father returned home with a stranger: from my room, where I was reading, I heard a woman's voice.

I straightened my clothes, ran my fingers through my hair, opened the door and ran down the stairs to the hall. Next to my parents stood a middle-aged woman. She wore tight leather trousers and a cloak of black hessian. Over her shoulder she carried a thick belt to which were clipped a water bottle, a bundle of clothes, and a leather satchel: she was a gypsy.

I completed my descent of the stairs. My father looked me over, nodded curt approval. 'This is my son,' he said.

The gypsy nodded and smiled. She was very self-confident. She looked perfectly at ease. She approached me. We shook hands. Her grip was firm. Her accent was strong and awkward-sounding: 'My name is Lilith,' she said.

Thomas,' I murmured, intimidated by her foreignness. My father explained: 'Lilith has returned to our city with maps of the surrounding countryside. It seems there are new places suited to the growing of vines. She wishes to sell her maps to our Association, and the Association wishes to offer her every comfort while the deal is struck. I have offered her our humble hospitality – with your sanction, as always, dear wife.' My mother curtsied, and disappeared into the kitchen to speak to Josey.

I ate little of the evening meal. I was fascinated by Lilith. A gypsy – an explorer! But why, I asked her, did she explore only the surroundings of our city – why did she not explore some other part of the world?

An abrupt and embarrassed silence descended. Lilith merely smiled and shook her head. My mother said, 'You will understand these things when you grow up, Thomas.'

But a while later my father, always eager for new information and insight, took up my lead and questioned the gypsy closely about her work, her beginnings, and her beliefs.

'I left the City,' said Lilith, 'when I was a child, to explore the world. The City had begun to feel too cramped, too little; I was a wild youngster and I had run out of places to explore. I left on the night of my thirteenth birthday. I was an orphan child – my parents died in a fire when I was eleven – and I don't suppose my disappearance troubled the seminary for very long.'

'Where did you go?'

'I worked for a time in the vineyards of the City, picking the grapes when that was the season, tending the vines – and in the winter months, other things.' A faint blush coloured her cheeks – I admired its prettiness. 'Soon, that life began to pall, and I began to hear of the gypsies who wander the wastes beyond the City's boundaries. As soon as I heard about them, I wanted to join them. I earned myself enough for a wagon and supplies and set out into the scrub.'

'What did you find?' I asked her.

She looked at me and smiled indulgently. 'Nothing,' she replied.

'Nothing?' A lame way indeed to end a story.

'Nothing,' she affirmed. 'What they teach you in school is quite true, I'm afraid – there is nothing beyond the City. No other cities, no roads, no people.' Her gaze held me. 'Nothing exists beyond the hills.'

How depressing it was, to have this romantic-seeming woman merely confirm my lessons. 'But the world,' I complained, 'the forests and the jungles and the snows—'

My mother laughed indulgently. 'Tom, you really are rather old to believe such tales.'

My father came unexpectedly to my defence. 'You have to admit,' he said, 'as tales go, they do tend to cling to one. Such wonderful notions! Oceans and ice-caps and foreign peoples …'

'Gypsies,' Lilith said to me, 'believe there were such places, once, but that we lost them.' Her voice was soft and unutterably sad. 'Lost them long ago. That is why gypsies search the borders of our bubble for a way back to the greater world – the world the legends say once was given to us, and which we have lost.'

'And have any of you – any gypsies, I mean – seen this "given world"?'

Lilith shook her head. 'Not a glimpse,' she said. Her voice was flat and dead and sure. 'Not one.'

3

'You know,' said my mother, as she tucked me into bed, 'those stories of a world bigger and better than this one – they're only stories.'

'I know,' I yawned.

'Good night, then,' said my mother; she kissed me on the forehead.

'Do try and get some sleep, now.'

I tried, but I could not.

It seemed to me that life in our lonely little city was unfairly restricted. Everyone knew it; but to make things bearable, no-one ever admitted it.

It seemed to me then that there were only two means of escape from our world – that 'little bubble', as Lilith called it. The first was despair – the ritual futility of Mr Stock's plunge from the bridge. The second was to search the borderlands for a physical way out: a door, a road, a bridge. This, obviously, was the more attractive response. But Lilith's failure to find any door into the given world – and the reported failure of all her kind – distressed me.

'If this is how you feel,' my father said to me, when I described to him these feelings, 'then perhaps my books will be able to help.'

The rituals his books described were invented, he told me, to make the world more bearable. 'They are curative,' he said: 'medicines for the uneasy soul, for the easily dissatisfied mind.'

On another occasion he said, 'You are young to have these doubts about the world.' He looked at me as though he were peering down at me from the mouth of a deep well. 'There is something special about your impatience and curiosity, something precocious, to be sure. But also something – not quite healthy.'

He spoke as though he were reading the future in my eyes, as old women at fairs read your fate from your palm.

He clicked his tongue, broke off his mesmerized stare, and went to his bookshelves. I stood watching as he rifled among his dusty, damaged, beloved books. 'No need to stand there gawping,' he said to me at last, irritated. 'This will take me most of the evening.'

In fact, it took him an entire day to find an observance appropriate to my malaise. In all this time he barely spoke to us, and left the running of the house all to my long-suffering mother and her maid – 'Business as usual, then,' Josey muttered in that low, conspiratorial tone meant for me alone.

'Here,' he said, the next evening in his study: he handed me a chap-book, so large and awkward I could barely handle it without risking its precious spine. Finally I got it steady under my hand and studied the page my father had marked. I blanched. 'A doll?'

He waved his hands at me, fussily. 'Read it, read it.'

The print was uneven and blotchy, the typeface cut by hand. It was illuminated throughout with colour plates and these, I realized with a start, were hand-coloured, with a sumptuousness that nobody bothered with these days. A design in gold leaf wove round the opening letter of each page. The pages were thick and soft, their edges ragged and furry. The book was laid out like a cook book, with a plate illustrating the ritual on one page, and instructions on how to perform it opposite. The book was open at a page headed thus:

Through THIS the Sufficiency of the World is Made Manifest to its Troubled Denizens

The book, being ancient, employed an arcane lettering system, with B's like G's and S's like F's without the cross-piece, but soon enough the page came clear: I was to make a doll, dress it in grey skirts and a woollen bobble-hat (I could tell already that this was one observance I would not be telling my school-friends about); next, I was to secrete this votive figure in the crux of two massive suspension ties, high up among the girders and beams of the road bridge—

I swallowed hard: *the bridge!* A smooth and level roadway,

gliding off into space as though it did not need banks at all; and might spin itself out to infinite length by the mere elegance of its engineering, the mathematical beauty of its taper, the spider-fine mesh of structural tubes and suspension ties which underlay it—

To climb the bridge – to ascend that recursive swirl of steel hawser and iron girder and crawl at last along those narrow, dirty I-girders barely four feet beneath the surface of the roadway itself, all the time the structure shuddering like a live thing under every cart or tram – to a mid-point some two hundred feet above the marble river—

'For the sake of a doll?'

'Not for its sake,' my father replied, testily: 'for yours.'

I could hardly tell him that I was afraid, now that he had spent a day searching out this observance for me. I kept my peace, and took the book upstairs to copy – with some foreboding – my instructions.

Climbing the cat's-cradle ironwork of the bridge was, after all, not so hard.

The higher I climbed, the more I came to trust my common sense and the instinctive movements of my body. Somehow the notion of plunging two hundred feet is far less frightening than the fear of falling twenty, so after a while the ground no longer frightened me – indeed, the sight of the marble river with its barges and yachts exhilarated far more than it threatened.

I clambered easily up the latticed braces. Either side of me rose structural tubes twenty feet in diameter; rusty and smeared, they curved under the immense weight of the bridge like the wind-warped trunks of great iron trees.

I reached a point some fifty feet beneath the road surface of the bridge, and rested there a while, curled around an old suspension tie, and listened to the rumble of traffic above my head, the distant creak and hiss of the barges as they heaved across the great marble river, the wind in the workings of the bridge itself ...

I had waited to perform my observance until the eve of the Ceremonies of Stuffing and Hanging, so as to be out of the way of all that jollity and enthusiasm: the wide streets about our house

17

cluttered with paint-pots and glue and papier mâché, banners and flags and women stitching, floats and decorations, wagons dismantled and the panelling strewn about under paper flowers and glutinous green varnish, gurgling infants half-naked and barbarously painted trying on costumes of wire and bamboo and cotton feathers and little foil disks with bird's eyes painted upon them, and all the other paraphernalia of the coming parade. My father understood, I think, my desire to escape all that; he gave my climb his blessing. 'You will see much from there,' he said to me. 'You will catch glimpses across the whole City of the preparations we are making for these great Ceremonies.' It was the nearest he came to criticizing me for my aloofness.

My mother was less sanguine. 'You'll regret this,' she warned me. 'It'll never come round again for you, this ceremony, not until you are an old man and not fit to enjoy it.'

'I'll be thirty-two,' I replied with dignity; 'that's barely half father's age, and I don't hear you calling him old – least, not to his face.' A clip round the ear was my mother's sufficient response. I was not well-disposed to my mother that day: the night before she had satirized the doll I had sewn and got my fingers all bloody for, and while tucking me into bed that night had murmured repeatedly – and in a tone of pervasive hysteria – that I was bound to trip and fall to my death in a very little while and what a waste that would be of all the years of care and suffering she had lavished upon me *et cetera, et cetera*. That morning, she had made a point of not seeing me off. My father stood by the door alone, watching me go.

As I turned the corner of the street I waved to him. He did not wave back – he was looking at me again with that strange intensity, as though I were hidden from him down a long, dark shaft ...

Recollecting myself, I stretched and rubbed vigorously at my calves, which had grown stiff after so much unaccustomed exertion, and began working my way along the I-beams towards the bridge's mid-point – and here I received my first check, for the wind that day was not light, and the bridge, being a fine structure, rocked, ever so slightly, with each and every gust. Of course, I was familiar with the sensation – I knew the bridge as well as anyone

– but it is one thing to feel the sway of the bridge with its balus-trades safely about you, quite another to feel it while balanced upon a shelf of metal no more than three feet wide. And where at first I had walked cockily along this makeshift pavement, now I crawled, and with my heart in my mouth.

I reached the junction at last – that meeting point of great iron hawsers. Here the main cables, each thicker than my waist, were tethered to their unimaginable loads. Of the great contest of forces concentrated in these workings there was no sign: I rested my hands upon the very screws and pins, some wider than my outstretched arms could encompass, and my stomach stirred at the thought of the forces running invisibly through them.

When at last these sensations eased, I took from my back pocket that paper I had drawn. My diagram was sloppy and inac-curate, but after much searching I found what I supposed was the correct resting place for my doll: a dirty, oily hole between the gears of two suspension ties. To my disappointment, there was not the slightest remains of any other doll there. No-one else had been here before me. No-one had been here in a very long time. It somehow cheapened the venture for me, to realize how little interest anyone else had in performing it.

I took the doll I had made from the pocket in my breeches. It was a sad, misshapen thing, the calico stained with blood from my pricked fingers, and somehow in the climb the stitching around its head had come adrift and some of the stuffing had edged out of its neck. I poked the stuff in with my thumb, wrapped the doll up in the paper and tucked it into the hole between the gears.

A squawk of trumpets – I would like to use a grander term than 'squawk', but the sound did not deserve it – interrupted my glum reverie. I clambered over the thickly nested machinery and sat down cross-legged on a small gridded iron platform. From here I could look out over the Baixa, whence the sound had come.

As my father had promised me, I had from this height an excellent view of the City's preparations. Flashes of wine-colour showed between the tenements as the Baixa's men folk, dressed in robes made from old velveteen curtains, awesome in veiled head-pieces six feet high made of balsa and paper dyed with beetroot.

Once more they lifted their cornets to their lips and blew, more tunefully this time. Their clarion mixed strangely on muddling breeze; it sounded old and melancholy, less like music than like the memory of music.

The cliffs beneath the Baixa shimmered strangely; that morning, the girls of the lower terraces had climbed up them, scattering shreds of blue tinsel over the rocks from sacks strapped loosely over their backs. It was a dangerous occupation, for the cliffs were rarely climbed and the stone was soft and loose. It was inevitable that one family or another would be celebrating the next day's Ceremonies at a daughter's graveside; but it was a ritual of attained womanhood among those people, and few resented or feared the challenge this rare celebration presented to them.

(Our maid Josey hailed from this parish and, having narrowly missed the previous ceremonies – she had been eleven at the time, and deemed too young to make the attempt upon the cliff – she was determined, though thirty-one that year and grown fat on her own cooking, that she would take part in the climb. To our amazement, she was among the first to crest into the Baixa, with its cheering women and their hail of stale rice – and to hear her for days afterwards, you would think she was a giddy seventeen-year old, just into her majority.)

Along both banks of the marble river the boatmen and bargees had buried their long-standing feuds and were working together to construct simple wooden workings for bridges. The bridges would not of course be able to span the great river, nor were they meant to. It was not even an object with the men to see how far their structures would reach out over the gleaming stone. It was the simple act of building that first half of arc, that outflung gesture of wooden crosspieces over the embankment wall and over the shore of the marble river, that occupied them. When they were done, these half-constructed things looked less like bridges than the launching places of sea-birds, or perhaps the embodiment of prayers – images of escape, perhaps, the bridge built in this world blending invisibly with the workings of a bridge in the next ... All along the river there were such structures. Some were mere toys, not much higher than a man; others towered twenty or thirty feet above the embankment wall, ornate designs whittled into their planked sides and bedecked with huge foil roses.

Vying for space among the partial bridges stood flagpoles flying proud black pennants. These were the poles that marked out the course for the next day's games of Tack, a complex and fiercely competitive racing game played at all the City's festivals. I saw parties of dapper grey-bearded men in white flannels and blue yachting jackets waving tape measures and thick pocket-books, remonstrating with each other over the positioning of the poles, whether one pole or another should be moved to the left or to the right, what was the regulation height for a pole, and so on and so forth. (Tack is a complex game, and its players and umpires are notoriously litigious.)

Every once in a while a train would rattle out from its lair in the belly of the Northern Hill, halt mid-way across the bridge, belch brightly coloured smoke from out its funnel, and trundle back again. The railwaymen's fireworks and pyrotechnic effects were renowned throughout the City. Each driver had his allotted hour on the bridge, to fuss over his special powders, adding them in various proportions to the coke that fired his engine's boiler. Umpires from among the signalling staff – little figures, waving flags from the glass roof of Central Station 1 – indicated their opinion of each belch of smoke by semaphore. There was a story at school that one pupil's grandfather, a driver of many years' standing, had once had the ingenious notion of packeting his powders together like the skins of an onion, so that his engine belched out regular pulses of red and green smoke, one after the other. Unfortunately, the core of the packet grew so hot in the furnace the entire fusillade exploded, cracking the boiler and spilling the driver off his foot plate and over the side of the bridge. A barge-load of salted popcorn, fortuitously bound for the Circus of Birds, broke that gentleman's fall and saved his life. I affected not to believe a word of this tall tale: nonetheless, I hung on, watching the trains for most of that afternoon, secretly hankering for some disaster to befall a railwayman.

The light waned. Reluctantly, I began my descent. I was in

21

better humour now, and determined to make the most I could of the morrow's Ceremonies.

4

'Tom, wake up. Come see Father on the roof!' I sat up in bed, sweating, tangled with troubled dreams. 'He's on the roof already!'

On the roof? For one heart-stopping moment I thought of Mr Stock, plunging to his death from the bridge. Then I remembered – today was the day of the Ceremonies! I sighed with relief, kicked free of the bed-clothes and padded over to the chair where my clothes were draped.

Father was balanced precariously on the sloping apex of the roof; arms extended, he minced gingerly up to the highest of our three chimney stacks. Strapped to his back by a leather loop was a long stave lacquered orange, topped by a plume of purple and silver tassels. When he reached the chimney, he swung the stick from his shoulder and planted it smartly in the leaden tube affixed to the chimney's side.

Mother and I cheered and applauded. My father smiled, gave a little bow, and slipped on a loose tile. His hands windmilled as he struggled to keep his balance. Mother screamed. His flailing hand at last connected with the pole: thus steadied, he was able to right himself.

Mother called up to him, pale and anxious.

Father laughed weakly and wiped his brow. 'I always wondered what that stick was for.'

In the beginning, my father once explained to me, the inventive powers of the Ceremonies were so great that the whole City was changed. Even before the scraps of poetry escaped between the ribs of the fish – even, indeed, before the sun had set on the Ceremonies themselves – the streets of the City would begin to shift. The usual hills were laid flat, revealing great, half-recognized vistas; elsewhere, great ironstone crags and grassy banks appeared from nowhere, with rivulets coursing down them, and at their foot ran waterways which gave onto canals which gave onto ponds, and with them all sorts of bridges and sluices and tatty terraced houses with overgrown back gardens; staircases and slip-ways would slide in and out of view of the celebrants as they left the Circus; sometimes the Circus itself would disappear only to repeat itself further down the road. You might never find the expected streets, but sometimes one of them would appear of a sudden behind you as you walked. People in those early days tried flagging their houses before the Ceremonies so that afterwards they might find their way home again. Whether the flags worked is not recorded, but the habit of making and planting them stuck, even when, centuries later, the City had grown too complex and well-realized for a single Ceremony to much alter its geography.

'Come inside now,' said my mother, plucking at the clothes I had thrown on. 'It's time we got you properly done up.'

My jacket was bottle-green velvet, rakishly ventilated with all sorts of pleats and tucks and false pockets: it looked like an expensive rag lying there in its tissue, but once it was on and the clasps were fastened, it came into its own, standing out at the shoulders and hips as though it had a life of its own. The day was hot, and I wore only a cotton undershirt beneath my coat; but that too was special in its way, trimmed with broderie anglaise and finely decorated around the buttons in swirls and paisley curlicues done in the finest cream silk.

I was inordinately proud of my trousers: a tartan of black and royal blue edged with gold thread, and fastened at the ankle by elasticated puttees encrusted with little silver bells. I was less sure of the shoes; they had ornate steel treads finely engraved with miniature city scenes, but the polished black leather uppers, being new, cut into the soft parts of my feet and while tottering about the gravel path in front of our house I discovered that the city scenes on the soles were already being rubbed away.

'They are supposed to do that,' said my father, blandly, when I pointed this out to him. I thought it a shame: my mother's toilette

23

was taking so long, by the time we were ready to join the procession there would be nothing left of these enchanting designs.

Father's black silk draperies fanned about his feet like a skirt; he circled serenely around the house, as if on wheels. He tried keeping me amused by pointing to parts of the small but meticulously manicured garden: 'See? The rhododendrons will soon be in bloom. There, by the water-butt.' I stamped my feet about in the gravel impatiently.

'She won't be long,' my father soothed; he came up to me and adjusted my cap of feathers.

'I have to wear it on the slant,' I complained, 'otherwise I can't see out.'

Father took the cap from my head and adjusted its plumage. 'There,' he sighed, handing it back to me. 'Now do stop fretting.'

The front door closed with a bang. We looked round.

How can I adequately describe the vision before us? My mother looked barely human – she had transformed herself into a faery, decked in diaphanous garb from a more frivolous, more decorative realm. Her dress was a marvel of sheer cream tissue and green sequins, the stuff swirled in the most fluid and artless fashion; it was as though a sea had decked her in foam and ocean glints. Gloves with tassels in green giving onto deepest red hung like rich baubles of seaweed from her pale arms. On her head, fluttering boisterously upon this living sea, was a hat in the shape of a boat, and a main-sail stitched with the family crest.

We stood speechless, my father and I; dumbfounded, we did not even smile.

My mother shuffled her feet, embarrassed. 'Well?'

Father snapped out of his reverie first, went straight up to her, took her face in his hands, and gave her such a kiss as I never saw him give her again. He whispered some niceties in her ear too low for me to hear, and she blushed very prettily. It was clear to me that they ought to be alone together, so I turned my back and took a discreet amble round the garden.

My mother's appearance stirred me strangely. I was so used to thinking of her as a pair of rough, useful hands, that to see her as an attractive woman surprised me. At the same time, I felt sorry for her: it was all very well my father making a fuss of her now, while she was all done up in her ritual garb (something that was bound to appeal to him), but at other times his affection rarely showed itself. I sighed (already I was something of a romantic): the look upon her face when he whispered in her ear!

We promenaded in our finery towards the nearest tram stop, some three streets away, meeting often with some neighbour or other, well kitted out (though, I fancied, not quite so properly as we) in one heady concoction or another. Dr Heinrich Schnurre, running a little late as always, waved his marking pole at us from his rooftop – it was tipped with shreds of pink and red velvet – and cried out, jocularly, 'By the end of today, who knows, we might be closer neighbours!' These days, the occasional swap of neighbouring houses was the most the Ceremonies could manage by way of altering the City's geography.

We reached the main road. The tram lines, catching the morning light, dazzled me. They had been newly polished. Overnight teams of boys with wire brushes and heavy leather gloves had inched a painful course along the roads of the City, leaving iridescent trails of burnished steel.

Everyone we knew from our neighbourhood, so it seemed, was waiting for us at the stop: the Jungs in their harlequin's suits, the Kyurkdjiyskis in meticulously finished cardboard armour, the Psmiths, ever aloof, on stilts. A cheer went up as the tram approached. Its livery was freshly polished and the paint work repaired, the driver stiff and proud, and not a little flushed, in his tight-collared navy blue jacket with regulation brass buttons.

The tram was crowded to the point of asphyxiation. Not a few costumes were ruined by the journey that followed, and the stilted Psmiths, to my secret delight, proved altogether too tall for the conveyance, and had to walk. For my own part, I found myself with my midriff pressed up against the protuberant buttocks of a large, elderly woman in peach taffeta, my neck cricked round the pole by the exit doors, and my feet, at every jolt of the vehicle, lifted an inch or two from the ground. I bore this for as long as I could, then, when the tram pulled to a brief halt at a junction, I wrestled free and shimmied up the pole.

From my eyrie, I looked out over a sea of hats, plumed, or with boats upon them, and even models of sea-birds, all caught in the dip and swell of the tram as it rolled towards the road bridge. I shimmied round to look out the exit doors at the marble river. The embankments were a mass of bunting and municipal black flags, under which strolled hundreds of party-goers, Tack officials, drunkards, and line after line of children from the City's orphanage, the drab brown of their every-day uniforms cheered hardly at all by sprays of bay and bits of silver tinsel.

I remembered Lilith, the gypsy. Her running away from the orphanage made more sense to me now, considering what a dull time of it orphans had in the City: bay leaves and tinsel – it was enough to make me ashamed of my finery.

We attained the Northern Hill and swept past Central Station: a shrine to the Goddess of Locomotion, its steps showered in confetti and great masses of lilies in plaster horns. The building shone cream and golden in the pellucid light: the tram eased away from it reluctantly, stealing itself for the long haul up to the Sé.

The slope was so steep, the tram made hardly any headway, and many who were near the doors offered to disembark and walk up the hill. The driver, cheerful and proud, demurred: it was a point of honour with him to bear us safely to the start of the procession, and that he would do.

He did, eventually, as we, many of us slumped and fallen upon each other in a hysterical heap at the back of the vehicle, encouraged his labours with a rousing chorus of the *Oubliez:*

> Oubliez les anges
> Oubliez les bossues
> Et partout
> Oubliez les professeurs!

Scant seconds after we disembarked from the tram, a blare of cornets signalled the start of the procession. The crowds in their dizzying finery – and we among them, holding hands for fear that we would be swept from each other by the jubilant press – descended Green Monkey Street towards the Circus of Birds.

The street was hardly recognizable from the street my father and I had walked down six months before. There were great papier mâché mobiles hung from wires slung over the street – clown's heads, with fiery hair and terrible, avid grins; big black alligators, cleverly articulated, so that as the breeze moved them they opened and closed their jaws and twitched their diminutive forearms. Among these grotesqueries hung gigantic representations of domestic objects: huge scissors cleaved the air, pigeons fluttered out from a huge cardboard garlic press as the levers swung shut in the breeze, a chair and a table and a teapot played games of perspective with each other down the street – all this, strung above our heads on steel wires. The buildings too had been made out of the ordinary. Rolls of bright cloth had been hung out the windows: makeshift banners that caught the wind and intertwined like fronds in storm-struck jungle. From every window, old women threw handfuls of confetti and paper streamers into the air: every once in a while the view ahead was obscured as though by flurries of parti-coloured snow.

Progress was slow: we stopped often so that my mother and father might drink from the wine barrels set all along the street under gold flags. I had never seen my father so animated, my mother so flushed and happy with him. They kissed often – it made me glad and jealous all at once, but more glad than jealous: how rare were such expressions of tenderness between them.

Needless to say, their pleasure-taking was in part a ritual thing. There was a sense of freedom, a licentiousness, about the whole occasion. Some of the women around me walked bare-breasted, eliciting much good-natured lewdness from the young men who gambolled among us, some of whom had astonishing jewelled cod-pieces stitched to their trousers: the sight stirred me strangely. Couples fondled each other uxoriously in doorways decked with grape vines with the fruit still green upon them. Children pulled at each other's clothes, stripping each other with a wide-eyed decadence as they ran about and yelled and barked and shrieked and all the time got underfoot, like so many enthusiastic dogs.

We marched down the street, my parents with their wine, me with my spun candy and my proud green jacket (not once seized and torn by another child, for I fancy its grandness intimidated them). Every once in a while my father took a broad-sheet from one of the many poetry vendors lining the streets in their distinctive blue wigs. He gave one to me. I glanced over it. It was by Ian Deeprose: a much-feted literary figure. Young as I was, even I had heard of him.

> The innermost desire of my erstwhile heart
> This shattering of windows
> This brave ache of the wheel and the span
> This brevity of sense ...

I tore a corner from the broad-sheet and folded it away. I examined the scrap I had torn off. It read:

> This brave ache
> This brevity

It behoved everyone who attended the Ceremonies to bear with them a scrap of paper, with some design or a few words upon it. It did not matter what the paper was: it might be a scrap torn from some learned treatise, or a sweet wrapper, or an old bus ticket, or a child's drawing of its pet dog, or the list of ingredients for stuffed aubergines. Indeed, the more heterogeneous the mix of scraps the better; for once the provost of the Academy had fed them to the Iron Fish, that subtle engine was taken up and hung from the top-most spar of the scaffold: the Vessel, packed with its Seed. And there the Fish hung, for many weeks, evolving out of all our scraps – those multifarious evidences – the City's next incarnation.

From leavings and from nonsenses, from hints and glimpses, it shaped our city, like some great and alien archaeologist of the future ...

We neared the Circus of Birds. The crowds grew more densely packed, the accumulated smells of the parade – wine, burnt sugar, glue from the mobiles softening in the heat, the perfume of the women, the sweat of so many over-dressed bodies, the sour breath of the children, almost naked now – all this made me faint, and weary, and though my father held me up to watch the Ceremonies as they unfolded, there were so many children sat upon their father's shoulders, my view was hardly less obscured, and I was anyway too tired to take much interest. The bucket passed me and I dropped my bit of poetry into it carelessly. The applause and the cheering disorientated me; they sounded deep in my skull like the in-rushing breath of some great animal: the City itself perhaps, drawing all its parts together for one great act of respiration.

'Can you see?' my father asked me. 'Can you? Can you see?'

I saw it all: saw the College of Makers carry the Fish onto the dais, saw the scraps poured into the Fish's mouth, and the jaws clamp shut – but I had lost my earlier enthusiasm, my cool enjoyment, and all my earlier doubts had come and gathered about me.

The City, hibernating for millennia, drawing breath once every twenty years … Were we citizens of this place, I wondered, or merely its prisoners – flotsam in the belly of a whale?

PART TWO

1

M y father died of an embolism, six years later. I was eighteen. The funeral cortège wound through the lanes of the Baixa to the Quiet Lake. The pall-bearers, drunk on my mother's cider, stumbled over the cobbles, muttering curses. Father, borne upon their quaking shoulders, slid about in a coffin two sizes too big because of an undertaker's mistake. Death delights in these tiny, vicious incongruities: it piles them on like a writer of bad farces.

A representative of the Academy attended the funeral: a gaunt young man with lips too small for his mouthful of gigantic teeth. Doctor Emmanuel Binns, deputy secretary of the Libraries Committee, had a face like a skull. It was impossible not to stare at him, and I had had many an opportunity to do so. Dr Binns had visited my father often in the weeks before the Ceremonies, in order that he might consult the ancient books on points of ceremonial etiquette. My father, I remember, was pitifully grateful that an academic had shown interest in him at last: 'And me, a mere self-educated man!' In this he was deluded: Binns was much more interested in my father's books than in my father. In fact, he could be rather off-hand. Father put it down to what he called 'the learned temperament'; but I'd not been impressed.

Dr Binns laid a wreath by the shore; I noticed that his shoe laces had come undone. The coffin slid down the splintered ash-wood ramp and disappeared with hardly a ripple into the grey, felty water. It was as though something monstrous had sucked it down. Binns came over and stood beside me. He did not seem to know what to do. He made to touch me on the shoulder, then drew back. He smiled at me; peeled back his lips to reveal dreadful, horse's teeth. I did not find him sympathetic: I looked away.

Sea-birds skimmed the surface of the lake. Ripples V-ed across the still water, slicing through the inverted reflections of the park. Binns pointed at them and laughed. There was no humour in the sound. It was just his way of trying to cheer me.

My mother came up to me, clasped my hand with limp fingers. I squeezed her hand, hard. Nothing moved on the lake. The birds settled on the far shore and pecked drearily about in the gravel: they had learned these gestures from the other birds, but had no real idea how to catch anything. I remembered my pockets full of bread, I remembered the smell of it, and my mother's gloves, scratching my neck.

No-one had had the heart to give Father the funeral he had asked for. The ancient rituals of death were too outlandish for my mother, who had never really sympathized with her husband's studies. It saddened me that my father would not leave this world in the manner he had chosen, but I was learning that the world had changed too much for the old observances. It had grown too busy, too rational, too plain for these strange antics to survive. The old rituals disorientated people, where once they had comforted them. Dress my father in those ritual robes, mark him with such knives and paints, recite those arcane chants? How could we have done such things, strange and eerie things, in the midst of our modern grief?

I recited some of my father's favourite poetry over the lifeless lake. Some other words were spoken, I remember nothing of them – and it was over.

We returned to the bridge, down cobbled streets. Women were planting salads in the allotments; behind the wash-house, the tramps were arguing over a game of shove-penny. On the marble river, boatmen were tapping limpets from the bottoms of their craft with heavy chisels.

Limpets: newcomers to the City. Six years ago they had not existed. It was the Ceremonies that had brought them. The limpet: it was their only gift. Surely, these Ceremonies had lost their potency, if all they could come up with was the mere and dismal limpet. It seemed to me oddly fitting that my father's death should coincide with magic's own demise.

Six months later, at the end of our mourning, my mother dismissed Josey and moved into a small apartment off Thaïs Avenue. Our old house was put up for sale. Soon, nothing of the family would remain: nothing of my childhood but my father's books.

I was angry with my mother for selling up: all my past was tied up in that house, and I grieved for its loss as much as I grieved for my father – in some ways, I think I grieved for the house more. But my mother, poor woman, wanted only some rest and ease in her declining years. She had been my father's help-mate – his servant, practically – for so many years, she had no desire now to be slave to a house too big for her, and too expensive for her to keep up. Why should she not have some freedom in her last years? I helped her move to Thaïs Avenue. It was a dispiriting place, full of a sort of people I thought unworthy of her: commercial travellers, petty government officials, insurance clerks. We ate with them the evening after the move, sat around the landlady's big round table – dumplings in a sweetish sauce. They asked me questions and I replied obscurely, with a barely-concealed arrogance. I was priggish and sullen and my mother was ashamed of me. 'My son,' she explained to her neighbour – a fat woman, sister to the local tax inspector – 'is going to the Academy this autumn.' It was less a show of pride than an explanation for my snobbery. I realized with disgust that my mother was perfectly at home among these people.

It took us some while after that to dispose of the contents of the old house. For several weeks I lived alone in my room there, greeting my mother each morning with cold courtesy as we met to sort out the disposition of the effects. We sat at opposite sides of my father's desk, working in silence as we drew up our lists, like generals on the brink of war grimly seeking the right words on a last-ditch treaty. Then we would walk through the house, taking and mending and packing and sealing all manner of things my mother no longer had any room for. Around us the house grew daily more empty and the echo of our voices louder, and more hollow.

On the last day, only the books were left. My mother sat in her housecoat, slumped over Father's desk, her head in her hands. Her fingers, teasing at her greying hair, were raw and rough; she could not have looked more different from the self she had displayed, seven years before, at the Ceremonies. She no longer dressed up, of course: she no longer had anyone to dress up for.

She looked up and surveyed the book-lined walls. There was no regret in her eyes, the way there was at other times.

'They are yours, Tom,' she said to me; and then, as if to spoil the gift: 'I never want to see them again.' She was not a particularly jealous woman, but these books had been her rival for her husband's affections for so many years, she would not be sorry to see the back of them.

'They will help me,' I said, wanting to be grateful, but careful to mute my gratitude lest she think that she would lose me to them, the way she had lost my father. It occurred to me, with a sudden poignant force, that I did not want to lose my mother, that I had no cause to despise her, or resent her desire for peace. Knowing now what it was I ought to have said, I leaned forward and kissed her cheek and murmured: 'They will remind me of him.'

My mother nodded, satisfied.

'Take them with you, Tom, when you go.'

2

Mother wept, of course, as we rode towards my new home – a room above the Academy's principal dining hall – and hugged me to her repeatedly. I was embarrassed, but I kept my temper. I was less afraid of the spectacle we made as we trundled over the road bridge – a fresher and his clinging mother – than of the danger to which she put us both by hugging so hard: we were perched in the back of a hired steam wagon, upon boxes of

34

my father's books, and at every jolt the boxes shifted dangerously beneath us. The driver of the wagon – a morose man who chewed incessantly on his unkempt black moustache – demanded that we disembark before he attempted the hill up to the Academy. Even then, he made slow enough progress and we had no trouble keeping pace with him.

We arrived at the main gate just as the clock in its tower above our heads struck Two. Through the chilly arch I saw the quad was a sea of utmost confusion, as students of all sorts, their parents and their servants, porters, beagles and ermine-gowned masters, wove about each other in a bad-tempered frenzy, so tight packed and without purpose they might have been one repulsive, pulsing organism, like maggots in a jar.

We looked around for some assistance, or at very least some sign telling us where we should go. There was no-one about but for four or five vagrant boys who, having attended and grown bored with the spectacle within, had formed a rough circle and were heaving loose cobbles at each other.

At last, from out a small door sunken in the wall of the arch, a short, rotund man approached us, dabbing his cheeks and forehead with a blue silk cravat. His shirt, I noticed, was open at the collar.

'Right!' he exclaimed. 'Get this thing turned round at once!'

The owner of the steam wagon, grumbling, put the wagon into reverse.

The little man stood, his arms akimbo, waiting for us to clear the arch.

'Where are we to go?' my mother asked him.

'Anywhere you like,' said the little man, and thrust out his chin with such accentuation I thought for a moment he must have dislodged his jaw from its hinges.

'But how do we get to my son's rooms?' my mother persevered.

'You don't,' said the little man, with obvious relish. 'Not until this evening. Don't you read your letters?'

My mother stared at him in confusion. I stepped down off the wagon, bristling at the man's rudeness, but my mother, catching sight of me, stepped in my way and said to the man, with more

35

civility than he merited, 'When are we permitted to enter?'

'Hand luggage only until six,' said the little man and, strutted, self-satisfied, back to his burrow.

'What am I supposed to be doin', then?' the carrier demanded, worrying over the dials and gauges of his machine.

'We unload here,' said my mother, suddenly. I must have stared rather, because she said to me, 'Don't gawp, boy: help the man!' And the three of us proceeded to unload the wagon in the street. When the carrier was gone my mother called over the five urchin boys. The two strongest she hired to carry the boxes in with us. The other three she paid a lesser amount to guard our goods as we carried them by hand through the mêlée within.

The gatekeeper rushed out at us. 'You boys, clear off!' he exclaimed. Our two makeshift porters stood and jeered at him from behind their boxes.

The gatekeeper turned on my mother. 'No-one but students and their relatives!' he exclaimed. 'Can't you read?'

My mother had had enough. 'They are my sons,' she said, with an acid inflection. She turned to them. 'Sammy, Reginald, come along, we have to settle your brother in before tea-time!'

The urchin boys whooped with delight at their new names and winked cheekily at the flabbergasted gatekeeper. They strutted past him. 'Do we get a bath, Mum?' Sammy demanded loudly of my mother.

'Will you wash my cock?' Reginald sniggered.

My hands were full, otherwise I would have clobbered them. But they served us well, their roughness forcing a path through the quad to the gravelled path that runs between the chapel and the dining hall.

A tall, grey-haired man with gold-rimmed spectacles stood at the entrance to the wing where my rooms were situated. He alone seemed unflustered that day, tall and erect in a dove-grey morning coat and a sleek black top-hat with a white silk ribbon. He greeted us with a smile, reacted not at all to the urchin boys (who, I fancy, were not a little overawed by his appearance and meticulous manner), and led us to my rooms. He unlocked the door and held it open for us. We hardly paused to look around, but straight away dumped our belongings and descended the stairs once more for our next load.

'I suppose he is some tutor,' my mother murmured, impressed, as we fought free of the crush at the quad.

'No, Mother,' I said; I had recognized his livery. 'He's simply the general footman of that wing.'

'Footman!' my mother exclaimed, startled. Then, 'Tom, cultivate that man; you may never again have such smart service!'

3

It was my good fortune to study under no less an authority than C.L.S., an exacting and uncompromising virtuoso. Over the years he had earned himself a fearsome reputation, both as an artist and as a historian, and it was in the guise of historian that I first came to know him; I thought him a fine tutor. I remember to this day his first lecture, which he presented in the unusual setting of the college's conservatory.

There we were, young men and women eager for knowledge, all of us determined to overcome our youthful proclivities, so that we might grow tall in the arid, bracing desert air of Learning. (What a dreadful lot of young prigs we must have been!) Around us, giant succulents (tended with pride by the botany department) wetted the air so that we were sweltering in our high collars and starched chokers. Summer sunlight entered steamily through wet windows.

C.L.S. entered, stripped off his coat, whipped off his tie, and prayed us be seated:

'Life in this city,' he began, 'is based upon the conventions of living. To live is, inevitably – unavoidably – to engage in a tradition.'

He was full of fierce energy. He must have been about sixty at that time, and he wore the years like a badge. All the softness of youth and middle age had been burned out of him, leaving a gnarled and fiery core. His dress was modern: he wore his hair cropped, and sported a full, pointed beard. His face was moulded to a negroid pattern, and it gave him a startling, earthy, seductive appearance.

His demeanour was direct, energetic, and not without humour. He was capable of astonishing intellectual dexterity. He adored complexity in all its forms; indeed, he did not so much teach as seduce, initiating us into the arcane realms of historical discipline as though he were a succubus teasingly revealing the fiendish mechanisms of Hell. I was from the first tremendously drawn to him. His words and his arguments were so elegant, so classically beautiful, that I found the man himself, the fount of these words, almost erotically attractive.

'Living,' he continued, 'is made possible by the existence of these traditions. You may, and probably will, all attempt to subvert them, but they form none the less the context within which your subversion takes place, as surely as breaking a promise is made possible by the convention of the promise.

'This notion leads, naturally enough, to the conceit of a life here which is not random, never haphazard, always comprehensible. We all need some ground against which to display our uniqueness: we have all, therefore, perhaps without suspecting it, come to some working arrangement with our environment.'

I was entranced; my brain and my heart were fired to bursting by the spectacle of C.L.S.'s deep and precise analysis of life. I felt that moment as if, by my listening to him, the course of my life were irrevocably altered.

'My dear boy,' exclaimed Henry, my neighbour in halls: 'what on earth are you up to with all these books?'

'They are my father's,' I explained, as I offered him my only uncluttered seat. 'He was a collector.'

'Was? He no longer collects?'

'He is no longer alive.'

'I am sorry.'

I went to the door and rang the bell. 'Where is that blasted man?' I demanded.

'He works to his own fashion,' Henry said, with his usual

patient irony. I am not sure to this day which of us had adopted whom: he me for my fire, or I him for his calming influence.

There was a knock at the door. I flung it open.

'Sir?' Footman Knobes, resplendent as usual in his grey frock coat, stood to attention by the door: in his hands he bore a tray set with cups of hot chocolate, a plate of toasted muffins, and a pot of lavender honey.

'About bloody time, Knobes,' I said. 'Put it down there, would you, on the table.'

'The table, sir?' Knobes repeated.

'There, blast you, there, there!' I jabbed impatiently at the pile of books I had assembled in the middle of the room, with a tea-cloth spread over the top of them. Most of my furniture was made of books; there were so many, I had to do something with them.

Knobes entered, set down the tray and departed in silence. I banged the door to behind him.

'Easy, Tom,' Henry rebuked me, kindly.

'The man is insufferable!' I exclaimed.

'This place is His kingdom,' Henry chuckled. 'He'll outlive the lot of us here, as no doubt he's outlived a hundred, a thousand, others. We're but lodgers.'

'Oh do stop being so infernally *understanding,*' I complained. 'It's not in any way amusing. Here.' I handed him a cup of chocolate. 'And how – since you would be *polite* – was your day?'

Henry grunted. 'Nudz in a fluster as usual.' (Henry, a second-year student, was studying human biology under the esteemed Professor Heinrich Nudz, whose anxious temperament was well known throughout the Academy.) 'It seems his assistant set up the wrong brain for this afternoon's experiment.'

'A bad business.'

'And you?'

I settled back in my chair and smiled. 'Ah.' Henry nodded, wisely. 'C.L.S. again.'

'Indeed?'

Henry wagged his finger at me. 'I can always tell; you're half in love with that man.'

I said nothing.

Henry subjected me to a quizzical stare. 'Is something troubling you, Thomas?'

I shook myself out of my reverie, reached forward and crammed half a muffin into my mouth. 'The content of today's lecture,' I muttered, through a mouthful of dough and melted butter, 'has made me philosophical.'

Henry settled in his chair. 'Go on.'

I wiped my lips. 'There are rituals which we use to maintain the City,' I began. 'The Ceremonies of seven years ago, for example.'

'Yes—'

'Now: in these unsuperstitious times, we think of these rituals as a means to disguise our city's smallness: they're distractions, flights of fancy; mummeries, merely. But no sooner do I begin aping this modern fashion than C.L.S. tells us these rituals really *are* magical. They hold our city together. Literally! As surely as the great beams and hawsers of iron sustain its twin bridges.'

Henry scoffed. 'What sort of world would it be, that needs magic to maintain it?'

I could but shrug.

'"The world as spell" – that I suppose is his notion.'

'I suppose so,' I admitted: 'yes.'

Henry tutted. He leaned forward and clattered his saucer against the tea tray. 'Is this saucer a magical illusion, Tom? Does it sound like an illusion? Were I to rattle it harder and break it, would its breakage be an illusion? Were you to kick me for my clumsiness, would your foot be a dream, my pain a phantasm?'

'Perhaps,' I replied, doggedly. 'It's a tenable argument.'

'But is it useful?' Henry demanded. 'Does it get us anywhere to suppose that all this—' his gesture took in the room, the Academy, the City '—is an illusion?'

'Only if you admit the possibility of a greater world,' I murmured.

'Ah,' said Henry, with gentle irony. 'The "greater world": my nurse used to fill me up with stories about it when I was little. Your teacher is becoming a mystic'

'Have you seen a sea, Henry?' I challenged, hoping to prick his complacency: 'A cliff, eaten by the tide? A forest? A she-leopard,

40

concealing herself in the undergrowth of a jungle floor? A mountain capped by snow? A river, swollen with melted frost? Have you?'

Henry frowned, made uncomfortable by my questions. 'You know such things do not exist,' he said.

'So why do we so often have these outlandish things in mind?' I demanded. 'Why do these images constantly visit us? Why do they infest our language, our poetry, our metaphors, our way of thinking even, if we never see them?'

'So we are hiding from these things?' Henry demanded; 'hiding from them in a city of dull dreams?' He cast around him for some prop by which to further his argument. He lighted upon his saucer. He picked it up and dropped it to the floor. 'What did I just do, Tom?' he demanded.

I blinked at him. 'You dropped your saucer.'

He gave a quick smile, and shook his head. 'No, the saucer stayed where it was: this entire room, the entire City in fact, must suddenly have risen three feet into the air!'

'Henry, I—'

He stopped me with a gesture: *'Prove I'm wrong,'* he insisted.

I sighed. 'You know I can't. It's possible, what you say, but it's absurd.'

He grinned at me, and retrieved his saucer. 'That is *precisely* the point I am making. You are supposing that reality is a dream and dreams our one true reality: the idea is "tenable" only for so long as one has the patience to think backwards the whole time. It's a coffee-and-brandy supposition, nothing more.'

I sat in silence a moment, quite deflated. 'You think the idea quite daft, don't you?'

Henry pursed his lips. 'No,' he admitted, 'not daft; in fact I think it is poignant and beautiful. But as an answer to our city's isolated state – it is an artist's, a *mystic's,* response, not a rationalist's. And I—' he puffed himself up with deliberate self-parody '—am a rationalist!'

Now and again, when we could afford it, Henry and I went and drank white port with crushed ice in the Bar Terminal, that hub and heart of the Baixa. I tended, as the evening progressed and my pockets grew lighter, to regret these outings; I found the Bar Terminal oppressive. It was also horrendously expensive: but that, of course, is why we went there (profligacy, for the poor, having its own irresistible glamour).

The waiters, for reasons I never fathomed, invariably sat us near a black-painted iron sheet cut into the silhouette of an eagle; this was mounted on the silver fascia of the bar. In our more unruly moments we used to shy its head with pretzels until threatened with summary dismissal by a frosty *maitre d'*.

A tremendous rail-station echo haunted this cavernous white and pearl-painted hall. The chandeliers above us, chunky and functional, cast a fitful fluorescent glare: it bleached the colour from everything it touched. The floor tiles – grey, flecked with red, as in a municipal bathroom – were cold through my shoes.

One evening we were joined by a newcomer: Henry's cousin, Blythe Maravell.

'She is an artist!' Henry had enthused, earlier that evening. 'Ever since she was a little child, she has shown some flair for painting. She was never one for the garish combinations children usually attempt when first confronted with a box of paints: cool washes, odd angles – she discovered perspective on her nurse's knee, a crayon in her fist!' One summer, Henry claimed, when she was four, Blythe abandoned her stick figures of Mummy and Daddy and began a three-quarters portrait in graphite and burnt sienna of the neighbour's dog. 'She still has the scar on her calf to prove it.'

'Oh?'

'She wanted it to hold its head at a certain angle.'

'Foolish.'

'She tells me her current models aren't much better.'

From these stories I had picked such elements as suited my romantic sensibility: the early talent, the sensitivity, the loneliness of the true artist; I had built up in my head a delicate, sylph-like image of Blythe: a waif-like creature, her gift rendering her too sensitive for the world, too delicate to withstand for long its harsh demands. I had imagined her to be one of those heartbreakingly gifted invalids whose early death is written in pale and shining letters on brow, and wrist, and in the limpid pools of the eyes.

Now here she was, the woman who wrestled dogs for her art – built like a fish-wife, and with something of a fish-wife's humour. Henry introduced me: but she hardly glanced in my direction before she rounded on her cousin, picking up an obviously stale debate they were having about some debut exhibition at Grabbinges's gallery. I was nettled by her rudeness and determined to ignore her.

Anyway, she wore tacking garb. Tacking, I should explain, is one of those pastimes whose true aficionados are few and far between; far more common are those whose main interest lies in the expensive clothing associated with it. I had reason, therefore, to expect the worst as I took in her peaked cap with the legend 'Taq Krayzee' stitched across it, a woolly jumper made of fluorescent purple and green squares, shiny skin-tight knee-length breeches that emphasized her stocky, over-muscular legs, and – of all things! – a pair of special, chunky tacking shoes (in the sole of each boot there was a ratchet system for attaching the special roller skates favoured by serious tackers). In such get-up she resembled all too closely the usual hearty Bar Terminal fodder, and I confess I was disappointed.

So, ironically enough, it was she who finally brought me into the conversation: 'Henry tells me you own lots of books,' she said. 'Have you read them?'

I met her insolence steadily. 'They are a resource I draw upon,' I said, and before she could scoff: 'You are an artist: do you use up every tube of paint on a single picture?'

I had never before heard such a pretty laugh: it caught me quite by surprise. It seemed to bubble up from the back of her throat before the humour showed on her face. Her mouth, which was large, and with lips that were too thick and wide, should have been ugly when she laughed, but there was a kind of feral curl to her lips which made her laughter exhilarating to watch. 'So, you use books and I use paints: now is that just a pretty riposte or is it true?'

Behind that confrontational manner, an interesting question

43

lurked: I am pleased to say I stepped down off my pedestal and answered her, explaining to her my father's interests, his books, and my own historical studies which seemed to touch upon them. 'Even now,' I added, pre-empting any charge of obscurantism, 'even as we preen ourselves in the mirror of modernity, our leading thinkers are turning back to the magic of the past; C.L.S. himself gives credence to the old myths – what an iconoclast!'

Such a naked appeal to intellectual fashion left Blythe unimpressed: 'It's our job to develop new myths,' she said, 'new images and archetypes, new strategies for coping with our lives; not preserve the old ones in amber!'

'You are one of those people, then,' I said, determined not to be outdone in this pugilistic encounter, 'who perceive no value in history.'

'I'd rather make history than study it,' Blythe replied. It was such an extreme claim, I had no choice but to take it seriously. Indeed, it demanded some respect – I have heard worse ambitions expressed with much less candour. I liked it – but I did not agree with it.

'You will find,' I said, 'that "iconoclasts" are often the most conservative members of their society: so conservative, indeed, they find themselves retreating into a vision of a romanticized yesteryear, where they imagine life was somehow more genuine than it has become. Their creations were most likely fired by a desire to recreate the glorious days of an imagined past.'

'That may be true for some artists,' Blythe conceded, 'but why elevate what you say to a general rule? I still don't see why an artist, or a philosopher for that matter, should not dissect the body politic the way a surgeon investigates the processes of the living body.'

'You see yourself as a knife, then,' I smiled, 'cutting cleanly through the world.'

'I see myself as an explorer,' she replied, 'taking what life has to offer.'

But I, with my bookish prejudices, could not allow the argument to go unchallenged. 'It is their very *disjunction* from the world which makes artists great. If they were truly of their time, they would not *be* artists; they would be judges, or teachers, or pamphletists.'

Blythe shook her head in vigorous disagreement. 'I consider myself,' she said, 'a pamphletist in paint.'

I thought she was naïve, and this, coupled with her absurd clothing, amused me. Here she was, victim of the City's most fatuous fashion of the moment – Taq Krayzee indeed – and believing herself in touch with the spirit of her age! Well, I thought, if that were the spirit of the age, it only proved us sour academics right to believe that the age was trivial!

I cannot remember what I said to convey these thoughts, but I cannot have been too abrupt because she simply looked down at herself and laughed. 'A girl needs distraction,' she said.

But the drink had made me candid about my prejudices. 'A rather facile sort of distraction, isn't it?' I said.

'Physicality isn't facile,' she replied, evenly. 'I enjoy exercise, competition, games. I never saw much pleasure in indolence: There's time enough when I'm old to puff upstairs, sleep overlong and lose my rag at every turn. You young men think building up your strength isn't worth the effort. Behold the consequence!' She gestured regally at her cousin, slumped comatose in his chair. 'Look at Henry, there. No stamina! He talks and talks and when he's done he's incapable! You young intellectuals stumble about like men in their dotage. You're too weak and indolent to do anything; you've no memories worth having, no real experience, just idle dreams you pass on to each other like used clothes.'

Her words pricked me: it was true, my experience of life at that time was paltry at best. So I laughed and shrugged and confessed myself defeated. 'You would have me ride off on my snow-white charger searching for adventure and damsels and distress!' I teased her.

Blythe pouted. 'I think the expression is "in distress",' she said, 'but, since you ask – is knight errant so bad a thing to be?'

I confessed that it was not.

4

'It takes two or three weeks,' C.L.S. explained, 'for the City's salty airs to eat through the finely worked iron scales of the Fish to the bronze lattice beneath.'

I yawned behind my hand. There is in any course of study some more or less tedious groundwork to be got over before the innovative part can begin. All that week in his lectures C.L.S. had been boring me to death with talk of the Fish – a subject already familiar to me, thanks to my father's frequent monologues on City lore.

'Hour by hour,' C.L.S. went on, 'from its interstices, teased out by these breezes, the scraps with which we fed the Fish emerge and flutter about the disturbed air. At night, we prowl the Circus of Birds, searching the gutters for these scraps. When we find one we take it up, sprinkle it with salt, and eat it. The next day the world is a little different, a little brighter, a little more strange. Seven years ago, for the very first time, limpets appeared on the bottom of the City's boats and barges. Twenty-seven years ago, the paint on the houses behind the shipyards became faint and brittle: the sea breeze had grown more salt and corrosive. Forty-seven years ago ...'

He glanced up from his lectern and caught me in mid-yawn. He gave a pained smile. 'But you have understood. Slowly, by this magic, our city transmutes, and that is how it transmutes.'

He fell silent a moment, weighed down, perhaps by his own boredom at having to give this mechanistic little lecture year-in, year-out. Then he looked up, and some of the usual sparkle returned to his eyes. He stepped away from the lectern and, with a sweeping gesture of his hand, he seemed to cast aside all he had said.

'Transmutation,' he declaimed, and he smiled, mischievously. 'The word implies two states: an original state, and a transmuted state. So here is a little problem for us to ponder: if our city, our little world, our little bubble of existence, is transmuted, every twenty years, into something a little different, what was its original state? And let there be no question about it,' he went on, 'there *was* an original state! If you asked me, "when did the sun first rise?" – I would have no answer for you. Perhaps it always rose, perhaps there was no time, ever, when it did not. But if you ask me, "when did this ritual begin?" – ah, then I might find an answer for you! For rituals, all rituals, however arcane, belong to human history, and human operations – be they customs, beliefs, political systems, or what-have-you – are short-lived beasts ...'

He paused a moment, until the massed scratching of over fifty pencils diminished and fell silent.

'It is true, however,' he conceded, 'that this ritual of Stuffing and Hanging has been with us for longer than our written histories record. How is this possible? How is it, that this ritual has survived so long? Why do we attach to it such import? Any suggestions?'

I raised my hand.

'Yes, Mr Kemp?'

'Because it works, sir,' I replied.

There was some laughter in the hall. C.L.S. raised his hand. 'Mr Kemp is correct,' he announced, evenly. 'It *works,* very visibly, to change our world. This is no small matter. We are encouraged to maintain the ritual *because it works.* But does it work quite as well as it used to?'

There was silence in the hall.

'It does not,' said C.L.S., very quietly. 'Not at all.' And then, with a grandiloquent gesture: 'Once the very fabric of our city shook with the transformation of the world! New streets appeared, old ones vanished – rivers – gorges – the very colours of the world slipped in and out of existence before our eyes!' He let his arms hang down by his sides. 'Now,' he said, 'what do we generate?' Then, in a silly, small voice: 'Limpets.'

Through the chuckles of his audience, C.L.S. went on: 'The world is growing stable, the changes are less marked. This indicates that the process of transmogrification is not an infinite series of equal transmutations, but a finite series of steps from one state to another. From a desert place to a great maritime city? Perhaps! – though it seems unlikely, given the small changes of the past years, that we will ever, desert-bound as we are, attain an ocean-going existence.

47

'What purpose, then, does such a world as ours serve – a tiny, bound, desert place, haunted by dreams of a realm larger than itself?'

C.L.S.'s cat-like gaze travelled over the students sat in tiers before him, as if from us he might – vain enterprise! – elicit some startling truth. The candour and hunger of that stare as it passed me caused me to look away, as from too bright a flare. I looked around me at my fellow students. They were a dull lot, and already, so early in the course, attendance at these lectures had slacked off markedly. One student I did not recognize: she sat one tier below me, and to my left; her bright red hair concealed her face. I saw that she was taking notes; her hand moved in great, clumsy sweeps, the way a child's does that is learning to form its letters.

'There are rituals, of course, many of them,' said C.L.S., 'by which our simple ancestors sought to impose a meaning on their existence. In this modern age, this age of enlightenment, such rituals cannot entirely comfort us; nevertheless, compared to them our modern politic seems parochial and mundane – it lacks the passion and ceremony of olden times. So it is that in our so-called age of Reason, many of our forebears's rituals survive today, all be it in a debased form: ancient psychological strategies, welded by the centuries into the pattern of our lives, so that to a stranger our social behaviour might at times seem quaint, strange, eerie – even sinister.'

The young woman below me brushed back her hair behind her ear – it was Blythe, Henry's cousin. What I had taken for her gauche, childish handwriting, was, I now realized, not writing at all – she was sketching C.L.S.! I wondered how I might acknowledge her and, as if the thought were a cue she had been expecting, she turned around and winked at me. I was flattered and pleased by the gesture, but I did not know why. Our one previous encounter, after all, had proved quite thorny.

'Let me share with you an example of such behaviour,' said C.L.S. 'The denizens of the City's lower terraces, like the rest of us, have never seen the sea. But theirs is a brutish and literalistic character: undeterred, they proudly tend wind-weathered mouldings of great ocean-going galleys above their doors. They make fishing nets out of old sacking and wine-bottle corks, and sell them to each other at exorbitant prices. Metal smiths fashion elaborate sextants and compasses, copying them out of old books written in an archaic tongue they cannot translate. They sell their seconds as curios to the richer families of the Southern Hill. Their finest work they keep for themselves, crammed together upon every fire-surround and occasional table!'

My fellow students laughed most heartily at this: I felt my cheeks redden. Was not my father the son of a bargee? Were not the rituals C.L.S. saw fit to satirize not the very rituals my father once talked of with affection and pride? And what was he thinking of – lampooning those very rituals which he'd said possessed a crucial power? Or were the bargees's rituals excluded from his magical system? Perhaps they weren't *polite* enough …

I glanced around me, embarrassed by the strength of my reaction. Turning to my left, I met Blythe's quizzical stare. She gave me a half-smile, then looked away. She seemed satisfied about something. Did she know of my commoner's background, then? Did she know that I would take exception to C.L.S.'s remarks? Or, knowing of my collection of books, perhaps she simply guessed that I would take such lampooning too much to heart.

'Such patterns of behaviour,' C.L.S. explained, with an air of patronage, 'are firmly ingrained in our society. Generation after generation has behaved in this way. For many, it is unthinkable that any other mode of behaviour exists. Only among the upper echelons of our society have Reason, Science and Investigation loosed us from our superstitious bonds!'

Unfortunately Reason, Science and Investigation were at that moment timed-out by the luncheon bell; we gave them a perfunctory bout of applause, and repaired to the blistering heat of the quad.

Blythe had already left the lecture hall by the time I reached the door. I was disappointed that she had not waited for me, but I told myself I would meet her again soon enough, *via* her cousin Henry. If I had not glimpsed her shock of red hair, bobbing briefly in the sunlight above the grey and black crush of masters on their way to High Table, I should not have given her much thought … I hurried after her, weaving as quickly as I could through the mass of hungry academics. I lost her at the entrance to the formal gardens, whose shady walks and little vistas separate the Academy proper from those annexes, offices and lodges which have accreted to it over time.

I had drunk somewhat too much with Henry the night before and could not face the thought of dinner, so I entered the gardens after her; at least the shade might cool me as I searched.

I turned down a trellis walk. Pea gravel sprinkled with dead rose leaves crunched beneath my shoes. The gardeners had trained Mermaid roses up and over the trellis. The golden glow of the rose blooms turned the sunlight to butter; it lent an unnatural, claustrophobic hue to the air. The roses were past their brief best: round the edge of each gaudy, bright petal there was a ragged brown line of decay. The leaves, too, had suffered – from drought, from the too-sandy soil. Their undersides were thick with black fly.

Further on, the rose bushes had expired, and had been removed; in their place dog-rose, on tough, pea-green stalks, was weaving its way around the trellis with cool, dark-green foliage and simple, small, starch-white flowers. It was darker here, cooler, less cloying, where the dog-rose had invaded the trellis path, as though this vigorously-sprung weed had gifted some of its power to the air.

I stopped a moment and plucked One of the small, white, waxy blooms, rubbed the petals between my fingers and examined, in the cool green light, the taper of each petal where it emerged from its bud, the thin green veins at the root of each petal, their flawless and simple arrangement.

I heard laughter – unmistakably Blythe's. I pushed aside the tangle of dog-rose and peered out.

Blythe hung from the branch of an old apple tree; the branch trembled as she pulled up with her arms until she could touch the branch with her chin. I heard slow, ironic clapping and looking to my left I saw a large, swarthy boy with a black beard applauding her efforts.

Blythe relaxed slowly, then, still clinging to the branch with her hands, she hooked her left leg over it, and then the right, then, tensing her haunches, she let go with her hands. She hung there a few moments, up-side down, chatting quite naturally with her swarthy friend, then, unconsciously perhaps, she began to rock, back and forth, trailing her outstretched fingers in the grass. Coins fell from her trouser pockets like silver rain. The boy came and sat cross-legged in front of her so that their heads were on a level and as she swung towards him he stole a kiss from her mouth.

I snatched my hand back, and the screen of dog-rose concealed them from my sight. So! I stood there some moments, dumbfounded by what I had seen, arms folded as though to deny those images which persisted behind my eyes.

And yet, when some moments had passed, I was amazed at myself, that I should have been surprised at Blythe's sporting with her friend. Why on earth should it have startled me? Why – had I assumed that Blythe lived like a hermit before our meeting? What an idiotic notion! She could have a friend, a dozen friends, a hundred, it meant nothing to me: it was not, I told myself, as if I had any reason to be jealous. Why, I hardly liked her!

She was, I told myself, too harsh for my taste, too childishly argumentative; I turned back towards the quad.

But why was I turning back, confound it! Had I not set off for a walk in the shade? And why should Blythe's having an intimate friend among the students of the Academy upset my plan? It was too rich – here I was, would-be sophisticate-*extraordinaire* of the Lower First, running away like a silly, love-lorn boy from someone I hardly knew!

I told myself to act naturally, turned a corner of the walk, and strode bravely into the sunlight, in full view of Blythe and her friend. I put my hands in my pockets and affected an air of most improbable unconcern as I sauntered along the brick-paved path, glancing now and again in Blythe's direction, then away – lest she catch my eye – miming some sudden show of interest in a distant leaf, a bird, the coping stone on a wall.

Given the sheer busy-ness of my casual passing, it is a wonder

Blythe's attention was not drawn to me. But it was not: she had righted herself on her branch and was swinging from her hands again: her Adonis had grasped her by her waist and was now pushing her, as you would push a child on a swing. Blythe gave a cry, fell from the branch and burst out giggling, rubbing her hands and blowing into them to cool them. Adonis reached down to help her up and she made a play of trying to kick him, at which he began laughing, too.

In a cloud of resentment so uncalled-for it was like the visitation of some malign spirit, I stalked off into another, much darker trellis walk – one which led to the annexes of the Academy – and came at last to a clearing, and at the centre of the clearing, a large, ugly, single-storey log shed.

The shed had been roughly thrown together, and it looked as though in a very little while it might be pulled apart again just as roughly and transported elsewhere. This unprepossessing shack lay empty now, and it would remain empty for another thirteen years, until the next Fishmaker took up residence. For this, despite its unremarkable location, was no temporary annexe, but a building founded on a site some said was older than the Academy itself: this was the workshop wherein the City's great Iron Fish was made!

Here she drew her magic engine. Here she smelted iron and copper. Every twenty years these walls rang with the chisel's clink, the screech of stencil against plate. A pleasant history for the place, and all that most folk knew. The truth was darker: Here stood a workshop merely: once there'd been a chapel, too; a place of dark and terrible resolve. Kneeling there, hour after hour, the Fishmaker practised her consolatory verses so that, come the Ceremonies, she'd burn to death with more dignity – a dubious rite at best, that immolation, and long since stricken from the canon.

I walked up to the shack. It did not look much of a place to meditate in. A blackthorn tree over-hung the path, and white blossoms overlaid the dusty gravel, as though a light snowfall had miraculously visited this desert realm. I reached the wall of the shed and peered in through low windows, the glass heavily encrusted with dirt and bird droppings.

I could but dimly make out a line of simple wooden trestles, strewn over with paper – 'Mr. Kemp!'

I wheeled round.

Thomas!' It was Blythe. I grinned and waved, overcome by an enthusiasm I did not understand. I walked towards her.

'Ferreting out the secrets of our foremothers now, are we?'

But I was by now used to Blythe's acerbic turn of greeting, and simply gave as good as I got. 'C.L.S.'s physiognomy interested you more than his lecture.'

Blythe's laugh caught me unawares once more, bubbling up through her large, endearingly ugly mouth.

'So may I see what you made of him?'

Blythe shrugged, and beckoned me off the path. We sat down together on a bank scattered with violets and coltsfoot and daisies. She had a pile of books with her, and her sketchbook was at the bottom of the pile: a thin blue cloth-bound tablet, dog-eared with use.

She handed it to me. 'I'd rather assumed Henry had told you about this wickedness of mine,' she said, as I flicked through the pages. 'Many's the time I've sat in with him, to watch Nudz.'

'And the lecturers never catch you?'

Blythe shrugged. 'I've had one or two scrapes. Though I don't suppose C.L.S., with his artistic sympathies, would have objected too strongly.'

'You should have told me you wanted to sketch C.L.S.,' I said, 'and we could have gone in to the lecture hall together.'

'Oh,' she said, 'it doesn't matter. I went with Boris.' *Boris* – there is something about that name which feeds animosity.

'Mind, you've gone past him.'

I turned back the pages.

'Well,' said Blythe, after a pause. 'What do you think?'

'There's certainly a lot of energy to them,' I admitted. Then, perhaps because I had overheard someone else say this in an art gallery: 'A good economy of line.'

The likeness was poor, but I did not like to say so. *Good economy of line?* I wondered. Of all the silly gibberish—

But Blythe seemed satisfied: 'He has a wonderful face,' she said.

53

'So gnarled, so lived-in. It would be fascinating to smooth it out in paint, to uncover his youthful image.'

'He may not thank you for it. Did you enjoy his lecture? Or were you too busy observing the man to hear his words?'

Blythe pouted – an odd gesture to make with so large a mouth, and not entirely successful. 'I was interested in him because of his art,' she said, 'and I think he is a better artist than a historian.'

Never having seen C.L.S.'s work, I could not comment.

'I was rather disappointed,' she said at last.

'It wasn't his best lecture,' I admitted. 'Last week—'

But Blythe interrupted: 'That's not what I meant. The content was riveting enough, to the lay ear. But it was *old* content. I've already read the lecture he delivered.' She turned and picked through her books and picked one out; she handed it to me. The golden stamp of the Academy was pressed into the red leather cover. I turned it and read the spine: *Transmogrification and the Perpetuation of Culture.* The title was enough to balk me – then I noticed the name of the author.

'C.L.S.?'

'It's his monograph,' Blythe explained. 'It's in the library. There's two weeks to go on the ticket, you can borrow it if you like; it's on Henry's ticket.'

I took the book from her and flicked through the pages. 'He takes his opening lectures from here, then,' I mused.

Blythe took the book off me and turned to the contents page, handed it back to me. 'And not just the opening lectures,' she said: 'look.'

I read the chapter titles: they seemed oddly familiar.

'Practically his entire course is reproduced from that book,' Blythe said, with disdain. 'A book he wrote years ago!'

It was true. Now I recognized the titles: they had been listed in my course notes, some weeks before. I wondered what to say. 'This will be very useful,' I offered. 'Thank you.'

Blythe sniffed. 'Can't say I think much of a man who still uses his old student notes to lecture from,' she complained.

Much as I was nettled by Blythe's superior air, I had to agree with her: it was disappointing of him. 'Still,' I offered, 'if a man pursues two careers, I suppose one or the other will eventually suffer.' It occurred to me that I had probably come under C.L.S.'s wing at the wrong time. How much more rewarding it would have been, to know him while his views on the world were fresh!

I looked through the book, and came upon a passage marked in the margin with red ink:

If our city is indeed a self-contained bubble of humanity, hived off from the Greater Realm by forces of artistic excellence, then we can begin at last to assign some motives to those who originally performed the hiving-off.

First, we may consider the possibility that the Greater Realm was dying: in order to survive the Greater Realm's death, a small pocket of humanity hid themselves away in this city. What form this death took – a natural death, a running down, or a more or less malicious destruction – is an important point of conjecture. More fundamental, however, is the ontological problem: if the City was created within the Greater Realm, and the Greater Realm is no more, where then is the City?

'"Magical thinking", as Henry would put it,' I remarked, and I showed Blythe the relevant passage.

She grunted. 'It gets wilder, listen,' and she read from the next page: '"Less perturbing is the notion that the Greater Realm continues to exist, and was simply abandoned by the City. Perhaps the Greater Realm has grown hostile to the presence of humanity, and this City is a refuge. Perhaps some human purpose in the Greater Realm is being served by hiving the City off."'

'He makes this place sound like a prison,' I commented, glumly.

'So it is,' Blythe replied, 'if you accept the existence of some huge and glorious "Greater Realm" outside it.'

'You see no value in the notion, then,' I replied.

Blythe looked at me in silence for a moment, pondering. 'I did not say that,' she replied, carefully, much as Henry had done.

Just then the tramp of heavy feet through gravel distracted us: Blythe's swarthy Adonis shambled hugely into view, flinging out his feet to right and left. 'Aha!' he exclaimed, rumbustiously. 'So here you are!'

We stood up. 'Thomas Kemp—' Blythe began.

Adonis grabbed my hand with his great, hairy paw and gave a shriekingly hard squeeze. 'Stock!' he boomed: 'Boris Stock!'

Boris. There was something teasingly familiar about the name—

But I was not alone in my confusion; Boris Stock crunched my hand even harder: 'Good God, lad!' he yelled, 'don't I know you?' – and behind my eyes, a naked man fell to his death from the bridge …

5

The years had effected an extraordinary transformation upon little Boris Stock. The gawky, timid schoolboy of my boyhood memories had flourished since I had last seen him, into a paragon of big-boned heartiness: muscular, plump, ruddy-faced, and of a lively and boisterous disposition.

It seemed extraordinary to me, talking with him later that day, that this could be the weedy child so over-awed by his father's spectacular death: why, at school we must all have stumbled across him at one time or another, weeping piteously at the strangeness of it all.

I supposed that deep inside himself, in his darkest and most defenceless hour, Stock had found some sort of compensatory strength – one which explained the ebullient personality he now exhibited to the world.

Blythe left the two of us shortly after our meeting outside the Fishmaker's workshop. She had a painting in progress, one which required the remains of the daylight to complete; her excuses made, she left us to our reminiscences.

Stock and I sat upon the bank and talked of this and that; before we knew it, it was evening. The air had grown chill and damp, and the gardens – which had before been lit by translucent gleams from petal and leaf – lay now extinguished and cold and eerie.

'Fancy a drink, lad?' Boris yelled. (It says something about the self-confidence he exuded, indeed, the sheer glamour of his physical presence, that I did not object to this 'lad' business of his, though he was a good two years my junior.)

'You know somewhere?' I asked.

'The very place!' Stock's bellow boomed across the chill and shadowy garden like the mating call of a rampant bull.

The Café Persil was an undistinguished building, cramped between the terraces of a steep, cobbled road leading to the Sé. It served the usual clientele of workmen, beggars and students. 'I would like,' Stock cried, as we entered the building, 'to introduce you to two pals of mine – poets!'

'Delighted,' I winced.

There were two rooms to the place. One was long and narrow, with settles upholstered in Nicol Street tapestry, and rickety oblong tables; the tall, dark-stained bar seemed to tower over you wherever you sat. You reached the other room by five steps: its round ironwork tables and incompetently framed prints suited more the poetic pretensions of Stock and his companions.

There were two. The first was a lanky man of indeterminate age; his ravaged, squashed, unsymmetrical face and pained, coal-black eyes contrasted oddly with the luxuriant, raven locks which, springing thickly from high up his forehead, spilled down the back of his hand-knitted poncho: a soft cascade of beautiful, deadly black water. 'Edwin Gross!' Stock announced, quite as if the man were about to leap up and perform a conjuring trick. But Gross, who was of a sullen disposition, supped his beer and would not meet my eyes.

Unfazed, Stock turned to the other gentleman: a petit man with a shaved head; dapper gestures, watery eyes and an inoffensive smile. 'Evelyn Christ,' said Stock.

We took our seats and sat in silence for a few seconds. Sensing that something was expected of me, I offered to buy drinks. 'Oh!' Stock exclaimed, flustered. 'Oh, right, lad. I was just about – ah, just a beer, ta.'

I turned to Gross and caught him giving Stock a nasty, insinuating wink. Stock affected not to notice. 'Mr Gross,' I said.

Gross turned his terrible black eyes upon me and said, rather tetchily I thought, 'The same, the same—'

I turned to Christ. He said nothing. 'Do you want a drink?' I prompted him.

'Oh,' said Christ, and blinked as if the light hurt his eyes. 'Thank you so much. A beer, thank you awfully. Do you want my glass?'

I shrugged and took it.

'Thanks awfully,' he said, again, eyes grey and glistening like the scales of a fish; I wondered if I was being lampooned.

The beer of the Café Persil was sweet and cloudy, with an after-taste of rotten pears. When the old woman behind the counter poured it, she flicked the foam from the top of the glass with a bone spatula. I returned with the drinks on a tray and took the one free chair for myself. This, to my gratification, was placed so that I had a clear view of the bar-room: when she wasn't pouring beer, I noticed that the serving woman played patience – a curious game, possibly of her own invention, that permitted no resolution – I never saw her take up or shuffle the cards once, in all the time she was there. Half way through the evening she gave a loud, bad tempered sigh, swept the cards together, deposited them in the till, threw on a shawl and left by the kitchen door. A few minutes later her husband came out – a glowering man with massive shoulders and a permanent stoop, as though the top half of his body were too heavy for the bottom half.

Stock and his companions drank with a passion. It did not take me long to fall a mug behind. Stock meantime had lost interest in me and was catching up on tittle-tattle.

'Weng has resigned from the *Quarterly*!' Gross crowed, his face a mask of malign delight, punctuated by dreadful black eyes. 'The pusillanimous little toe-rag has been *expunged.* I went round this morning, I presented my *sickest* work to the surviving crew of that listing publication – And. They. *Took it*!'

I was to learn, in the coming weeks, that Gross was a most talented man, all be it a filthy-tempered one. Something of that bile which infested him informed his art, rendering it bleak and painful and tortured: of its formal excellence, however, there could be no doubt.

'My dear Gross,' Stock boomed, 'you have reached the *Quarterly*? Well then, today's a sad day for poetry! Oh, you're clever enough, lad, I don't doubt it, you deserve your sale: but the more popular you get the more the copyists will take note of you: impoverished descriptions of blood and sickness – those things you've made your hallmark – will flow across our pages, cheap as the ale we spill across our tables!'

'But they will never replicate the *technique*!' Gross cackled.

'Erm …' Christ began.

To my surprise. Stock and Gross both stopped and listened to him.

'If you'll excuse me, my dear Mr Gross, yours is a claim (I'm sure we would agree) that no one would cross, of course. But our dear Mr Stock is right. The tastes of "vulgar" readers rarely look beyond the surface of a poetic narrative – they are as well contented by the formulaic spew of a Bax epic (will you forgive me that malign description?) as with the maimed writhings of a Gross *qasida*. Your ascendancy, if (if! what am I saying? *When* –) it comes, shall bring forth, I think, a glut of derivative horripilations.' Christ then gave a little bob of his head to indicate that he had stopped speaking and thanked everyone for listening.

Stock and Christ paused a moment while they untangled Christ's remarkable syntax, then nodded, sagely. (Christ had a talent, I was to discover, for rounding off conversations.)

Gross repaired to the latrine: Stock lent over the table towards me. 'You see that poncho of his?' he murmured.

'Yes?'

'Oh,' Christ began, waving his hands about ineffectually, 'I say—'

'He wove that during his last internment!' Stock announced, delighted. 'Great, eh?'

'Stock,' said Christ, and screwed up his watery eyes in the vain attempt to give his look some fire: 'Really!'

'They say,' Stock went on, unabashed, 'he wove it from his own blankets, but Gross can't remember a thing about it!'

I gave a weak smile: Stock's tale had embarrassed me.

Christ came to my rescue: 'Mr Gross's wits are independently

59

minded,' he explained, his fingers all the while playing cat's cradle as he sought for the most inoffensive pattern for his words. 'They abandon him from time to time, in the pursuit of strange grails!'

Neither Stock nor I could think of anything to follow this: we sat in silence until Gross returned.

'Well,' said Gross, 'we going to eat or not?'

'Good idea!' Stock exclaimed.

'Please!' Christ exclaimed, 'allow me!' And the little man rushed off to the bar to collect a handful of paper menus.

'You wouldn't think he was a talented man,' said Stock, 'would you?'

I gave Stock my most polite smile: I wished heartily that he would not keep characterizing one friend in front of the other.

'Such a pale little chap!' Stock screamed. 'And yet,' he added quickly, perhaps sensing my discomfort, 'there's intelligence there, oh yes! Feed it modestly from your own table, it will bloom. Sure as shot! Behind that modest front sits a bloody great *furnace* of enthusiasm!'

On cue, Christ returned, toddling up to us with his menus and his facile smile. 'Look!' he cried, 'look!' He handed me a paper and stabbed daintily with his finger at the first entry—

Cozido. Now that was a rarity – one of the very few dishes native to the City I had yet to try ...

As a body, we plumped for it; Gross stood up from his chair, turned and bawled into the bar-room for service.

A slovenly boy shambled up the stairs and looked about him, vaguely.

'Here, fool!' Gross declaimed. The boy gave him a gap-toothed smile and slid his feet over the dusty boards towards us, lapping at the stub of his pencil as though it were a candy stick. Stock announced our choice with firm hand-movements and a sober glare.

Christ hummed and ha-ed in an embarrassed fashion and turned to me. 'Please,' he began, 'do not think too ill of us at this juncture. Normally, we are kind, almost jovial, to the most incompetent serving staff, but this poor lad – it only makes him cry if one shows him kindness.'

'Indeed?'

Christ nodded. His eyes, the colour of cloudy water, held a suspicion of tears. 'It is a strange affliction,' he admitted.

The boy opened and closed his mouth like a fish. 'Off...' he whispered, at length.

A satanic gleam entered Gross's tortured eyes. 'Off where?' he asked, with chilling calm.

The boy wailed: 'Off!'

'Certainly!' Gross cried, with great gallantry, leapt out of his chair, and offered the boy his seat.

The boy fell to his knees and banged the floor with his fists. 'Off!'

'Why, my dear fellow, I didn't know puce offended you, of course!' Gross rushed round the table, seized Stock's coat from the back of his chair, and threw it to the ground.

'Bloody hell!' Stock shouted, outraged.

'Oh dear ...' said Christ.

The boy leaned forward over the coat and keened as if he were worshipping the material (as well he might – I saw the label). He foamed a little.

Gingerly, Gross toed the coat out the way of his spittle.

The boy fell to his knees and scrawled on the floorboard. I left my place, greatly entertained, and crouched down to read what he had written:

OF

I sighed. 'Oh, very well. I'll have a Calzone, instead.'

'And me, lad,' said Stock.

'Yes, yes, yes,' Gross snarled, his eyes so black at that moment they might have been holes drilled into his head; he returned to his seat.

The boy panted, and scrawled on the floorboard:

IIII COLD SONY.

He stood up, grinning, and tottered to the kitchen.

'I suppose we want another beer?' said Stock.

'Gosh,' said Christ. 'Thank you.'

Gross drained his glass and said nothing.

'Kemp?'

I pointed to the two full mugs in front of me.

'That's four, then,' said Stock, disregarding my earnest head-shake. He reached into his coat pocket, brushing the dust off the material as he did so with much tutting and fussing, and brought out a paw-full of dull brass coins. 'Ah,' he said, 'I've got a bit of a problem here.' He sent a look of blank appeal around the table.

I sighed. 'Here,' I said, reaching for my wallet, 'allow me—'

'Watch your pennies!' Gross wheedled.

'I pay my way,' Stock replied, and, lowering his gaze to the puny coppers in his paw, muttered: 'foul-mouthed beggar!'

'Behold!' Gross croaked, in a ridiculous parody of an *annuncio* at a ball – 'Stock, the Gentleman Pauper!'

Stock said nothing, but it was clear from the angry flush on his face that Gross had found a chink in the rumbustious man's *bonhomie*. 'Kemp,' said Stock, 'do you suppose I could borrow ...?'

Gross put his hands behind his head and put his feet up on the table. 'Time you learned the bloody accordion, mate, and did this begging job properly.'

'Time you sewed up your mouth!' Stock bellowed, whipping round in a sudden fury. His chair creaked ominously.

'Time you sewed up your wallet,' Gross replied, quietly.

Stock struggled, red-faced, for a riposte. 'Fuck off!' he exclaimed, at last.

Just then the idiot boy came out the kitchen. He was leant at an odd angle, as though pulling something out from the kitchen – something which resisted, and fought against him with sharp, violent jerks.

The row between Gross and Stock straight away evaporated and we watched, fascinated, waiting to see what struggling behemoth the boy had caught for our supper.

It was, it transpired, the right arm of his uncle, the manager. The manager himself inched into view, yelling vociferously at the boy, who in response grinned even wider than before, chittering and squeaking like a contented guinea-pig. I will say this for the boy: despite the manager's best endeavours, he kept up his grip.

Once the manager was in full view (for indeed the boy's hold upon his uncle's arm was prodigious), it appeared that he (that is, the manager) likewise had hold of something and dared not let it go.

The procession moved forth somewhat jerkily along the bar; something had got itself tangled up in the manager's wristwatch – it was caught in the interstices of the bracelet.

What was it?

The procession shuffled a little further.

It was the lace edging along the top half of a basque. The basque was even more intimately fastened around the waist of a young lady, and as she was revealed to us, it was clear that she was in a state of even more considerable distress than the manager. Her generous and shapely breasts bounced about in a jolly fashion as her artful fingers sought to disentangle the undergarment from her burly paramour's timepiece.

We contained our laughter as best we could: the manager was built like an ape, and his frown bespoke an apelike temper.

At last the young lady gave up the unequal struggle. With a lightning gesture born of long practice she disengaged herself from the flimsy garment and fled in high dudgeon back to the kitchen. The manager, thus released, charged at his nephew; the boy stumbled across the bar-room, scampered up the stairs and, once more ahead of his irate master, pointed to the floor by our table. The manager came over, drew himself up to his full height and scowled at what was written there.

'Four Calzone,' he observed.

The boy whooped.

A savage glint appeared in his master's eye. 'Why *thank you!*' he cried, grabbed the boy's ears, and kissed him most passionately on the forehead. The poor lad went quite white, his eyes filled with tears, and he began wailing most piteously.

Thus discommoded, he did not see the blow. With a resounding smack, the manager catapulted the boy across the room to the foot of the bar. The boy sprawled and gurgled. The manager strode over, picked him up by his trouser belt, swung him over the other side of the bar and, rather daintily, dropped him.

He strode back to the kitchen. By the door he stopped and turned to us. We could not see below his waist, for the bar was in the way, but he seemed to have gained a few inches. 'Five minutes,' he announced, with great sobriety – and vanished into the kitchen.

A ragged rush of indrawn air accompanied his departure.

'Well, then,' Stock sighed, when we were done laughing and the place had grown calm again. 'What's it to be, the same all round?'

'Dear Stock,' I said, 'let me get these, and keep your pennies.'

Stock cast a sidelong glance at Gross; Gross, exhausted by his taunting sport with the idiot boy, sat slumped in his chair, eyes firmly shut.

'Thanks, lad,' said Stock, and gave me a wink.

I trotted down the stairs into the bar-room, elbowed my way through the mass of drunken labourers newly gathered there, and bought my beer. When I returned, it was to find Stock cajoling Christ into a pre-dinner reading of his latest poem.

Christ simpered.

'Come along!' Stock insisted.

'Well,' Christ explained, 'I'm not quite sure whether it's really quite—'

'Please,' I said, a trifle unctuously – drink has that effect on me – 'I'd be most honoured.'

Christ smiled at me, warmly. 'Well … thank you,' he said, and for the first time, behind his pale eyes, I saw a gleam of sleepy intelligence. He stood up, cleared his throat self-consciously, drew a paper from out the breast pocket of his coat and began:

> He would not cut his hair, mother
> Lay his head
> (He loves his hair)
> In a cooling pan
> He would be mad to cut his hair
> (On the dairy window sill—)
> With silver scissors!

Stock and I applauded politely. Gross was still sulking, his terrible eyes hidden under waxy, mismatched lids and his arms folded upon his sunken, poncho-clad chest.

Our meal interrupted any further forays into the poetic art:

four luke-warm salty Calzone, served with extremely bad grace by our ape-like host.

'It's full of lard,' Gross complained, unfolding the bread and picking at the insides with a fork. 'That's lard, not cheese.'

'Oh dear,' said Christ, staring doubtfully at his leathery meal; he gave it a quick, embarrassed smile, as if to encourage it, but the thing gave no response and sat there still, swimming in its own grease.

I sawed away at the bread base with my knife but the knife was blunt and I was drunk and between us we made little headway.

Stock tucked in and said nothing.

'Cold grated lard,' said Gross again; then, when he saw no-one would rise to the announcement he shrugged, folded his Calzone back up, lifted it to his wet misshapen mouth two-handed and proceeded to force-feed himself. Not once did he take it away from his face: not to drink, nor even to breathe. The leathery bread gave way at last under my knife: half my Calzone flopped off the plate and into a puddle of beer.

'Cheers,' said Stock, and he snared the mess up with his fork and dropped it onto his plate without so much as a glance in my direction.

'And now, Mr Stock!' Christ exclaimed, when our meal – if it can be called that – was done: 'perhaps, you too – forgive my impertinence – but I think perhaps—'

Gross muttered an oath, tightened his grip on his poncho, and curled in on himself like a snake.

But Boris Stock needed no greater encouragement than Christ's enthusiasm. He drew a sheaf of crumpled note-paper from his trouser pocket, and prepared to read.

Stock's poem was a long, highly coloured ode upon the gloomy theme of despair. I remember quite clearly, and with a chill, the millennial crescendo of the last stanza:

> … memory and meaning
> Lie across this land
> Like the liver and lungs
> Of some colossal animal!

Christ and I applauded wildly: truly this was a virtuoso performance!

'What I liked particularly,' I enthused – when drunk I am given to embarrassing *encomia* – 'was the way you made concrete the alienation of your poetic voice through the medium of body imagery!'

Stock blinked at me. 'Aye,' he said, rather at a loss, 'well, lad, I don't know about that. I just write what I feel!'

Gross unwrapped his limbs and stretched in his chair: a particularly poisonous reptile, uncoiling. 'Nil-rhetoric,' he informed me, nastily, 'is Boris's speciality.'

'Fuck off,' Stock snarled.

Gross smiled sleepily and, his point proved, he wrapped himself up again.

'Have you anything to read?' I asked Gross, hoping to draw him out of his foul mood.

He opened one terrible black eye at me. 'Do I look,' he enquired, in the coldest tones, 'like a performing bear?'

Just then the labourers in the bar-room struck up a song: the beloved *Oubliez.*

'By heck!' Stock exclaimed, bouncing his meaty fist upon the iron table. 'Bloody appropriate, eh?! Listen! The true poetry of the people!'

'Good grief,' Gross muttered.

The drunken party slipped up on the second line, burst out laughing, and began again.

Stock leapt from his chair, flinging out his legs to left and right, swept up his tankard with a meaty paw, and with a grandiloquent toast to the men in the next room, joined in:

> Oubliez les anges!
> Oubliez … 'Come along, you lot!'
> … bossues
> Et partout …

Gross, sickened by this display, slipped out of his seat, adjusted his poncho and slunk out of the cafe. His luxuriant black locks bounced softly against the back of his neck, incongruous and beautiful, like the mane of a young girl.

The workmen cheered and laughed at Boris, who stood splay-footed there saluting them. They raised their mugs to the friendly giant and sang the chorus once again.

'Be brave!' Stock exhorted us: Christ cleared his throat and struck up, an embarrassed little whine that could not hold a note for more than half a second.

'Kemp, for crying out loud!'

There was nothing for it. I tottered up from my chair, mighty unsteadily, and, lifting one of several full mugs set before me, I struck up:

> Oubliez les anges
> Oubliez les bossues
> Et partout
> Oubliez les professeurs!

6

'Blythe, mind you,' Stock bellowed, selecting a bloom of *Frau Karl Druschki,* 'is right fascinated by the New Poetry.'

I had not heard of the movement and supposed it was Stock's own description of himself and his cronies. 'She's a champion—' he went on, and he broke the stalk of the largest rose he could find – 'of modernism.'

I looked around, uneasily. We were in the private grounds of the Goldsmith's Union; Stock claimed he regularly used their park as an illicit short-cut from the Sé to the Opera.

'But the Opera will have already begun,' I'd complained, as we left the Café Persil.

'No matter, lad,' Stock had urged me, drawing me along with him with the flat of one meaty hand; 'they never check tickets for the second half.'

Quite why I went along with him I do not know. The blessings of that evening had been mixed at best, and Stock's moneyless state was draining my own pockets quicker than I could afford. I suppose I wanted to see how far Stock, with his 'lad's and his 'aye well's, would go. Was he really a plain-spoken master of the City's cafes and theatres, or was he merely, as Gross had proclaimed him, an empty-pocketed virtuoso of 'nil-rhetoric'?

Stock tucked the rose into the button-hole of his expensive puce coat and straightened his collar. 'Come along!'

I followed after, obedient to the supporting role in which Stock had cast me. Stock led me along a gravel path which led to the Goldsmith's hall. The sound of the stones beneath our boots made an awful din, but Stock was undeterred by the threat of irate grounds men. 'This city's small enough without silly artisans hiving land off for themselves,' he complained.

I was far too drunk to put into words why I thought Stock was wrong: but to my mind, were it not for these distinctions of place and persons, these privy grounds and private privileges, would not the City seem much smaller than it already did?

It occurred to me then, by way of metaphor, that a maze, once its high hedges are erased, is revealed to be an inconsequential blot of land, where once it seemed huge and mysterious.

The image so startled me with its clarity, I made to share it with Stock, but he had stopped a little way behind and was urinating copiously into a bush of Peace roses. 'This way,' he snapped, beckoning me with his free hand, while with the other he adjusted his trews, 'or we'll be in sight of their silly hall!'

We emerged from the Goldsmith's garden, somewhat the worse for wear, through a gap between two bent railings on the corner of Crisp Street. Stock stood picking leaves out of his hair and beard. I wiped muddy crusts off my shoes against the edge of the kerb. This was one of the wealthier areas of the City, and the flagstones, brought to a high polish by light rainfall earlier that evening, glittered lemon yellow under ornate gas lamps. Beyond the lighted street, set back from it by a formal walk and a fountain, stood the Opera. Its ostentatious green cupola gleamed against a deep blue sky; yellow glints caught on the burnished trellis work at the top; rose marble crenellations around the cupola cast a glow of their own, soft and pink, as though the cupola was a deep green jewel and the marble was its setting.

'God!' Stock exclaimed, 'I'm right in the mood for a bit of skirt after all that.'

I blinked at him.

'Come on!'

We arrived at the Opera just as the bell sounded for the second act. The formal elegance of the men's evening suits, the sumptuous finery of the ladies's gowns and muffs, intimidated me. I was all too conscious of my cheap cream jacket and my green brogues smeared with muddy residues and leaf-mould. Stock, his confidence bolstered perhaps by his expensive puce jacket, brushed away my hesitations and drew me after him, like some timid country cousin, past chattering dignitaries under ribbons and pince-nez, past gaggles of flighty middle-aged womenfolk, all teases and winks and fluty laughter, up three flights of stairs and into the red plush corridor which led to the boxes at the very rear of the theatre.

'These chorus girls are bloody gorgeous,' Stock insisted; he stopped at each box and peeked through the baize curtains to see if it was free. 'Fantastic costumes!'

I was beginning to wonder if Stock had meant to bring me here, or whether he had at some point confused the Opera with some Vaudeville in the Baixa.

'Tits under sheer silk!'

'What's the opera?' I asked, quite unable to share in Stock's prurience, and half expecting him to say 'What opera?'

'Werner's Trunk,' Stock replied, offhand: 'Here we are!'

Werner's Trunk: all I knew of the piece was that it was old, popular, a supernatural love story too passionate to be a gothic piece and too eerie to be a romance. Had I not drunk so much earlier in the evening, and had I not sat next to Boris Stock, and had I not walked in half way through without a ticket, I might have enjoyed myself. But I did not enjoy myself: not at all.

First there was the opera itself. Werner's Trunk is a play upon the story of the king who turned all he touched to gold. This story is not a demanding one and if Werner's Trunk had stuck to it I could probably have watched it quite happily. But at some point in the libretto half a dozen other themes had snuck in, all of them vying for equal attention, all of them begun several scenes before, all hopelessly intertangled before I, with my bleary eyes and blearier head, arrived upon the scene.

What, after all, was I supposed to make of the tableau which greeted me when the curtain lifted on Act Two? A stage madman manipulating arcane electrical apparatus in one corner – I presume this Nudzian vision updated some alchemical original, for electricity is a relatively recent discovery – a life-size golden nude sculpture in the other corner, stood upon a black marble plinth for all the world like some outsize trophy, a party of sylphs in diaphanous robes in the centre, holding a candle in one hand, a book in the other and a stuffed raven perched upon each shoulder, and – most incomprehensible of all – a gigantic papier mâché goat suspended by its neck from the ceiling. While the sylphs danced, something within the body of the goat stirred and trembled. I stared, fascinated, as Werner – at least, I think it was Werner, but it turned out there was some play about mistaken identities and breeches parts and identical twins swapped at birth and heaven knows what else and I cannot therefore guarantee who was who – sliced open the goat in which he hid, stuck his head out, and peered down with trepidation at the dervishments of the sylphs.

'Look! Look!' Stock exclaimed, pointing excitedly at the sylphs: he made me slip a coin into the device in front of him to release a pair of cheap opera glasses then kept insisting I take them and examine the sylphs' chests. I could barely focus as it was and every time Stock handed the glasses over he contrived – perhaps because by this time I was swaying back and forth rather badly – to hit me on the forehead with them.

I did not focus on the sylphs – they whirled about too fast for my stomach to bear – and watched instead the antics of 'Werner', as he gazed around the hall, his face a melodramatic mask of fright and awe.

The dance of the sylphs went on, and on, and on, and on, and it was a wonder that 'Werner' sustained that pained expression for so long, though no doubt being cramped up in a paper goat twenty feet up in the air put him in the appropriate mood. I turned my attentions to the set itself: the sumptuous hangings with their devilish designs, the pattern of lights upon a backcloth suggesting the catacombs of a great castle, the electrical apparatus with its spinning wheels and bubbling fluids, and that great golden statue upon its plinth, blinking at me through eyes the shape of sloes.

I started, looked up from the glasses, peered again.

The woman – for woman it was – gazed glassily back at me, delicate arms upraised, hands frozen in an elegant, wilting gesture, fingers straight and taut.

Just then another character appeared on stage: a comic maid with country skirt slit to the thigh and full bosom laced high so that it strained its stays. The dervishes took fright and fled. 'Werner' leaned out perilously far from his goat and peered curiously down the maid's cleavage.

Quite how the poor woman was supposed to sing laced up like that I have no idea, but she managed a creditable comic lament; meanwhile. Stock had snatched the glasses back and was examining her with the intentness of a farmer at auction.

He scowled, and passed judgement. 'Seen better legs on a dog,' he sniffed.

'Oh, really!' I exclaimed, quite as ineffectual as Christ (such are the effects of beer at the Café Persil).

'Told her the exercises,' Stock went on, unperturbed. 'Nancy, I said, if you don't do what I showed you you'll have hams like bladders and calves thicker than your thighs.'

'You know her?' I asked, startled.

'Once sat at her feet,' Stock quipped. 'Fancied my chances, I did. Me! Sat at her feet, of all things!' He chuckled, humouring his younger self: 'Well, it's what she liked, so I'd heard. You know, love-lorn boy stuff. We were alone, her dressing room, lights out, all ready for a rollicking good fuck. She flexed her thighs ... *Phaaw!* One whiff was enough, I was off!'

Nancy slipped a feather duster out of her voluminous slit skirts, bustled over to the living statue and began to dust it. My admiration for the statue's self-control increased apace, as the duster probed the corners and nooks of her lithe flesh.

'Bet she enjoys that!' Stock guffawed, and, eyes glued to the glasses, he began to recount some other ungallant tale about his 'younger years'.

I put my hands to my temples; if I surreptitiously blocked my ears, I thought, I might gain a few minutes' peace. But the cacophony *inside* my head – the thrum of febrile blood, the foetid gurgle in my stomach as the Calzone enacted its terrible revenge – proved no better than the row *outside* my head; I dropped my hands to my lap.

'—little hairs round her nipples and got me to pick them out with my teeth.'

'Oh God!' I muttered.

'Good? Fucking *fantastic,* mate – LOOK!' Stock seized me by the shoulder and shook it; in my inner ear I heard my stomach fizz. Meanness enveloped me and I decided that if at any point that evening I threw up I would make sure it was over Boris Stock.

Nancy bustled off, Werner leaned out his goat further than one would have thought humanly possible and intoned a spell – and the statue moved.

I was entranced: Stock with his nasty stories, the box with its rickety seats and chipped gilt rail, the space between me and the stage – the stage itself, even – disappeared: only the golden dancer remained: naked and superb. I gazed, and gazed, and gazed. Stock, of course, kept the glasses all to himself, but I did not grudge him: before me danced the quintessence of all beauty and grace, and it was enough to see it from afar, see the patterns it made in space, the power of its gestures, the grace and sudden violence of its passage back and forth across the stage. 'Werner' sang in accompaniment: an eerie and painful expression of male desire; astonishing, moving, and as far from the cruderies of Boris Stock as it is possible to get. Soon it became impossible for me to separate the dance and the song, the glow of the woman's body, the echo of the man's passion-clotted melody, and I was suffused by a tremendous surge of goodwill towards my fellows, all my fellows – even Stock, who did not know how to be happy – and fell to contemplation of some perfect state, the glow of the woman, the melody of the man, radiating through time to some infinitely far off, infinitely worthwhile union …

'Wake up, you silly prick!'

I raised my head from the balcony rail. I had the most appalling headache. I sat up, blear-eyed, and rubbed my forehead. I felt the impress of the rail there, the skin sore and sticky where it had been embossed.

'Back-stage!' Stock exclaimed. 'Back-stage!'

'Ba— what?'

Stock went behind my chair, leaned over me and with his great fists he lifted me up by the collar of my jacket.

'Steady on!' I yelled, feet paddling as Stock lifted me clear of the ground.

All around us, wave after wave of applause sent thanks to a cast lined up on a set quite different to the one I had examined: bushes, a sandy path, a backdrop of dawn over some wide sylvan landscape, the effect enhanced by red-filtered lights behind the cloth—

'Are you coming or aren't you?'

'All right!' I exclaimed. 'All right!' put out of temper by Stock's bullying, my disorientating snooze, the pains in my stomach.

Once upon a time the Opera had boasted a suite of principal dressing rooms, finely carpeted, the walls covered in rich velvet, green for the principal female, red for the principal male, with plaster mouldings in the corners, picked out in gilts and oils; and for the chorus two sumptuous halls, one for the ladies, one for the men, each with its tiled anteroom upon which a herd of large enamelled bathtubs stood passive and patient on their brass claws, while servants fed them buckets of steaming water scented with restorative oils – pine, geranium, patchouli.

Today, crippled by falling attendances, the Opera boasted but a single, cramped dressing room, once the preserve of the male chorus. The bathtubs had been rounded up and driven away. A massive stretch of canvas, torn rudely from some backdrop, had been strung up along the centre of the room, dividing the tiled

73

part – which was now the men's sole preserve – from the carpeted part, which was reserved for the women. All this I learned much later: by the time Stock and I arrived, this huge makeshift curtain had been drawn back, and all distinction of territory between the sexes had been lost (if, indeed, it had ever been maintained, which I secretly doubt). Half-clad persons of both sexes chatted happily and unselfconsciously to each other in light cast by a few chilly electric light-bulbs. There were clothes everywhere, both costumes and the daily wear of the cast, slung over chairs, trodden underfoot, hung from the curtain wire, thrown carelessly over tables already cluttered with open pots of make-up, squashed tubes of lip gloss, discarded cotton wool, balls of screwed up tissue paper and trays stuffed with cigarette butts. The air was an oily fug of warm make-up, cut through here and there by the acid reek of spilt skin tonic.

'Here,' said Stock, and with a twist of one ape-like arm he hauled me into the room. 'You must meet Maera LaCouche!'

'Who?'

Stock stared at me, as at a village idiot. 'The dancer, you fool! The dancer in gold paint. You never heard of her?' He did not wait for an answer, but hauled at my sleeve once more.

The great LaCouche sat in state in the middle of the room, quite still, in a high-backed scroll-work chair, naked to the ministrations of her maids; they worked from her head to her feet, wiping the gold paint from her skin with scented oils, and caught the dribbling residues with swatches of cotton wool. The drops they missed trickled down LaCouche's paint work, leaving trails of greenish slurry in the shimmering surface; if she were a statue in truth, one might suppose that her innards were made of some base metal, and that this had begun to corrode and seep through the golden veneer. For all that, the sight of her was far from displeasing. There was much pleasure to be had in the sight of a woman so young, so lithe and well-constructed, taking rest after worthy labour. Her face, though streaked by odd greenish smears, held a healthy pink around her lips and cheeks; the graceful column of her neck, in the shadow of her chin, held a deeper, more roseate, more carnal glow. Her shoulders and breasts moved gently and evenly in response to her deep and steady breathing. There was about her physique, as much as about her kindly, slightly supercilious smile, an aura of self-confidence and command I have rarely seen equalled.

'So, Boris,' she coo-ed – she was a singer of high repute, and yet she had the most extraordinary voice when you met her, almost childlike. 'Who's this pretty young man you have with you?'

I dare say this was the most outrageous flattery. No drunk looks his best at half past one in the morning. No matter: her flattery shook me out of my daze: I straightened my back, wiped the hair from my forehead, smiled, and bowed low.

'Mr Timothy Kemp,' Boris announced, with such authority that I did not think to correct him.

'*Tim!*' LaCouche smiled and nodded at me. 'A poet?'

Lest Stock invent a history to go with his invented name for me, I hastened to reply, 'No, madam, a student merely.'

'And what do you study?'

'Social history, ma'am.'

Her face froze, as she racked her brain for some gracious reply. At last: 'We had need of you here at rehearsal. These old libretti can be so damnably obscure.'

Now that LaCouche had set her seal of social approval upon me, the rest of the room made efforts to draw me in. Three giggly girls – I suppose they had played sylphs – talked about their lodgings, and how hard it was in winter, in the damp and cold of their attic rooms, to do their exercises. 'The best thing is the sparrows,' said one called Arabella. 'I feed them crumbs on the window sill. They cheer the place up so, on a dull morning!' Someone handed me a glass of champagne, which I drank off at a gulp, under the dangerous assumption that any more alcohol could not worsen my condition. I was surprised to discover that the drink settled my stomach quite quickly, and went off to hunt for another glass.

A number of equally innocuous conversations followed, for which I was quite content to play the passive partner. The life of these people seemed a poor one, but with its own modest glamour and companionship, and I was not surprised that Stock (who did,

I had to admit, write rather good poetry) found this company stimulating.

I had forgotten, of course, that Stock's motives for being here were not exactly artistic. When I enquired after him one young man, whom I later learned was the scenarist, replied carelessly: 'in some broom cupboard with an understudy with no tits.' I should not have been surprised, but I was.

It seemed unfair, I thought, looking round me at these tired, happy, ambitious young people, that Stock should use this place as his private knocking shop. I wondered what benefit the company derived from his visits: perhaps they liked his verse.

The more champagne I drank, the more estimable seemed the people around me. They really were, I thought to myself, quite astonishingly good looking. I knew, moreover, that I would never be as well trained, as confident in my body, as lithe or as elegant as they. The more I drank, the more of a privilege my being here became, and I determined to make the most of it.

My stomach pains returned, but I was determined that they should not hamper me; I struck up a conversation with the scenarist again – a slim, diminutive young artist who went by the name of Allingham Nye. 'Some argue,' he explained to me, *apropos* the performance just gone, that Werner turns up at the castle in a *boat*. But Massey's handwriting is notoriously illegible and the first printed edition says "goat". We stuck with that. I've seen the manuscript, it's in the Academy library. It quite clearly says "goat" to me, but–' he shrugged '–scholars are divided on the matter.'

So it went on, my belly hurting more and more, my head beginning to pound in response, on and on; glass after glass of champagne hit the back of my throat, as I tried to quell the pains inside me.

So enraptured was I by this world, so drunk was I on the exempla of beauty surrounding me, I found myself avidly pursuing any conversation that would bring me closer to them all, whether I knew what I was talking about or no.

The pains in my stomach redoubled, and strange movements gurgled in my inner ear. But I was too besotted to take heed of them, and noticed them only in so far as they drew an odd, feverish veil over the proceedings around me. As my sickness worsened I found that I had somehow split into two: there was the inner self, peering intently through the windows of the eyes at the beauty and grace around me; and there was – strange apparition! – what I may call my *outer* self, that shell of me that moved my eyes and opened my mouth and pulled the air from my lungs, shaping them into words my inner self found quite incomprehensible.

A lancing pain in my side made me stagger. When I recovered, I was to find to my consternation that the two halves of me were even further divorced than they had been a moment before. The inner me sulked behind the clouded eyes, the fetid mouth, the glued and furred confusion of the skin, lost to the party going on outside itself, the beauty it had glimpsed and loved. All it could perceive of the world was the noise made by the outer me, that silly shell. 'What nonsense it talks!' the inner me said to itself, in disgust. 'And its laughter! No better than a hyena's—'

A voice, deep and kindly and unintelligible, insinuated itself into my ear, and something warm clasped my arm. The intensity of these sensations woke me somewhat, brought my inner and outer selves sufficiently together, and so I returned to a smeared sort of consciousness. 'I am being led away,' I thought, and if my head were not flopped upon my chest already I would have hung it for shame: 'Of course,' I thought, 'they are ridding themselves of me, I am unworthy.' A bolt of freezing air swiped my face. I started mumbling something about death and prepared to be thrown like the trash I was into the nearest gutter, punishment for my hubris, my glimpse of the Gods—

It is astonishing, is it not, how much self-pity wells up ahead of a good vomit? I am not one of these reductionists who relate all humours to the stomach, but occasions like this really do make one think. Who knows what ridiculous notions, what foibles, what elements of character, what structures of thought and even of memory, were expectorated in that climactic, blind, gargantuan heave? And what, after all, can be the motive that leads the young and virile to abuse themselves so as to cause such violent sickness, if not that, out of a need to put away childish things, we needs must expel them from our viscera? Drink, then is our enema, our weak toxin; it aids our evacuation of more bitter poisons, the rottenness of old obsessions, the soggy and corrupted remnants of dead complaisance—

In brief, I threw up.

'How are you now?'

I looked up and saw Allingham Nye, leaning over me, his hand out to touch me gently on the shoulder.

I waved him away, ashamed. 'Thank you,' I muttered, 'thank you, I'm quite all right now, I'll just—' I looked around me, vaguely. 'I'll just go home.'

'Without your coat?'

'Yes,' I replied, abstracted. Now that I had my breath back, I felt as refreshed and invigorated as though I had emerged from one of the City's excellent municipal pools. I looked around me for a way out: the ground was a mass of bird dirt, broken glass and dead pigeons. We were surrounded on all sides by four walls of brick, black with accumulated soot. Two walls were completely blank, their only feature a lead gutter, broken mid-way so that one half leaned out into space. The other walls had windows in them, many of them broken, and the paint was peeling from the joinery: these were the tallest walls, and I could see the eaves and gables of yet higher terraces beyond them; this, then, was the rear of the Opera. 'Is there no way out?' I moaned, and Allingham laughed gently at my distress.

'None,' he said, 'unless you want a tour of the cellars.' He beckoned me to him and led me to a door I had not seen, set in the tallest of the walls. 'They say,' he said, 'that you can walk from here to the Circus of Birds through the cellars beneath our feet. I do think, though,' he added, and he opened the door for me, 'that we ought at least get you your coat first.'

I sucked at my teeth. My mouth tasted as though some small, bilious rodent had pissed into it. Allingham led me down a cold and gloomy corridor towards a shaft of light. I heard laughter, women's voices – I held back.

'Come along,' Allingham urged me.

I shook my head.

'What is it?'

I found my voice: 'I've been a damnable fool,' I said.

Allingham shrugged. 'Oh,' he said – the irony in his voice was soft and rich, like honey: 'I wouldn't worry about that.'

Just before we reached the light, Allingham stopped and opened a small door to his right. He gestured for me to follow him inside, and he hunted around in the gloom for some tap or bracket to show him where the gas-light was. He gave up: 'Wait here a moment,' he said to me. 'No point taking you back into that crush; I'll get you something to steady your head.'

So I waited, just inside the gloomy room, which was stuffy and smelled of felt, and listened, in the half dark, to the laughter and chatter of the Opera cast.

I was calmer now, but still I felt ashamed of myself. The events of that night had shown me how inexperienced I was for my years. I could not hold my liquor; I was easily led; I was something of a fool, socially – and now here I was, listening at some remove to other people's pleasure, much as I had, as a boy, looked on as my school fellows tore joyfully about Green Monkey Street ripping each other's party clothes during the Ceremonies of Stuffing and Hanging. Was I still, I wondered, that sheltered, untouched, untouchable little boy? Was I still so incapable of engaging in the world?

Little had changed with me, it seemed to me then, except that I knew more, and was more capable of doing harm—

'Here you are.' Allingham returned, with a lantern, a bottle of malmsey and a small goblet of blue glass. He poured me a mouthful of the rich brown syrup and handed it to me. His fingers were cool as he brushed them over my hand. 'It will freshen your mouth.'

'Thank you,' I said, and drank.

Allingham turned up the light.

The room had smelled close, like a cupboard or a boudoir, but now I saw how much my senses had deceived me. We were in a great gallery of red brick, with a simple vaulted ceiling. The room extended far beyond the reach of the lamp: all the doors along the corridor must have given onto different parts of this same, gigantic hall, whose curious, close smell and damped sound came from its contents: rail upon rail of sumptuous costumes, ranked as far as eye could see. The sight, so unexpected, sobered me at once. 'Why,' I exclaimed, as much to myself as to Allingham Nye, 'they're beautiful!' I walked forward to touch the dress on the nearest rail: a kimono, embossed with pink wisteria on a ground of amethyst. Allingham came with me, carrying the light so I could see more clearly.

'And this!' I exclaimed, catching sight – at the edge of the lamplight's bright circle – of a velvet harlequin's suit. Allingham accommodatingly walked over to it and held up his lamp: the costume had a ruff of raw silk, and silver bells down the arms. 'The silver is real,' Allingham confided. 'Theodore Netting wore it for *Petruchio Exposed* some ten years ago. Silly egotist, what with his costume and all, cost more than all the rest of the production put together; needless to say he went down with laryngitis in week two of the run.'

So it was that Allingham Nye and I whiled away a half hour, perhaps more, quite lost in this seemingly endless space, me charging forth to examine this or that pretty costume, Allingham with his lantern following behind, companionably explaining this or that. Each costume for him had its own history. 'Oh that!' he would exclaim, with a laugh, 'that was from *Erasmus* – a very silly musical. I got to operate the curtain: I must have been the only one in that production some critic didn't slate.' Or, with a whisper, he would intone the name of some great singer, retired, sometimes deceased, whose dress I had found. 'Lea!' he exclaimed, as I fingered a gown of green shimmering stuff. 'Lea Potteridge – the finest alto in history, so they say – you must have heard of her. She died soon after the gramophone was invented. Her singing voice – ah, that was long gone! – but someone took the trouble, anyway, to record her speech. Some poetry, Swingewood's *Odes* I think, and her voice all cracked and broken. But the rhythms!' He sighed. 'You see, she had learned to express herself in pauses. Remarkable.' Allingham sighed, put down his lantern, came up to me and kissed me on the mouth.

'Remarkable,' he said.

I blushed and stuttered.

He sighed and picked up his lantern again. 'Come along,' he said, 'there is still much to see!'

But he no longer had stories to tell me, and without his tales I soon grew weary of the costumes: I had seen too much, I was glutted. Allingham walked closer to me now. When I bent to examine this or that material, motif, decoration, he placed his hand upon my back. When I stood up, there was his face, on a level with my own, that gentle, ironic smile, those lips in a perfect bow—

I broke from his kiss. 'I don't—' I began.

'Hush,' he whispered. 'Hush!' And he turned out the light. I felt his hands upon me, unlacing me. I put my hands upon his shoulders: I did not know what to do.

His tongue probed gently at my mouth, teasing it open. The slight stubble of his upper lip ground against my skin. His lips, luxurious and wet, sealed themselves around my mouth.

Desire, long-unacknowledged, flooded me. I pushed my tongue against his, unwrapped it into his sweet-tasting mouth, ran it along the sharp edges of his teeth, with it felt the trembling of his jaw.

We chewed at each other; the kiss ended in a frenzied tussle, a barely restrained game of teasing bites and lunges. We kissed again, and again. I do not know how long it lasted: the moment seemed timeless.

At last he turned me with my back to him and pushed down my trousers and trews. He kissed the back of my neck and bit gently into the muscle behind my collar bone. I reached behind to stroke him, and touched naked skin; he had already unlaced himself. My fingers stole towards his groin, then lost their nerve and slid back again to his cold, smooth rump.

He reached round for my prick and squeezed it enough to hurt. I gave a gasp of pain. My heart-beat thundered in my groin and my organ swelled. His hand teased it to its full hardness, then, very slowly, he pulled the foreskin back from my prick. From it oozed a trail of moisture. He pressed his fingers to my bulb, to stem the dissipation of these juices, then rubbed them around my glans with gentle circular motions of his thumb. It was as though my whole body were expanding, exploding, threading and splitting, meshing and intermeshing, a billion surfaces recombining.

He stroked down the length of my prick, further and further, and at last his fingertips gently kneaded my testicles. His other hand left my waist and slid sideways down the crack of my arse, deeper and deeper until his forefinger lay pressed tightly against my arse. I responded instantly to his questing finger, my sphincter softened by alcohol, excitement, desire.

He edged forward, I felt a hardness that was not his hand against my buttocks, and suddenly he was upon me, his hands clasped like a vise around my chest, bending me forward so that I staggered under him like the drunk. He nudged my legs apart with his knee and shuffled closer, reached between his legs and lifted his cock up against my fundament. He thrust, I gasped and fell forward, and we landed, him on top of me, on the floor. The hems and skirts and trains of a dozen dresses swathed my head and shoulders in their musky folds.

'No matter,' he murmured, 'no matter,' and placed a few deft kisses on my back and rear.

He stroked me from the base of my spine to my knees, back to my trembling hips, along my sides to my shoulders, his hands warm upon my skin; then he took my arms and pulled them, took my hands in his and bent my arms behind my back so that I was stretched and pinioned against his wiry frame, my face pressed against the dusty carpet, my buttocks stretched, my fundament proffered to him. Holding my hands like reins, he shuffled back onto his knees and began kissing me, more intimately than before: his spittle cold and soothing against my arse. He rose up, shuffled forwards, clasped both my hands in one of his, and with his free hand guided his cock to its target.

At last his hardness was inside me. I rocked back against him with pleasure and, fraction by fraction, he penetrated me to his full extent. The tip of his organ nudged my prostate and I shuddered at the unfamiliar pleasure of it. My prick grew distended; and as he rocked, my prick, with its newly acquired weight, swung back and forth and side to side, moist and swollen like a ripe fruit. The shiver in my loins flowed to my testicles, began to dribble, as his thrusts became more wild, into the bulb of my penis. The tissue there grew so sensitive, it felt as though I were copulating with the very air.

Allingham began to gasp; saliva dribbled from his chin onto my back, and trickled along my spine towards my neck, my arse grew suddenly slick and succulent for him, no longer the dry and makeshift shaft it had been, the sensations in my groin redoubled, poured freely into my prick and burst – powerful strings of milky mucus shot from my cock into the carpet, my legs buckled, and I collapsed, shuddering with delight and wonder at this unlooked-for and bizarre initiation into adulthood, and the pleasures of the flesh.

Allingham stayed in me a while longer, his long shaft teasing me slowly as he built to his own climax. He began to shout: mad, beautiful things came out of his mouth—

'Tom! Good grief!'

I heaved round so that I could see out from my grotto of skirts and coat bottoms. Stock stood there in the open doorway, transfixed, a lantern in his hand.

'Boris,' I said. (I noticed that his shirt was open, the buttons of his fly askew and half-undone.)

'I was just—' he began, then: 'Do you—' At last the enormity of the situation overcame him: he mumbled some apology and disappeared.

7

I walked home. The journey was long, but I had been anaesthetized by the alcohol. The night was clear and cool: perfect for contemplation.

Allingham Nye had said that a path might easily be forged through the cellars of the City, all the way from the Opera to the Folded Rose Hostel; no such easy route was to be found above ground. I skirted the gardens of the Goldsmith's hall and walked up to the Sé. From there I descended to Central Station. Cabs and milk wagons were already abroad. Their carriage lamps cast strange shadow-patterns over the waste ground to my left, and I glimpsed a screen of scrawny trees, behind which lay two ghostly bordellos. I wondered, with pleasurable disorientation, if after tonight I would ever want to visit such places.

Allingham Nye had been a superb and gentle lover, and while it was clear from his manner afterwards that our encounter meant no more to him than that, I could only be grateful to him for my initiation. It had not occurred to me till that night that my Uranian tastes were capable of fulfilment; now that Allingham Nye had fulfilled them, I was overcome by a heady and confused sensation of power and freedom. If fate had dictated that I would favour my own sex, then, I believed, I was equal to my lot.

The way to the City's road bridge lay through the region of the Folded Rose Hostel. I screwed up my courage and set off, furtively, threading my way through the alleys, my hands in my pockets and the lapels of my coat drawn up around my ears. The firebrands at the corners of these defeated streets had burned out hours ago: starlight alone guided me. My feet slipped in slops and turds and snagged in broken paving stones. I heard footsteps, scampering, a baby crying, and a long way off, a man's screaming fit. I inadvertently kicked an empty bottle across the pavement: it fell into the area of a tall tenement and shattered. The stench of bathtub gin rose from the blackness. A light went on in a high window. I hurried on. I heard the window open. Something soft and wet hit the ground behind me: I did not look back to see what it was.

Soon enough, I found myself on the broad road which led without check or incline onto the City's road bridge. There I rested, leant up against the rail, savouring the harbour air, while the strange, salt damp collected on my drink-flushed face.

I knew by now the streets leading to my rooms; knew them so well in fact that my progress would have been quite automatic, were it not for a curious incident: for just as I was about to turn into the aptly (if prosaically) named Academy Avenue, I heard a woman's whimpering. I glanced back, and noticed an unlit foot-passage leading between two large, gloomy houses. The sound came again.

Emboldened by my safe passage through the terraces of the

Folded Rose Hostel, I retraced my steps and peered down the alley.

The houses here were built into the side of the hill; the alley descended by flights of narrow stairs to connect my street with one running parallel to it, some thirty or forty feet below. Above me, and not far distant, a figure clung half-way up the right-hand wall.

It turned its head: 'Please—' A woman's voice. She was standing in pockets where the brick had rotted away. Her ankles were trembling. Her fists were wrapped round an iron spar, which stuck out level with two small balconies, one either side of her.

There was a lead gutter on my right. I drew off my coat and threw it aside, and took hold of the pipe. It seemed secure enough. I ascended it a little way, until I could lean out and take hold of the balcony's iron rail. Gingerly I straddled the gap between the pipe and the balcony, and pulled hard on the rail. It squealed and shifted. I tugged harder, panicking, and drew myself over to land most untidily – indeed, head-first – on chill, dew-damp flagstones.

'My hands are all sweaty! Oh God!'

I scrambled to my feet and looked down. These balconies either side of the climbing figure had once been one; they had been crudely separated, and wooden palings had been fixed with wire over the open sides. The spar to which the climber clung must once have supported the interconnecting part.

'For heaven's sake!—'

I wrestled with the palings. They came loose. I threw them over the side. It took some seconds before they hit the ground. Surely I was not so high up as all that? I leant over the balcony rail and looked down.

I had not, of course, taken account of the incline of the alley: The climber was suspended some fifty feet above the steep, glistening steps! I knelt, leaning over the open end of the balcony, and extended my hand.

'I can't!' She looked up at me: her eyes were blank with fright. 'I can't let go!'

I lay down and anchored myself as best I could; I leaned further down and gripped her trembling wrist.

'Oh God!'

She refused to let go. I gave her wrist a gentle tug.

'No!' She gripped harder; and her fingers slipped on the slick metal. Her whole weight yanked my arm. Pain shrieked through my shoulder, so sharp I thought for a moment it was dislocated. She pulled hard on my arm, let go with one hand and grabbed for the edge of the balcony. She missed, teetered, swung in again, grabbed the stone. She scrabbled for purchase and got one foot up onto the spar. She let go my hand, grabbed the rail near my head, pushed up with her foot and heaved herself on top of me. Exhausted, she belly-flopped over my back to safety. I lay flattened, winded, afraid to move in case my shoulder had been put out of joint.

'Tom,' the woman panted, 'thank God you happened along!'

I peered at her in the blue light cast by fading stars. 'Blythe?'

'Bloody stupid thing to do,' she gasped out; 'Lost my key.'

I remembered she had been playing with Stock in the Academy gardens earlier that day: perhaps she had lost it then. But why, having lost her key, had she not climbed up by the route I had taken?

'It looked too easy,' she explained, when she had regained her breath. She sat up against the balcony rail and stretched, luxuriantly. 'The brickwork under the balconies is all pocked and broken and I wanted to see how easy it was to climb: I fancied the challenge.' She shook her head. 'The brick's all soft; it crumbled under me as I climbed. Once I began there was no way I could climb down. I had to keep moving up. It was stupid of me.'

Recovered somewhat, Blythe stood up, pushed open the patio doors and went into the house. I waited on the balcony, peering blindly into the darkness, while she hunted for a light.

'There!' She turned the screw of the lamp and gentle, buttery light filled her room.

There was a threadbare grey carpet on the floor, blotched and criss-crossed here and there by dribbles of paint. There was an easel, turned away from me, and a large stained rag hanging from a hook on its side. A divan bed, largely hidden under rolls of raw canvas, stood in one corner. A large, ugly bureau lay open: its drawers were stuffed with tubes of beaten lead, brushes, rags, letters, torn envelopes. The walls were lined with paintings – some framed, some on their stretchers – cartoons, sketches in charcoal, prints and, pinned to the wall with rusty drawing pins, lithographs printed with blue and mauve inks.

Blythe folded her arms, stepping backwards towards the divan, and watched me warily as I surveyed the room. They were defensive gestures: few ever saw this collection of hers. Each piece had personal associations for her. It was as if I had entered into a private part of her mind—

I did not know all this then, of course: and I thought I could make her feel at ease by praising her work. She was as her cousin Henry had described her, a brilliant technician. Her nudes, portraits and city scenes were enlivened here and there by grotesque gestures. 'These faces!' I exclaimed. 'This one here: the corruption expressed in the line of its mouth – are these the children of the Folded Rose?'

Blythe gave a grudging nod.

I went on like this for some time before I realized she did not enjoy my praise: She sat upon the divan, her head turned from me, her arms folded. 'I owe you a great deal,' she said, in a flat voice. 'You took a great risk for me.' It was the nearest she could come to dismissing me.

Sensing that I had wrong-footed myself, I took my leave. 'I look forward to seeing you again, under less extraordinary circumstances.'

She managed a weak smile and led me to the door: it was easily opened from the inside. 'Goodbye,' she said. 'Thank you again.'

I found my coat in the alley where I had dropped it; it was soaked through. I draped it over my arm and walked up Academy Avenue to my rooms.

The beery warmth of my blood, which had up to now sustained me, chilled quickly in the morning air: by the time I got home I was frozen through. I swung my door to with a bang and stripped off where I stood. I lit a fire in the grate, wrapped myself in a towel and warmed myself in front of the flames. A bath would have served me better, but it was barely six and the recalcitrant Knobes would not yet have surfaced.

I stared into the flames as daylight gathered strength outside my window, and let the night replay itself behind my eyes.

It is extraordinary, after weeks of more or less rote existence, how much life will pack itself, quite unexpectedly, into the compass of a few hours. Much had come upon me all in a rush, and now I did not know what to celebrate, what to regret, what lessons to draw from it all, or what the likely consequences would be. Would my lovemaking with Allingham shape my life? Or was it a mere drunken aberration? I considered its social consequences. Stock knew of the incident, and so – unless Stock was very circumspect, which I knew he was not – Blythe would get to hear about it. And through Blythe, Henry: not that Henry mattered, since, by his sly remarks concerning C.L.S., he had demonstrated a nice phlegmatism towards male love.

It was, as time wore on and sleep stole up on me, the image of Blythe which most concerned me. Behind my eyes I watched her, arms folded, step back towards her bed: defenceless, eyes averted, body trembling from her abortive climb. It was Blythe as I had never expected to see her. It was Blythe without the brusque surface – that surface I had found so off-putting at our first meeting.

None of it made any sense. I rubbed my hands over my face, discarded the towel, and got into bed: the starched sheets were stiff against my skin. Something banged against the head-board. I reached up with my good arm – the other though it did not hurt much had begun to stiffen – and felt for the offending object. It was the book I had removed from the pocket of my sodden jacket. 'Transmogrification and the Perpetuation of Culture.' C.L.S.'s monograph, still damp.

Blythe—

Once more, images – of her room; of her face, averted from me – filled the spaces behind my eyes.

Why was I worrying so much about Blythe? Did I suppose she would be particularly outraged or disgusted by my activities the night past? No, it was not that—

I closed my eyes.

It could only be – *Are these the children of the Folded Rose?* – that I cared (my last thought, then sleep snared me) for her good opinion.

8

I saw nothing of Blythe for several weeks. When at last I went to visit her a middle-aged woman – the landlady of the house – answered the door. She wore a little silver fishing boat round her neck, hung from a thin chain. I asked after Blythe, and she shook her head, smiling conceitedly.

'She's not in?' I prompted.

She shook her head, more firmly.

'When will she be back?'

'Gone away,' she smiled; she shut the door in my face. I asked after Blythe in a casual, off-hand way, and Henry, taking his cue from my tone, told me little. Blythe had moved: the landlady had objected strongly to her climbing escapade and the damage done to her balconies, so Blythe had left, owing a month's rent. Where had she moved to? Some southern back street near the new tram workings, said Henry, as dismissive with his answers as I was with my questions. I asked him, with studied neutrality, whether he intended to bring Blythe along to any more drinking sessions at the Bar Terminal. Henry replied: 'Of course not, dear fellow, if you two don't get on.'

I was hoist up by my own circumspection! Did Henry suppose I didn't like her? Or was he protecting her from me? Had she taken an aversion to me, perhaps because of something Stock had told her? I had no way of finding out: not now I had paraded my indifference whenever her name was spoken. Henry, taking my professed lack of interest in women as gospel, dutifully kept the two of us apart. I kept an eye open at the Academy for signs of Blythe with Stock, but I saw neither of them. I went back to the Café Persil on several occasions, but no-one I recognized was there. What had seemed at the time to be an evening of great import for me was turning out to have had no consequences whatever: I might as well have dreamed it, or slipped into someone else's life entirely. It was uncanny.

When I went in search of Blythe, wandering the sorry developments of the City's southernmost suburbs, I told myself I was not so much looking for her as for that evening, that other life: the Café Persil, the poets, the Opera, the costume hall, Allingham Nye, the room full of pictures.

One overcast Sunday I followed the new canal from Quiet Lake all the way to its indeterminate end among the estates on the hill's southern face. Averted from the City, these rough, naked suburbs confronted a drear prospect of scrub and sterile rock terraces.

If the City was indeed a prison then here, at its southernmost prospect, it revealed its bars most brutally.

The buildings here were not so much homes as challenges to an unkind land. Few people dwelt here, those who did were rarely to be seen. In places, such was the general dilapidation of the region, it was impossible to tell what had been recently erected, and what abandoned. The towpath at the canal's furthest end, though recently built, had already fallen into disuse: there were weeds in the cracks between the flagstones, and the stones themselves had lifted, affording a treacherous prospect to the walker. The canal lay to my right: to my left, gantries for new overhead tramlines stuck up out the ground, their parts so oddly connected, like something a child makes out of clothes-pegs, it seemed the merest shudder would cause them to fall apart.

Further on the tram line rose up on an old railway embankment. Works forced me off the towpath and a little way up the incline. Ahead of me, the gantries, bare and useless as grass stalks, had temporary signs fixed to them: 'Drive Slowly', 'Ramp Ahead'. There was a metal pole, about fifty feet high, thin enough that had I embraced it, my hands would have met easily round its back. There was a ladder set against it and a crosspiece at the top, the spars tipped with lights like petals of some gigantic, Spartan weed. It was an eerie landscape – the sort of landscape you might imagine someone concocting who had never seen a city, and had no idea what it was for.

Not long afterwards I found steps which led back down to the canal. The steps had been roped off and a 'Danger' sign hung from the string. I snaked under the barrier and picked my way down. Some flagstones, as I trod upon them, wobbled dangerously beneath me and I glimpsed, in the wide gaps that had formed between them, the dank and flooded foundations of the stairs, glistening under stray motes of damp, late-afternoon light.

Some hundred yards further down the towpath there was a playground. I had not seen a single child that afternoon, and it did not surprise me that the place was empty. It was a nasty, soulless construction: a maze of low, shin-cracking red brick walls, irregular terraces and slopes of rough cement. In as much as it might have had a purpose, it seemed designed to scrape as much skin as possible from a child's knees.

In one corner there was a small amphitheatre, no more than twenty paces across, with semicircular benches made out of brick, two brick walls for wings, and a miniature concrete balcony. What sort of performance, I wondered with a shiver, would *that* inspire? Over it rose old railway arches; they were bricked in, and windows set into them some eight feet above the little balcony impended, black and glassless, portals to some urban evil. I ascended by steps too narrow for me: the balcony stank of old urine. The brick of the railway arches was all rotten: ants and spiders had eaten holes in the mortar and dead moss gave the wall a mottled, barnacled appearance. Once, there had even been bushes, growing out of the brickwork, but someone had sawn them back and painted the stumps with creosote. I turned to descend, and saw half a dozen old women enter the playground, dressed in the voluminous black shawls and skirts of beggars. They were cackling and arguing, and passing from hand to hand an old bottle full of some brown, murky stuff. Behind them, at a discreet distance, came Blythe, a sketch book under one arm, and over the other a bag stuffed with rags.

I descended the steps. The old women ignored me. They came and sat together in a semicircle at the bottom of the amphitheatre. From out their voluminous black drapes they drew stuff to make a fire: Blythe came up to me, glowering, and drew me away.

'Out on a stroll?' she demanded, *sotto voce,* when we were out of earshot. I wondered at her precaution. We held little fascination for the old women; they were arguing – as far as I could tell from this distance – about the best way to light a wet match.

I sat down on one of the stupid little brick walls crisscrossing the playground. 'Well,' I said, with a shrug, 'it's a strange region, sure enough, and I wondered what it was that attracted you to it.'

'You were looking for me?'

'I was curious,' I admitted: 'What are you doing?'

Blythe said, 'I'm making a study of these women: sketches, portraits–' she waved her hand, vaguely '–just to see if anything will come of it. But they're distrustful of strangers, and garrulous.'

'Oh?'

Blythe beckoned me up. 'Come with me,' she offered, 'but say nothing!'

We took our seats near the balcony, where Blythe could see the women's faces. Their fire was by now well alight; their faces, creased and lined and idiosyncratic, pulsed oddly in the firelight. They were toasting marshmallows speared on the handles of old sable brushes. Once in a while the tallest of their number reached over to the rubbish pile and threw onto the fire discarded sketchbooks, sliced canvases, snapped frames, lacquered panels with the paint chipped off, abandoned sachets and packets, cloths stained with flammable mediums, empty paint tubes, wool scraps with which they had reamed out discarded tins of thinners and varnishes—

'You give them their fuel,' I remarked.

Blythe shook her head. 'They pick it for themselves: from tips, from rubbish bins, from the detritus of galleries, the leavings of private auctions.' She was silent, then, intent upon some gesture of the women, some angle of the light. Her hand flashed across the page. 'This city,' she muttered 'is fuelled by art. Is it any wonder there are so many leavings?'

True, I had witnessed many artistic upheavals. The City's artists had, over the years of my growing up, developed more and more grandiose ways of redecorating our frozen, immutable home. Not a week went by that did not see new banners strung across the streets, fresh auctions of outdoor sculpture, a handful of pottery festivals in the parks, an evening of readings by the latest poets. But it had not occurred to me before, how all this work – new at first but soon surpassed – must somewhere, somehow, find its end.

Like ash filtered through a busy furnace, forgotten art found its way at last onto the City's rubbish tips. How long would the Opera, whose popularity was already waning, hold on to its treasured costumes? Would the next few years see these too ripped to rags, and fed to beggar women's fires? No doubt. Such was the way of life here.

I had not given it much thought before; now, faced with the fire the old women had made upon the puddled concrete – this final resting place for art – I grew morose and uneasy. 'How have you been?' I asked Blythe, to disguise my discomfort.

'On edge,' she admitted. 'That night you rescued me, I felt tremendously excited and alive. I'd faced death and come through! The exhilaration was tremendous. But—' she shook her head. Some of her hair came free from its velvet band. Three locks: they licked around her ear like flames.

Her eyes were tired. There were creases under them, which softened the startling directness of her gaze. 'I've been having nightmares,' she admitted. 'As I fall asleep I keep reliving my danger. Climbing the stairs to my apartment makes me dizzy.' She went back to her drawing. 'Stupid, isn't it?'

For a moment she looked as defenceless as she had when I had examined her private pictures; but it was not the modesty of the expression that appealed to me. It was rather the willingness with which she showed this weaker side. There was a candidness about her, more palatable to me than the rather silly bravura she sometimes displayed.

She brushed her hair back behind her ear.

'Come climbing with me,' I said, before I knew what I was saying. There was a lump in my throat: I felt it there all of a sudden; it surprised me.

'Funny,' she snapped; she thought that I was lampooning her. Some of the steel returned to her gaze. The muscles around her jaw tightened. It was as though her face were putting on armour.

'Up the road bridge,' I said. What was it, this lump in my

throat? 'To recover your nerve, if that's the problem. It's quite safe to climb, I went up it once as a boy; unfit as I am, I'm sure I could climb it now.'

She was silent, looking at me. Her hair had come loose again. I realized with a lurch that I desired her.

'You should have no problems,' I offered. 'Really, it's like climbing stairs.'

'Oh,' she said, disappointed.

'But it swings a lot,' I added hurriedly; 'the bridge I mean, so it's exciting. In the wind.' I ran out of words. I had so confused myself I simply stared at her.

She stared back. 'Oh,' she said. 'I see. Right then. Yes, all right. Let's do that.'

Her tone was so unenthusiastic, I mistook her meaning. 'Well, no matter,' I shrugged. 'It was just an idea.' I looked back at the crones, at the column of sorry smoke rising from their fire. It hung there in a mustard fog above their heads, reluctant to disperse.

'No, I said let's do it,' said Blythe.

'Sure,' I said. Then: 'What?'

Blythe smiled to conceal her irritation. 'Eight o'clock tomorrow morning.'

'Oh,' I said.

'Let's climb the bridge/ she said. 'You can show me how.'

And as she was leaving she gave me a kiss on the cheek. A friendly kiss.

9

'I thought you said this was easy!' Blythe yelled. Fear and exhilaration caught at her throat; her speech was thick and clogged. She looked down at me, panting. Her hair fell down around her face: it threshed about in the wind like flames.

'The holds seemed so much bigger when I was a boy,' I hollered back.

'More likely when you were smaller you found it easier to bear your weight.'

'You sound like your cousin,' I teased her, to take my mind off the chasm beneath us. 'This is no time for physics!'

'Come on, then!' Blythe cried, and we began once more to ascend the road bridge, where it spanned the marble river.

Minute by minute the wind picked up, plucking at our clothes, buffeting us. The bridge began to vibrate, the wind coaxing it moment by moment into new, nauseating harmonics.

Blythe clambered powerfully, but her weight played to her disadvantage; she began to tire. I caught up with her about half way to the top; we rested a moment on a wide, gently slanting beam, then, before the cold could stiffen us, clambered together up two sides of a square trellis, urging each other on with smiles and facetious jibes. Without such companionship, the wind and the trembling of the structure would surely have panicked us, and as the wind grew worse something desperate entered our laughter and our language.

The storm grew violent. Thunder clouds rolled in from the west, blue and black, primitive creatures from a deep ocean come to raid the hostile desert. The wind became a solid thing; it nudged and tripped us. There was nothing malicious about it; it was unaware of us and our plight. If the wind plucked us off and cast us into the air, no injustice would be done. Nothing stood between us and death but chance and our own skill.

My heart beat loud in my throat. At first I took the sensation for fear, then I knew it for joy. Terror is but one side of danger's tempting coin: the other is a sensation of absolute freedom. No wonder that we laughed!

'Wait!' Blythe cried. She linked her powerful legs round the junction of two spars, held on tight with one hand, and with the other reached under her jumper to her cotton undershirt. She tugged hard at the material. It gave. She tore off a wide strip. She adjusted her position on the beam to free both hands and tied the strip around her unruly hair, to keep it from her face.

'I'm freezing!' I called across to her. My fingers, chilled by contact with the fast-cooling iron of the wind-swept bridge, had passed the point of numbness. Hot aches crippled them, intermittent pins and needles made it feel as though I were climbing in gloves made of raw wool and thorns. The rest of the time, it was as if I did not have hands at all, but heavy bone claws clothed in felt – cumbersome, insensate, lethally unresponsive.

'If it rains,' Blythe exclaimed, with a worried glance at the clouds, 'we're done for!'

'We'll be sheltered by the surface of the bridge,' I called back, to encourage her.

'If we get that far!'

'We've no choice,' I replied. Down-climbing in the wet would be the end of us. I pressed on; Blythe stayed close behind.

The bridge set up a new and tremendous harmonic: I felt it thrum in my bones. Its sway became more regular, the 'give' in each metal limb grew more abandoned. The air filled with a terrible sound, like the massed call of a thousand metal birds: the bridge was singing. Battered by its incessant cry – a cry of pain perhaps, or of infernal pleasure – our minds grew dull. Terror and joy faded from our hearts, replaced by thudding fury. It was the fury of the ant, wrestling up some steep dirt bank with a leaf in its jaws: it is checked every time – by the gradient, by the weight it bears – but it will not desist. It is gripped by the blind and stupid determination of living things. So it was with us as, deafened, windswept and bedraggled, we reached the final leg of our breakneck climb.

But the danger was not yet over.

The beam along which I had crawled as a boy – that beam which ran mere feet beneath the surface of the bridge all the way to its mid-point – had shrunk to half its width, while its length appeared to have doubled. So much for objectivity: as I stared, fear and uncertain memories stretched the beam like taffy. Appalled, I did not move for some minutes: at last Blythe, huffing under the burden of her superb musculature, caught up with me.

'Problems?' she said.

I gestured at the beam.

She swallowed.

It was our only route across: all the multifarious spars, beams and ties by which we had ascended came together in this one beam. It and it alone spanned the stomach churning-gulf between us and the bridge's central pivot.

Straddling the beam as best we could, we pulled ourselves along with our hands. I felt honour-bound to lead the way. As a consequence, Blythe received what can best be described as an intimate view of my posterior – but this immodest perspective was the least of her worries at this point. Her superior physique showed every sign of finishing her off: burdened by her weight, she was near to dropping with exhaustion, the wind had near blinded her, and her clothes – adequate enough, no doubt, for tacking on the marble river – were long since damped through by the stormy air.

I reached the end of the beam and clambered to safety in the crow's nest of platforms and gantries. Blythe was no longer behind me. I turned back. She was still on the beam. Her face was pale, her eyes half-closed, her arms trembling. She was about three feet from safety.

'Kemp,' she said, in a tone I had heard before.

My heart beat in my throat: I clambered back to the beam and leaned toward her.

'I can't move!' she cried.

But I had reached her in time: with my hand upon her jacket collar, I pulled her forward. Had her hands been warm enough they would have clung stubbornly, like limpets, to the sides of the beam, and then I don't know what I would have done. As it was her fingers were frozen through and had little grip left. I pulled, and Blythe toppled forward. With a cry she saved herself – easy enough, for the beam was not as narrow as all that. I took her hands, put them on the rail, guided her up and over it and clasped her at last, my hands round her waist, as we shuffled forward towards the junction of great hawsers – our quarry.

It took some time for Blythe to recover. I would not let her rest too deeply for fear that she might fall asleep and lose some of her heat to the winds whipping viciously about us. She was tetchy with me, which was only to be expected, but she soon revived. We were much sheltered from the worst of the wind, and as sensation returned to her skin and her wind-bleared eyes recovered,

Blythe grew excited. She was proud at what we had achieved. 'So far, Kemp!' she exclaimed, over and over. Amazed at what we had done, awed at the sight of the City laid below us under glowering cloud, I happily shared her enthusiasm.

'Of all the people to lead me here!' Blythe laughed, then added quickly, 'I'm sorry, that wasn't meant as—'

I waved off her apology. 'I was thinking the same thing.'

'I would never have thought of this!'

'I'd never have attempted it again were it not for you.'

Blythe said nothing. My words hung there, pregnant. A pledge of sorts. We exchanged glances. We did not smile; we did not have to. Our glances spoke: some message, some thing that did not need words to express it.

I broke off first, my body trembling. It was as though some physical connection had been made between us; a thread or fine wire, looped through our eyes. It took force to break the connection, and even then, if was not wholly gone.

'There is a doll,' I mumbled. 'That doll I told you about.' I found it at last, still wrapped up in its paper, and bore it like a trophy back to her. She unwrapped it and examined it. 'You see?' I said, 'it's hardly weathered. You can even see the stains where I pricked my thumb on the needle.'

Blythe glanced over the paper. She looked over her shoulder, and frowned. 'I didn't see you go up there,' she said.

'What? Up where?'

'Up there,' she said, pointing to where the two halves of the bridge met above a gigantic hinge. 'Why should I go up there?'

Blythe looked back at the paper. 'Well, that's what's been drawn here,' she said. 'There's an arrow pointing right at the hinge. Isn't that where you should have put the doll?'

I came forward and looked over her shoulder. The paper was creased and stained, but my clumsy sketch was still readable. 'Good God,' I said, and blushed heartily. How on earth had I picked out such a trifling hole for my doll, all those years ago? My diagram was clear enough: it should have been inserted underneath the massive central hinge!

I laughed to cover my embarrassment. 'Why on earth did I not see that? I suppose I must have been too short to see over the top of the suspension ties.'

Blythe smiled: but she was not listening. She was gazing past the City, to the distant mountains – mountains that marked the edge of the world.

'I must look up what the doll means again,' I said, preoccupied. 'My father said it was a ritual to banish melancholy, but I wonder if he simply thought the adventure would do me good.'

Blythe said nothing.

'Blythe?'

She started, and half turned towards me. She said: 'I'm sorry.' Then, 'I was wondering: what lies beyond the mountains?'

'Nothing.'

'Nothing?'

'Nothing,' I assured her.

'No rivers? No woods? No lost lands?'

'Nothing.' The melancholy in my voice surprised me. Blythe turned back to the mountains. A minute passed and she said: 'How can we be sure?'

'The gypsies,' I said, 'they tell us there is nothing there.'

'And if they're wrong?'

I should have been irritated by Blythe's question, by her calling into doubt, the way a little child does, so basic and self-evident a truth. But I was not irritated.

I remembered Lilith, and her determined search for the 'given world'. In the beginning Lilith, too, must have asked that simple, shattering question.

And it seemed to me then that the attitudes Blythe and I held that moment said much about us: here sat I, my child's doll cradled in my hands, a timorous investigator of trifles; and there, beside me, stood Blythe – questioning the very fabric of the world!

I took the doll, climbed up and placed it where it should have been placed all those years ago, under the gigantic hinge. This gap was as filthy as the other, and as untenanted: who else but I would ever have performed such a silly observance? No doubt about it, I belonged to the Academy, to father's dry and bookish world.

But Blythe?

I gazed at her, at her shock of fiery hair. She sat cross-legged on the platform below me: Ah, Blythe! I thought, warmly: you have a gypsy's heart!

PART THREE

1

One summer noon five years later, Blythe and I met up at the Café Persil. We compared our lists and our baggage, and on the stroke of one, having satisfied ourselves that we had everything necessary for our adventure, we said farewell to our friends, and set off on foot, along the marble river – out of the City.

All that afternoon we weaved through the City's great complex of docks and wharves, pausing occasionally to watch antique barges trundling by on wheels taller than a man; patched sails the colour of tobacco snapped in the breeze.

Small craft wheeled about the barges: pleasure rigs ridden by the wild boys of the City. Bright noon light glanced from their chrome fittings and glittered upon the surface of the marble: a tantalizing, liquid sheen.

'Tom,' Blythe said, grinning into the wind that was blowing up from the east. 'Now that we are engaged upon this adventure, it amazes me we ever hesitated over it.'

'Our elders and betters taught us it was wrong to leave the City,' I pointed out. 'Such strictures have a lasting power. Do you not think that part of our enjoyment now is derived from a sense, however repressed, that we are doing wrong?'

Blythe giggled. Her laugh still surprised me; her too-wide mouth seemed at once ugly and desirable, just as it had on our first meeting. 'Yes, Tom, I agree. Why, I feel like a school-girl, playing truant!'

So we were – truants from that serious business of city life! Explorers, no less; but from a city that put no store by exploration.

When we neared the edge of that bustling district, home to bargees, we clambered down some stone slabs sunk into the embankment wall. Below the steps there was a wooden pier, resting upon the smooth marble surface of the river, and tied up to the pier were many sorts of small craft. River men lined up there, plying for trade. The baulks from which the pier was constructed were black and rotten, the cable binding them frayed and soiled. We stumbled often, and the men around us cast us glances of withering professional contempt. We hoped to find a boatman willing to bear us along the 'river', but we were soon discouraged. No-one here proved of any use. Not even the jangle of a money-bag could induce one young tar from his pipe and his rope-coil seat. The marble, we were informed with no great politeness, was strewn with rocks a mere seven miles from the City's municipal boundaries, and unnavigable. One did offer to take us as far as he safely could, but he demanded a price so outrageous that I sent him away with a flea in his ear.

We returned to the embankment. A dapper, chinless man in a smart, blue suit tended a stall stacked with arcane navigational devices. We examined them, thinking that they might prove useful, but none seemed necessary to our purpose.

'We're wasting time,' Blythe fretted. We quickened our pace, and in an hour or two we got beyond the maze of jetties.

After five years's study I had graduated from the Academy. I still did not know Blythe very well. Hearing Stock's tales of my pursuit of male love, she had decided to preserve a certain distance between us. This distance, far from souring the bud of mutual trust, had given it space to grow. Unburdened by the usual amorous expectations, our friendship grew candid and generous. Such temperate friendships can bear much. How else would we ever have dared concoct together an adventure as unorthodox as this upon which we were now embarked? *To leave the City …*

We were afraid, of course: as children we had been taught that the countryside was stuffed full of all sorts of brigands. Worse than the fear though, was the sense instilled in us that by leaving the City we were somehow demeaning ourselves. A man who left the City was a brigand himself. A woman who left the City was a gypsy, and as such no better than the lowest sort of drab.

But at last the thing was done – our lodgings were given up, our effects lent to friends or sold outright. My father's many books (for I had grown out of patience with my father's impotent arcana) I had given over to the Academy library, handing them in person to the custodian: Dr Emmanuel Binns. A fitting end for them, I thought: returned to the dust and darkness!

Quitting the City is difficult only in the mind. If childhood bugbears can be overcome, then leaving is easy: there are no fences, no guards, no watch-towers, no forbidding placards. It was with a sense of anti-climax therefore that Blythe and I found ourselves, quite soon, outside the City.

By three o'clock we had entered a valley of rich, well-tended farmland. Three o'clock! And we had not been robbed once! The road we followed ran roughly parallel with the marble river. Where the road and the river met, there were small hamlets, inhabited by vinegrowers and labourers. We passed through them without incident, and camped in a grassy dell. Five o'clock, and not a single brigand had made a test upon Blythe's virtue! Clearly, the dangers of the country were much exaggerated.

A grey penumbra cast by city lights dominated the sky as the daylight diminished: we were not yet outside the City's protective halo. But already we felt as if we had left the old life a thousand miles behind. The air was so fresh, and yet so rich: one felt nourished by it. It was clearer, too: transparent to a degree which astonished us, used as we were to the City's perpetual haze. And now, as evening descended, the air revealed another quality – substance. It was like a solid thing: a yielding tegument of crystal. It made objects shine, as though it had gellified into a lens that lends to every object, however distant, a preternaturally sharp edge.

'An extraordinary thing just happened,' said Blythe, returning from the stream where she had been washing the dust off her face.

'Oh?'

'A man just emerged from that spinney over there, and came right up to me. A young man, with a knife in his belt.'

'Why didn't you call me?' I exclaimed. 'What did he do?'

'He invited us to dinner,' she said. She frowned. 'Do you think we should go?'

I looked across to the spinney. On the rise above it stood a small-holding and a hut at its centre, warmly lit. 'Well,' I said, 'I think we should.'

'Will it be safe?' Blythe insisted.

'You know,' I replied, 'wishing for perfect safety is rather contemptible, isn't it?'

So we went. And drank. And talked, and ate, and – unless extreme culinary generosity ever enters the statute books as a method of murder – the cheerful farmer and his heavily pregnant young wife made not one single attempt on our lives. A happy anti-climax to our strange and peaceful day.

The next day brought us to the first mountain range. There were trees here, which afforded some shelter from the blast of the sun: but they were not the generous chestnuts of the valleys. These were dense-packed conifers. They filled the air with stale musk. Under them the ground was a mass of slippery pine needles and loose shale. It took us two hours to clear the forest; then, free of the obscuring foliage, we looked back and saw the City. How small it was! It glittered in the distance, newly washed and polished by a storm. Banks of blue-black cloud hung in the sky to the south of the City; we watched as the hungry sun swallowed them up.

It was a magical sight: these isolated clouds did not belong in the desert sky, but something had engendered them, had blown them across the City, and swallowed them up again—

What?

What strange providence, in all this inferno of scorching heat and splintered rock, saw to the care of our cool, well-watered municipality?

But such questions were, for the moment, a luxury we could

not afford: it was vital we crack our ascent of these slopes before the heat and glare became unbearable.

Progress out of the tree line was more difficult than before; for an hour we slipped and wobbled about on pale, filthy scree, snatching for purchase at the trunks of stunted firs whenever they came within reach. At length the gradient eased slightly, as the slope rounded towards the summit; but far from making progress easier, this convexity served merely to block out the spaces below, making it impossible for us to measure what progress we had made. Chutes of grey scree lay all about us, so without feature that each time I looked around, it seemed as though we could not have moved forward more than a few feet. After an hour of this, it was hard to escape the infernal notion that we had somehow stumbled upon a gigantic wheel, and were walking merely to stay still.

The top, when at last it came, opened out before us with the suddenness of a miracle: a smooth green lawn dotted about with flowers, and here and there a plant I did not recognize: a clump of serrated leaves, and half-hidden in its centre a single, fleshy bloom that smelled of dog rose.

'*Calatheae*,' Blythe called them. 'You find them sometimes in botanical gardens.'

'Are you bearing up?'

'Oh yes,' she smiled, 'I'm quite well.' My gallantry amused her. It was obvious that she was fitter than I, and better suited to back-packing. My wiry body, on the other hand, was a mass of aches and sore joints, and it was Blythe's constant refrain that I should not push myself too hard. 'If you must prove your manhood to me,' she had jibed, 'at least do it next week, when you have some muscle. Do it now, you'll cripple yourself and ruin the adventure for both of us!'

Remembering these words, I took off my pack, lay down upon the grass, put my hat over my face and did absolutely nothing for about half an hour.

'You'll fry,' Blythe warned me, when my time was up, and tipped the hat from my face with the toe of her boot. I sighed and sat up. The air quivered in the heat as though it were alive.

Half an hour's walk brought us to a dried-up river bed. We followed it into a broad ravine. It was not the season for rain. The bed was quite dried up. Water was just a memory; its course had left no mark on the surrounding stone. Even the oleanders, with their bright green sheaves, seemed sustained, not by past waters, so much as by faith in storms to come.

Wide semi-circles of bright pebbles showed where the winter flow ran smoothest. Elsewhere, the boulders barring our descent seemed an impenetrable barrier to any flood; come winter, they would turn the chill waters to writhing snakes of spume and spray.

The river bed opened out into a pebbly estuary. The ravine walls fell away in a mass of boulders and thorny scrub. There was a cave here, walled up into a pen for sheep and goats. Plane trees sheltered the opening, and beneath them lay a party of shepherds. To one side of the pen, a woman stirred a cauldron over a thorn fire. From the branches of the tree beside her hung dripping cloths full of wet cheese. A papoose of heavy green cloth was strung like a hammock from another branch: a child lay asleep inside it.

The woman called and waved to us. The shepherds stirred themselves, watching our approach in lazy silence. Then, when we were almost upon them, one of their number, a man with a fearsome moustache and silly, crooked teeth, leapt up, welcomed us with a great gabble of archaic compliments, and offered us the shade of the tree in which he had been sleeping. We accepted gratefully. Half-calabashes of warm milk sprinkled with rock salt were thrust into our hands, and nothing more was spoken until we had drunk our fill.

They could not understand what we were doing in these quiet regions. I spoke to them about the edge of the world, and they shrugged: there was nothing there. Why were we going all that way, when there was nothing to see? Put like that, our expedition did seem rather spurious.

What sort of nothing did they mean? A hole? A wall? A general or personal collapse?

No – simply nothing! they replied, vexed that city folk made even nothing sound complicated.

Their provincialism was seamless; there seemed no way to crack it, and little point in making the attempt. So I smiled and shrugged and pretended not to notice their looks of suspicion. There was probably some ingrained distrust of city folk among these people. When we told them of our walk, however, they took delight in describing their native landscape. We asked if there was a village nearby – and they replied with a list of precise directions to the village nearest the world's edge.

When we left, our pockets were stuffed with pears and almonds; our throats tingled from the sweet strong coffee they had insisted we drink. For as long as we were in sight of them, they called farewell, as though we had been their guests for a whole season.

Another day's trek brought us to that village which they had called Last Place. We had planned only to take a few days's rest, but the place proved so enchanting, we practically settled there.

2

The walls of the only café in Last Place – a long, barrel-vaulted room, sunk half into the ground – were covered over with posters and prints scavenged from the City. Flyleafs advertising dance companies and long-defunct orchestras vied for attention with scraps torn from a hoarding, a political manifesto on fluorescent pink paper, wrappers from bottles of champagne and port – there was much else besides, but I cannot remember it all. Having no pretty baubles of their own, the villagers here were careful to preserve and display any colourful scrap that came their way. It was moving and sad, this scavenging of colour.

Blythe had once said she wanted to be a 'pamphletist in paint': now she had her chance. Where better for her to set up shop than here? The townsfolk provided her with an appreciative audience, and many willing subjects. Free, now, from the weight of the City's past, she had set about recording the lives of these simple people: harvests, funerals, births, weddings, feuds, men shepherding their flocks, women gathering rock salt from the terraces above the village—

And why not a picture of this very tavern? I made a mental note to suggest it to her when she arrived. (She was off sketching the crippled shepherd's daughter; she lived a mile outside the village and I did not expect Blythe back until late.) In itself, the room encapsulated much about the simple, gentle life to be had here. Three men in thread-bare black suits – the only customers – were sat round a tin table, playing cards and listening to a gramophone record so scratched it took me a while to recognize the music. Vulgar ditties from the City's low cafés echoed about the half-cylindrical room; barely a single lyric came out unmarred, which may have been as well: what would these sober-looking gentlemen have thought if they knew what they were listening to?

The gramophone stood upon a wooden trestle at the end of the room; its bell was the shape of an amaryllis bloom, the dented brass petals painted over with faded nosegays. Near the gramophone was the cooking alcove. A thin woman was arranging twigs under a frying pan, easing them into the flames with a care typical of those who live in treeless regions. I ordered a meal, then took a seat at a table not far from the card players. The woman came and set before me a green glass carafe of white wine fortified with pine resin. I poured myself a drink and knocked it back in one swallow, raising my glass in honour of my hostess. She smiled, pleased that I knew the custom, and returned to her pans. The rest of the wine I sipped more temperately, and while I drank I glanced through my leather-bound notebook – all battered and dog-eared from the journey.

Blythe and I had been in Last Place for some months. We had not yet travelled to the edge of the world. This was partly due to Blythe's artistic fascination with the village. Partly, though, it was because we had become infected with the villagers' parochialism. Why travel to a place where there is nothing to see? Why look out into nothing when you can look in: upon your home, your family, your hearth? The wider issues played no part in the lives of the villagers, and they found it strange that Blythe and I talked so much, and about such abstract things.

It would have been easy to conform to the kindly mindlessness of these people: how close we had come at times! Work, when there was any, was hard. But companionship sucked the ache from our bones, and everything was so new and strange to us we were glad to participate in whatever was going on. I remember how at the end of autumn we knocked fruit from the trees with sticks of bamboo, and lay fresh-picked olives in an outspread blanket under the trees. I remember shelling peas. I remember covering tomatoes with gauze to dry in the sun. I remember the wine harvest; how Blythe joined the women of the village and helped pour baskets of grapes into the huge stone trough set in the village square, and how I was picked, an honoured stranger, as one of the first treaders. My fellows pulled my boots off and threw jugs of water fresh from some chill cistern over my feet. The old men grinned with toothless mouths. Pity to wash off the dirt, they said: it gave the wine flavour. Dutiful laughter accompanied this joke, which I imagine was as old as the village itself. Blythe put a garland of wild flowers around my neck and my fellow treaders helped me up, over the lip of the trough, and onto the grapes. They bounced, resilient under my feet, a hundred grape skins burst under me, and the first juices bled up from between my toes. The elders of the village struck up a song: a dreadful cacophony, with much drumming of hands upon the stone sill of the trough. The first mouthfuls of thin, dark liquid trickled down the long stone spout to the waiting bucket. The trickle swelled, filled up the channel; bucket after bucket was brought to the trough, and borne away full with pink-foamed juice. More grapes were added, a new team of treaders climbed into the cistern, and we who were done sat in the sun and sipped from cups of blood-red juice: already, one could detect in it the corrupt tang of must.

All in all, Blythe and I had led dilettante lives. When time came to harvest a crop, gather a herd, plough a sick man's field, repair an aged woman's house, erect a barn – then we were there, turning our hands to whatever we could. But the silly bustling ways the City had taught us had no place among these gentle people. For them, labour was a simple necessity: they did not need to make it into a first principle, the way the City's merchants and traders did. The hot country sun boiled away such cheerless philosophies, so that by the end of the year I dare say Blythe and I were quite as indolent and easy going as anyone in the village.

But thought is a habit we are loathe to break. I drained my glass and read from my notebook:

'The dawn light, cut by distant mountain passes into mathematical shafts of blue light, criss-crosses the barren plains. Where two or three beams cross each other, the land beneath glows twice as bright: a parallelogram of premature day. The beams's cool passage across the land proceeds with the slow stateliness of an alchemical demonstration, the lattices of watery and gentle light broken only where a shattered rock cone casts a perfect, elongated green-black shadow. Dawn here is a dance of numbers, a courtly game of rulers and compass, played with counters of light.

'Such regal entertainment ends by mid morning. By noon, under the blast of a savage day-time sun, all is cacophony: a shadowless abomination of mineral stains and broken structures.

'Not until sunset is the landscape humanized again: evening casts healing washes of turquoise, peach, and pale lemon over the cooked hills. The colours soak into the stone, soften it, so that at length the view becomes indistinct. It is a melancholy effect; under it, the land seems unknowable, unreachable, the fey glimpse of a declining paradise.

'Where dawn's geometrical games speak to the rational eye, sunset circumvents the eye altogether, and pierces with a fine flame the observer's soul.'

I closed the book. Why, I wondered, could I not simply observe? Why must I always be *scribbling*? Why did I insist upon imposing these clever-clever patterns upon the simple, inchoate experiences of my life? But there it was: I could not change now. Thought was a habit with me. A bad habit, perhaps, but an unbreakable one. The interlude to our travels was over; and our minds cried out for change.

'Have you finished?' the woman said to me, offering me another carafe.

I handed her the empty one. 'Yes,' I sighed. 'I've finished.'

*

The next evening, Blythe and I packed our belongings and walked out of the village. From here, we enjoyed for the last time a panorama of the village's fertile terraces. We recognized Patrick, a farmer and carpenter who had taken us in under his roof when we had first arrived at the village. He was hidden under a straw hat as wide as an umbrella, balanced precariously upon a sled as he drove three mules linked by a yoke around and around a threshing floor. The floor, perfectly round, shone bright as a gold penny in the evening light. On the terrace below, his wife and daughters were winnowing grain upon bright blankets, the chaff whirling about them in a soft copper cloud.

'We should have said our good-byes properly,' said Blythe, sadly. We had chosen to set off at evening, so our departure would not be noticed.

'If we had told people we were leaving,' I reminded her, 'they would have made such a fuss – we would never have left at all.'

'I will miss this place.'

I said, 'Perhaps we will come back here.'

She shook her head. 'No, we won't,' she said.

We began our climb in guilty silence. We knew we would not get far before the light failed us. We would camp above the village gardens, at the mouth of a defile they said led straight to the world's edge.

The pattern of fields and terraces vanished, obscured in a mass of shadow cast by the stony and rippled ground. But here and there the smooth discs of threshing floors, bright gold in the evening light, lay like loose change dropped by a careless god. The golden discs formed a unique constellation, brighter far and more intense than the few watery stars which hung above them in the dusk. A constellation that might, once understood, guide one to this or that homestead; to a path, a grove, a washing place. 'I wish I had been born here,' I sighed.

Blythe said, 'You only say that because you were born in the City.' She was right of course: dissatisfaction is the price one pays for thought.

The shadows of the peaks grew longer, their progress more stealthy. One by one, the threshing floors went out.

We ascended the mountain up long slants of rock, and at each angle new vistas opened below us. The foothills were already full of inky shadow, but across the great valley the mountain slopes glowed gold and green in answer to the evening sun.

We followed the contour of the hill, round to a cleft in the steep mountainside. This cleft was so deep and narrow, the bluffs to either side so rounded, I do not suppose the fiercest gale stirred more than a few grains of dust here. Thus sheltered, Nature – normally so hard pressed – could demonstrate her wares unhindered. Watered by a steep series of cataracts, the cleft was a mass of plane trees, sycamores, and figs. We followed a narrow path around the steep, rock-strewn bluff and arrived amongst a patch of flowering oleanders. A steep line of rocks indicated where, after winter rains, the nook swallowed huge torrents of run-off from the plain above. Of these cataclysmic down-pourings only a thin trickle was left.

I bent and put my mouth to the trickle where it splashed over a large limestone rock into a shallow basin. It was fresh and sweet. It had been explained to us by the proud townsfolk how the ground was so drought-hardened on the plain above us, the water just slithered off it down this notch. Every drop for miles around came through here: a minor miracle, without which the village could not have sustained itself. Blythe led the way up the water-course to the mouth of a cistern, hewn from a natural hollowing in the rock. We sat on the lip of the opening and gazed down upon tiny terraces crammed with tomatoes and chickpeas and beanstalks. We were above the level of the trees now, and I could see clearly how, fed by lines of hollowed tree trunks and crude notches in the rock, these terraces, extending in tier upon tier to the very bottom of the cleft, supped from countless basins and cisterns, artfully placed to catch and preserve the seasonal waters. Where the slope was too rocky to be cultivated, clumps of trees provided twigs for fires, figs, and shelter from what few winds penetrated the place.

There was, I remarked to myself, an intelligence and a genius to the region and its people: a secret wisdom I had yet to penetrate. I think if Blythe had said then, 'Let's stay,' I would have returned with her to the village. But all she said was: 'It's too dark to go on.'

We pitched our tent among the peas and convulvuli; we struck camp early the next morning, and set off for the edge of the world.

3

As the massive walls of the ravine closed in around us, towering ever higher as we ascended the gorge, the tops of the walls tallied so closely with each other, it was as if the earth there had cracked like an eggshell. At its narrowest part, the gorge was spanned by a sequence of old wooden bridges. Fat drops of brackish water, condensed upon impending ledges, fell with a dead sound among the creepers and vines at our feet. The place was a mass of spider's webs. I was continually having to wipe them from my face and out of my hair. The plants around had a primordial quality: there were blankets of moss, and ferns of all shapes and sizes; and *calatheae*, some with liquorice-black stems, which Bythe said were *lucifugae*, the rarest of all that species; from chinks in the rocky walls sprung shapeless succulents over which scurried nameless grubs. The place smelled of old evil; in its presence even the parched crags seemed preferable, and I regretted that we had not attempted them.

The ravine petered out quite suddenly in a great mound of loose scree, and when at last we attained the upper air we found that it was evening, and the light lay like fur across the buckled land. We camped under the lee of a tall rock.

In the morning we crossed the plain. Shattered spires rose all around, like the talons of some great beast, imprisoned beneath the gigantic scarp. Their knife-sharp edges stood out wickedly in the pitiless noon light; the air, blasted by heat, seemed to tremble with fear.

It was impossible to tell what lay at the foot of these spires: their roots lay many hundreds of feet below, swathed in intense shadow that never lifted. These mysterious caverns yawned hungrily; I fancied they might be the lairs of dragons. There was no life; the only motion the gelatinous trembling of the air. No wonder, then, that I began populating this place with beasts of my own invention; terror of the unknown, however intense, being always preferable to certain and complete isolation.

There was no obvious way down: We walked south-west along a ridge between two shattered towers, shielding our eyes as best we could from the terrible metallic glare. A dip in the ridge concealed what we had long since given up hope of finding: a spring, overhung by a fig tree. We dropped our packs and crawled gratefully into the shade. Some enterprising shepherd long ago had harnessed the water of the spring, laying a hollow tree trunk down to catch the water before it trickled into a green and sickly mat, down through fissures in the rock some feet below. I knelt and drank deeply from the cold, sweet reservoir, then leant back against the tree and took out of my knapsack some of the food I had brought with me: cucumber, garlic, paprika, onion, tomatoes, and two rock-hard biscuits of twice baked bread. These I tossed into the hollow log to soak for a time. I stood up and plucked a fig leaf to serve as a plate, rescued the bread and wrung it out, tore it and sprinkled it with slivers of garlic. Blythe and I ate in rapt silence. No meal in the City had ever tasted like this one, no olive sparked so sharp on the tongue as those Blythe had wrapped in a kerchief in her knapsack pocket, no cucumber quenched a thirst so quickly, no oil was ever so rich and savoury as the oil I dribbled sparingly from a little clay bottle onto the ripe and bursting tomatoes.

The descent which followed was a break-neck affair that saw us surfing half out of control on a landslide of scree through an absurdly tilted landscape of shattered towers. The towers set up a sinister echo which doubled and redoubled the noise we made, filling the air with an outraged and terrible susurration.

When at last the slope levelled off, we found to our consternation that the going was harder than ever. Where once we could simply surf the rubble beneath our feet, now we had to pick over it, in mincing, unsteady strides, fearful every moment of breaking an ankle.

All around us in the neutral evening light loomed the shells of shattered towers. A hissing sound from within a circle of these towers distracted us. We paused a moment, listening, then approached the circle. The going was easier here, the scree smaller and more compact.

When at last we came up to them, we found that the towers were much smaller than we had imagined, stuffed with cactus and overgrown with spider's web. They surrounded a depression in the earth, and from out of it crept two shadowy figures: mother and daughter, folded up in the shapeless black gowns that gypsies wear; old straw hats, almost a yard across, were balanced upon their heads. They were gathering rock salt in wicker baskets. They told us they lived in a cave not far away, where there was a little spring of brackish water for them to drink, and for moistening their twice-baked bread. There was not a trace of misery or bitterness in their tale.

'Why do you suppose they live like that?' Blythe asked me, when they were far behind us. Then, twisting up her face, she spat upon the ground. 'They are in love with this place!' She made it sound like a perversion.

'They deserve pity more than suspicion,' I replied, 'and anyway, they have directed us to our quarry.'

'The edge of the world?' Blythe smiled, ironically. 'I do not think we'll have much bother in finding that!' And she pointed down the ever more gentle slope, at blank, interminable wastes of desolation.

The ground became smooth, scattered over with pebbles and glassy shards. Our feet told us that the slope had all but given out, and yet before and below us, the desolate rocky basin – curved at its edges now as though its vastness were causing it to collapse upon itself – promised us days of wearisome descent. No new peaks were revealed to us; the very absence of feature wormed its way steadily into my heart, until I could barely walk, gripped by agoraphobia. The day ended early. Sharp shadows cut the landscape into a billion shining fragments.

We slept that night huddled together, dwarfed by the immense spaces around us, frightened by the sheer scale of the emptiness surrounding us, and the great yawning sky.

The next morning we opened the flap of the tent upon a landscape so alien it took all our courage to step outside and confront it. The great depression in which we had camped had curled tighter upon itself during the night. To our left and right, and miles distant, walls of rock several times higher than the highest mountain tilted up in absurd, liquid curves. Indeed, it was impossible for us to say how high these walls really were, for they overtopped the air itself, dissolving in a misty effervescence as their sloping surfaces approached the perpendicular. Even to call them walls was not sufficient, for if they had been walls, then the sunlight would have caught them obliquely. As it was, both were lit plainly by the sun! Light itself was conspiring in the illusion that these great curves or waves of land were but the basin floor perceived strangely, as from the air. It seemed to us then that we were entering the lip of some gigantic jug: a lip whose curvature was rendered so utterly seamless and gradual, that air and light as well as land were warped in the effect. Our minds all in confusion, Blythe and I pressed on, and at every step it seemed to us that we were pouring ourselves out of the world into some scalding oblivion. The ground lost its smoothness. It became serrated, the swirling jags of stone knife-sharp under our boots.

Towards evening, dune replaced the rocky floor of the mesa. Sedges and gorse – the first living things we had seen that afternoon, glimmered in the waning light. I stopped and looked about me. Behind me, Blythe gave forth a sharp cry – of warning, or dismay.

There was nothing to see now but this great listing plateau of sand and gorse and sedge.

Blythe hurried to me, and took my hand.

Her skin was dry, a mere prickly pressure on my palm. She squeezed my hand, shouted at me, but the sound came through to me shrouded by the hiss of dust on the air, the insistent, unintelligible whisper of a billion grains of sand. The sun bloodied the dirt all around us.

Something strange happened to the bushes. As the sky grew black so their colours seemed to burn more fiercely. They grew more pure: shades of russet turned primary red, brown went black, and leaf on the turn changed from chrome to purest daffodil yellow.

Shapes too grew more jagged, their geometries formal and stylized, as in a child's picture book.

I turned in amazement to Blythe.

She was no more than a doll, a wooden doll, life-size, with woollen hair.

I turned and turned and turned: shade by shade, subtlety by subtlety, the world was going out—

Blythe pulled sharply at me, and I fell back into the world. I sprawled there in the dust, afraid to open my eyes.

A wooden doll ...

'Thomas!'

Blythe's frantic breath wetted my cheek. I opened my lids a crack and peered at her – at her tears and the dust streaked in her hair. 'Oh!' I gasped, and flung my arms around her, shaking.

When at last I let go of her, Blythe stepped forward gingerly and extended her hand into that spot where I had stood. Her outstretched fingers went pink. She snatched them back and examined them. They were as they should be. She extended her hand again. Again, her fingers turned pink. She flexed them. I peered closer. Her fingers had been transmuted into some other substance – hard, pink, and smooth. There was no skin on them: the joints were quite visible, flexing on little metal pins.

Blythe snatched back her hand, put it to her mouth, and held it there, whimpering. I extended my own hand into that invisible, metamorphic zone. My fingers went pink, then, as I extended my arm further into that space, turned brown. From flesh, to plastic, to wood. From crude forms to yet cruder forms, until – what?

From my knapsack I took out my notebook. From it I tore a pencil portrait I had made of Patrick, our host. I edged it into the zone. The picture disintegrated. Lines vanished. Subtleties dissolved. A breeze picked up and carried the picture a foot or two further into the zone. Blythe shuddered with horror. I stood transfixed. On the paper, where the portrait had been, was a stick-man, such as very young children draw. A stick-man, scrawled in black crayon. Then that too decayed. We had reached the border of our illusory little kingdom. We stood at the limits of its trifling power.

Beyond lay an abomination. A plain: smooth as a table-top,

more inimical than Hell. A place too desolate to sustain meaning, let alone life.

Of the Greater World there was no sign.

PART FOUR

1

'I enjoy the light: the open spaces of the squares, all deserted in the afternoon; the silence here.'

'It sounds haunted,' I said, with a shiver. We had left the canal just past the playground and were walking up a grey and winding street towards her house: a modern cream and grey apartment block set among low, box-like houses, cracked through with subsidence.

'Of course it's haunted,' Blythe replied. 'That is the point.'

Blythe rented three rooms on the ground floor; they were square and without feature, like the insides of cardboard boxes. The drawing room was separated from the kitchen by a wide sliding door, which was stuck solidly open. There was a large north-facing box which Blythe used as a studio. Its cheap floorboards – many had dried and split down their whole length – were spattered with paint. Blythe used the third, and smallest, box for her bedroom. Here she hung her private pictures. She did not invite me to look at them.

Blythe and I had stuck closely by each other since our return from the world's edge, sensing that alone we might not be able to bear the truths our adventure had confirmed.

In our prison-world, our box-room city, we struggled to find some meaning for our lives.

'It seems to me,' said Blythe, handing me my marjolaine, 'that since we know, you and I, that the world is really so limited, and there is no actual door to some great outside – then it is only by enriching the little world that we can expand it.'

'But I never thought of you as a mere "embellisher",' I said, wryly. 'I thought you wanted art to be a knife, cutting through the world.'

Blythe smiled; she was pleased with my acuteness. 'If we use art to enrich the City, then it must be an honest art, one that confronts the world's limitations. An art that is rooted in smallness and bareness. A brutal art, of necessity, because we live in an age of brutal truths.' She stood up from the sofa and offered me her hand. 'Come into the studio; let me show you what I've done.'

Pinned to the walls, Blythe's drawings of the City's beggar women stared down at me with baleful ferocity.

'Good God,' I said. I was taken aback: I had assumed her new work would refer to our journey to the edge of the world. Instead, Blythe had gone back to her earlier sketches: of beggar women, turning the art of the City into the rubbish of dead bonfires.

There was no denying their eerie, oppressive power: you caught it in the way Blythe had drawn their eyes. In the first pictures, they were illuminated, widened and made wise in the glow of incinerated canvases. Then, in mid-series, they became suddenly empty, dead, even terrible. In the final picture – different from the rest, and nakedly emblematic – the City itself was portrayed as a beggar woman: twin bridges formed the ragged shawl which framed her haggard face; her features were made of intersecting alleys, stucco mouldings, pigeon's wings: she sat upon a pyre of broken frames, rent canvases and twisted, broken plaster-casts, wreathed in flames ...

I was shocked. 'Why've you returned to this drear stuff?' I insisted. 'What happened to all those sketches you made in Last Place?'

'Oh!' she exclaimed, and flung her hands into the air. 'Don't be so obtuse, Tom! Didn't I say art must be honest? It must tackle the paucity of the world, not hide from it. The rustic life is no more than another veil, shielding our eyes from the truth: what would you have me do – prettify goat-herds for a sentimental clientele?'

'That's not what I meant,' I replied, hurt. 'I just think it's a shame that our travels haven't made you think differently about the world.'

'Differently? How?'

I thought of Patrick, Last Place, and our friends, all left behind. But just as I was about to speak of them, I remembered what had followed: our terrible encounter with the world's edge. Blythe was right: Last Place, and the rustic life generally, was – for all its human worth – a distraction. A warm, human bauble, placed in the way of a most chill, mathematical truth. I said nothing.

Blythe said: 'You know, I've always found it dull work, living in this world. Always, since I was a little girl. To live and not to know where the fish come from, why the gulls queue for bread, why we live in the desert yet dream of seas and snows … either you know why you're alive or it's all rubbish.'

I looked at her pictures once again. 'Does this mean that you must only paint the rubbish?'

'That's right,' Blythe replied. 'I must paint the rubbish – there is nothing else worth painting!'

The bronze cast of a nude woman reclined luxuriously upon floorboards pale and bruised, like skin too long under a dressing. Her stomach was flat and well-muscled, her legs strong, like a cyclist's. The left leg was crooked, revealing finely worked genitals. Looking up from the bronze nude, I saw, hung upon the walls of the gallery, five large etchings, and a portrait in oils.

I wandered from piece to piece for a few minutes searching for some unifying principle to the works. None sprang to mind, even though these pieces were all by the same artist. I ascended the generous and creaking staircase to the next floor, and found myself in a light loft-space, bare but for some large display cases. In them lay some remarkable and unusual pieces: a porcelain violin painted over with an exuberant scene of fiddlers and rustic dancing, a thirteen-storey china pagoda with spouts at every corner of its tiered roof, a jug covered in mandalas – but from none of them could I have guessed the identity of the artist.

A creak on the staircase made me turn. Blythe was there.

'Is there nothing Allingham Nye can't turn his hand to?' I demanded.

Blythe shrugged.

However fiery our disagreements and misunderstandings, it flattered Blythe to teach me about Art. Each morning she would take me through winter rain to one or other of the City's many private galleries. If the work we saw was poor, I grew waspish and sarcastic, and Blythe grew short with me, like a baited school-ma'am. If the work was good, then Blythe's childlike enthusiasm was infectious.

Allingham Nye's exhibition prompted no strong reaction either way: we left the gallery and repaired to the Bar Terminal. The waiters sat us down at the table by the black iron eagle bolted to the front of the bar. I toyed with a pretzel but felt too self-conscious to throw it. I racked my brain for something sensible to say about Allingham Nye's exhibition.

Allingham Nye was one of the most popular artists of those days. It turned out that, shortly after our passionate encounter, he had left his post of scenarist at the Opera and been taken up as a protégé by no less a figure than my old history tutor, the multi-talented Mr C.L.S. Since then he had come out from under that man's shadow to pursue a career so fecund it was an uphill struggle for his audience to keep up with his shows, which were constantly opening all over the City.

I was shy of meeting Nye himself – I had a wilting notion that he might be embarrassed to see me again, or worse, that he would not remember me. But I had eagerly accompanied Blythe to this, his latest show.

'He has an extraordinary facility!' I declared, though without much enthusiasm.

'Precisely,' Blythe muttered. 'That is precisely what is wrong with him!'

'What?' I said, 'that he is facile?'

'Don't you think so?' I was about to reply when Blythe nudged me under the table with her foot and said, 'To your right, you see who's just arrived?' I turned and saw a small party – two men and two women – take their seats at the neighbouring table. One of the men was Evelyn Christ; his companion I recognized as Maera LaCouche, the opera singer. The second woman I knew vaguely as the author of 'Mouth and Memory', a good-natured but fatally confused edificatory pamphlet.

The grey-haired gentleman accompanying her was C.L.S.

Christ gave me a shy nod when our eyes met, and must have mentioned to C.L.S. that he knew us, for C.L.S. took an interest in us thereafter, and acted up a little for our benefit. When he said something witty, he would glance across at us, smiling, as though we were to be included in the joke. Eventually he came across to us with a basket of strawberries, and offered us some.

We exchanged pleasantries. It turned out that he had retired from the Academy, the better to devote himself to art.

'Then I had better count myself lucky I was in time to hear you lecture,' I said, meaning to flatter him.

He waved my words off: 'Too stale, dear, too stale by half!' It was not clear whether he meant his lecturing, or my compliment. He turned to Blythe. 'Miss Maravell, if I'm not mistaken.'

Blythe blushed, pleased that he had recognized her.

C.L.S. turned to me. 'Historians should always consort with artists, don't you think? The pleasures of miscegenation!' I explained to C.L.S. that, however mediocre I had been as an historian under his tutelage, Blythe, nevertheless, was very much an artist.

'A pity we did not speak before,' said C.L.S. 'There was a private view of *Island* last night at Grabbinges; you could have come along. Still—' He smiled '—it seems to me you both might like to visit my studio, sometime. This time next week perhaps? If your curiosity about me holds out that long. A picture tells a thousand words, and anyway, artists are no good at explanations unless they have pencils in their hands.'

A few days later, Blythe and I went to view C.L.S.'s new show.

Island was laid out to appear as though it were a museum exhibit of crafts and treasures from a lost people – a half-invented, half-real culture whose artefacts were assembled from the City's detritus. There were exotic crowns cut from cans that had held sauerkraut. Tiny ornamental jugs made by weaving copper bands round coloured light bulbs. Toys made from coat hangers and old tram parts. Doors inset with shards of coloured glass, arranged in mosaic patterns. Flutes and drums and simple, single-stringed violins fashioned from pipes and tubs and broken furniture. Stone crosses and totems lay in a row along one wall, hung with beads and toy spiders and strung together with stripped wire. There were plaster skulls with faceted glass eyes and beaks made of beaten catering drums.

Some exhibits were arranged in more complex ways. In one lay a guitar made out of old electrical components. Its frame was made of wood, covered in tin foil and beaten coffee tins. It had no strings, and an old switch-plate took the place of a fret-board. Buttons were nailed into the fret-board; wires trailed from them in colourful bundles. The choice of materials made it not so much a model of a guitar as its memory. In another cabinet, a couturier's plaster dummy lay in state, wearing full evening dress. It grinned madly, gripping in its hands a clear glass cross set with ball bearings. The mannequin was surrounded by burial goods: wooden swords, Bakelite models of railway engines, and insects made out of painted wire, stuck together so that they seemed to be mating. At the mannequin's feet was a plaster gargoyle.

My heart thudded with excitement, not from anything that C.L.S. had made here, but – on the contrary – from what he had *not* made. For amongst his own work were ornaments and artefacts I recognized from elsewhere. Those light-bulb flagons, those plaster skeletons, those paper flowers and gaudy crosses – those were not C.L.S.'s creations: I recognized them for the folk-art of Last Place! C.L.S. had scavenged much of his exhibition from the villages surrounding the City. In so doing, and in creating his mythical *Island*, he had done what I had hoped Blythe might do: he had created a wholly new vision of the world, one that turned the detritus of one city into the artefacts of another – one as yet unborn.

A thrill went through me: an intensity of excitement I had not felt since I was a child.

Blythe sniffed. 'I cannot imagine what you see in *Island*,' she said, as we walked to Central Station. 'It is the worst, most unthinking sort of embellishment.'

'No,' I insisted, put out by Blythe's reaction. 'That's not true. C.L.S. has imagined a way forward for our city. He imagines that we enter new and alien lands through time, rather than through space. The foreign and surprising lands we were seeking exist in future times, rather than in distant valleys.'

'And we travel to those foreign realms by idle speculation and the throwing together of other people's work, I suppose!'

'That,' I replied, coldly, 'is a most unkind interpretation.'

'I see no other,' Blythe replied, belligerently. I glanced at her face: it was stony, sealed up: it was not the face I liked, or thought I knew.

I said, 'You could at least give him credit for travelling outside the City: like us, he had the courage to put aside petty prejudice and see those lands for himself!'

Blythe shrugged. 'That's as may be,' she said, 'but what did he do with what he learned? It was all mere raw material to him: stuff from which to build fantasies. Fantasies! The cheapest sort of art.'

'*Island* wasn't fantasy!' I protested. 'It was history – a speculative history, a history of the future. It reminds us that the historical process is not yet over, that change is possible!'

'Is it?' Blythe demanded. I see little real evidence of it. To my mind we are at the end of history. Everything points to it. The loss of magic, the littleness of everything. There will be no more change. Only better understanding of our miserable existence.'

'And then?'

'Despair,' she said, unflinching.

'Is that all you can offer?'

She looked at me – a blank, nihilistic gaze, in which I recognized her pictures of the beggar women: I was chilled through. 'That, Tom, as you well know, is all the world has to offer.'

'You dislike hopeful work on principle,' I said, to prick her armour.

'Fantasies aren't "hopeful",' she replied: 'they're an admission of failure – mere masturbation.'

'You and your bloody knife-like art,' I grumbled; 'you murder the world as you dissect it.'

'I simply dislike lies,' she retorted, raising her voice: she was losing patience.

'Even necessary ones?'

'There's no such thing.'

'Blythe,' I sighed, 'the world can only have meaning if we give it one. How else can we hold it all together? Trams, the Ceremonies, *Calatheae*, "Werner's Trunk", stucco, Bakelite, grey gulls, black-clad women, tin guitars ...' I found myself trailing off into nonsense. It seemed to me suddenly as if the world was like a deep dark mouth, and every thing a misshapen tooth. The feeling unbalanced me: I didn't understand it.

'The world's not big enough to sustain a human meaning,' said Blythe, as if she'd read my mind. The smile on her face was chill, even malevolent. 'You would like us all to lead fantastical lives, wouldn't you? Lives of high drama! Well the world's not big enough for that. You'll see. This world is neither comic nor tragic. It is merely farcical. There can be no great joys in this world, no potent tears. Only horrid laughter!'

The following week found me crossing the Circus of Birds on my way to C.L.S.'s rooms on Green Monkey Street. I was alone. Blythe had chosen not to accompany me: we had had a falling out.

One felt certain, walking across it, that something momentous was about to happen in the Circus of Birds – though nothing did any more. The sky was grey, like a great metal lid shut over the world. Trapped and reflected by the metallic sky, light lost all its colour and softness; it boiled away, distilled into a trembling, intense luminescence. Though it was late evening, I could see clearly every rivet and strut of the ancient scaffold. Beyond it, the guttering and cracked paintwork of the deserted terraces stood out with the bleak intensity of a photographic print. If daylight paints a landscape, then this light etched it, scraping its shapes into the varnish of my eyes with a needle-sharp point.

Eerie breezes circled the Circus of Birds, carrying strange hints and sighs. The Circus, once the City's magical centre, was never at rest; it was as though it were raging against its own impotence.

The air was haunted by half-snatched rhymes, lines of the *Oubliez*, the muttering of old women, the cry of gulls.

Only as I ascended Green Monkey Street and glimpsed the sugar-confection spires of the Sé did the sky take on its proper hue of deep, winter blue. I turned off Green Monkey Street at a small arched alley and entered a cobbled courtyard. I looked around for the stairs to take me up to C.L.S.'s apartment. A light in an attic room guided me to the steps. The clack of my boots upon the stone must have alerted C.L.S. to my arrival; when I reached the top of the winding staircase he was standing at the open door. In his guise of artist, there was nothing formal about C.L.S. He wore a simple skin-tight jersey with a broad blue lateral stripe, and rough denims. His clothes contrasted oddly with his aged and dignified face; the effect was exotic, and vital.

'Come in, come in,' he bustled. I entered a narrow hallway which ended in a large arched window. Exotic birds pecked at the bars of wicker cages hung in rows along the hall.

I noticed that the floorboards, which were smooth from much scrubbing, were dotted here and there with splashes of bird dirt.

'When I'm on my own, I let them fly around,' C.L.S. explained. 'A messy eccentricity, but my own.'

He led me into another room, whose size would have been impressive had it not been littered with so much junk. There were sofas with the stuffing half knocked out of them, and wooden chairs with broken legs propped against each other in one corner. On the sofas lay several sculptures of guitars, which I recognized from the *Island* exhibition. When I asked him about them he explained that they were new acquisitions. He himself, he explained, made the guitar for *Island*: but he had since learned of an old man in a small hamlet to the north of the City, who made guitars just like it. These guitars were the old man's work.

'To tell you the truth,' C.L.S. confessed, 'eighteen months into this project, and I'm getting in a dreadful muddle about what I acquired and what I made. The techniques I learned from these rural craftsmen are relatively crude, you see. A bulb-flagon by the great C.L.S. is indistinguishable from one made by some goodwife up in the mountains. And just as worthless, or as valuable, depending

127

on your point of view. Even I can't tell them apart.' There were several trestle tables ranked along the back of the room. These were piled high with newspapers, photographs, umbrellas and other assorted rubbish. Under the tables lay piles of rocks. C.L.S. led me on without comment and ushered me into his studio.

Dominating the room stood the cold-clay original of his 'Man with Fish'. 'I made the fish out of an old vase,' he told me, 'and a spray of dried flowers, dipped repeatedly in plaster slurry, for the tail. You see the set of the man's shoulders, the furtive stoop? What object do you suppose hides under that lot of clay?'

I could not guess.

'Bicycle handle-bars,' he said, matter-of-factly. 'That, you see, is the key to my work, for good or for ill. I do not make: I find.' (Later, and in bronze, 'Man with Fish' could be found set up in a little square near the Folded Rose Hostel, under a tree particularly favoured by the local sparrows.)

Around the room lay numerous busts and plaster reliefs – women's heads. 'Your face,' he told me, 'reminds me of a young model called Jean Hegutine. Here—' He picked up a small plaster head – no bigger than his fist – from a tin bucket full of similar heads. 'You see here, and here?' he said, pointing to the base of the plaster neck. 'The angle between the line of this tendon and the jaw fascinated me. But that's all done with.' He threw the head carelessly back into the bucket. 'Come along, the tour's not done yet!'

The next door was propped open with a small bronze bird's skull.

We entered a large loft. Canvases lay stacked four or five deep against the wooden supports. The room, which was lit by oil lamps, was white, and even the floorboards were a kind of off-white, so that it seemed the whole room ebbed and flowed around us as we moved, with a total disregard for perspective. The effect must have been even more disconcerting in the day, when there were fewer shadows, and an even daylight filled the room from the many skylights.

At the end of the room stood a group of six men in evening dress; they were admiring some large canvas which was turned

128

away from me. C.L.S. paid them no mind, and did not introduce us. He walked across the room and sat upon an ornate but much abused antique dining table, set under a north facing window. 'I hardly ever use this room to work,' he told me. 'I do my painting downstairs and my sculpture in another studio I have, off Trout Street. Do you know Petersen's *Beatitudes*? The covered spiral stairway up to the Trout Street studio is where Margory meets Richard Speng, the poet nobody understands, and tells him she's had an abortion.' He shrugged. 'The area is full of all sorts of literary and artistic allusions, if you can be bothered with them.' He jumped up from the table. 'Come and have a look at some of what I did when I lived at Tierney Street!'

I followed him across the room, and he showed me some of his early paintings – expressionist still-lives in a brutal palette of greys and ochres; he piled them on top of one another, carelessly, as though he were stacking up a bonfire.

The bell from the Sé struck midnight. The group in front of the painting took their leave of C.L.S. They paid me no attention. C.L.S. said his good-byes carelessly. When they were gone he said, 'I'm tired, now. You'll have to go. And if you want to come back, come as you came tonight, because you were interested in me. Don't be like those silly starch-shirts out there.' He thumbed at the open door through which the gentlemen had just departed. 'I have no time for cultists.'

2

All that winter and the following spring I tried my hand at art: doubtfully at first, but as time went by, with greater confidence. I found I had a native talent of sorts, and an eye for perspective and scale; C.L.S., amused to take so raw a pupil into his charge, fostered my experiments, leading me around the wide and empty dockyards and having me draw what I saw.

The clean lines of the barges and cranes were simple enough, and drawing them gave me confidence. Later, C.L.S. got me to sketch the same scene at different times of day, so that I began to take account of the passage of light, the differences of suffused and direct illumination, and so on. He never criticized me directly, but would rather say something like, 'always work below your means. If you are given a paint box with eight colours, throw four away. If there are two brushes in your drawer, discard one. Ingenuity only ever flourishes under privation.'

Advice like this encouraged as much as it informed, and inspired in me the strictest self-discipline and the most grand ambition. I developed quickly.

I said nothing to Blythe about my new calling. I feared she might laugh at my pretensions. I did not find it hard to keep my activities from her; she herself had tired of me. She had lost interest in my opinions. I had refused to indulge her in her gospel of despair, and this made me appear trivial to her.

'You see now,' said C.L.S., examining a harbour scene I had brought him, 'that your single sable has produced a multiplicity of effects you would not have thought possible a month ago. That is because you have trained your hand, made it supple and smart. But the strength of this piece lies, not in the multiplicity of its effects alone, but rather in the tension between them and the necessary crudity of your brushwork. You are up against the stop here, forcing your medium – your single brush – to perform to the very edge of its capability. Therein lies true strength. In the artist: and in the man.' He clasped my shoulder, and squeezed it, hard.

The touch – the firmness, the power of it – was familiar. I remembered Allingham Nye.

I had always found myself drawn to C.L.S. the teacher. Now I was drawn to the man. All through that spring C.L.S. was testing me, to see how far I would let our relationship develop. If I arrived in a rainstorm he towelled my hair dry. If the rain had penetrated my overcoat, he would insist that I let him dry my shirt in front of his stove, and wear a smock of his in the meantime. I stripped in front of him with no thought that it meant anything to him. I admit it seemed odd to me the way C.L.S. always contrived to get us pressed up together in the dusty corners of his rooms. Whenever he needed this or that tool, or resin, or paper, he could not lay hand to it straight away, but had to enlist my help: diligently, I searched with him amongst the scraps and cobwebs that had collected in the corners of his rooms, hemmed in beside him as we fought through the dust and litter, and just when I came upon whatever it was he wanted, he seemed to spot it first, draping himself over me in his eagerness to lay hold of it. And when we got back to the work-table it was never any use, or it was the wrong size or it was broken or empty and C.L.S. would go back to using whatever there was to hand, without complaint or apparent difficulty.

One day he led me through the loft to a door which led to another wing of the tenement: the passageway was thick with dust, and apparently derelict. Through another door C.L.S. led me into his 'museum'.

There was a complete and impenetrable darkness. C.L.S. lit an oil lamp and held it above his head, revealing the shabbiest enclosure I had ever come across, with bare plaster barely clinging to the walls, and a wooden beam showing in the far part of the room where part of the ceiling had fallen in. 'Come and see,' C.L.S. said, going further into the room. I followed closely, so as to stay within the circle of lamplight.

The walls were lined with shelves and glass cases. The flame in the lamp was low, and I had to lean up close against C.L.S.'s arm to be able to see his treasures at all. 'These are things I did before you were born,' he said, holding the lamp above five small portraits of seated nudes. They were done in relief work: little bits of cardboard had been stuck on top of each other to make the figures, and the chairs on which they sat were built up out of knotted string. There were profiles, too, built up in the same way, then dipped in glue and sanded, so that they had the appearance of ancient carvings, half eaten away by wind and time.

As I looked, C.L.S. slowly drew the lamp away. The closer I had to peer, the closer I fetched up against him. At last he insinuated a hand around my waist. I had no idea what was going on. He kissed the top of my head. I assumed the kiss was avuncular: and felt slighted accordingly. I turned to protest, but he stifled my words, pressing his lips impetuously against mine. His lips pressed steadily upon my mouth. I didn't know what to do, so I simply pressed my lips back against his. It never occurred to me that I should open my mouth. We stayed like this until my teeth grew numb. He broke away from me and peered at me, curious, as at some exotic captive bird. 'I wonder,' he said at last, 'whether that was enjoyable for you.'

'Very,' I assured him.

He looked somewhat taken aback. 'Oh?'

He wanted me to demur – even to resist: but I was too naïve to understand why.

'You are attracted to me, then?'

'Yes,' I replied; and when he frowned: 'Very.'

'Ah,' he said, nonplussed. He made to kiss me again. I gave him a broad, inviting smile; it put him off his stride. 'I don't know how you expect me to seduce you if you're going to behave like this,' he said, disgusted.

I shrugged helplessly. 'Just tell me what to do.'

My pliability had quite unmanned him. He mumbled something about having to think things through; crestfallen, he led me out from his 'museum'.

C.L.S. and I rarely left his atelier now: work was his life, and he was determined that it should be mine. We rarely went out to enjoy ourselves. I did however persuade him to go with me to Blythe's debut exhibition at Grabbinges's gallery. Her show had the overall title of *Ennui*. It consisted for the most part of her pictures of the black-clad women.

I had hoped to meet Blythe at the gallery: a rapprochement between us was long overdue; anyway, I was confident enough now that I wanted to tell her what I was up to. But she was not there.

I glanced through the visitor's book. Blythe's work had so far drawn positive responses from her public. Those of C.L.S.'s technical persuasion admired her economy. Those of a more spiritual bent admired the intensity of her subject matter.

'I suppose you disagreed with her work quite strongly,' I said to C.L.S., as we walked back to his studio.

C.L.S. frowned at me. 'I don't know what you mean by that.'

'I mean her choice of subject matter: all those scrap heaps, those ragged canvases. The place she paints – "her city", if you like – can never be more than a surf of transient images, destroyed just as soon as they are made.' C.L.S. said nothing.

'In *Island* though,' I went on, doggedly, 'your view seemed so much more optimistic. Your city, by recycling its own detritus, makes a genuinely alien future for itself.'

C.L.S. walked in silence for some moments. At last he said to me: 'You are wrong to look at my work in so programmatic a function. I work to no hidden agenda. My work is not a metaphor for my thinking.'

I mumbled something conciliatory. Obviously it was not sufficient, for C.L.S. added, acidly: 'If you want an aphorism, here it is: Artists do not argue: they emote.'

At the time, this declaration seemed very profound, my own analysis embarrassing and facile.

I visited C.L.S. daily. It was a bright spring: the air was abnormally clear, the outlines of the City razor-sharp. Dry breezes freshened the alleys, swept up scraps and dust from the pavements and whirled it away through the little squares. Early each morning I walked to my local rail station: a primitive platform knocked together out of unseasoned planks, opposite a disused wash-house. From this bleak suburb I travelled round the Southern Hill and over the rail bridge into Central Station.

Light burned through the glass roof; warped, broken, tinted green, it lent a freshness to the flowers arranged in tubs all along the concourse.

At the end of the platform there ran a stone fascia; each morning, it glowed with a rose light as if it were turning molten. Through the station's glass roof, above the battlements, dust swirled restlessly like steam in a pan of water coming to the boil.

Indeed, on a bright day the whole architectural confection burned and dazzled my eyes as if there were a furious little sun belting its molten heart out behind each pane in the roof. Ornate trellis work spilled irregular rivulets of shade across the gleaming platforms; gazing at those patterns, it was as though someone had spattered droplets of india ink into my dazzled eyes.

From there, though the walk took nearly an hour, I preferred to approach C.L.S.'s apartments on foot. Once out of the station, I kept to the shady side of Green Monkey Street. The footpath was crowded with peep-shows, toy stands, wax-works, inspired monsters, quacks, thimble riggers, knick knack vendors and readers of Fate. I dodged and feinted to keep up a good pace but was forced often into the road. My feet sank into the dust, staining the turn-ups of my white breeches quite ochreous.

'What an extraordinary concoction!' C.L.S. exclaimed, when he saw me.

I adjusted my cravat, self-consciously.

'All in white like a newly-wed, even. Is this the dress of someone come to learn engraving?'

But over recent months, I had grown bolder. I told him that, as his interest in me was no longer entirely teacherly, so I had dressed in accordance with his real agenda.

'Come again?'

'I wanted to look pretty.'

C.L.S. slapped his forehead in frustration. 'How on earth do you expect us ever to get together if you won't fall in with my game?' he demanded. 'If you insist on accepting my attentions, I can't imagine how you'll ever get the benefit of them.'

I told him that was a risk I was willing to take, for the sake of an honest relationship.

'Honesty, hmm?' he echoed; he beckoned me inside. 'Honesty is a harsh supper.'

'That,' I told him, 'is the only diet I'll settle for.'

C.L.S. shrugged, at a loss.

It took some hours poring over some old etchings of his – I had my lesson, after all! – before he regained his old confidence.

'These,' he began, opening a book of prints to a picture of birds mating on the wing, 'are made using the very simplest techniques. Varnish is applied to the copperplate and the design is scratched in with a stencil. The copperplate is dipped in acid, and the acid eats into the copper wherever the point has scratched away the varnish. Once the plate is inked and the excess wiped off, you're ready to print: ink gathered in the grooves of the plate comes off on the paper.'

He turned the page. The subject was the same, but now the birds were mating above the spires of the Sé: white silhouettes against a black sky. The spires looked as though they had been rendered with a brush.

'You don't have to dip your copperplate in the acid, of course,' C.L.S. said. 'You can paint it on, as I've done here. It's a very direct way of working – very exhilarating. Frightening, too: you can really bugger things up if you're not careful. Now look—'

He turned over some more pages and came to a third treatment of the same subject. There was a new sense of depth to the picture, which I traced to the quality of the sky. No longer uniformly black, it was speckled with tiny white dots. 'Resin granules,' C.L.S. explained. 'If you sprinkle them on the copperplate then hold the plate under a candle-flame the grains burst and tiny circles of resin protect the plate when you dip it in the acid. It gives this wonderful speckled effect. Using a small flame like a candle means you can control the amount of varnish that bursts, and hence the density of the black. You see in this picture how some spires of the Sé appear distant and some more near?'

He showed me more examples. Most striking was a series of naked male forms. The figures, whose faces were either obscured by hair or were averted from the viewer, stood naked in deserted night-time streets. The gloomy, anonymous background leant a strange glamour to their well-lit forms: marine flowers, unfurling in the night. I guessed why C.L.S. had shown me them.

'Come with me,' he said, and he led me once more through the loft and down the dusty passageway to his museum. He took me by the hand. 'Follow me,' he ordered, drawing me through the dark and straight to another door – in the centre of the room beyond stood a gigantic four poster bed. C.L.S. put the lamp on the floor, and sat down on the edge of the bed.

'I want you to do something for me,' he said. 'I want to see whether your body really resembles the image I have of it.'

The implications of that remark were clear. I reached for the top button of my freshly laundered shirt.

'Also,' said C.L.S., I want to see how your neck relates to your waist. Only in some men is there this resonance. I want to see if you are such a man.'

I slipped off my shirt.

C.L.S. sat further back on the bed. I unbuttoned my trousers and slipped them off. My penis swelled under the cotton of my pants. C.L.S. gazed at me. I gazed back. He stood up, came over, and took hold of my pants. He freed my erection and stroked the pants down my legs, then, kneeling before me, he began to stroke me, all over: a sculptor feeling for hidden proportions and correspondences. Under his hands I grew relaxed, refreshed, aware of my flesh but not self-conscious of it.

'There,' said C.L.S., 'now at last you are looking like a model. You are holding yourself as a model should.' He went back to the bed and sat down.

We remained like that for some minutes. I watched him, waiting for some sign. None came. I stooped, ready to pick up my clothes, when it occurred to me that C.L.S. had changed the tactics of his game. He was no longer the pursuer, nor I the pursued. Where I had refused to act as prey, now he was refusing to play the hunter. I stepped up to him. His face, weather-beaten and beautiful, glowed in the soft red light of the lamp. I reached down and stroked his cheek. He nuzzled against my hand like a cat. Encouraged, I pressed the tip of my forefinger to the corner of his mouth. He licked at my finger. I drew his head towards my penis. He left off sucking my finger and drew back. A shudder went through me. I reached and put my hand behind his head, crushed his snowy stubble into my palm, and drew his head forward again. His lips brushed my cock. I thrust at his mouth. It opened for me, there was a moment's pain as his teeth scraped back my foreskin, and in the sudden heat of his throat I found a wet release.

C.L.S. gave me an attic room to work in. There were no rugs; the floorboards were covered with a thick black resin. Two easels stood either side of the window, to catch the best of the light as the day progressed. Rags, paints, oils and thinners covered the floor under the window. A bed lay lengthways along the opposite wall, behind a beam which ran at head-cracking height across the room.

C.L.S. made it clear to me at once that the bed was not for sleeping in. 'I am not a modern man,' he warned me. 'If we are to live together, then we must share everything: my bed, especially.'

I said the arrangement pleased me.

Of course it did: mine was a position with many privileges. Together, C.L.S. and I drank the best wines, dined at the most expensive restaurants – and all to court the sycophancy of the City's richest art dealers.

All this was not, you must understand, thrust upon me all at once. C.L.S. initiated me only little by little. He was a secretive man, and to begin with he was careful to conceal from me whole areas of his life: his trade as a dealer, his work as consultant to the Grabbinge brothers and to Dr Binns of the Academy. I lived and worked closely with him for some months before he dared disclose to me the full scope of his career, and he did so with the nicest care. He demanded that I exhibit an extreme guardedness about his work. If a Mr Mcllvanney arrived to take photographs of C.L.S.'s sculptures, I was to give whatever assistance needed to be given, but without so much as a hint that *I knew what was going on*. I was not to mention the word 'photograph'; I was not to mention the word 'sculpture'. If a Miss Pagels were to collect a plate for the lithographers, I was to wrap it up in such a way that it resembled something different: a loaf of bread, say, or a bird cage. I handed it to her in complete silence, or with some words which would throw any hidden spy off the scent: 'And another half-pound tomorrow,' I might say, or 'Mr C.L.S. says they're too short.'

Everyone who had daily dealings with C.L.S. learned sooner

or later to enjoy these charades. No-one crossed C.L.S.'s obsessive need for secrecy, which extended to the communication of the simplest messages.

By early autumn I had become something of a 'secretary' – in the precise sense – fielding the most extraordinarily arcane business with a positively Machiavellian élan.

My greatest troubles were the letters. I have never had much time for word puzzles, and puzzles such as those his letters afforded would have taxed the patience of a saint.

If Christ, for example, wanted to invite C.L.S. to Boris Stock's poetry reading on the fourth of the month, he would write a letter (in the form of a reply to some mythical inquiry of C.L.S.'s) recommending a bulb grower (*bulb* as a synonym for *stock*) who, he claimed, had tulip-growing down chapter and verse and would, Christ felt sure, be only too happy to hold *forth* upon the subject to C.L.S.'s edification.

Of all these hermetic correspondents, Allingham Nye was the liveliest. I remember once he was involved in some protest with Grabbinges's gallery, who had varnished over a new series of portraits without his permission. He wrote a four page letter to C.L.S. about how he had 'gone on a binge' and fought a 'pair of drunken braggarts' for the attentions of a tart whose skin was so 'ingrained' with dirt (hence *varnish*) that he had dragged her protesting into a municipal wash-house and dunked her in the nearest tub before he so much as loosened her stays. The letter, so garbled and drunken-seeming, concealed all sorts of names and dates in cypher form, but its cleverness remained for a long time hidden, as neither C.L.S. nor I could for the life of us work out the basic facts of the case. I was put to wonder if the thing were in the customary code at all, and suggested that Nye might really have written it when he was drunk. 'In which case,' I added, 'Nye is no gentleman – indeed, he's lower than the blaggards that he fought.'

'Not blaggards,' C.L.S. murmured, preoccupied, 'braggarts—' Then: 'Braggarts!' he fairly screamed in my ear, rushed to the inkwell, and began scribbling. Those *brag-arts* of Nye's having run foul of our hero's *binge*, the step to Grabbinges's gallery was simple enough: once C.L.S. knew this, he was able to decode the rest of the letter with relative ease.

Of all C.L.S.'s acquaintances, Allingham Nye seemed to hold the most constant place in his affections. Such was C.L.S.'s high regard for his former pupil, so often did he mention him with warmth and respect, I became quite jealous. My position as C.L.S.'s bed mate was not so secure as it outwardly seemed: because I was always to hand, I became the natural and frequent butt of C.L.S.'s outbursts of temper and impatience. Not only had I to smother my own irritation at these outbursts, it was down to me to smooth the troubled waters his petulant moods set up among the dealers and sycophants with whom he was almost continually surrounded. I was, in my own way, C.L.S.'s wife, and my lot was the lot of any wife of a great man. I was ignored as much as I was cherished; and when I was not thought a pliant enough help-mate, I was treated as a hindrance.

Inevitably, in thinking about my lot I was reminded of my mother, and her patient, acquiescent behaviour towards my father. It occurred to me for the first time that those who are subservient in love have made a choice: they are less victims of another's injustice, but have rather suffered a certain failure of the will. That others take advantage of it is not surprising, and it did not surprise me in the least that C.L.S. took advantage of me. I too had made my choice: I had elected to stay and be his wife.

Hardly surprising, given all this, that I felt jealous of Nye: Nye who had once been C.L.S.'s pupil, but had since come out from the great man's shadow to earn respect as an artist in his own right. Until I met him again, indeed, I entertained the most uncharitable thoughts towards poor Allingham Nye. Thinking of his exhibitions, I had him down in my mind as an *idiot savant* – a mere calculating machine into whom C.L.S. had poured the contents of a dozen art manuals. Nye was free of C.L.S. because there was nothing in him C.L.S. could use. C.L.S. had not fed off Nye the way he fed off me – thus I phrased my absurd boast – because there was nothing in Nye to feed off. I realize with a shudder now how far gone I must have been in subservience: to think I took pride in being C.L.S.'s prize milking cow!

Eventually I got to meet Allingham Nye again. One night in mid-summer he invited C.L.S. and me to dinner.

Nye's house bordered the Quiet Lake. I was struck immediately by the rich variety of the plants in his garden, framing the house on all sides with splashes of vibrant colour. We ascended the paved path to Nye's front door; C.L.S. told me the garden was Nye's passion; he was regularly found leaning over the fence separating his garden from the municipal park, deep in intricate debate with one gardener or other.

I made some appropriate sound; I was not really listening. I was nervous: would Allingham Nye remember me? And, if he did, what would his reaction be to seeing me again? Would he be embarrassed, or cruelly amused? Would he tell C.L.S. of our encounter, and would C.L.S. take offence at the tale?

Nye opened the front door himself. He was shorter than I remembered him, almost dwarfish about the shoulders. He wore a plain shirt, a paisley waistcoat and full black trousers, like a diminutive matador. His eyes, smiling a welcome, startled me: their slight protuberance gave him an air of perpetual astonishment.

'How do, C——,' he greeted C.L.S., warmly. I had never heard C.L.S. addressed so informally; I didn't dare do so myself!

Allingham turned to me. 'Thomas!' he exclaimed. 'How are you?' He shook my hand warmly, and turning to C.L.S. said, 'I met your young friend once before, C——, at the Opera. "Werner's Trunk", wasn't it?'

I nodded, and blushed deeply.

Allingham Nye's living room was cluttered to bursting with the strangest bric-a-brac: an ornamental china brandy cask with a brass tap, a tasselled table lamp with a Bakelite stand; an elephant's foot, a rusted pump, countless jugs of no particular vintage or interest, a brass diving helmet with a little grilled window, a hand plane, wicker baskets, a hand-painted paper lantern, some crepe decorations, a stuffed fox in a glass cabinet, two workman's lamps, a straw hat, a dragon mask, some rustic musical instruments, a pair of polished bullhorns, a paper model of an albatross, a watchman's helmet, and, screwed into the door of the room, a plaque which read 'The Home Governesses's Institute' – the collection weaved its way drunkenly from table to table and disappeared down the hall to metastasize through every room of the house.

'Mr Nye,' C.L.S. explained, redundantly, 'is a compulsive hoarder.'

Just then Nye walked in, bearing a baked fish on a platter. 'An extraordinary thing happened to me this morning,' he said, as he served the meal. 'I was in Mario's Seafood Depository when three old ladies all in black came up to me and started telling me off.'

'You pushed in front of them, I expect,' said C.L.S. 'You never look where you're going.'

'It was the contents of my shopping bag they objected to. They took one look at the mullet you're eating and they started on about its not being cod.'

'Not cod?'

'That's what they said. They tutted at me. "It's not cod," they said. "What's wrong with a nice bit of cod?" Then they started rifling through my shopping basket.'

'Good God!'

'They really had it in for me, I can tell you.' He switched to a silly voice: '"*Spring onions! Cornflour! Root ginger! Ooh, you don't want to go messing round with stuff like that!*"' He said, 'You know, I was shaking by the end of it. And then one of them followed me to the train station. She was wearing work boots. I noticed that because she sat opposite me on the train and kicked me in the shin.'

'I trust you assaulted her?' said C.L.S.

Allingham shrugged helplessly. 'Well, no, I didn't do anything. She did it so casually, I supposed it was an accident.'

'Maybe it was,' said C.L.S., bored now with Allingham's tale.

But now that he had started upon it, Allingham couldn't let it drop: 'You know,' he said, 'she had a comb and paper in her pocket. It was the strangest thing. Whenever the train stopped, she took it out and played *Crab Annie*.'

'Did she play well?'

'No,' said Allingham, frowning. 'Very, very badly.'

We visited Allingham about once a week. While C.L.S. sat picking over his food, muttering cryptically about the effrontery of this or that dealer, Allingham and I ignored the food altogether and winked at one another over the top of whatever exotic plant graced the centre of the dining table.

Allingham Nye guessed from the first that I could not really love C.L.S.; that I was a kind of impostor. But the interest I showed in his garden endeared me to him. At every meal the dining table was furnished with a different and ever more exotic centrepiece: *Calathea makoyana* with its leaves like raised peacock tails; *Orchis glauca* with petals like burnished steel; *Platycerium alipes*, its asymmetric leaves like ruffled feathers; and, one special night, a unique example of the rare and notoriously delicate *Calathea lucifuga*, its shoots black and sticky as liquorice.

C.L.S. was unimpressed: he was not going to be upstaged by a mere plant.

Allingham told me that his grandfather, an avid collector of *Calatheae*, had brought the first *lucifuga* back with him from the desert when he was a young man, given to journeys outside the City. In speaking of his grandfather's treasured plant, Allingham adopted the diction and manner of herbals and astrological gardening books. Whenever I asked him a direct question, he would say something like, 'Today in mountain channels the blue hibiscus blooms as in the days when they laid the blossoms beside the dead on the shores of the Quiet Lake.'

He was enchanting.

That autumn C.L.S. took up lithography; he needed to escape from his hangers-on and the cool, damp anonymous gloom of Klemperer's lithography shop was an ideal sanctuary. The more he worked there, the more interested he became in pushing at the frontiers of the medium. This meant many hours spent in the chill fug of Klemperer's basement works, which were situated in an alley near the Opera. The place was uncomfortable – necessarily so.

Without the damp, the lithographic paper would have dried out, and the coolness of the basement kept the lithographic inks at the right consistency: heat would have made them too runny.

But there was another reason for my dissatisfaction. C.L.S.'s work had turned purely representational: it lacked the imaginative fire of *Island*.

'Projects like *Island* are the sum of many years' effort,' C.L.S. retorted, when I hinted at my dissatisfaction. 'They can't simply be knocked together in a matter of weeks, or even months. What you see me engaged in now is the very first stage of a new project: I mean the gathering of materials and techniques. This process must begin modestly. Look here.' He beckoned me into that workroom Klemperer reserved for his best clientele. I saw that C.L.S. had rubbed a crayon over a piece of lithographic paper so that the grain of the workbench showed through – a technique called 'frottage'. Now he took up a pair of scissors and cut from the paper the silhouette of a running man. He took this silhouette, knelt down on the floor, which was paved with white mosaics, and rubbed a crayon over the reverse side of the figure, so that a criss-cross pattern developed, and the figure was nearly all blacked in. Then he stood up and applied the figure to the paper he had cut. Now there were two figures: a white figure formed by the cut-out, and a black criss-cross figure which was the cut-out itself, reversed and applied to the paper. These figures were placed against the wood grained background so that they appeared to be running away from each other.

It was a novel effect, its doubling of the figure a good example of C.L.S.'s principle of economy – it put him in a good mood for the rest of the day – and yet I hankered after the plaster heads, the gimcrack toys, all the extraordinary paraphernalia of C.L.S.'s imaginary *Island*. 'Don't you miss those rustic crafts you used for *Island*?' I asked him.

He replied, 'The world of art is too vast ever to be keeping everything you learn in your head at the same time.' He was speaking, as was usual with him, in aphorisms.

I was disappointed that C.L.S. no longer had time for 'his *Island*', that bizarre and hopeful vision. 'Then you did not find your attitudes changed by your sojourn outside the City?'

'What sojourn?' C.L.S. demanded, sharply.

'I mean that period you spent researching *Island*,' I said.

'Good God, man,' he blustered, 'surely you don't think I left the City, do you?'

I was speechless.

He stared at me, and burst into unpleasant laughter. 'My dear boy, you must really be out of your mind if you think I, of all people, would go tramping off into all that dust and muck – who do you think I am? I paid a few gypsy tarts and peasants and traders and folk of that sort to do my leg-work for me.' He chuckled and wiped his eyes. 'As if I would soil myself by such a journey.' And then, putting his hand on my knee, 'some sacrifices, sweetie, are too terrible – even in the name of Art!'

We still visited Allingham Nye.

The food he made for us never varied: Red mullet in a hot and sour sauce; and spaghetti, baked in a dish wetted with garlic oil. Dessert consisted of Allingham's 'special' rice pudding crusted with nutmeg and currants. The entire meal was disgusting.

Allingham's plants made up for the food. They were a continual delight, reminding me of the garden my mother had so carefully tended, when I was a child.

After our meal we left C.L.S. in the house, chuckling over some of Nye's caricatures – Nye had a cruel eye, and he sometimes condescended to put it to use in some deserving newspaper or topical journal – and Allingham showed me his hothouse. An *Aechea caudata* held pride of place on a table by the door. The impress of older leaves had left dark lines in the pale blue bloom of the younger growth. Nested stars of thick serrated petals guarded magnolia-coloured stamens.

Sweat trickled down my neck. I loosened my shirt. The place smelled heady and delicious – the unmistakable scent of *Calatheae*.

Allingham led me to a shallow tank. Floating on an inch or two of cloudy water were eight *lucifugae* – descendants of his grandfather's original plant. Allingham said, 'According to the botanist

144

Jonas Merryl, the *lucifuga* is a symbol of perfection. It makes the figure of a circle, you see – leaves, flowers and fruit, a perfect circle. Like the sun's rays.'

I bent my head to drink in the sweet, salivatory scent.

'The *lucifuga* represents the past, present and future.'

'Oh?'

'It bears buds, flowers and seeds at the same time.'

I smiled. 'Of course.'

He reached past me into the tank and plucked one of the plants and broke it apart. He offered me a fleshy petal. 'Eat it.'

I don't know why I felt so uneasy.

'It's all right,' he whispered, lifting it to my mouth. 'It's quite edible. You can flavour rice with the flowers.'

Afterwards, as we left his hothouse, he took me by the arm and said, 'I like your visits. If you wanted to, you could come here–'

'Yes?' I prompted.

He gave me a nervous smile. 'Without C——.'

4

Modelling for Allingham Nye was easy enough. He built up a huge fire in the dining room of his spacious house, and he had me stand naked before the flames. He did not sketch me in all that time; he simply stared at me, for about an hour, with that expression I remembered my father had used when I was a child: as though I were far away from him, in the depths of some deep pit.

'That's all,' he said, at last. 'That's enough for now.'

A few days after that, Allingham sent me a *Calathea*.

It was a different sort to the black and sticky *lucifuga* which he had fed me that night in his hothouse: this plant – its stems and leaves and flowers – was all pure white.

There was a letter with it. 'I bring thee the flower which was in the Beginning,' he wrote; 'the Glorious Lily of the Desert.'

C.L.S. suspected nothing.

*

When business engagements – and there were many – took C.L.S. off to the Academy, or to Grabbinges's, or some like place, I visited Allingham Nye and watched him while he worked. These visits were a sort of holiday for me – a way to escape the increasingly oppressive shadow of my master.

Allingham, while respecting his old teacher, had the measure of him: 'If it's technique you want,' he told me one day, nailing canvas to a stretcher for his first painted portrait of me, 'then C.L.S. is your man; but there's less real imagination in him than you might suppose.' Though the same might have been said of Nye himself, that didn't detract from the truth of his words.

'I'd reluctantly come to the same conclusion,' I said.

Allingham wrestled some more with the stretcher.

'I discovered the other day,' I added, 'that C.L.S. has never once stepped outside the City.'

Allingham smiled at me, quizzically. 'You expected him to?'

I blushed. 'I suppose *Island* caught my fancy so much, I thought him more of a romantic than he really is.'

'C.L.S. as knight errant, eh?' Allingham suggested, amused. 'Riding off in search of adventure and romance!'

The remark reminded me so sharply of something Blythe once said, I missed the parody in Nye's remark. 'Is there not a certain dishonesty in what he did?'

Allingham Nye put down his stretcher. 'Dishonesty? No, I don't think so.'

'Have you ever left the City?'

Allingham laughed: 'The very idea!' he exclaimed, just like C.L.S. – I felt somehow cheated – 'No, no: I'm not the adventure-some type!'

'And yet your grandfather left the City to find his plants.'

'And the family damn near disowned him because of it,' Allingham added, sourly. 'The shame of it! As if he needed to go himself. There were plenty of low-lifes he could have used for such an errand. I don't know what it is they teach you at the Academy these days: but such travels – well,' he ended, weakly, 'they just aren't done!'

Rotten and refreshing and delicate, dawn breezes weaved up mistily from the harbour.

I had not slept: memories flooded me: old mysteries, unanswered questions. They guided me along cobbled streets ribboned with tram tracks to the embankment. I walked towards a dawn the colour of embers, and haunted the spattered slipways of the City's harbour. I ran my hand across the brick walls of the warehouses, felt the salt and wet against my fingers, and for a moment felt – as I had felt often as a child – an almost insupportable yearning to understand the mysteries of this place: this seafaring town, set in the centre of this tiny desert world!

Why, I wondered, for the ten-thousandth time, was it founded upon a river of marble?

Why did its traditions play upon a seafaring life?

Why did a salt and kelp-laden breeze tease its desert stillness?

Why must we feed the gulls?

Not since I was a child had I felt so keenly how this city frantically tried not to know itself. From my childhood meeting with the gypsy, I had always supposed Exploration was the cutting edge of the search for knowledge: so why was it treated as an aberration?

There was something terribly topsy-turvy about the world. It had all gone terribly wrong.

The following winter, the city filled up with black-clad women.

No-one knew where they came from. We didn't think much of them at first. We saw them without seeing them: blocking shop doorways, pushing ahead of the queue at a tram stop, stamping on the feet of importunate beggar-children. They walked around in threes and fours, talking all at once in high, rasping voices. The existence of others was a source of vague but persistent irritation to them. Early on we thought ourselves inured to them; it was easy enough, after all, to laugh at Allingham's tales of arguments over cod.

To come up against them oneself was, I discovered, an altogether different proposition.

Allingham Nye and I were out scouring that triangle of waste ground which stands between the Sé and Central Station, picking over the rubbish heaps in search of what C.L.S. called 'raw material'. Nye, more robustly, named it 'crap', and, being a compulsive hoarder, he took to gathering armloads of the stuff. Where C.L.S. would, say, stumble across a pair of bicycle handle-bars and use them for the furtive stoop of the shoulders of his 'Man with Fish', Nye would purposely go tramping about the City and drag back to his atelier, not just the handle-bars, but anything else that happened to be lying around: the bent-up frames of old perambulators, lead piping, fragments of clay pipe, a rusted-through Harvey & Robespierre biscuit tin ('Provisions for Gentlemen'), a threadbare shaving brush, discarded underwear, china figurines with missing limbs, snapped peacock feathers, half-used canisters of paint, obsolete timetables, rotted leather goods, curtain fittings and certain grades of gravel.

The triangle we were scavenging had once contained a warren of mean terraces, but these had been demolished long before I was born. In some places the crushed remnants were swirled into meaningless mounds and shoals, as if by some hugely complex estuarine current. In other places, I could trace the plans of whole streets, house by house and room by room. It was as though I were examining a long-drowned city unexpectedly pushed up to the surface.

In the centre of the slope, partly hidden by sickly fir trees, stood two bordellos, their gay paint long since faded, their desolate black windows like eyes.

'The daylight won't hold for much longer,' Allingham urged me.

The sky was a sickly colour, neither grey nor brown; it threw false shadows.

I quickened my pace on ground that was a mulch of weeds, clods, tiles, broken bottles, clay pipe, sacking, unravelled dressmakers' ribbon, tatters of newsprint—

Nye had an idea for a sculpture made entirely of artistic scraps – a work of great ambition: one which its broken-down materials were not equal to. It would fail, of course: viewers would see immediately the huge gap between the artist's intention and the finished object. 'By this, I mean to imply that a recycled culture must by definition be a culture in decline.' (I had lent him my catalogue of Blythe's exhibition, *Ennui*, and Nye was keen to explore similar territory.)

'What if they simply accuse you of incompetence?' I objected.

'Let them,' Nye replied, carelessly. 'Until now people have complained that I've been too restrained, too modest, too facile. If they argue the opposite when I change my style, well then, it shows them up more than me.'

Allingham believed that this region was much frequented by Blythe's black-clad women: with some half-charred picture frames, a few tubes of paint, maybe a brush or two, he could make an immediate start on his project.

'These hags clear the chaff of Art away. I will turn that rubbish back into Art! There's a primal quality about this adventure, don't you think? It smacks of something revolutionary!'

I did not venture an opinion: much as I liked Nye, it did not escape me that he was merely refining a statement Blythe had already made.

As we neared the brothels we heard the clatter of generators: the air smelled of burnt rubber. Workmen were installing electric lights along the street up to the Sé. Arc lamps on flimsy poles cast a cold, theatrical light. Allingham was delighted. It meant we could stay out longer. To my mind, it was just this sort of pitiless glare that might accompany the end of the world.

Allingham posed heroically upon a pile of rotted timber and beckoned me on. 'Kemp!' he cried, 'stop dawdling!' Next to him, an abandoned rocking horse – his best find so far – wobbled restlessly in the wind. I joined him on the rise: there were camp-fires all around us – great greasy black pocks, as though the earth had contracted some infection. 'Well,' said Allingham, his cheeriness somewhat muted – the view was truly miserable – 'here we are.'

I led the way down the slope to the nearest bonfire. A scrap of old wallpaper, its glue reactivated by the humid air, stuck to my shoe. I bent to pick it off. A stone sailed over my head. It whistled through the air and clattered off an old coping-stone into a puddle.

'Allingham?'

'Yes, Tom?'

'Did you …?'

'Did I what?' he asked me, coming abreast.

'Careful,' I said, 'you just kicked something past me.'

The burnt tyre smell grew stronger; nearby, draped over an old scrubbing-board, a black scarf fluttered.

'It must be a regular haunt,' Allingham observed, poking about the ashes with a stick. 'Look – yesterday's newspaper.'

A stone struck him between the shoulder-blades. 'Really!' Allingham exclaimed. 'I knew you were in a bad mood, Tom, but that's hardly any reason—'

'Fuck off!'

On a rise of fallen-in walls and warped cart-wheels stood a dumpy woman, dressed all in black.

'Fuck off !' she said.

Allingham drew himself to his full height – about five feet. 'We are gentlemen! Desist!'

'Go away, or we'll spit in your eyes!'

The royal 'we', no less!

I said, 'I'll thank you to display a little more—' A brick whizzed past my ear and shied the scrubbing-board, knocking it flat. I wheeled round, but saw no-one.

'I say!' Allingham exclaimed, as he ducked a second missile.

'We'll pull yer legs off!' came another cry, from behind the bonfire.

'We are surrounded,' Allingham observed. 'We are artists,' I cried, 'we mean no harm.'

'Bleedin' know-alls,' yelled another. 'Painterly pricks!'

Over the heaps emerged lines of women dressed in black rags. They numbered nearly a hundred.

'Good heavens,' Allingham exclaimed, 'it's a convention!'

A stick whizzed through the air and landed at our feet. It was studded through with nails.

'Not a convention,' I exclaimed, 'a rout! Let's be off. They're drunk: capable of who knows what frenzy.'

Someone threw a bottle at Allingham's head. 'All right,' he muttered. 'Here, give me a hand with the horse!'

We took a runner each and, staggering a little under the load, we retraced our steps.

'Oh no you don't!' the first woman exclaimed, bearing down upon us in her heavy workman's boots. 'Thieving buggers, put that down!'

Her sisters followed after her; they were not the harmless derelicts Blythe and I had met by the canal. They were younger; and the hunger in their eyes was no pale gleam. It was a savage flame: they were eaten up with something, some unquenchable appetite. They were not drunk.

'Go on! Drop it!'

'Shan't,' Allingham retorted. 'It's mine!'

'No it's not!'

'So it is!'

'No it isn't!'

'So it isn't?'

The beggar woman blinked. 'Yes, it is,' she said, put off her stride.

'Good!' Allingham barked; he slung the horse over his shoulder and set off again down the hill. I hurried after. My ankle turned on a broken brick.

'Just keep up,' Allingham muttered, 'for heaven's sake!'

Something thudded against the horse, and it slipped off his shoulder. We looked: there was a barbed stick buried in its rump.

Allingham looked up from the horse to the women sliding over the rubble towards us. His face suffused with blind, petulant rage.

'Please,' I begged him. 'Do what you like, of course, but I beg you, no more circus patter!'

'It's rubbish, therefore it's ours,' the dumpy woman cried.

'If it's rubbish,' I replied, eager to get in before the raging Allingham, 'then surely it's anybody's!'

The woman smiled and shook her head, patiently: a woman explaining her trade to the ignorant. 'If it's rubbish, we tend it,' she said, with quiet dignity, and drew her moth-eaten shawl about her black-clad breasts.

'What futile imbecility—' Allingham began, but the woman cut him off.

151

'We have enough trouble with you nincompoop artists,' she mewled. 'It's up to us to clear away your leavings, so don't you start snatching them all back again! If it's garbage, let it remain garbage!'

There was a murmur of approval from the women ranked behind her. There was something about their good order and attentiveness that chilled the blood.

Allingham puffed himself up. 'You filth!' he expostulated. 'Do you presume to dictate how I should conduct my affairs?'

The beggar woman put her hands on her hips and screwed her face up into a shrewish mask. The women behind her stirred uneasily: ready, I feared, to strike at her command. She said, 'And are you tellin' me how I should tend my tip?'

'*Your* tip! This is insuff—'

'Let it go, Mr Nye,' I said. His anger was silly; it would only inflame this mad crew.

He shuddered: 'Very well,' he gasped, almost too furious for words. He kicked the horse where it lay at his feet. He turned to the women. 'I bid you good day!' he cried – a last flourish of bravura.

I followed him out of the waste ground. The harsh electric light cast sharp shadows across his face, it turned the flesh blue-white like alabaster. He neither spoke nor looked at me.

The women, meanwhile, said nothing, nor did they move, till we had quite lost sight of them.

5

One of my most exacting wifely duties was to get C.L.S. up in the morning. He invariably awoke racked by self-doubt and depression, and until noon he took it out on anyone he came across. He was appallingly petulant. When I came in with his breakfast he would complain that after nearly nine months of sharing his bed, I had no idea how to make his coffee. Did I not know that he always drank *café au lait* before dinner? The next day, I brought him *café au lait*, and he demanded to know how on earth he was supposed to be revived by that insipid concoction: espresso was required, had I no common sense? The next day he decided that he was ill, and moaned for a cup of hot water with half a teaspoonful of honey dissolved in it: 'Can't you see I am a sick man? Can't you smell it on me, for heaven's sake?'

The mornings when he was ill were the worst. There was nothing ever the matter with him, of course: illness was merely the cover for an extended ritual of complaint. It would start with his many illnesses, proceed to insulting his doctor and thus by extension everyone around him, descend into the bitterest self-pity, and conclude with some despairing line to the effect that every day his abilities were fading, and that with a life like his there was no point in going on.

Then it was my turn. For the next hour I threw together as many reasons as I could for him to carry on (though after his tirades, it was hard for me to find any purpose in my own life, let alone his). I told him his doctor loved him, that his dealers and public respected him, that his work was as remarkable as ever.

Such Polly Anna-isms did not always brighten him up. My glibness sometimes angered him. 'No-one knows what I am going through,' he said. 'No-one understands the suffering that attaches to my work. I have no-one to talk to – no-one! Everyone around me is so stupid; I can hardly expect them to understand.'

Fortunately, thoughts like these would drive him into such a rage he would forget he was sick; and then he would fling himself out of bed and rush off to his loft in search of a visitor he could insult.

The window of our bedroom looked out over a small courtyard where the washerwomen came to scrub their sheets and pillow-cases. Each morning, all through the summer and autumn, we awoke to their songs and gossipings, and to the sounds of the games their children played, their bells and musical sticks. Sometimes I used to lie in bed an extra quarter-hour, just so I could watch glints of light play upon the ceiling, where the sun was reflected off tubs of grey, sudsy water.

Winter ushered in a less sportive morning call. The homely sounds of the busy little courtyard vanished: in their place, every morning, regular as clockwork, came a rhythmic thumping: unreal, like the heartbeat of some great monster. The effects on C.L.S. were terrible. One morning I came in with the breakfast tray and found him gripping the sides of his bed, trembling and straining, as if at any moment some motion of the earth might pitch him onto the floor. When he saw me he gave a mighty groan, and insisted he was dying.

I went to the window and eased the lace curtain aside and watched them; black rags twitching, metal heels sparking upon the age-smoothed pavement. The curtain shivered in my grip.

'They have taken to marching round and round the Circus of Birds,' Stock had written to me. 'The City authorities claim they are powerless to stop them.' That was a week ago. Now there were drills in almost every courtyard in the City: eddies, spiralling from the central gorge.

I turned back to the room, my fists clenched in frustration. The sound of their marching filled my head. 'I have heard they sew death's heads on their petticoats and pick together their love-lips with iron rings!'

'These cursed parades!' I muttered. I went to the phonograph at the foot of the bed and placed a disc on the turntable.

'Tom,' C.L.S. groaned, 'for God's sake, I'm dying; must you celebrate the fact with that bloody pop music?'

I cranked the delicate mechanism so furiously, I had to let it run down a little before I dared lower the needle. 'You are not dying,' I said, sterner than usual.

'A pity,' C.L.S. moaned. 'Death would be a comfort.' The morning ritual had begun.

I settled the needle upon the surface of the record. Maera LaCouche's abandoned, *impassionato* interpretation of the final bars of 'The Lost Life' filled the room, drowning out the noise of the courtyard.

'Listen, C——!' I exclaimed. 'What terrible, delicious self-consuming energy resides in Maera LaCouche's soul!'

C.L.S. sniffed. 'What does she know about the fires that burn the heart?' He sat up in bed. 'What do you know, for that matter?'

It was my cue. Once again I embarked upon my Sisyphean task; rolling C.L.S.'s rock-like ego out of its slough of depression.

'Young fool,' said C.L.S., gently, when I was done. 'Don't you understand why those women march round and round outside our window? Don't you understand why they light their bonfires, and why they delight so in burning up our work? Has it not occurred to you they might understand something about the world that you do not?'

'And what would that be?' I asked him, reluctantly.

C.L.S. lay back on the bed and closed his eyes. In a tone of utter defeat he explained: 'We've been playing with this infernally small world for so long now, there's no longer a world to play with: we're merely poking around in its scrap-heap. Those old women you're always lampooning, those hags with their appetite for waste and rubbish: they are our heirs. Not Mrs LaCouche, not Christ, not Stock, nor any of your modern friends. These women are our inheritors: old before their time, embittered, despairing. Picking over trash.'

I was quite beaten. I could think of nothing to say. I stood up and left the room, without a word.

C.L.S. did not get up that day.

I had originally been attracted to C.L.S. by his powers of concentration. He once told me that everyone is born with the same level of genius, but that most people frittered theirs away in numerous little ways; he, on the other hand, lived and worked in the same breath. When I first moved in with him nothing he did seemed wholly separate from his role as an artist. He turned everything to account. In the past year, we had hardly left his rooms; unless it was something to do with his business, we never went out of an evening.

That winter, everything changed.

C.L.S.'s fits of depression grew unbearable. On some days he was bed-ridden, incapacitated by a nebulous despair. When these fits passed and he rose from the bed, he would rush about, trying feverishly to compensate for the hours lost; and he would make up for them not, as formerly, by extra hours in front of his canvases and plates, but by a frenetic round of partying, theatre-going, boxing meetings, even visits to the Café Persil. Sometimes we were out on the tiles until gone four in the morning, and if this happened C.L.S. would sniff and say, 'Hardly worth going to bed now; we might as well have breakfast,' and the next day would begin there and then, without so much as an hour's rest. Where formerly C.L.S. had contained his genius and funnelled it into his art, now he was frittering it away on the most juvenile pastimes; in music halls and indecent theatres, and on drink.

C.L.S. had begun to be afraid of death. His own increasing age was something which distressed him terribly. 'You are so lucky to be young,' he said. 'I would give my eyes, I think, to be twenty years younger. If I were superstitious I would leach you and drink your blood in wine to revive me!' He hated me for my youth; if after an all-night carouse I dozed off in front of him, he shook me roughly awake and delighted at my weariness. 'You won't live half so long as me,' he would say. 'Why, I feel as if I could live forever!'

He did everything he could to be young again. His behaviour grew extreme, even raucous, and our evening companions, were they dealers, critics, or mere hangers-on, stared at him with brittle amusement.

He seemed determined to prove his prowess upon me. Some mornings I got up so bruised and sore it was a trial to step into my clothes. I would have borne these attentions better if they had been ardent; on the contrary, they were spiteful. C.L.S., of course, interpreted my consequent frigidity for loss of vital strength. 'Your generation has no fire!' he complained, one night. (He had begun to use me as an emblem for everyone born after him.) 'You're too weak for real passion.'

Over the next few months, this was to become his favourite *recitative*. There was, apparently, to be no great generation of thinkers or artists after his own. The world was a prison and he had mapped its walls; the edifice of Art was complete and he had set its cap-stone. He belittled the work of young people to their faces. My own work he refused to comment upon, I suppose because he felt it to be too minor to vent his spleen over. In his desire to be young, C.L.S. felt he had to undermine everyone who really was young: the young were for him a constant reproach, and only by belittling them could he maintain his shaky equanimity.

When the black-clad women took to burning books, he was delighted. 'Have they started burning any poetry?' he asked me; and 'Do you think Mr Stock's verse is good enough to burn?'

'The fad will pass,' I said, trying not to be drawn.

'Really?' he said, tucking the covers up around himself. It was mid-afternoon. 'Pity. There are too many fucking poems in the world.'

Where once I had seen a great artist, there was now an old man so immature he was behaving no better than a giddy adolescent. I was repulsed.

Now was my chance to turn life to account. Everywhere we went I took my sketchbook with me. I was methodical: I kept some pages for restaurants, some for drinking houses, some for theatres, and so on. At the back of the book I did crude sketches of C.L.S. when he wasn't looking. (I had been practising caricature with Allingham Nye, and had picked out C.L.S. as my first victim.) Looking at them later, I was pleased to see that I had accurately recorded the looks of contempt C.L.S. was giving me.

(I had captured something else, too, though I did not spot it until much later: C.L.S.'s eyes were pregnant with muted horror, like the eyes of Blythe's black-clad women.)

More interesting to me at the time were the sketches I made of dancers, acrobats and erotic performers. C.L.S. would more and more often resort to the City's low theatres, less out of prurience than to gloat over the younger generation's moral debasement.

I was not so embittered: I saw nothing failed or contemptible about these shows. On the contrary, they filled me with delight. The lithe legs of a dancing girl as she wrapped them about the head of a man in the front row, the proud thrust of some well-accoutred gentleman, piercing the fundament of a squealing barrow-boy, delighted my aesthetic sense. C.L.S. dubbed this attitude of mine 'excruciatingly naïve'; undaunted, I kept my sketchbook open on my lap, and with pencil and with charcoal I celebrated what I saw: the fragile glory of the human form; lust's animal grace. I drew my low-life subjects with the same warmth and sympathy I would have applied to anyone else: I had not the faintest idea that I was doing anything revolutionary.

But the moment I translated my sketches into lithographs and watercolours, Nye and some of his dealer friends became tremendously excited; they promised me instant success, and commissioned a whole series of these portraits to be hung – great honour! – in the vestibule of the Opera, to accompany a run of Runciman's celebrated melodrama *Ruth in Red Light*.

There was even a private view, and a small but flattering coterie came to wish me *bon chance*. (C.L.S. refused to attend; but his resentment was predictable.)

'A pamphletist in paint, no less!' Blythe toasted me with a near-empty glass.

I fetched her a replacement: 'I've not seen you in so long.'

Blythe tossed her shock of red hair. 'We followed different paths,' she said; and looking around at my prints, 'and we reached the same place, more or less.'

I confessed I had not seen her recent work.

'I've been down among the bargees,' she explained. 'They're even more unlikely subjects than your belly-dancers!'

'No more black-clad women?'

She made a face. 'Listen, about our misunderstanding: I think we were both right.'

'Oh?'

'The world *is* too small for people to be people: but that doesn't mean we shouldn't try.'

'And the black-clad women?'

'There's nothing human in them, no substance, no sympathy.'

'You grew bored of painting rubbish, then,' I teased her.

'They're more self-conscious than that,' she warned me. 'They're burning books …'

As the evening progressed, so the makeshift gallery filled up more and more: workers from the Opera slipped in uninvited, turning the view into an enormous impromptu cast party. The new arrivals brought with them an odd feeling of tension: the atmosphere grew strident and shrill. The room filled to bursting.

Drawings were knocked from their hangers; but no-one thought to move to another room. The air grew thick and sour. Looking about me at manic grins and anxious eyes, I imagined a gathering of doomed aristocrats: here, in the top room of their castle, they play and dance, determined to ignore until the last possible moment the peasant revolutionaries, who even now are storming the redoubts ... I shared my fantasy with Devlin, a plump little baritone who over the course of the evening had taken quite a shine to me. He hummed and haa-ed at my pretty conceit and did all he could not to meet my gaze.

'Well then,' I said, and I put down my glass, 'I for one find it all rather unsettling. It's too hot in here now – I'm going for a walk.' I eyed Devlin up, and remembered the chamber of costumes. I said, 'Do you fancy taking a turn with me?'

Devlin's eyes nearly started out his head. 'A turn?'

'A walk.'

'Out *there*?'

'Just round the Opera.' Aside from my casual designs upon the plump baritone I was – believe it or not – genuinely keen to wander round the place. I had been too drunk, that night with Boris Stock, to appreciate the finer points of the building: the *fin de siècle* elegance of its tiers, balconies and mezzanines, the crumbling grandeur of its plaster mouldings, the poignant beauty of its wall-paintings, all flaking now and half-obliterated by neglect—

'You can't go out *there*!'

'For God's sake, man, why not?'

'Haven't you heard?' Devlin hissed; 'There is a creature abroad in the Opera!'

'Oh come—'

'A shadow, but not a shadow, either – a phantom!' A sweat broke upon his forehead.

'Are you sure you're not too old for this?'

'Ask anyone!' he challenged, puffing himself up. 'Ask someone from *Ruth in Red Light* what happened to the lighting rig last Thursday!'

'Well, what?'

Devlin went back to his sinister hissing, so that I had to lean in close to hear him. 'It plummeted! Smashed to so much broken glass and melted foil! Arabella from the chorus was standing right underneath it. It broke her legs. It will be months before she can even walk again – and the burns!' Devlin shuddered. A waiter walked past with a tray of champagne. Devlin wheeled round, snatched two glasses, and drank them off in hasty gulps. 'We saw the shadow of a sinister figure, cast upon the back wall of the auditorium!'

I mused. 'It was some trick of the light. You said the lighting stack had fallen: perhaps it cast that shadow as it fizzled out.'

Devlin sneered at my rationalism. 'And the missing props? And the trails of blood?'

'Good God.'

'Little spots of blood, leading along forgotten corridors, disappearing under doors sealed with heavy iron bars and pad-locks rusted shut! And what of the fish-guts we found blocking the drains in the dressing room, the skeletal reflection Madame Pompadour glimpsed in the glass of her French window – an image so hideous, it sent her plunging with a scream from her third-floor balcony?'

'My good man,' I exclaimed, relieved, 'your tall tale has come unstuck! There is Madame Pompadour, over there, by the canapes!'

He glanced at her, and shrugged: 'Fortunately,' he embroi-dered, with the quickness of a spider repairing a rent web, 'she landed in a net strung by the renovators to catch loose masonry. Look – see the heavy powder upon her forehead? That's to cover an unpleasant bruise she sustained as a consequence of her fall—'

'—from a third-floor window.'

'*Ask* her, if you don't believe me!'

But I had wearied of the game. I said, 'I'm off for my ramble. You can add my disappearance to your stock of jolly tales!' I made for the door, pausing only to greet one or two of the more important dealers, come to see what I was capable of. I got to the door – and found the way barred by Madame Pompadour.

'Madame!' I bowed before this giant of the stage. Her hair was cropped: she spurned rococo adornments and wore a wig only in performance. Her neck was so shapeless and gargantuan the pearls that encompassed it might as easily have clasped a belly-dancer's waist; her enormous gold-trimmed slippers were like scatter-cushions, roughly customized. Age and greed had pumped up her flesh to such a degree, one might have mistaken her for some over-stuffed chaise-longue.

'DO NOT STEP OUT OF THIS ROOM!' she declaimed: a gun could not have silenced the room so suddenly. 'TO DO SO WOULD BE CALAMITOUS!' I fancied I heard the hairs bristle on two hundred necks.

'But madam,' I protested, 'a little air—'

'USE THE BALCONY!'

I strutted and fumed, but she would not let me past. I wondered what on earth had occasioned this siege mentality among the people of the Opera. Some sort of mass hysteria? Some elaborate and unfunny practical joke? But to persevere with this ridiculous altercation threatened to ruin my proudest evening: I bowed to her and retreated. She smiled at me for my submission. Her forehead cracked open. A great wad of make-up splintered and fell, revealing an unsightly bruise. She gasped, covered the mark with her hand, and repaired to a corner of the room, scattering guests, plates and glasses as she lumbered past, off to repair her face.

'You see?' said Devlin.

'Go away!' I fairly shouted at him.

Allingham came up to me.

I said, 'Have you ever heard such outrageous poppy-cock in all your life?'

'Some ghost, they say, or vengeful sprite,' Allingham replied; 'thespians are supposed to be highly-strung. You should be pleased that they care so much for your safety.' He patted me on the shoulder.

'You know,' I said, shaking him off, 'I find being kept in perfect safety perfectly contemptible!'

I edged towards the French windows and waited my moment. Unobserved, I slipped out of the room. The balcony ran along the entire wing of the Opera; many rooms had windows which gave onto it. I found a pair that were ajar, slipped through and, after a short and absurd battle with a pair of heavy brocade curtains, disappeared from view.

The room was in pitch darkness, but as my eyes adjusted so I saw a thin bar of light coming from under a door. I padded carefully towards the chink, and barked my shin on the corner of some chest or other. I hopped about, cursing. When the pain was bearable, I edged more circumspectly towards the light. I reached the door and swung it open. Steam billowed past me: a great gale of sweet vapour, with an undertaste of Turkish delight.

'Ah,' I said; the clouds dissipated to reveal a man and a woman, pink and flushed like new-borns, intimately conjoined on a rug in the middle of an extremely well-appointed bathroom.

Their screams rent the air like paper. I whirled round, ran blindly away from the door, and barked my other shin. One or other of the amorous pair had got to the door of the bathroom and was swinging it shut, cutting out the light. I just glimpsed the door I should have picked before the light disappeared completely. I sprang towards it. It was locked. I fumbled madly at the doorknob. The bathroom door opened again. I quailed: the man had got his courage up, and was coming at me with a makeshift club. I tugged madly at the handle. The door was so rotten, the entire mechanism came away in my hand. The man raised his weapon. I tried to speak, but my tongue, in imitation of a bad novel, cleaved to the roof of my mouth.

The man struck.

'Ouch,' I said.

He hesitated, then struck again.

'Ouch,' I said again.

The man wailed, flung himself headlong back into the bathroom, and slammed the door behind him, gibbering senselessly. He must have thought I was indestructible. On the contrary, I am eminently mortal. The fault lay with him: in his panic, and luckily for me, he had snatched up a loofah for his weapon – an item not highly rated in an assault. I felt for the hole in the door where the handle had been, and gave the door a tug. It opened for me, and I stepped into the corridor. Free at last! I allowed myself a fiendish chuckle. If there had not been a phantom before, there was now, and I was of a mind, suddenly, to exercise a phantom's privileges! Where, I wondered, should I begin my haunt?

The corridor was unlit, but there was a gleam to my right: I followed it.

The light wavered oddly, like antique gas-light: but the further along the corridor I went, the further the light receded. Then the light came not from some lamp mounted upon a wall, but from a hand-lantern!

Whose, I wondered? I quickened my pace.

The corridor made a complete circuit of the Opera, maintaining a steady curve all around, breaking off only where it gave onto some balcony or lounge. Here there were lights aplenty – bright cold electric bulbs under frosted glass shades, the pride of Heinrich Nudz and the Opera House Improvements Committee. There were a few posters on the walls, here and there a bust, a picture, a hanging, a costume or two in a glass case. I did not stop – ahead of me rushed my quarry, just out of sight, luring me on.

I came to a fire door: it was swinging shut. I leapt and caught it just before it clicked to. I paused, catching my breath. Devlin's silly tales echoed in my mind with renewed force, but I could not turn back: not now I had sneered so openly at Safety! I wound up my courage, and opened the door.

I found myself in the bowels of the building – a service corridor with walls of drab, untreated plaster, scaffolding poles stacked along one wall, and signs on every door that read:

STRICTLY OUT OF BOUNDS TO CONTRACTORS
AND LOW PERSONS GENERALLY

A door slammed to my left. I edged cautiously round a corner, and entered a corridor indistinguishable from the first. I picked my way over discarded lengths of wood, coils of electrical wire and cigarette butts, and came upon a door, arched, with fluted panels, and set in an alcove of dressed stone. I knew instinctively that behind this strange door – this intrusion of some more ancient, gothic structure – lay my quarry. I laid a trembling hand upon the tarnished brass knob. It vibrated strangely. I turned it, and opened the door a crack. Distant music trembled in the darkness beyond the door: grandiose harmonies, as much felt as heard, sprung from some unearthly organ.

I stepped into the darkness. I found myself at the top of a stone staircase, lit by firebrands mounted in iron brackets along one wall. The steps led to the floor of a gigantic cavern; its looming dimensions made me dizzier: they were greater even than those of the auditorium. It was then I remembered Allingham Nye's assertion, on the night of our youthful debauch, that the Opera was founded upon a nest of interconnecting cellars and passages and supporting structures: this cavern must be the remains of some ancient and forgotten building. I descended the stairs.

Music swelled from the cave: everything became bright. The great hall leapt into focus like a lantern slide. I stumbled on the stairs and gripped the balustrade, shaking with surprise.

Someone, somewhere, had turned on the lights. They were strung up on wires, from pillar to massive pillar, across the hall. Their glare hid the ceiling, which must have stretched at least a hundred and fifty feet above my head. The columns supporting this gigantic space were so massive I saw they had been made hollow. There were doors in them: they were riddled through with passages like wood-worm in a table.

Part of the gigantic hall was screened by a red velvet curtain. Gilt-framed pictures hung on the walls – mythical scenes, greater than life size, full of blood and terror, the clash of antique weapons, and serpents the size of trolleybuses. Arranged about the hall were three pulpits, each with its eagle. I went round them all, and found upon each lectern a book bound in new red leather, of the sort used in the Academy for re-binding—

'Good God!'

My exclamation boomed around the hall, in muddy syncopation with that imperturbable procession of grand and distant harmonies. No movement answered my involuntary cry.

I turned the pages of the book back and forth. There, that brown stain all down the marbled edging – Josey Hugg tripping over her laces one Sunday dinner time, flinging gravy everywhere. I remembered it as if it were yesterday! And there, that dog-eared page, that graphic and educational plate I had pored over on many illicit midnights, showing how in olden times men used to—

But how came my father's books here, and new-bound?

A door in the pillar behind me banged open. I whirled round.

I am not sure which of us screamed louder – he from the shock of being discovered, or me from horror. That skull for a face, that sinister black garb, why this could only be—

'Doctor Binns!' I exclaimed. 'What are you doing?' He held a bucket of fish in his left hand. 'What?' he barked. 'Oh, hullo, Mr – uh – Camp?'

'Kemp.'

'Kemp. What? Me? Nothing. Why?'

'But—' I looked around me. 'What is this place? What are you doing here?'

'Oh, said Binns, and shrugged, 'just passing through.'

'*Passing through*?' I fairly shouted. 'Doctor Binns, you have, if I am not very much mistaken, crippled a chorus girl and trauma-tized an entire opera company! And you say you are just *passing through*?'

Binns shuffled his feet. 'Uh—' he began. 'Well, it is a *bit* more complicated than that—'

'I am sure!'

'But – I say, Mr Kemp, would you mind terribly coming down off that pulpit? You are reminding me of my old headmaster during school assemblies.'

'Oh,' I said. 'Yes. Of course.' I descended the creaking wooden steps of the pulpit and offered him my hand. Binns experimented with a smile, peeling his lips back – I couldn't watch. 'You have found some use for my father's books, I see,' I said, and when Binns did not answer: 'Why are you holding a bucket full of fish?'

Binns shuffled his feet some more. 'That's – that's quite a tricky question,' he confessed.

'You must have some idea.'

'Well—' Binns scowled, pursed his lips, and came to a decision. 'Camp,' he began.

'Kemp.'

'Kemp: you are a man of honour, are you not?'

165

'I suppose so,' I said, uncomfortably: my afternoons with Allingham Nye …

'Can you keep a secret?' Dr Binns demanded.

'Is it an entertaining one?' I asked him; then, when I saw my humour was of no account here: 'Dr Binns, for pity's sake, do let me in on this business, or your bucket of fish will haunt me for the rest of my days!'

'Very well,' said Binns, and in a theatrical tone: 'Follow me!' He shuffled past me, bearing the bucket towards the red velvet curtain. A cord hung by the wall to the left of the curtain. Binns bade me pull it. 'Mind,' he said, darkly: 'what lies beyond might startle you.' I pulled upon the cord.

The curtains parted smoothly. An unearthly turquoise light flooded the hall, illuminating the ornate stressed ceiling of the vault. Beyond the curtain, the room was bare and unfurnished, the floor was pitted stone. The walls were a mosaic of bricks, tile and flint, some mortared, some loose in the socket; this was a place repaired and demolished successively over many generations. At the heart of the room, supported by wooden scaffolds, nesting among countless pipes, coils, cables, condensers and funnels, lay a fish made of iron, some twenty feet high. Its belly was set with windows from which issued a brilliant blue-white light.

My mind quaked.

Dr Binns slipped the handle of the bucket over his arm and carried it up a rickety step ladder, which was propped against the side of the terrible fish. The fish in the bucket, sensing some imminent event, floundered about, beating the sides of the bucket so that an eerie and sonorous clanging filled the chamber.

Binns gained the top of the ladder and swung himself up onto a railed deck which ran along the topside of the fish. He edged past the gigantic dorsal fin – all filigree and silver effulgence – and knelt by a small hatch in the head, which he undogged. Taking up his bucket, he poured its contents into the beast's iron recesses. The light from the windows in its belly pulsed once; I shielded my eyes. Dr Binns closed the hatch, scampered back to the top of the ladder and slid down it. He hurried to the cord and pulled the curtain shut.

I turned to him, speechless.

'You are startled by these wonders, Mr Kemp. Put your mind at rest: these things – even that majestic fish, behind the curtain – are perfectly in accord with the conventions and stipulations set down in your father's books of lore.'

I would have been more comforted if I had had the remotest notion what he was talking about.

'I have, you see,' he went on, oblivious to my confusion, 'taken it upon myself – at first as a hobby, and later with greater seriousness – to enact the various arcane procedures set down in your father's ancient books. What today we think is superstitious nonsense – so much mumbo-jumbo – can still wreak extraordinary effects. Take this place, for instance! What extraordinary power is mine, that I have fashioned such a palace for myself, out of a mere broom-cupboard!'

I stared at him. The trivial little librarian had gone quite mad. I wondered how best to deal with him.

He said, 'From what I have learned, I hope to revive – indeed, to accelerate! – the City's progression from a desert waste to a bustling, sea-faring port!'

I nodded sagely: failing all else, perhaps I might be able to humour my way out of this chamber!

'We may suppose,' Dr Binns began, 'that in the distant past, people regularly wielded such power: wielded it, indeed, in a democratic manner – Kemp, if you keep wagging your head up and down like that you'll burst a blood vessel.'

'Sorry,' I murmured. He was not so daft, then.

He continued: 'With time, however, this power became concentrated in the hands of a very few demagogues – self-styled priests, or wizards. And because their status depended upon secrecy, they saw to it that the knowledge fell out of general use.'

I thought about Dr Binns's fish. It had all the appearance of a madman's folly, but the fact remained it had been built. If Dr Binns was deluded, then his delusion was a complex and diverting one.

'Kemp, you're not listening.'

I apologized.

'I believe,' he said, 'that the City has got itself into a rather piddling and unsatisfactory shape because certain magical tools have been lost. I believe, for instance, that everyone once owned a gigantic fish, by which they shaped and enlarged their domestic spaces. The knack of it has been lost, but with good fortune I will re-educate the populace: one day everyone will have a fish like mine! A modest beginning, from which who knows what wonders will spring—'

'Jolly good,' I said, thinking a rote response better than an appalled silence.

'Mr Kemp,' he glowered. 'I believe you are not taking me seriously.'

'On the contrary,' I exclaimed, frighted: 'I have never felt so serious before in my entire life.'

'Ha!' He strutted around the room, beating his fist into his palm. 'You are a lightweight, Mr Kemp, and I should never have entrusted you with these secrets!'

'But Dr Binns,' I pleaded, 'I am a child of a rational education. I'm at a loss to know what you're talking about. If my father's books have proved useful to you, I'm glad; if your studies are secret, I will be discreet. But unless you tell me in clear language what you think you're doing, you can hardly expect me to comment!'

From above came a great hammering.

Dr Binns raised haunted eyes to the fluted ceiling of his eyrie. 'Good Gods!' he exclaimed. 'I am found out!' He scampered about, digging his clawlike hands into his robes. 'Ah!' he exclaimed, with relief, drawing from the voluminous folds an old stick.

All the while blows rained upon a distant door, more savage now than formerly.

'Sir, don't you think I ought to go let them in? I expect some of the cast from *Ruth in Red Light* have come looking for me.'

Dr Binns fixed me with a withering glare. 'Don't be a fool, Mr Kemp,' he snarled. 'Do you seriously suppose I have let anyone in here but you? You think I *advertise* my presence in this place?' Sarcasm gave way to hysteria: 'I'm found out! I am undone! The dogs have sniffed me out at last! Out the way—' He held the stick aloft in both hands and in quivering cadences began: 'For this rough magic I here abjure, and when I have required some heavenly music—' He tapped his foot impatiently, then, when nothing happened, muttered thickly: '*which even now I do—*' at which point whatever invisible sprite had missed its cue woke up, and the air filled once more with grand, unearthly arpeggios – 'I'll break my staff!' Dr Binns exclaimed, gripped the stick in both hands, and brought it crashing down over his upraised knee. '*Shit!*' he bawled, hopping around the room, rubbing his leg with one hand and flailing the stick in the other like a dervish. 'Here, Kemp, give me a hand!' I took the stick and broke it across my knee. The lights went out.

I took a pace forward and barked both shins. Something soft enveloped me, impeding all movement. I floundered about, tripped, fell, bashed my forehead against something sharp. The thumping and hammering started up again. I fumbled for the door, knocked over a bucket: water sloshed round my ankles.

'MR KEMP?'

A lock rattled, matchwood snapped and tore, and the door juddered open. Firm hands took hold of the enveloping thing and pulled it off me. I blinked, as the light of the corridor streamed into the broom-cupboard.

'Good heavens!' Devlin exclaimed, his hands fluttering about under his face like the mouthparts of an insect. 'Are you all right?'

'Quite,' I said. 'Quite, thank you.' I stood up, brushed myself down, straightened my tie, adjusted my cuffs, shook out the creases in my trousers, slicked back my hair, stepped out of the closet and tripped over a mop.

6

While my work progressed well, my private situation was slipping steadily into crisis. I had begun to despise the man to whom I was, to all intents and purposes, married. I knew that to preserve my self-respect I should come out from under his shadow; but I did not know how it could be done. As a consequence, I found myself playing out my personal resentments on the page.

I drew scenes of figurative rape: I composed dramatic scenes, dressed my erotic dancers in diaphanous classical drapery, and had them put to flight and terror by grotesque, lustful satyrs – satyrs with C.L.S.'s face. When finally I paused for a day or two and took stock of what I had done, my consternation may be imagined.

I was afraid of C.L.S., who was so celebrated and so adored, and shied from thoughts of what might happen were I to walk out on him. I had recently heard tales of how, in his bitterness towards the young, he was using his influence to stultify the work of new artists. Were I to leave him, would any dealer dare take me on? I saw, as clearly as if it were a lantern lecture my new career and ambition stifled by my jealous husband.

Allingham Nye was unsympathetic: 'You got yourself into this situation,' he upbraided me, 'it's up to you to get yourself out of it.'

'You might at least say how,' I complained, doing up my shirt.

Allingham got out of bed and picked his clothes off the floor. 'I've been telling you how for weeks,' he replied. 'Tell him.'

'Oh for God's …'

'Tell him about us, it's the only way.'

'Because you're too scared to do so yourself!'

Allingham rounded on me: '*Because*, you stupid boy, I've no desire to show you up for a cheat!'

'It takes two,' I sneered, turning from him.

He walked round the bed and took me by the arm. He shook me: 'Why don't you do something, damn it? Why do you leave it to other people to adjust themselves to you? All right, I wanted you. It's true. And you wanted me. And while we were unsure how things would turn out, there was no point in telling him: it would have caused needless pain. But now – Good God! How long has it been?'

I shrugged.

Allingham threw up his hands in exasperation. 'What is that supposed to mean?'

'It means we've got by so far,' I said: 'there've been no problems.'

Allingham went back to his clothes. He would not look at me. 'You think by playing the innocent you can get away with anything. Look at you: your clothes are C——'s, your home is his, the food in your belly—'

'I don't deny any of that.'

'Yet you complain—'

'Because he's grown insufferable!'

'Then *leave* him!'

I said, 'If I leave him, I'm finished. You know that as well as I do.'

'You have allies: there are those who would defend you.'

'Indeed?'

He sighed. 'I would—'

'*You*?' I exclaimed. 'You stole me away from him; much weight your opinion would carry!'

Allingham stared at me, his face flushed. 'Stole you! You talk about yourself as if you were some trinket, some ornament. Some commodity to be bought and sold!'

'It's how I feel!' I groaned.

'It's how you *want* to feel,' Allingham insisted. 'It's easy to complain, harder to do something about it. You have no moral courage. None!'

'And what,' I asked, softly, 'will he think of you, if I tell him?'

Allingham was checked by that: 'I don't know,' he said.

'It seems to me,' I went on, conceitedly, 'it wouldn't do you any good either, to have him know about us.'

'I don't suppose it would. But I care for him.'

I scoffed: 'If you cared for him so much, why did you bed me?'

Allingham stared at me. 'Because I love you,' he said, as if it were the most obvious thing in the world.

Like a fool, I did not believe him.

'Here,' said Allingham Nye, snatching the rim of a shattered pot from the gutter. 'Grab hold of this!'

Nye had once more enlisted my help in dragging back to his rooms all sorts of heterogeneous rubbish. It lay mouldering in heaps for months, even years, before Nye found a use for it. I

171

resented these expeditions. Anyone else, seeing my weakened and anxious state, would have sat me down in a soft chair with a cup of weak tea and a plate of Garibaldis, but not Nye. He dragged me out in all weathers on 'crap-hunts', and had me bear back to his apartment trash that was even more decayed and useless than usual: fire tongs, a mug-tree, a cot-frame, half a dozen empty cutlery canteens, a charred picture frame from one of the women's bonfires.

Days spent scrabbling over old rubbish heaps had unexpected consequences, however: they sped the blood, warmed the brain, and began at length to dislodge my paralytic gloom. Coming away from Nye's house at the end of a day's scavenge, I was exhausted: I slept well, woke early, and had no time for C.L.S.'s fits of depression. I grew more resilient, and better tempered. While there were problems in my life, I felt that I was strong enough to face them at last. I began to assert myself.

C.L.S. hated these changes in me. 'Look at you!' he exclaimed one morning, deep in a bed-ridden depression. 'You look no better than a greased-up barrow-boy!' I paused in my dressing and turned to the fly-spotted mirror screwed into the bedroom door. I saw that C.L.S. was right: I had grown fit, from my daily scavenges, and my arms and chest were filled out with neat, compact little muscles. My face and arms were tanned by winter winds; my posture had improved; my stomach was flat and hard. I liked what I saw.

'Like a bleeding navvy.' He sniffed. 'I don't know what I ever saw in you. I thought you were a boy with some talent, but there's nothing in you but the desire to impress. To think that I could have been flattered by so trivial a person!'

I saw my opening: I asked him whether he wanted me to leave.

'Don't even think about it,' he grumbled. 'You wouldn't last five minutes in the real world. Without me you're nothing. I suppose I made you a gigolo, and so I'm responsible for you. We both have to live with the fact.'

'Why sacrifice yourself?' I said. 'Your first duty should be to yourself. Throw me over: I'll take my chances.'

He sneered. 'If I threw you off you would wither, like ivy torn from a tree.'

'If I'm like a creeper,' I retorted, 'if I am draining you, would it not be better for you to throw me off?'

C.L.S. shrugged, embarrassed by the extreme pass we had come to. 'You drain me, but so do others. I am surrounded by syco-phants, and they all want part of me, and it's horrible, horrible, I don't know how I've borne it for so long, and now that I am an old man, the last of my generation, it delights them to leach me of my remaining powers, to feed off me and make me one of them, and I would much rather be dead than let that happen.' He broke into aphorism: 'Better the pot that's cleanly smashed than the tin tub drilled through for a colander.' It was not one of his better efforts. Still—

'I think you're right,' I said.

C.L.S. stared at me.

I said: 'I see such little cause for hope, indeed, I fear in later years we shall think these times happy in comparison.'

At this C.L.S. flew into a rage, reiterated every point of com-plaint he had ever made of me and of his life, and threatened suicide. 'If it would please you,' I said. 'Your first duty must always be to yourself.'

C.L.S. stared at me in silent hatred.

I turned on my heel and walked out the room.

'All set up for our little jaunt?' Allingham asked me heartily, later that morning. Hail battered the glass roof of the station and a cold gust of air, thick with coal dust, blew in from the mouth of the tunnel. I was so worked up by my confrontation with C.L.S. that I could think of nothing to say. Allingham took my silence for agreement and set off. I trailed after him.

Allingham was arranging a mid-winter concert – an open-air affair in protest at the outrages of the City's black-clad women. He hoped to inscribe the name of Maera LaCouche at the head of his programme book.

We set off up narrow cobbled streets into the vertiginous terraces of the Baixa. Maera LaCouche lived in the northeastern quarter, in a splendid ivy- and buddleia-strewn mansion set like a jewel in a maze of mean terraces: streets which had slid into disuse under the baleful influence of the marching women. The ground-floor windows of the tenements were boarded up. Rubbish lay strewn across the pavements. Cobbles had been torn from the street. The hulk of a burnt-out tram impeded our progress.

Allingham and I walked with military briskness; this had become a dangerous place for artists.

The wall surrounding Maera LaCouche's mansion had been daubed with graffiti – hanged-man symbols, the broken cross that was the women's emblem, and other hateful signs and slogans. The gate was padlocked. Allingham went to the pillar to pull the bell-wire, and found it was torn from its socket. He cast me an anxious glance, then turned and announced our arrival through cupped hands.

A figure in blue and white peered cautiously from behind the front door.

'Whayer wan?' the maid demanded, raucous and uncouth.

'She must be new here,' I murmured.

'We have come to see Madame LaCouche!' Allingham cried.

'She's not seen anyone.'

'All the more reason why our visit will lighten her day!' Allingham bellowed back, with great gallantry.

'I *said*,' said the maid, and stamped her foot, 'she's not seein' anyone.'

'Oh. See-yin. Forgive me, I misunderstood.'

The maid disappeared.

'Hai!' Allingham yelled.

The maid poked her head out again. 'It won dooyany good!' she snarled, defiantly.

'Our names are Nye, and Kemp!' I yelled back.

The maid lifted up her pinny and wiped her nose on it.

'Ugh,' said Allingham.

'You sellin' somefin'?' she demanded.

'No!'

'Oh.' She stared at the ground a while, mulling it over. 'Whayer wan, then?'

'We have come to see Madame LaCouche!' Allingham screamed. 'We are friends of hers!'

'She's not seen anyone,' the maid bawled back.

This went on for about ten minutes. At last, Maera herself appeared at the door, covering her face with her hand. She spoke to the maid. The maid bobbed and shuffled over to the gate. She unlocked the padlock, untied the chain and opened the gate for us.

Maera went back into the house.

The maid led us to an atrium. At the centre of this room there was a finely worked bronze fountain. Maera sat running her hand back and forth over the spout. Her gown was a dowdy thing; it bespoke a certain melancholy. Her hair was dishevelled. She swept her hand through the water and dabbed at her eye: it was bruised and swollen.

'What on earth happened?' Allingham demanded.

Maera winced at the touch of the water. 'My critics have grown more forthright, I think.'

'But—'

1 was struck down: by a turnip, I am told. God! How undignified it all is! Jennifer, a glass of port for Mr Nye. And for – Mr Kemp, isn't it? I liked your sketches for *Ruth*. What's your poison?'

'Marjolaine,' I replied, pleased at her flattery. 'Not too much honey.'

The maid Jenny bobbed and shuffled from the room.

'Please forgive her the altercation at the gate,' Maera begged; 'My usual staff have abandoned me. They grew fearful of those stick-wielding hags. I can't say I blame them. Jenny looks after me now.' She dabbed at her eye again.

'What on earth happened to you?' said Allingham.

'It was those women, of course,' Maera explained. 'They entered the auditorium with pans hidden in their skirts. In the middle of my favourite Petersen duet – you know, the second act of *Beatitudes* – they whipped them out and started drumming.'

'But why on earth were they allowed in to start with?' Allingham protested.

'First, because they bought tickets. Second, because we were afraid they might otherwise torch the theatre. Now don't start getting all heated up about this, Nye,' she warned. 'I'll have you know the staff back-stage were wonderful. Five minutes later not a single one of the dears remained in the auditorium. There was little violence.'

'But your eye—'

'Alas, though they moved quickly to suppress the disturbance, they were not quick enough.' She dabbed gingerly at the bruise. 'Benchling was my tenor – never again will I work with him! I fell when I was struck. Some members of the audience screamed. Benchling thought I'd been shot. He fled the stage—' She burst out giggling '—the little worm.'

'And left you defenceless, I suppose!' Nye glossed, outraged.

'Poor man,' Maera sighed. 'We found him three hours later. He had locked himself in the lavatory behind Madame Pompadour's dressing room. We hammered on the door and he started screaming. All sorts of things he thought might propitiate our attackers. He begged us not to kill him, declared that he'd never read a difficult book in his life, didn't understand fine art, only sang opera because he'd been done out of a job in a bank and – oh, all sorts of nonsense!'

'But you went on with the performance?'

'Benchling's understudy came on for the rest of the opera. *Devlin*. He felt he needed to look after me, protect me – *shield* me, if you take my meaning. The little rascal upstaged me every chance he got! We tussled and manoeuvred for position so much the whole evening turned to farce. For most of the final act we were teetering on the edge of the orchestra pit. The libretto had us clinging to each other in the extremities of passion.' She sighed and shook her head: 'More likely we were trying to push each other off the stage! But enough, forgive my trivial preoccupations! How may I be of service?'

Nye explained about his concert, and his reasons for it.

Maera was not immediately impressed. 'It seems a pity,' she mused, 'that we protest against these women before we even know what they want.'

Nye was shocked. 'You say this, even after they have assaulted you? Maera, look reasonably at the thing, the streets outside this chateau are made a slum by these viragos! The community of the place is all broken up—'

Maera held up a hand for silence. 'And yet,' she said, pointedly, 'can anyone tell me, please, what it is they want?'

I said, 'Nothing.'

'Nothing?'

'Nothing,' I said again. 'The movement is without a political motive. It has no ideological ground; it needs none. It is a movement of negatives and denials.'

'How intriguing!' cried Maera, delighted.

'Oh, yes,' Allingham exclaimed, bitterly. 'Intriguing is the word. But does it not occur to you, Maera, that we citizens may have grown so used to thinking of life as Art that we cannot see the very dangers which threaten us?'

Maera peered at him. 'You are getting terribly worked up about this, aren't you?'

'Oh!' Nye leapt up from his seat and paced about the room. 'Maera, you are like everyone else!'

'I am?'

'Everyone I speak to seems determined to treat these women as a joke. Maera, I tell you, they are not a joke, and I for one will not stand applauding the tidal wave as it towers, foot by foot, over our heads!'

'I see,' said Maera, coldly. She was not used to being spoken to like this. 'And where, pray, do I come in?'

Nye came over, took up her hand, and kissed it: his misjudgement of her mood was spectacular. 'We would be honoured if you would consent to head the bill of our proposed concert!' he exclaimed.

There was a long silence. Maera shook her head. 'I really don't think that will be possible,' she said, in tones of professional regret.

'But why ever not?' I pleaded – a token gesture, but I felt I had to do my bit.

Maera glared at me. 'Don't be obtuse, Mr Kemp.' She turned to the fountain and bathed her eye again.

I tried to convince her that to show herself, disfigured as she was, would be a show of strength, and not a prompt for derision, but she cut me off: 'I am not a martyr, gentlemen,' she said. 'This is, perhaps, not to my credit, but there it is. Perhaps I should turn the other cheek, as it were. Perhaps I should make witness of last night's shameful assault. But it is not my nature to show myself in public in a dishevelled state.'

'But—'

'Forgive me,' she said, and raised her hand once more – an imperious gesture. 'I am a hot-house flower. My beauty constitutes half my art. I would not inspire respect in an audience, any more than a rose afflicted with the green-fly inspires pleasure in a gardener. I would excite mere contempt, or pity at best, and would only depress those you wish to fire with rebellious energies.'

At that, I stood and bowed, but Allingham could not let the matter rest so easily: 'You are wrong,' he said, brusque. 'The time for such nice distinctions is past. It is time to act. Those who do not act with us are by their very inaction against us.'

Maera turned on him: 'And what cause, pray, would your concert serve,' she demanded, 'other than to draw together all our bravest citizens in a single easily surrounded venue, and at night at that?'

Nye was struck dumb. 'I—' he began. 'I must confess, I hadn't thought of that.'

'Well,' Maera LaCouche crooned, 'when your plans are more evolved, perhaps you will be so good as to approach me again? Then perhaps I will join you. I am not an ideologue, Mr Nye: it is not my job to originate ideas.'

Our interview was over.

'Bloody woman!' Nye exclaimed furiously, as we walked back to his apartment. '*Bloody* woman.'

'Allingham, really!' I chided him. 'Not so boisterous, please.'

'Well, really,' Allingham replied, 'did you ever hear such giddy complaisance? It's enough to make one sick, it really is.' Indeed, Nye was so hurt by Maera's snub, it put him out of sorts for the rest of the day.

As for the concert, he never mentioned it again.

C.L.S. did his best work at night. He could not bear gloom, and insisted every lamp in the apartment was lit after sundown. In this manner he frittered away a good part of his fortune on paraffin. But when that evening I reached his apartments, there was no light in the loft. I supposed he was out on an errand. Wearily I climbed the iron stairs to the front door, and turned the key in the lock. It would not turn. I tried the handle and the door opened easily. Before I could register surprise at C.L.S.'s carelessness, something leapt out from between the door and the jamb and hit me full in the stomach. Another blow landed, and then another; they hailed my head and chest. I staggered back against the rail. The blows rained down, though they were softer now; so soft indeed, that when my initial shock was past I had the confused notion that I was being attacked by a squadron of feather dusters. Something fluttered at my breast. I swept it away, revolted and afraid. It fell at my feet, flapping feebly. It was a small bird, a canary perhaps, though in the gloom it was impossible to be sure—

'C——!' C.L.S. had left his cages undone. Now I had come and re-leased all his darlings to the less-than-tender mercies of the City's gulls! 'C——?' I swept in through the open door, my foot slipped from under me, and I fell into the hall. I lay sprawled, winded, berating myself for this comic entrance: the clowns of Marvyn's Merriment Theatre could not have bettered it. 'C——?'

There was no answer.

I got to my feet and felt for the lamp on its nail by the door. I lit it. I was covered in bird shit.

'C——,' I shouted, 'you *silly* old bugger!'

I went into the loft and crossed to the dingy and unswept wing where the museum and our bedroom were. I entered the bedroom. On the table by C.L.S.'s side of the bed stood a dead pot-plant. A *Calatheae*: it was my present from Allingham Nye. It had lost its leaves – they lay white and damp and crumpled all over the table and the floor.

I scooped up some leaves from the table. They were fleshy, healthy – crumpled.

C.L.S. had picked off every leaf.

I looked around. The desk on his side of the bed – normally invisible under a sea of unopened correspondence – was bare, but for a single book. I walked around the bed and bent over to examine it. It was my sketchbook, open at its last page. Cruel satyrs with C.L.S.'s face stared back at me, vengeful and irate.

I had shown him the plant with such insouciance, 'Look what Mr Nye has sent us', then put it on an out-of-the-way sill in the kitchen so his mind would not linger upon the likely meaning of the gift. I'd kept my sketchbook hidden under my work-things in the studio C.L.S. had given me. Now and again, in a malignant fit, I added another caricature to my collection. The book, the plant: evidence of my betrayal of him.

The plant – disfigured. The book open upon his desk, its drawings – added to. I put my hands to my mouth.

C.L.S. had sketched in arrows, piercing every satyr's heart.

'C——!'

The door to the museum was ajar.

'C——?'

There, in the gloom at the back of the room, stood C.L.S., peering into a glass case.

'C——, for heaven's sake!' I exclaimed, anger concealing my shame. 'What on earth are you hanging about in there for?' But he was in a sulk, and kept his back to me.

I turned up the lamp. Impressions flooded me so fast – the dejected slant of his head; the chair overturned; flakes of ceiling plaster on the bare wooden floor; the worn leather soles of his shoes; the stench of his evacuated bowels; last—

Like some bumbling detective in a bad farce, I noticed last the rope around his neck.

7

After C.L.S.'s funeral, I moved into a house by the Sé. It stood at the end of a sunken alley, behind the square where old men sat and smoked.

Every day, while I tried to sleep away my troubled conscience, workmen dug up and remade the pavements around the east gate. The noise kept me awake: iron on stone, a terrible din. I lay in bed and in the gloom I studied the paper hanging from my ceiling. The noise of the workmen's picks and their crowbars and their rattling carts beat at my ears; I searched the shapes in the ceiling and begged for rest, but it did not come. Then there was a lull in the noise, and I noticed that my whole body was stiff and straining, as though it were trying to rise out of the bed and float out the room.

'I've gone to them,' I explained to Evelyn Christ, early one evening in the Café Persil. I was already drunk. 'I've asked them how long they'll be working, how many days this must go on, and they push past me, muttering to themselves.'

Christ swallowed painfully on his beer. His watery grey eyes seemed misted over even more than usual. 'Why, if you'll excuse me for asking, do you suppose this is?' he said.

I stared at his vacant, abstracted little smile; I put my face in my hands. It seemed to me that they would never stop tearing up the pavement, that they would always be hammering new stone into place with their heavy wooden mallets. 'They keep watch on my house now.'

'Maybe you should invite them here for a drink,' Christ suggested, with a perky little smile. 'Perhaps, by gaining some sympathy for their work and their lives, you might be able to cope with their noise more philosophically.'

'Is that the best you can do?' I snarled.

He blinked at me, tried another smile, put it away again and shrugged. His eyes were so indistinct, they might have been pencilled in.

I visited the Café Persil every night. I told myself I went there to forget, but really I was punishing myself. Here, among the drunks and the navvies, I was continually reminded of how far I had fallen. I remembered all the evenings I had spent in C——'s company: evenings spent with the best writers, the most celebrated artists, the most renowned thinkers of the City. Of course, I had been no more than C.L.S.'s gigolo, and these people had no time for me now. One or two had sent me flowers; then rumours got abroad of my relationship with Nye, and I received nothing, not even a letter.

Blythe did her best for me, for old time's sake. She even invited me to her new studio – that same log cabin into which I had peered, that day I met her and Boris Stock. This cabin was now Blythe's, for she, of all the woman artists of the City, had been chosen to make the Iron Fish for the forthcoming Ceremonies.

When she first told me, I was confused. 'The ceremonies?' I echoed, dumbly. 'What ceremonies?'

'The Ceremonies of Stuffing and Hanging, of course.'

'Next year?'

'Indeed!'

Those astonishing costumes, my parents' fervent kiss – was it nigh on twenty years since that memorable day? Was it possible? Memories flooded me, so sweet and sharp I could hardly bear them. I pretended an interest in the studio, turning away from her so that she might not see my face.

Windows ran along the length of the cabin on both sides. Those facing south looked down through screens of lavender and dog-rose to the marble river; those facing north let in the soft, green-mediated light of the Academy's formal gardens.

There were papers everywhere, scattered over benches, in box files, pinned to the walls, crammed into the large tin waste-basket in the corner. Blythe had been showing me her work, explaining how she had planned her engravings on seventeen different kinds of paper: banana hemp, tea leaf, papyrus, rye grass and others whose names escaped me. She showed me some of her sketches. The illustrations and figures were a myriad of different styles, executed in greys and browns and creams with the occasional hint of ruddy sienna. Making an Iron Fish was no easy task. There was such a weight of tradition to be subsumed, such a burden of received ideas, and glosses upon them, and glosses upon glosses!

'And all for a bauble that rusts in the rain,' I sighed.

'Ah, but Tom, it's such a bauble! Come and see.'

At the end of the room stood a wooden trestle. Upon the trestle lay Blythe's fish, hidden under a square of cheesecloth. Without ceremony, Blythe drew off the cover.

'My God!'

'You like it?'

'It's – it's hideous!'

Blythe's fish was about four feet in diameter, bulbous, with bloated eyes and wicked spines along its back. Its mouth was gigantic – a rictus grin, lined with row upon row of primitive needle teeth.

'Recent fish have been so very stylized,' said Blythe. 'I felt it was time to return to basics.'

'Well you've certainly done that!' The engraved carapace was unfinished: the fish's belly was still in its skeletal state. I hunkered down and examined the gothic fluting and intricate joinery of the mahogany skeleton. 'How you can bear to think of all this work rotting through, I'll never know.'

'Oh come, Tom,' Blythe laughed. She picked up a small chisel from a tray beside her and began sharpening it absently on a piece of oil-stone; 'It's not as bad as all that. I'll have my drawings, my roughs and my casts. The Fish may decay, but the galleries will be stuffed full for months to come with my leavings and my scribbles!'

I stood up and from the table picked up a leaf of banana hemp. Sketched roughly in charcoal, two figures – rough silhouettes, one black and one white – ran from each other. Mirror-images of each other, they were connected at the left heel. Behind them, the surface was roughly scribbled over, in a wood-grain pattern.

I said, 'There was a time all the workings were burned you know.'

'Indeed?'

'After the Ceremonies, a torch was put to them all. Along with the artist. On a pyre of mobiles and bunting.'

'You think my premature cremation might make the Fish more effective?'

I shrugged. 'Might be worth a try.'

'Well don't tell Dr Binns,' Blythe laughed.

I picked up another sketch – two birds, mating on the wing above the spires of the Sé. 'You have dealings with Binns?'

'He was recently appointed provost of the Academy. Who else do you suppose is co-ordinating the Ceremonies?'

I dropped the papers back onto the work-bench. 'Then be on your guard – he owns my father's books, so he probably knows about the rite already. He does take such things terribly seriously.'

Blythe finished with her chisel and came over to the table I was poring over.

'Are these for the Fish?' I asked her, indicating the drawings.

'No,' she said. 'Don't you recognize them?'

'They're C——'s.'

'Some things I picked up at auction.' ,

'Auction?'

They broke up his collection. He had no family to bequeath it to.'

'He said he'd bequeathed it to a gallery.'

'He did. The black-clad women burned it down.' We were silent a moment, each with our thoughts.

I blamed myself for C.L.S.'s death; but I blamed others, too. There was Allingham Nye, my co-conspirator – and there was the world; it was easy to blame the world. I said: 'I think C—— could not bear the thought that there was nothing more to be done. He saw the world was a prison; in the end he lost patience with papering its walls.'

'Your influence kept him young,' Blythe assured me, kindly. 'He would have not been able to sustain himself for so long without you.'

I knew it wasn't true. 'I wasn't any help,' I said. 'Heaven knows, he told me so often enough!'

'Nonsense,' Blythe retorted, 'Mr Nye has told me what a lot you did for C.L.S.'

I stared at the Fish.

'It distressed him to see how much it drained you, helping C—— face the world without despair.'

'I suppose I earned my board,' I mumbled. I could not bear to think of Allingham Nye.

'You were devoted to him; Mr Nye said so.'

I could not stand it any more. 'Mr Nye and I cheated on him,' I announced, hoping my brutality would silence her.

'Mr Nye told me that, too,' she said, unfazed. 'He blames himself for that: he loved you very much.'

'Oh?' I said, and with heavy bitterness: 'Is that what he says?'

Blythe frowned. 'It's true,' she said. 'I know Nye loved you.'

'Loved me?' I echoed, struggling to maintain my shell of cynicism. 'How would you know a thing like that?'

'Because he visited me,' said Blythe. 'Nye, I mean. He poured out his troubles to me each evening, when you had left his bed to go play housewife to C.L.S.'

'You?' I breathed.

'He knew I was your friend. He told me he wanted the key to your heart.'

I stared at her.

'You did know Allingham loved you, didn't you?'

I shuddered. My protection was all undone.

'Tom? You surely realized?'

Some months went by before Allingham Nye and I met again: since C.L.S.'s death we could hardly bear the sight of each other.

Allingham chose our rendezvous – a cheap café, newly opened that spring. It was built into the arches under Central Station. Huge and empty and cold, little distinguished it from the surrounding warehouses. There were no plants, no decorations on the walls. The chrome tables with their circle of blue slatted seats were spaced far apart on cheap grey carpet; round the edges of the room were tables strewn over with leaflets for small exhibitions, concerts, rallies.

Allingham was late. I took a seat in a corner by the bar, which had been fenced off with a metal grille, and ordered a coffee. It arrived lukewarm and sour-tasting; the milk was old. The sound of the trains rattling over the café came through in a muffled and gurgling bass, as though there was a plumbing problem behind the high white ceiling.

Allingham came in at last. Almost the first thing he said to me was, 'I'm due at Grabbinges in an hour.' He didn't meet my gaze. 'Did you know those blasted women broke all their windows yesterday? Threatened the receptionist with a knife.'

'Really?'

'It was only a butter-knife,' he said, 'but even so—'

We bantered away for a few minutes, but we both knew what

our meeting was about. It was about blame. 'You look terrible,' said Allingham.

'I haven't been well since – since I found him,' I said.

'You should try and sleep.'

I shrugged. It was my turn not to meet his eyes. 'I have bad dreams,' I said. 'I didn't tell him. He found out about us himself. I feel I killed him.'

'No,' said Allingham, 'both of us did that.'

Tears stung my eyes. 'What on earth were we thinking of?'

Allingham had no answer.

'Why on earth did I let you persuade me—'

Allingham started. 'Persuaded you to do what?'

'Share your bed,' I replied, testily, 'what do you suppose I meant?'

Allingham shook his head. 'I persuaded *you*?'

I could not bear an argument. 'That was how it seemed, but what does it matter?'

But Allingham would not let the matter go so easily: 'I told you to tell him about us!'

'What good would that have done?' I demanded; then, with deliberate cruelty: 'It would merely have finished him off faster. If you'd cared for him that much, you'd never have bedded me.'

'I wanted you,' said Allingham helplessly. 'I wanted you for my own.'

'Well, then,' I said. 'You had me.'

He reached out across the table – a clumsy, hopeless gesture – then withdrew. 'You know I wanted more,' he said.

'You seemed happy enough with our afternoons,' I said.

'It was you who wanted to keep things as they were,' Allingham said. 'It was you who chose your double life, not me. If you had told him about us as I wanted you to, he would have let you go.'

'And what good would that have done?'

'Then you would have been free to come to me.'

I shook my head. 'You can't convince me of this now,' I said. 'We both know what it was you wanted—'

'*Me* again?' said Allingham, furiously. 'Why me, why not you? Oh,' he exclaimed, warming to his speech, 'it must be so easy for you, sitting there, so *passive*, so *innocent*. Did it never occur to you that you should have done something? But oh no, you simply sat back and let your beauty wreak its damage.'

I said, 'I don't know what you're talking about.'

'*It was not me at all!*' said Allingham, in a parody of my own voice. '*What did I do?* You did nothing, Tom. Nothing. Why else do you think things turned out the way they did? You, and that lethal beauty of yours – your neck, and your hands—'

I could bear no more. I dropped a handful of coins into the saucer, and walked out.

The men were working all through the night now, breaking up the pavements just outside my window. Arc lamps illuminated their work; when they paused for rest, the buzz and rattle of the generators was like the sound of wasps, battering the skylight of an abandoned attic.

I wrote to my mother. 'I have become important to these men: a part of their work, a necessary witness.' Of course, I couldn't send her that. Later: 'It seems to me that by my prevarication, I have committed a triple betrayal. I have cheated both gentlemen. Worse, I have cheated myself out of whatever happiness they might have given me.' I read over the letter and, disgusted, tore it to pieces. How could I write such things to her?

I sat in front of the clean tablet and worried at it until the following morning. 'My rooms are clean and the landlady has lent me a new coverlet!' It was light enough that I did not need the lamp any more: I snuffed it out, turned back to the desk and read over what I had written. I tore it up. I took a fresh sheet of paper, scribbled out my new address and asked for some money. Then I tumbled into bed.

I had maybe an hour's peace; then the workmen started up again.

I went to the window and twitched the curtain aside.

They were standing in a line, smiling up at me under an arc-light glare, despite the daylight. They were dressed all in black. They were women; and they all looked exactly alike.

PART FIVE

1

A year went by; then one day – a day like any other – a party of black-clad women entered Grabbinges's gallery.

Allingham Nye was there. As usual, he was arguing with the staff about some picture or other: this time, he insisted, they had hung it upside down. One of the women went up to the reception desk, picked up a pencil and walked over to where the men were arguing. She tapped Allingham Nye on the shoulder and when he turned round she pushed the pencil into his left eye as far as it would go, nailing it in firmly with the heel of her hand.

Blythe sent me a letter, inviting me to the funeral.

I threw it away.

I abandoned my artistic calling. I had grown weary of the black-clad women's insults and their threatening letters. I was sick of finding obscenities daubed over my windows, of turning up to a gallery only to find it torched.

Scraps of canvas, lodged between loose pavings, fluttered spasmodically like the wings of trapped insects. Scraps and shards: nothing new was left to amuse our late and laggard generation. Screwed up manifestos bowled across the Circus of Birds: mementos of the world's littleness. I remembered the sketch I had sent fluttering across the world's frontier, the lines disappearing, growing simpler, simpler, a stick figure-man …

Maybe the black-clad women were right after all: the time for art was past and the time for bonfires was upon us.

Set against the women's energy and determination, the lettered world I inhabited appeared trivial and conceited. There was not a manifesto declared or movement met that within the week was not overtaken by some upstart ideologue, riven by internal dissensions, vilified by the critics, set upon the plinth of finished history by academics, or repudiated by its founder the moment its name was abroad. The work was secondary: the greater part of it destined for some squalid bonfire – a fire tended, no doubt, by women dressed in black.

My despair and self-hatred took a dissolute form. I gloried in my purposelessness, and took up with some dissolute, witty fellows from the Baixa. Together we searched out hedonistic escapades, the better to lose ourselves.

We spent most of our time munching popcorn in indecent theatres. My companions went hoping to be shocked, or titillated. I was more sanguine: I had always esteemed erotic performers, ever since I had begun sketching them. To my mind their acrobatic escapades were a celebration of life – all the more poignant now that the City had grown grey and inimical. Eat drink and be merry – this was their message. Such was my enthusiasm, that when my drinking friends grew bored with our visits and found some other thing to distract them, I let them go rather than relinquish my daily attendance at Maisie May's or Reggie's High-Class Vaudeville. I became a regular at Maisie's. I was accorded red-carpet treatment: I had my own seat in the front circle, and a private understanding with the ice-cream boy who, for a modest sum, would with his agile fingers release some of the erogenous tension which built up in me from time to time during the show. The manager made an especial point of greeting me in person. Sometimes he condescended to entertain me in his tiny, yellow-painted office: a converted broom-cupboard which, leading directly off the urinals, smelled of bleach and mice. He made me a cup of tea on a small gas ring, and, having set the pot down between us as though it were some accoutrement of high office, some gavel or rod, he consulted with me as to which of his acts had a future, which needed more development, which had grown stale and should be replaced. Afterwards, while he was cleaning the tea things, I would steal up behind him and put my arms around his waist. What ensued required all our ingenuity: the little wooden table where we drank our tea filled up nearly all the space. There was no room to lie down. Once or twice I lay across the table and he stood on a bucket to be at the right height. But the bucket broke so we gave up.

'You really would be better off with one of the girls,' he told me, turning the broken bucket nervously around in his hands like a hat.

'I would?'

He shrugged. 'A small audience at first, hand-picked among discreet friends; the girl of your choice, assuming she was amenable—'

I laughed. 'I am an artist,' I told him, 'not an actor.' With the quickness of a true entrepreneur he then suggested that I sketch him some promotional material – but I refused. I had no desire to go back to the old life.

Mr May (his mother Maisie had begun the business) shook his head; his habitually worried look intensified. 'I cannot bear to see a young man waste himself.' He chewed on his thumb and stared at the ground. 'I don't know why,' he said, 'but I feel you have great potential.'

It was a potential Mr May was pathetically eager to tap – but I resisted him. I had done enough damage in my short life, and blown too many hopes. My sole desire was to become as inconsequential as possible.

There is a curious atmosphere to this underworld profession that has nothing to do with prurience. It is much closer to the spirit of a circus, with its lion-tamers, clowns, jugglers, tumblers and ladies on horses.

Maisie's boasted an intriguing variant of the last-mentioned act every Wednesday: one fateful night the horse in question – a sprightly young stallion well versed in the erotic arts – panicked at the sight of its intended paramour. She was clad in straps of leather and wide copper chains, and must I suppose have put it in mind of some hated bridle from its training days. It bolted up the aisle, trod on the ice-cream boy's foot, sent half a tub of best vanilla over the naked lap of his most recent client, and punched a horse-shaped hole through the plasterboard frontage of the rickety little theatre.

The ensuing crisis drew me further into Mr May's business.

'Lunatics!' Mr May exclaimed, when I arrived at the theatre the next morning. He was standing under the portico, pacing up and down like a demented doorman. I thought for one dreadful moment that the black-clad women had sacked the theatre, but he was referring to his own employees. 'Impossible, absurd demands!' he expostulated, over and over again. I spooned tea into the pot and poured on the water. The smell of mice was even stronger than usual.

'Even the sodding caretaker!' May cried. 'Sympathetic action my arse!'

It took a lot to make Mr May speak like this.

'Is anyone left?'

'I won't back down, I won't!'

'*Is anyone left?*' I repeated, and set the teapot down on the table. Its presence there – the gavel, the rod of office – calmed him. However bad the crisis, at least the niceties were being adhered to.

He licked his lips. 'Angelica. Rosalinda. Wilhemina—' He counted them off on his fingers. 'Archibald, Reginald. And young Miranda.'

'I thought they'd taken all your young players with them?'

Mr May shrugged. 'Miranda's thirteen – they're obstinate at that age. Besides, she's got a taste for it.' He licked his lips again, this time with more appetite.   .

The withdrawal of the juveniles was but a secondary issue as far as the striking players were concerned. It was merely part of their attempt to impose upon Maisie May's the rules of established theatre, viz., *that they should not be expected to work with animals or children.*

According to Mr May, such demands were simply impractical. 'What industry do they think they're working in?' he exploded, slopping his tea into his lap. '*Commedia del* bloody *Arte*? You can't do anything without animals. Animals are the *point*—' (Some of his best acts involved miscegenation.)

All afternoon, while disgruntled patrons traipsed in and out of a half-price show of under-rehearsed striptease, Mr May and I worked furiously on a new show. The office was a sea of brown paper bags – the only paper to hand – on which I had sketched idea after idea for Mr May's approval. Evening approached – the busiest evening of the week.

'They'll need coaching!' Mr May wailed, and pulled at his mousy hair. 'We give our boys and girls this—' he shook the plan of our show (a brown bundle tied together at the corner with a broken lace garter) ' – they won't be able to make head nor tail of it.'

He was right of course, but I could not see any solution to the problem. There was no way we could rehearse them all in time, no means of translating my frantic scribbles into polished stagecraft unless someone who knew and understood—

'No.'

Mr May's smile was predatory. His eyes glinted.

'No!' I exclaimed. But I had been lax in my self-protection; I was in too far and Mr May, the good entrepreneur, knew it.

For a time I was happy; I thought exhibitionism a gallant challenge to the greyness of the world; anyway, mine was a job with many pleasurable compensations.

I had thought myself bound to a life of male love; now I became, of necessity, intimately acquainted with members of the fairer sex, and I discovered just how universal is the language of the flesh. A night's public roistering with Angelica differed little from a night with Reginald; in the aftermath, stretched like cats across goat-skin rugs in the communal dressing room, I found that our more private dalliance was even less determined by anatomy: Rosalinda's mouth was as satisfying as Archibald's, her cunt squeezed as tight as his fundament, her climax was as raucous and savage as his.

Love of one became, in the general tussle of half a dozen participants, love of all. The finest-spun spirituality seemed beggared in comparison to this tough and savage lust of ours. Good, upstanding men might speak of charity and trust, philanthropy and care, but it was we – so far gone in what men chose to call iniquity – who practised all these virtues, and with an athleticism that a good, upstanding man could never hope to emulate.

What more disarming love and affection was ever tendered to a child, than was tendered by us all upon little Miranda at her bedtime? What bookish lesson in trust could equal in force or elegance the trussed strictures of Wilhemina in her leopard-print briefs? What love might be so nakedly expressed in goodly society, as was expressed by Reginald, Archibald and I over Rosalinda's breasts?

Of course, people being what they are, love of the general good often comes to be expressed as love of one representative sample. Human beings are not good in generalities: they need emblems and saints. Eventually, then, I took Wilhemina as a favourite. Perhaps it was because, under the luscious difference of her sex, she resembled most the men I was more used to. She was immensely strong. Her energy and power excited me: many is the time I quaked with awe at her superb musculature. She was very patient with me, for I had much to learn about the fairer sex; one lapse of concentration and I found myself flailing about like a drunk in the arms of a quick-stepping wrestler. Often I simply could not keep up with her demands; and then she indulged in masturbatory games of such alien and terrible beauty, that I imagined she had sprung fully formed from the pages of some particularly racy myth.

Little Miranda, who lived under Wilhemina's incestuous care, was gentler fare: a girl for whom the erotic arts were not yet much distinguished from all the other childish games.

Her favourite was dressing up: 'Sit on the bed,' she said. 'Close your eyes!'

She delighted in showing me her new dresses.

I lay back on her truckle bed and put my arm over my face. I heard a rustle of heavily dressed fabric.

'Now,' she said. 'Open them!'

The dress stopped just short of her knees: a figure-hugging black silk slip with a bright red net of embroidered flowers stitched over the top. I opened my arms for her. She reached down with her left hand and tugged up the material so she could straddle me without tearing the dress, then she slid down on the bed on top of me. I reached down, smoothing my hands over her boyish buttocks, and pulled the dress up higher so I could stroke her flesh. She pushed her tongue deep inside my mouth and slumped to one side, so that I might clamber on top of her.

I pushed myself up on my arms and admired the dress. I saw there was a zipper under her right arm. I lifted her arm, bit into her armpit, and pulled at the zip.

The dress opened from the side. I pulled the material aside and exposed the shallow, undeveloped curve of her breast. I licked and chewed at her nipple till it was swollen and red.

She groaned and lifted her legs into the air. I felt inside her knickers, pulling the elastic aside and rubbing my fingertips along the hairless folds of her cunt to where they met just above her clitoris.

She gave a little scream, and lifted her legs higher.

I leant forward, bending her double, her knees above her head, then let myself slide off the bed, kissing her flesh, the dress rucked up above her waist, the band of her knickers, the smooth skin stretched over her pubic bone—

She stretched her legs in the air like a kitten that is being tickled, then slung her knees round her arms, pulling her pale, thin thighs apart for my tongue.

When we were done, Wilhemina came in and sat beside us on the edge of the bed. 'I never see you dressed these days,' she complained.

Miranda snuggled deeper into the crook of my arm.

'There is nothing outside the bed,' I replied, luxuriously. 'Nothing that matters.'

'Well,' said Wilhemina, brandishing the cheap newspapers she was addicted to, 'that's the way things are going, for certain. When I think of poor little Miranda here, the sort of future she has to look forward to—' But the general diminution of things was beyond her expressive powers, and she fell into a morose silence.

I stretched out on the bed – my feet slipped from under the coverlet and I drew them back quickly to keep them in the warm. Wilhemina's meagre rooms were situated above the theatre; they were impossible to heat. 'If the papers disturb you,' I said, 'don't read them.'

'It won't stop things happening, will it?' Wilhemina demanded.

'No,' I admitted. 'No, that's true.'

'It says here they beat up a washerwoman for hanging out bright clothing. Poked her eye out.'

'Oh, really!' I muttered, and snuggled further under the covers. 'You really do pick the most inopportune moments—'

'Well—' she shrugged. 'You're the one always going on about how you and your clever friends spotted them before anyone else. I thought you'd be interested in what they're up to.'

'They are a fad,' I said, not believing what I said, but keen to change the subject. 'They will vanish soon enough.'

'They burned Mr Christ's new pamphlet yesterday. It's in all the papers.'

'Oh?'

'You said you knew him.'

I shrugged. 'Maybe.'

She stood up; she was growing impatient with me. 'Up with you – bath time. You can do my hair. Miranda – Miranda, wakey, wakey! Hang up that dress.'

Maisie May's theatre had been a bath-house. During the conversion Miss Maisie had preserved the warmest pool for her artists. Many a dancer and entertainer had refused offers from rival establishments, because they had no bath to equal Maisie May's.

The roof of the bathroom was all of glass: the metal framework was painted dark green: it cast lines of shadow across Wilhemina's brow, her face, her pendulous, half-submerged breasts—

'Those people what write for the papers, you heard what those bitches did to them?'

'You told me already,' I murmured, preoccupied.

'Dragged them round in a net, they did. The bargees made it for them.' She scowled. 'Nasty little pigs, bargees.'

'Mm?'

'Three of them died. Journalists.' And when I didn't respond: 'Soap my back, dear.'

I did as I was bid. There were freckles, running in a line from the base of her neck to her left shoulder, like a string of tiny brown pearls. 'Is this,' I said, 'leading to something?'

She shrugged. 'Just thought you might want to know what's happening outside Miranda's cunt.'

'And your cunt,' I countered.

'And mine, yes.'

I thought about what she had said. 'If you feel that I spend too much time with Miranda—'

'Miranda's got nothing to do with it. Let her have her little adventure.'

'With pleasure.' I dispensed with the soap and massaged her shoulders. Absently, she reached behind her and stroked my legs under the water. 'Mr May came up to me yesterday, asked if I thought you were "fulfilling your potential".'

I made some sarcastic response.

'I told him you didn't have any.'

'Thank you!'

'I told him you were like a little boy, run away from home after a scolding.'

I snuffled at her neck. Her skin smelled of almonds. 'And what did he say to that?' I asked her.

'He went on about your potential again, same as he always does.'

But I had done with this baiting: 'What potential?' I demanded, out of temper. I levered myself out of the pool and flung a towel about my shoulders. 'What is this potential everyone keeps on about?'

'Buggered if I know,' she said. She gazed up at me: 'I reckon you're running away from something, only I don't know what.'

I folded my arms. 'I don't know what you're talking about.'

She shrugged. 'You've been getting uptight lately.'

I was mystified. 'What makes you think that?'

Wilhemina pushed herself from the pool – water slid from her superbly muscled body. 'Well,' she began, wiping the water from her hair, 'there's the bruises on Mira's arms—'

197

'So this is about Miranda!'

'I'm not jealous of her, Tom.'

'Think,' I insolently persisted, 'of the passion those marks commemorate!'

'Tom, you bite her because you're bored.'

'Oh,' I said, affronted. 'You think so?'

She said, 'I've been in the business long enough to know when people start using it the wrong way.'

'*The wrong way*?' I couldn't help but laugh. 'What kind of tart's philosophy is this, Willy?' I knelt by her side. 'You know I have the highest respect,' I exclaimed, 'for all of you! You are my home and my family. I was nothing before I joined your troupe. Before I met you all, my life was a sham. Hollow! Meaningless! It signified nothing—'

'In a month's time you'll be saying the same about us,' said Wilhemina. 'I've seen it all before.' She soaped her face and splashed it clean. 'Tom,' she said, carefully, 'I reckon you joined us to prove something. Whatever it is, I don't want to be a part of it. And I don't want Miranda to be a part of it, neither.'

I was stumped. I had no idea what I had done to deserve such a rebuke. 'What is it you think I'm trying to prove?'

'That you can lose yourself,' Wilhemina replied. 'It's like you want to make yourself as nasty as possible. You thought living with us would make you bad. But we ain't different to anyone else, so now you're casting round for something worse.'

This was too much: 'Worse than you lot?' I sneered, and in my best thespian manner: 'Is't possible?'

'At least we stick up for our friends,' she said.

'And I don't?'

'Not that I've seen.'

'Oh?'

'That Mr Christ for one,' said Wilhemina, harking back to her bloody newspapers. 'You were always boasting you knew him. And that singer, the LaCouche woman. She can't sing since they tried lynching her outside the Opera. You ain't been to see her either, and her larynx is broken.'

'So that's it!' I'd been half-expecting her lecture to boil down to a demand for money, but this was even more imbecile! 'You expect a little reflected glory, do you? Pissed off that I want to lower myself, instead of raising you? So what's it to be, eh? What is it you're after? A little social one-upmanship, perhaps? "I know Thomas Kemp, confidante of Lady X and Y the sculptor." Or is it fame? An introduction, maybe? "Miss LaCouche, while I bandage your throat, do let me tell you about this *darling* little mother-and-daughter act"?'

'I thought you was a gent,' she said, levelly. 'But I don't think so no more.'

I laughed: I couldn't help it. As though being a gentleman mattered any more! The age of such nice distinctions was long past. All those oh-so-glittering figures who dazzled me in my youth – Maera LaCouche with her vanity, Evelyn Christ with his complex pretensions, C.L.S. with his proud despair – they seemed grotesquely comic to me now. The world was grown too small for such passions. Even my own youthful enthusiasms seemed ridiculous to me now, and I was pleased that I had put them behind me, that I had 'lost myself'.

Wilhemina said, 'You don't give a fuck about anyone, do you?'

'So?'

She hadn't expected so bald an admission. 'Well,' she said, at a loss, 'is everything a game to you?'

'Of course,' I replied, put into good humour at the thought of precious Maera LaCouche, squawking like a duck.

'And what you do here, with us? Is that a game, too?'

'The purest, most honest theatre that ever was.'

'What about Miranda?'

'Children's theatre!'

She stood up. Water ran from her breasts into my hair. I leaned forward, to kiss her, but she pushed my head away, roughly, the way you might push away an importunate pet. 'Well I'm not your sodding puppet,' she snapped.

'We're all puppets,' I chuckled; I drank in the sight of her damp loins.

She covered herself with a towel.

'No, don't,' I said. 'Stay with me.'

'Piss off,' she said.

I stood up. 'We know each other too well for that,' I said. I pulled off her towel and seized her hips.

'Tom—'

I pulled her to me.

'Mind!' she said, 'the floor's slippy.'

'Kneel, then,' I said. She had riled me; my blood was up. I nuzzled at her neck.

'Oh Tom—'

'Do what I say!'

'For heaven's sake—'

'Do it!'

She pushed me away. 'You *are* desperate!'

I said, 'On the marble. Kneel down.'

'Let me get a towel,' she offered. 'Let me—'

'No.' I pushed her. She slipped on the marble and fell to the ground. I leapt on her, laughing, and twisted her onto her stomach. 'Give me your hands.'

'Tom—'

'Give me your hands.' I took her arms from underneath her; my time in the business had made me strong; at last I overcame her resistance. She slumped, her cheek pressed to the cold marble. 'You are magnificent,' I panted, gazing at her broad, rippling back, her up-thrust buttocks. 'Magnificent!' I held her wrists like reins and slid inside her.

Later, when I was done with her, and we were lying next to each other, I said, 'Your breasts are swollen.'

She hid them with her towel and stood up again, away from me.

'They swell when we make love,' I said.

'Fool,' she snapped at me.

'But you care for me,' I smiled.

'Care for you!'

'That's why you're crying.'

She wiped her face, angrily. 'I'm crying because you hurt me, you sod.'

I lay back on the cold marble floor. 'No,' I said. 'That's not why you're crying. You're crying because you find me melancholy. Well I am, I suppose; there is no – Wilhemina?'

But she was leaving the room.

'Willy—?'

'Rapist!' she hissed, at the open door.

'Oh, Willy,' I chided her, 'don't be a silly bitch!' I got up and went over to her. 'Come here, you don't really think—'

She slammed the door in my face.

2

Mrs Cowie, my mother's landlady, was an obese, bad-tempered woman with dewlapped cheeks and liver spots on her hands. It was she who told me about my mother's illness. She visited the theatre in person and asked for me. She handed me an envelope written over in my mother's handwriting. Her smile told me she knew what was inside: my mother had been contributing to my living expenses for some time.

'Lost faith in the postal service?' I sneered at her, counting the notes out in front of her face. There was a paper with the money: my mother, with her usual heart-broken brevity, had written: 'Keep safe. Love, Mother.'

'Just thought I'd better tell you, dear,' said Mrs Cowie, simpering. It was then she told me. 'Just thought you ought to know.'

It was the day of the sweet market. Apiary stalls, piled high with hunks of soap, liqueur in china bottles and candles the shape of hives, lined the pavements. Slabs of liquorice hung on hooks around the pastry sellers' stalls clouded with flies like sides of rotten beef. I paused by the stalls, thinking to buy my mother a present of some marzipan fruit – sweets to say sorry for years of arrogant neglect – when I spotted, out the corner of my eye, a grotesque yet familiar figure. Binns! Dr Emmanuel Binns, smiling his dreadful smile and sweeping the busy lane with his long black gown like Death on a day trip. I quickly turned my back to him, and hunched up my shoulders – I had no desire to meet him after the last eerie and farcical episode – but I was too late.

'Thomas! *Thomas!*' He trotted up to me and clapped me on the back. I turned in feigned astonishment and greeted him as warmly as one can ever greet a skull. 'What happened to you at the Opera?' I urged him. 'Was it all lost, or did you save your books?'

'Shush!' he hissed in my ear. 'Do not speak of such things here. My illicit researches are still unsuspected, but the trail grows dangerously warm. Come, let us find a more private place to talk!'

'Oh,' I exclaimed, 'but Dr Binns, I regret I cannot—'

'Tom,' he urged, 'you are the very person I need to talk to! Extraordinary developments, unlooked for, cataclysmic in their significance—'

I shook my head. 'I am sorry, Dr Binns.'

'Mr Camp,' he admonished me, glowering terribly. 'The future of our city may depend upon our little talk! Will you refuse me now?'

I stared back at him in an agony of irritation. I decided to play him at his own game.

'For a little while, then. Doctor Binns,' I said, importantly, and then, in a patented *Binns Hiss*, 'for if I am long about this, my absence will be noted.'

'Ah – !' Binns nodded. 'Very well; I will be brief. There is a discreet café nearby. Come with me!'

I followed him, all the while watching for a chance to dodge and lose him; but he was assiduous in his beckoning on, and the crowds granted us an easy passage along the winding street.

Binns led me into the City's principal market. It was enclosed within a large rectangular mews, several storeys high. As a boy I was deemed a prodigy by my fellows, for I was able to filch fruit from even the most jealously guarded stalls. I was not as quick as I once was but I had grown more wily: a peach pumped its sweetness into my mouth as we toiled up sun-blasted steps to the upper part of the mews.

I wolfed the peach, for I knew that when I reached the top level my appetite would vanish: the meat stalls were situated there.

The butchers of the City were of diseased stock. How else might one explain their predilection for basketfuls of peeled chicks, whole flensed lambs with clouded eyes, buckets of spew and intestine, panniers of bullock teeth with the quick still red and juicy in the sockets, and all their other carnivorous obscenities? I kept my eyes averted till we reached the café.

We ordered espressi and I firmly declined the patron's offer of a filled roll.

'I have made great strides!' Binns exclaimed.

'Indeed.' So much had happened to me since I had last seen Dr Binns, I could not even begin to simulate interest in him.

'But I need help to wreak my emancipatory designs!'

'Indeed.'

'Let me show you.' He hunted in the folds of his voluminous black gown, waited till the patron had set down our coffees and turned his back; then, and with excessive caution, he revealed to me his latest engine. Not a fish, this time, gigantic or otherwise: something altogether more homely. 'You see?' he hissed.

'It's a child's doll,' I said.

'Or so it appears!' Dr Binns exclaimed. 'In truth, it is a *booby* or *fetish* prepared in accordance with strict magical principles—'

'The stuffing's falling out.'

'This doll has been made following ancient instructions set down in one of your father's books! Your father,' he declaimed, unctuously, 'was a great man.'

'He trawled second-hand book shops,' I said, 'what's so great about that?'

'This doll,' Dr Binns insisted, and buried the silly article under his cloak, 'is a golem of high price! Placed in the correct fashion and with due propriety in the junction of two huge spars, beneath the very centre of our road bridge, it is a catalyst for wonders!'

'Really,' I sneered.

'As you know, the Ceremonies take place later this year. On the day the Iron Fish is stuffed and hung this doll, planted by some athletic young man in its proper nook, "makes manifest—" I am quoting my source, mark you – "*makes manifest the sufficiency of the world*"!'

'Binns,' I sighed, 'you insufferable dupe – your doll does no such thing!'

'Really?' said Binns, put out. 'I'm sure that's what it said in the instructions.'

The sheer triviality of the man, with his glib rites and his facile librarian's credulity, were too much to be borne. I said, 'How many years it has taken you, my friend, how many long and lonely nights of slow and diligent study, for you to reach the point I reached at the tender age of twelve!'

'Eh?'

'Surely you don't think you're the first to come across that business of the doll? Why, when I was a boy, my father taught me that very rite – and I performed it, too!'

Binns blinked at me, uncomprehending.

'Throw your doll away, Dr Binns,' I laughed, 'your magic operation has already been performed. I myself performed it, twenty years ago! I made a doll, like that you're clutching so jealously to your breast. I made it, and wrapped it, and tucked it into my belt just as you want me to do with yours. I climbed up the bridge with it, and planted it, and thought perhaps, just perhaps, that something would happen! But nothing did, Dr Binns. Nothing did and nothing ever will. It is probably the most useless among the many thousand useless operations in my father's bloody books.' I laughed bitterly. 'Great strides, indeed!'

'Oh dear,' said Binns at last. He looked so deflated, like a dejected crow in the rain, I couldn't help laughing at him.

'Never mind,' I said, clapping him on his thin, bent back, 'there will be other rites no doubt. Why, it would take several lifetimes to sort through them all! Sticks and dolls, paints and cloths and foil flags, dances and feasts, jamborees and jubilees, pastries and cakes and ritual ways of baking bread. And when you die, Dr Binns, if you like I will cut you about in the ritual manner – my father taught me well you see – flay your cheeks and thumb blue paint on your forehead as they did in the olden days. Then you can die as you have lived: in the toils of a broken-backed past!'

'You know, Mr Crimp,' said Dr Binns, 'you really are a rather snide person.'

'It's Kemp, blast you.'

'Kemp. Sorry.' And when I said nothing: 'I am sorry to have

troubled you.' He stood up, dropped a coin into his saucer, and left me sitting there, grinning into space like a skull.

Ordinarily, Mrs Cowie spent her days in a wicker chair by her kitchen window, drinking sloe gin. But tending the sick awakened in her a belligerent, egocentric energy. She moved my mother out of the boarding house and into a small apartment she had recently inherited, between the allotments and the Opera. 'Now I can watch her,' she told me. 'Now I can watch her properly!' The place smelled of cooking and rancid soap. She took me aside and sat me down and told me the most terrible things. 'Your mother fiddles with herself,' she said. 'I've seen her.'

'For God's sake—'

'She fiddles with herself: sit down!'

The doctor told me my mother had contracted Bowles Syndrome – a rare variety of relapsing fever.

He said, 'She will need constant attention.'

I went in to see her.

My mother had the attic room. The air in there was dry and heavy, like the onset of migraine. She lay sprawled across the bed under a pink eiderdown, half-conscious, sweating profusely. Her body odour was sour and sickly; it pervaded the room, its bitterness combining with the smell of over-cooked vegetables. She lay with her arms outside the covers; the bed-jacket had ridden up her forearms, accentuating her blotchy, elephantine hands.

She said, 'Mrs Cowie will look after me.'

'You can't stay with her!'

She said, 'Mrs Cowie's always there for me.'

I held her hands, feeling for the tell-tale nodules, manipulating her outsize fingers, mapping in my mind the delicate architecture of her tendons. The flesh of her wrists and palms felt cold and clammy and fat.

Meanwhile, Mrs Cowie made coffee. The aroma of it filled the close air, mingling with the tang of sweat. 'Mr Kemp,' she called me, as if I were some specialist or other. The coffee was burnt and thick as treacle.

I could not bear the sight of the stuff she fed my mother for lunch: sprouts cooked to a grey opalescence, a ham-knuckle, thin gravy that smelled of fur. She insisted all three of us have lunch together in mother's room. She ate clumsily and greedily, as if to impress on us her animal vitality. She ate platefuls of kidneys; they swam about on her plate, eluding her fork. A drop of gravy dribbled from the corner of her mouth. She chewed on, oblivious: the drop hung from the hairs on her chin. Every so often she turned to my mother and stared at her. 'Poor thing,' she said, *apropos* of nothing. Then, with a movement too fast to dodge, she reached forward and clasped my mother's hand. Mother smiled weakly at the ceiling: Mrs Cowie tightened her grip.

However sincere our emotions, we remember clearest the farcical moments of funerals; long after the eulogies have faded from our minds, we carry the memory of countless trivial incidents around with us, and uncover them again with a twinge of embarrassment, as one might remove a crumpled paper flower from a winter overcoat.

I helped my mother's friends from the boarding house carry the coffin up to the Quiet Lake. This quarter of the City, with its terraces and its dirty washing, its derelict squares full of rubbish and its cobbled streets polished smooth in the rain, had always seemed to me such a curiously impermanent place. Its buildings had over the years been botched and gerrymandered so many times they had lost their original natures. That day the rain-transmuted light turned the most stoutly built brick facades into slabs of sodden cardboard.

Just as we turned in at the gate of the municipal park I lost my footing on the slippery cobbles. My fellow bearers staggered about under their unbalanced load; for a moment, it looked as if the coffin might fall. A small boy, watching us from the pavement, stifled a giggle.

I have never been able to shake off this moment. Its very triviality has assured it a place among my memories. Blythe joined me by the edge of the lake. 'How are you?'

I shrugged.

'Thomas?'

I did not want to look at her. 'I have been – unlike myself,' I said.

'Are you still at the theatre?'

I shook my head. Wilhemina had grown to hate me. She had been ready to throw me into the street, when news of my mother's death had stayed her hand. I had saved her the trouble; the day before I'd moved into a room above the bordello on Tierney Street.

'You know about Allingham Nye?' Blythe asked me.

I nodded: I could not meet her gaze.

'I wrote to you about him.'

I said, 'I'm sorry I didn't reply. I – I was busy.' But that was a brutish excuse, and I was sick of brutishness. So I said: 'It seemed – impossible for me.'

'I would have liked you there,' said Blythe. She was so studied in her refusal to accuse me, she reminded me of my mother. I felt giddy and sick.

After the funeral we ate boiled meats in a wood-panelled function room above a grocer's shop. Every slice of meat tasted exactly the same. I stared out the window at the rain. A gull settled on the sill outside and tapped on the glass. I shivered and turned away.

'Say you had lived these past years differently: what would you have done?'

'Been a gypsy, Blythe.'

'A moth, battering the sides of its glass jar?'

'Better to be a moth that breaks its wings trying to escape, than one who spends its life trying to crawl back inside the cocoon.'

'Why Tom, that's worthy of C.L.S.!'

I shook my head. 'His aphorisms were more pithy.' I could hold back the tears no longer.

'Oh, Tom,' Blythe sighed; she leaned against me and put her arm around my waist.

I turned to her; we held each other close. It struck me how much Blythe had aged, in the time I had spent hiding from myself. There was grey in her hair, and her once firm musculature had turned to fat. I felt it under my hands—

'Not so tight, Tom,' she murmured.

Reluctantly, I let her go.

Blythe took me under her wing. She treated me as though my recent brutishness were a sickness, more than a cause for blame. Books, papers, hours spent talking: these were the medicines she administered. Sometimes I wept, to think how little I deserved her ministrations.

I thought of Wilhemina, and poor little Miranda. We had been a kind of family, but I had brutalized them both. I thought of my mother, of how neglectful I had been of her, and how I had come to her sick-bed too late to be of any use. I had known for some time that my life was in ruins: now I began to understand why. I had ruined it myself. I had shied away from tragic truths, and had descended into farce. Knowing that the world was too small to requite much passion, I had refused passion when it was offered. In a world where to be human was a struggle, I had chosen instead to be a brute.

I thought about Allingham. Among the books Blythe brought me were some of his pamphlets. I wondered at his bravery, his resolute campaigning, the hostility he must have stirred up against himself with his angry and righteous attacks upon people's complacency. He had written: 'As for the women I have known them too long – known them, indeed, before they knew themselves – and so I may say I can cope with them; but the commons! The vulgar politic is all confusion; it displays such giddy complacency as may stir up the puke in even the most phlegmatic commentator's guts! We citizens have grown so used to thinking of Life as Art that we cannot see the very dangers which threaten us. We applaud the tidal wave as it towers, foot by foot, over our heads.'

His voice had gone largely unheard of course. He had been too brutal with his truths. He had lacked the guile and smoothness of the truly effective politician.

Reading Nye's pamphlets I came to understand that many symptoms of the time – from C.L.S.'s egomanic despair, to my own escapist flight into prurience, to the far more significant and terrible scourge of black-clad women – were rooted in a common despair. We were, as Allingham had written, a city so convinced that Life was Art that we had forgotten how to act. Rather than attempt to escape our cell, we had chosen instead – each in their own way – to paper over its walls.

Mrs Cowie wanted me to remove my mother's things.

I asked Blythe to come with me. 'I don't think I could bear to go on my own.'

There was nothing left in the boarding house. It had all been moved into the attic room of Mrs Cowie's apartment, stacked haphazardly around the bed where my mother had died.

There was little enough to sort out. In the years since my father's death, my mother had learned to cope with less and less. The few sticks of furniture she had saved from the house were missing. I suspected Mrs Cowie of keeping them for herself, but I couldn't bring myself to quiz her about them.

Blythe kept Mrs Cowie away from me as best she could. The old woman stood at the door to the room the whole time, slurping on the genever she'd splashed into a tin mug: she would not let us alone.

'Not many clothes,' she said. 'Not very sanitary, that.'

'Perhaps she couldn't afford them,' I replied, nettled.

'Wonder why,' Mrs Cowie crooned.

Blythe laid her hand on my shoulder; I tried to remain calm.

'There's china ornaments in that box.'

'Thank you, Mrs Cowie,' said Blythe.

'Never saw much point to them myself.'

'Thank you.'

'Well?' said Mrs Cowie. 'Aren't you going to look at them?'

Blythe's calm wore Mrs Cowie down in the end: with Blythe there, she knew she could not rile me as she wanted. She made one last attempt to catch my eye over Blythe's shoulder, then went off to make some coffee. 'You like my coffee, Mr Kemp,' she called back as she descended the stairs.

'Thank you, Mrs Cowie.'

'Brightens you up, I shouldn't wonder.'

'Thank you, Mrs Cowie.'

She said something else, but she was so far down the stairs by this time I couldn't make it out.

Beneath the box of ornaments was a small wooden trunk. Blythe helped me with the catches. I opened the lid. The inside had been packed out with tissue paper. I drew the tissue back and uncovered yard after yard of black silk, gathered into complex pleats and velutes. They met at a heavy black brocaded collar, decorated with jet. I drew the garment out and held it up.

'It was my father's,' I said. 'He wore it for the last Ceremonies.'

Blythe pulled back another layer of tissue. 'Oh Tom, look,' she sighed, 'it's beautiful.'

My mother's costume lay carefully folded in the bottom of the trunk. Green sequins swirled in fluid patterns over the sheer cream silk.

'May I?' said Blythe, and without waiting for an answer she drew it from its box. 'It's magnificent.'

It was so carefully made, to see it was to remember my mother's shape: the line of her hips, the narrow waist, the modest swell of her breasts—

I rummaged about in the tissue at the bottom of the trunk. 'Here,' I handed Blythe a pair of gloves, tasselled with carmine velvet and green and black lace, like seaweed.

'Tom, it's so beautiful,' said Blythe, holding the dress against her.

I couldn't bear to look. 'There's no hat, I'm afraid. It must be somewhere else.'

'Tom?'

'Do you see a hat box around here?' I asked her.

'Tom, hold your father's costume against you.'

'I don't see one …'

Blythe slid my mother's dress back into the trunk. 'I'm sorry.'

I smiled and shrugged, hiding as best I could the pain the sight of the dress had caused me. My parents' kiss …

'Here we are,' said Mrs Cowie, bustling in with a tray. 'Clear the bed.'

'Please, Mrs Cowie, not in here,' I said. 'We'll come down to the kitchen.'

She ignored me, side-stepped Blythe and came up to me. It was late in the afternoon and she had grown unsteady. Her hands shook: coffee slopped from the pot over the edge of the tray. It missed the trunk by inches. 'What are they?' she demanded.

Blythe tried steering her away. 'Nothing, Mrs Cowie.'

'Ooh! Costumes!'

'No, Mrs Cowie.'

'Yes!' Greed made her tremble violently. 'Yes!'

It was evening by the time we extricated ourselves from Mrs Cowie's apartment. In my room above the brothel on Tierney Street, I unwrapped the costumes and offered my mother's to Blythe.
'I couldn't.'

'Please,' I begged her. 'Who else have I got to give it to?'

'Tom, Tom,' Blythe fretted, embarrassed. 'Anyway, it wouldn't fit me.'

'You could let it out.'

'Tom.' Blythe faced me and drew her Tacking jersey around her middle. 'See? It would never go on.'

She was right: she was far too heavily built to get into it. 'Hang on to it, Tom.'

'Is there anything else you'd like?'

'Nothing, really. There were no books, I noticed.'

I explained: 'She had enough of them when Father was alive.'

'Binns will be disappointed.'

'Binns? What in the devil's name has Binns got to do with it?'

Blythe shushed me down. 'Nothing, nothing, he just told me to be on the look-out for any old books.'

I was outraged. 'I gave him all my father's treasured volumes, the ungrateful little sod! Isn't that enough?'

'Tom, you're jumping to conclusions. He didn't mean your books – he meant books in general. Calm down, Tom.'

'What does he want more books for, anyway?'

'He's trying to prepare the Ceremonies as authentically as possible.'

'Fussy little twit!' I said, still put out.

But Blythe had more time for him: 'He thinks he can rediscover lost magic. He's had some success, he tells me.'

I would have liked to scoff, but I remembered his gigantic fish, his magical chamber: 'He has, yes,' I admitted reluctantly, and remembering the doll: 'But it's a rather hit and miss affair.'

'At least he's trying to open up the world.'

'I'd sooner trust the gypsies,' I grumbled.

'Tom,' said Blythe, 'the gypsies have failed. Maybe it is time to look elsewhere.'

Only when she had left could I admit to myself that Blythe might be right. Maybe, somewhere in my father's books, there was a way out of our cell-like world. But how ironic it was that I might, in my desire to escape the world's narrow boundaries, have thrown away the very books that would have released me!

But these were idle speculations. There was a more immediate question: what was I to do with my parents's costumes? I toyed with the idea of keeping them. Perhaps if I had children—

I shook my head free of such nonsenses. It was hardly likely I would ever have dependants. I had rendered myself unfit for family life. What woman was there would marry a veteran of male love and erotic theatre?

But that of course was the solution! I wrapped my mother's dress and gloves carefully in some brown wrapping and addressed the package to Wilhemina. Blythe could not have let-out the dress enough for herself, but Wilhemina would have no problem taking it in for poor Miranda.

I owed them an apology. I had not been humane. I had slighted Wilhemina's kindness and been a brute to the girl. At my lowest, they had offered me the comforts of family. It seemed only right, therefore, that I should offer them a family token.

Miranda, I remembered with a pang, adored new dresses …

What of my father's costume? I held it against me. It seemed I had grown into my father's size.

I hesitated. I was reluctant to try the garment on. It seemed somehow unscrupulous of me. It was true I had no costume for the Ceremonies—

I took off my jacket and slipped the black gown over my head. It settled comfortably around my shoulders. I took a few paces around the room. It fitted perfectly.

It was an uncanny moment. I looked at myself in the mirror, and saw my father's face. It had not occurred to me before how much I looked like him. I felt self-conscious: I hid my hands in the voluminous pockets of the gown. I found a paper in the right hand pocket. I unfolded it carefully: it was brittle and yellow around the edges. It was a page torn from a wants list of second hand books. There was a hole torn out of it: my father must have thrown the scrap into the silver bucket, nigh on twenty years before. I folded the paper back up and slipped it back into the gown.

I looked at myself in the mirror again; my likeness to my father was even more startling a second time around.

I knew now why I had not wanted to put the gown on. The gown was my father's work. He had fashioned it according to the rules of some ancient book or other. My parents – all I had ever done was take from them. I had given nothing back to either of them. It was too late to redress the balance now. But perhaps some gesture ...

If Blythe was right, and Binns was on the trail of some discovery involving my father's books, then perhaps I could help him. It was ironic, that I should come to such a pass, and return to what I had first repudiated. But I knew I had to earn the right to wear my father's gown.

I looked in the mirror a third time. My father looked back at me, noble and severe in his ritual garb. I sighed. 'Oh very well,' I said; 'you win!'

4

'It'll take more than limpets to renew our hope for the world,' said Dr Binns, when I volunteered my services: 'I aim for nothing less than the City's total transformation!'

All that month Dr Binns and I spent buried in books, hunting the storerooms and cellars of the Academy library, first for this detail, then for that reference, now some variorum instruction, now another commentary, and a note, and an appendix, and now yet another gloss, all in the hope – the slim hope, certainly, but hope nonetheless – that between us we might be able to organize Ceremonies so true to their original state, so richly enacted and so carefully prepared, that the magic in them might transform the world into something rich and strange and – just possibly – given.

We cast about for others to help us. Response was meagre, as we had feared it would be. The black-clad women had much of the City cowed before their spiked sticks, and complacency was rife among the commons. Help sprang at last from an unlikely quarter.

'Good heavens, lad, how have you been?' boomed Boris Stock; his hearty laughter set the dust atremble on every shelf. Behind him filed his coterie – pale young men with cravats and pale, tonged hair. They lined up, noses quivering in the dusty air, like mice that have chewed through a wainscot and find themselves in an unfamiliar cellar. Among them I noticed a face more grey and unremarkable than the rest.

'Christ!' I exclaimed. 'Evelyn Christ!'

Christ simpered and stared at his feet. I remembered the women had burned his poems: I did not know what to say. I did not deserve his help.

As we worked, we discovered that many parts of the ceremonial were recent accretions, and therefore worthless. The climb of the cliffs beneath the Baixa, the dazzling display of fireworks from the trains upon their bridge, even the dance of the red-crowned buglers – none were vital to the Ceremonies.

This was as well. The City's enthusiasm for the coming day was decidedly damp. When Stock's men had wearied of their book-work – for it was a point of pride with them to ape their master and spurn anything so sedentary as 'book-learning' – Stock sent them off into the City to report on the City's preparations. Off they went: pale-skinned young students for whom Stock's brand of gruff nil-rhetoric was an exotic antidote to years spent cramming in private schools. When they returned, shivering and out of breath – for, try as they might to shake off their bookish pallor, they were not of Boris Stock's ruddy disposition – they had little enough to report. On this street there was a float abandoned in the rain; on that stretch of river there was a single ceremonial half-bridge lashed to the embankment wall, but it had no decoration, and anyway it was so carelessly built it would collapse in the first real gust.

The conclusion was inescapable. Disillusioned by a world that had lost its magic, and prostrated before the black-clad women, people had lost all interest in the Ceremonies.

There was a knock at the library door.

I opened it and stared into black and hellish eyes—

'Ah! St Thomas, I presume?' said Edwin Gross, pushing past me and into the hall.

'Let me take your cloak,' I said. He handed it to me. Beneath it he wore a new poncho, longer and louder than any I had seen him in before: his last sojourn in the sanatorium was the longest yet.

From out the poncho he drew an armload of books. 'I don't suppose you have these,' he sneered. Dr Binns scuttled over and examined them. I caught a glimpse of the titles. They were the most common sort of modern compendia, and we had long got past the need of them. Binns caught my eye: I shot him a warning look, which he interpreted correctly, saying, 'By Jove, Mr Grass, these are of tremendous value, I thank you sincerely.'

'Where did you get them?' I asked him, quickly, before he could take umbrage at Binns's mispronunciation.

'Nicked them from the landlady,' Gross sniggered.

'Oh, really!'

'Desperate times call for desperate measures,' Dr Binns reminded me.

'Yes,' said Gross; 'anyway, the obstreperous old tart had it coming to her.'

Dr Binns cleared his throat. 'Ah, yes, well I'm sure these will prove very useful, Mr Grass, thank you.' He bore them away to the reading room. There, Boris Stock's coterie – recovered from their outing and with their honour satisfied – pawed and scribbled their way through the great pile of books set before them. They yawned assiduously and exchanged filthy stories of the sort they knew Stock enjoyed, but in attempting to disguise their natural studiousness they fooled no-one, except possibly Boris Stock himself. By the seat of each young man lay a small pile of books already seen to.

'Come along then, Mr Gross,' I said, 'if you are here to help, let's get to it: help me reshelve these books!'

Gross retreated to the corner by the door. 'I've done my bit for charity,' he sneered, and folding his arms upon his chest, he fixed us all with his chilling black stare. I turned from him in disgust. 'Dr Binns!' I called out. 'What next? What would you have me do?'

Binns came up close to me and took me by the arm: 'Come with me,' he murmured, and led me like a stage conspirator up spiral steps to a mezzanine full of journals.

'Doctor,' I protested, 'I have looked up here, there's nothing to our purp—'

Binns pressed his finger to his lips, and beckoned me into the shadows between stacks of dissertations.

'Mr Kemp, this business of burning ...'

'Burning?'

'Yes.'

I frowned at him. 'You'll have to be more precise.'

'This – this pyre of bunting and stuff, rubbish from the Fishmaker's rooms thrown upon it, and so on ...'

Again he left his sentence incomplete.

'Good heavens!' I exclaimed. 'You're surely not suggesting we incinerate Miss Maravell, are you?'

Dr Binns grimaced. In the gloom, his teeth were like tombstones in a ghetto cemetery. 'Well,' he said, 'the most ancient of our books are quite insistent ...'

'Dr Binns, for all that's decent! We can't go setting fire to people just because it's recommended in a second-hand book!'

'But if the rites demand it ...'

'No! No, no, and a thousand times no, Dr Binns. Good God!' I took him by the shoulders and shook him. 'Get a hold on yourself. Think what you're saying! I'd sooner we abandoned your scheme in its entirety than countenance such an outrage.'

Dr Binns shook his head to clear it of the nightmare: 'Forgive me, Kemp,' he begged. 'I have been too hard at it, you see. Proportion is hard to come by when you're as tense as I ...'

'Then go home,' I insisted, 'and get some rest. You can be of little use to us in this state.'

He shuddered and ran his fingers through his hair. 'Tom, I shall do as you advise. Exhort those fellows! Keep them at it. Every minute counts.'

'I will be as the whip-hand on a gaol grinding wheel,' I assured him; 'now go to bed.'

We finished with the books at last, and gave what we had learned a solid form. Stock's pale young men were delighted. Day and night they hammered and pincered and sawed and sewed, laughing with practiced joviality, greeting each other with 'how do, lad?' and parting with cries of 'fuck off!', in the manner of their mentor. They were inexperienced craftsmen, and work was slow. It is a measure of their dedication that, despite numerous minor injuries, they managed to get all the various daises, ladders, and other sundry erections ready in time.

We left the stringing of the mobiles until the last minute, lest the black-clad women take exception to their bright colours and fanciful designs. It was dawn the day before the Ceremonies before we processed down Green Monkey Street, knocking at every door. We met with reluctance – even hostility – but the district's burghers were on hand to enforce the ancient rights of access. In we trouped, and secured strong wires to those ancient hooks and gears my father had pointed out to me twenty years before.

The mobiles themselves arrived mid-morning. They were of ancient, unfamiliar design. Gone were the clown heads, pierrots, twelve foot long pink kazoos and outsize balsa kitchen equipment I remembered from my childhood. These decorations were far more fearsome: balsa shark skulls stained with wine, a bacon rasher impaled upon every triangular, serrated tooth; mermaids with claws for hands, wild staring eyes and squid-beak genitals; cockroaches made of bent wire; rats with coats of burlap pressed with dung.

At the end of the sloping thoroughfare, glimpsed intermittently through a light sea-scented mist, gulls whirled uneasily around the Circus of Birds, or perched upon the newly assembled flag-poles. 'And I say they must come down!'

Dr Binns was in a state again: Heinrich Nudz had taken it upon himself to string gaily coloured electric lights along Green Monkey Street. The two of them – Binns gawky and pale-skinned, Nudz short and barrel-chested with cheeks aflame and sensuous woman's lips – were at loggerheads over the affair.

'You are a scientific illiterate!' Nudz screamed, tearing at the tufts of hair which sprang, like some alien growth, at each side of his otherwise baby-bald pate.

'Your new-fangled seditions will be the undoing of our sacred—'

'Mumbo jumbo! My media are clean and efficient!'

'A fig for your efficiency!' Binns cried, quite out of control, and snapped his fingers under Nudz's nose.

But Nudz was too busy extolling his discoveries to notice the insult. 'Hygienic lines of luminiferous aether, harnessed with the utmost probity through—'

'Bollocks!' Binns screamed, losing himself entirely. It was time to intervene.

'Gentlemen, please!' I exclaimed, stepping between them, 'why such commotion? Why such animosity?'

'This librarian thinks I wreck all with my fairy lights,' Nudz sneered.

'Apostatical gee-gaws!' Binns snarled: his teeth were blunt and greasy-looking like the tips of dirty butter-knives.

'Look!' said Nudz, and pointed to the little cases packed in tissue at his feet. In each nestled a thin green wire. From the wire hung small coloured bulbs. 'Little lights of green and red and blue, for children to coo at. But your Mister Binns, he trembles before them.'

'*Doctor* Binns, to you, Professor Nits.'

'Enough!' I cried.

'Enough!' Binns wailed, and jumped on Nudz's boxes. They shattered and spilled their contents into the gutter.

'Binns, that is not what I meant!' I admonished him, and seized him by his collar. He pulled himself free and started jumping up and down on Nudz's bulbs. Bright shards crackled under his patent leather boots.

'Visigoth!' Nudz screamed, knocked him into the gutter, and threw himself on top of him. 'Philistine!' Nudz made to hit Binns full in the face, but Binns caught his hand. Nudz wound his knee up to the level of Binns's testicles, but Binns caught Nudz's leg between his own so tightly, Nudz could not hurt him cleanly. Then Binns got an arm round his neck, but Nudz pinned his other arm behind him and pulled.

A plump man in a new grey suit leapt into the fray. He tugged at Professor Nudz's arm. It wouldn't budge. 'For heaven's sake!' he shouted at me, 'do something to help, can't you?'

Reluctantly, I stepped into the mêlée and wrestled Binns free of his assailant. Nudz lunged after him, but the stranger in the suit grabbed him by the collar and yanked him back.

'Sir!' he yelled. 'Professor! Sir! We have more important things to do.'

Nudz turned on his rescuer. 'Nincompoop!' he exploded. 'It is my honour ...'

'You were throttling the provost, sir.'

Nudz hesitated. Questions of academic tenure scudded across his engorged face. He slumped. 'Take down our lights, Henry,' he sighed. 'It is a lost battle.'

The man in grey went off to see to the removal of the fairy lights. He reminded me of someone. I followed him. From behind, the resemblance was more clear – 'Henry?'

The man turned.

'Henry!'

He frowned at me. 'I'm sorry—'

'It's Tom, Thomas Kemp.'

He stared at me. 'Good God.' He took my proffered hand and shook it vigorously. 'Tom!'

Henry had changed much since we were at the Academy together. He had put on weight, especially around the jowls: fat softened every line and curve of his face. His hair was receding: his pate was smooth as a baby's. He was like a gigantic new-born.

'You're still under Nudz?'

219

'Partners,' Henry corrected me. 'Next month we're electrifying the Sé!'

'You're in business then.' His suit was expensive and well cut.

'And you?'

I wondered what Blythe had told him. 'Research,' I replied, with an ironic smile.

'Ah yes, the Ceremonies. Is Binns quite mad?'

I shrugged. 'Enthusiastic, more than mad.'

'I'm relieved to hear it.' He glanced at his watch. 'I won't keep you any longer. Tomorrow – where will you be?'

'I'm meeting your cousin at the Fishmaker's cabin,' I replied, 'at daybreak. Will you be there?'

Henry shook his head. 'I've an appointment. The Bar Terminal, after the Ceremonies?'

'I'll bring Blythe,' I promised him.

That night in my room above Tierney Street, I undressed slowly: I was preoccupied. The sounds outside my window were not the ones I had expected. It was the night before the Ceremonies, and yet I heard no celebration. Hard as I tried, I caught not one chorus of the *Oubliez*. Once a bottle smashed on the pavement below, but there were no drunken cheers. In the distance, towards the Baixa, came the occasional beat of drums. I thought of the black-clad women. The sky was orange over the Folded Rose Hostel: a building was aflame. The black-clad women again, perhaps, but I could not be sure. Fires were not uncommon in that slovenly parish.

I went to the window and looked out. Shadowy figures criss-crossed the pavements: brothel clientele. They moved furtively, like conspirators. It was not like a normal night. Not a single whore braved the pavements: perhaps they were as ill at ease as I.

The City grew tense: I sensed it, winding itself up like a spring. My head throbbed. I looked into the sky. The stars glittered: there were movements in the air. I thought, There'll be a storm soon. I stayed up, waiting for it: I knew I would not be able to go to sleep before it broke. The stars flickered and blurred. The clear night air wobbled like jelly. I imagined some malignant hand, screwing the sky down over the world, pressing us in, tighter, tighter …

A bicycle rattled over the cobbles towards the brothel. I looked down.

The messenger dismounted and let the bike drop in the gutter. He ran over to the brothel. Behind me, the bell rang. I leant out the window and called down to him.

'Telegram!' the boy yelled back.

'A moment.' I threw on my coat and did the belt back up around my trousers. Business in the brothel was slow; the women were lounging about the narrow stairs and velveteen-papered corridors, smoking and chatting. I weaved my way between them and got to the door. I tipped the messenger and read the telegram as I went upstairs.

DAWN TOMORROW AT APT NOT CABIN STOP APOLS LOVE BLYTHE

I cursed. However was I supposed to get to her apartment by daybreak? Back in my room, I fished my watch out of its coat pocket. It was gone two already. It was hardly worth my going to bed.

I thought idly of the brothel beneath my feet – but virtue prevailed; I undressed and lay on my bed, staring out the window until the clocks struck four.

The stars shivered and whirled: the sky was on the boil.

PART SIX

1

Dawn, hesitant and grey as feathers, ushered in the day of the Ceremonies. There had been no storm. The pressure upon the City was palpable. I lay in bed, straining to hear some sound of bustle, of cheeriness, of bands tuning up, girls skipping, boys singing as they burnished the tram tracks. I heard nothing. I sighed, got up, splashed water over my face and draped myself in my father's costume.

I stepped out into Tierney Street, normally so vibrant and loud, thick with tarts and beggars and street vendors.

There was no-one about.

It was still dark. I glanced at my watch. It was nearly five. The trams were running in one direction only today: inwards, up to the Sé. There were no trains. I headed for the station anyway, hoping to hail a cab. There were none – only urchin boys, dozing under the canopies of their rickshaws. The one I came to first was fast asleep, his feet propped on the handle-bars of his bicycle. I shook him awake and waved a handful of coins under his nose. He yawned and sucked at his teeth. I bullied him out from under the canopy and took my seat.

The boy pedalled quickly through the district of the Folded Rose Hostel. The gloomy streets frightened him; he flicked his head from right to left, fearing an ambush. Smoke rose from the looming tenements, veiling the air like net curtains. The streets were silent and empty, as though a plague had cleared them. I saw no sign of the fire I had spotted earlier that night.

An old woman limped over the road in front of us, a load of bread under her arm. The boy hissed and catcalled as he pedalled past. In the next street, an ass harnessed to a milk wagon had balked at the entrance to a back street: it trembled under its master's flail.

We came to the road bridge. Below us, the black river stretched into the distance, stark, undecorated, unreflective: it might have been a fissure through the earth. There were no Tacking flags, no partial bridges, no gold pennants to relieve its black monotony. The embankment was empty. No-one was abroad.

We reached the Southern Hill. The rickshaw boy laboured up the gentle incline. Litter blew about the street in front of us. I studied the houses: a few of the windows were decorated. One or two of the doors had bay sprigs nailed above them. An old man was climbing a ladder onto his roof. He moved one limb at a time, carefully, as if part of him might give way at any moment. A tasselled pole was slung round his bent back. But he was alone in his piety: the houses around his were unflagged.

The boy left off pedalling and we descended in a broad curve around the Southern Hill. The bourgeois avenues of the Academy gave way to a familiar expanse of bleak, box-like houses. The boy slowed to a stop and looked around him. 'Where to?'

I gave him the directions again. He scratched his head, and set off. Street followed street: nothing distinguished one from another. There were no squares, no shops, no steeples to navigate by.

'It's near the canal,' I reminded the boy, but he was as lost as I.

I didn't have the heart to be angry with him: he had done his best. He pumped the rickshaw to the top of a small rise and we looked out over the district: it was like a hive for geometrically inclined insects. I pointed to some overhead power rails. 'That's the new tram line!'

We set off again, but as we neared the canal, we found our path blocked by a field of neglected allotments. We had not seen it from the hill, but from here it seemed to stretch for miles. The boy tried to cycle around it, but the streets kept leading him away, up sharp ascents and unmarked cul-de-sacs.

We admitted defeat at last. I got out of the rickshaw and tipped the boy for his trouble. I walked back to the allotments. I gathered my father's costume up around my knees and let myself in through the wicker gate. With mincing strides lest I dirty my costume, I followed a cobbled lane through a confused and over-grown muddle of weeds and canes and old fishnets, derelict sheds and rusted water butts. In amongst the general chaos lay a few meticulously-tended patches. Others were laid fallow for a season, the soil hidden under old cardboard and rolls of carpet.

The lane came to a dead end in front of a high brick wall. I walked along its length, swishing my way through the tall grass, until I reached a gate. Behind lay a footbridge, spanning the canal. To my relief the gate opened easily. I crossed the bridge and orientated myself: I was barely ten minutes's walk from Blythe's apartment.

When I got there, she was not at home. 'Gone away,' said Mrs Cowie.

There was in Mrs Cowie's face – in the fat-heavy line of her jaw with its few black curly hairs, perhaps, or the maggoty whiteness of her cheeks – something unyielding, something sour. That and her black garments made me uneasy.

I said, 'What are you doing here?'

'Tidying,' she replied.

'This is Miss Maravell's apartment.'

'And I'm tidying it.'

'I don't understand.'

'Mr Kemp,' she said. 'Come in.'

I stepped inside and she closed the door behind me.

'Why did Miss Maravell—' I began; but she was not listening. She was busy gathering things – old furniture, holed clothes, piles of dog-eared sketching paper. She enlisted my help. 'Come on,' she said. She marched me to the kitchen door. 'Give me a hand with these boxes.'

'Where's Blythe?'

'Never mind.'

'I spent a long time getting here, Mrs Cowie.'

'Those boxes.'

'But my costume—'

'Bring them outside!'

We carried them out and threw them onto a bonfire made of old papers, broken stretchers, empty lead tubes, canvas scraps, orange boxes and tattered gallery programmes.

'Will she be back soon, Mrs Cowie?'

Mrs Cowie danced round the bonfire, shaking turpentine out of an old milk bottle. 'Mrs Cowie,' I said, it'll burn anyway. It's all cloth and paper.'

'Don't interfere.'

'But you just asked me to help you,' I protested.

'Don't interfere.'

I studied the things piled up before me. For a second I was overcome by aphasia. It was as if, deprived of their usual setting, these things had lost their individual natures.

'Mrs Cowie, why did Blythe ask you—'

Mrs Cowie struck a match.

I moved to stop her. 'Mrs Cowie—'

She touched the match to a rag soaked in paraffin, and poked the flaming rag deep into the bowels of the bonfire with a long stick. The fire caught.

'Did she say when she'd be back?' I asked her, and I wondered: why did everything burn so fast? Why did it boil away so eagerly?

Mrs Cowie began running round and round the bonfire. It was such a strange thing for her to do.

I walked up to the edge of the bonfire. There was something burning near my feet.

It was a book, bound in black leather. The top right hand edge was alight.

I picked it up, read the spine, dropped it as the flames brushed my fingers.

'Mrs Cowie, why are you burning Massey's *Libretti*?'

'Load of shit,' said Mrs Cowie, rushing past, out of breath.

There was another book, near the first one. 'Evelyn Christ's *Leartes Laughs*?'

'Load of shit.'

There were books everywhere.

'C.L.S., *Historical Process for the Lay Reader*? But I bought her that!'

'Load of shit.'

Mrs Cowie was not talking to me at all: she was chanting.

I retreated carefully back into the kitchen, then, out of sight, turned and rushed through Blythe's apartment. Her box room was bare. The pictures had been torn from her walls. Her private gallery was gone. I looked out the window. A black cord of smoke from Mrs Cowie's bonfire climbed into the trembling air. Strange currents pressed it in, flattened it into a disc through which the sun gleamed – a pupil in a mad eye. I stared at Mrs Cowie. She was rushing round and round the bonfire, yelling something. In one hand she was waving a stick. In the other were a handful of drawings. I yelled and hammered on the window pane. The glass snapped. I sucked on my grazed knuckle and watched helplessly as Mrs Cowie consigned Blythe's drawings to the fire.

I let out a strangled cry of fright and revulsion.

Mrs Cowie turned. She looked up at the window. Her eyes were blue and terrible. She was grinning.

She raised her stick. It was spiked through with rusty nails.

I let out a scream of fright and bolted from the room. The kitchen door banged shut.

'Yoohoo!' Mrs Cowie sang. 'It's mee-hee!'

A drawer slid open and banged shut. '*Oubliez les anges!*' she sang. '*Oubliez les bossues!*'

She entered the living room, skipping. Her black skirts weaved about in the reticular light. '*Et partout, Oubliez les professeurs!*' There was a meat cleaver in her upraised fist.

I ran to the front door, swung it open, leapt out and swung the door shut behind me. Mrs Cowie smashed her cleaver through the glass panel of the door. Shards burst at my feet. I stared at the black-clad arm.

It did not move. It did not even tremble. Blood dribbled down the blade.

I turned and ran as fast as I could back the way I had come. I reached the canal and ran headlong down the towpath. I sprinted past the horrid concrete playground, afraid of the women that might be hiding there. Above me I heard the squeal and spark of a tram, pulling into a halt on the newly opened line. I sprinted up the stairs from the towpath to the street. The tram had already begun to move off. I chased after it, yelling. The driver saw me and stopped. I leapt on.

'Like the gear, mate.'

'What?' I panted.

'I like the gear!' the driver shouted, above the rattle of the wheels. He nodded at my costume.

'Oh,' I said, 'thanks.' I looked around me: two families and a middle-aged woman in a check scarf. Only the family nearest me wore costumes, and they were hardly worth the name. The driver too had made no effort: the buttons of his tunic were unpolished, and he had left the top button of his shirt undone. So much for the festival: I looked out of the driver's window: the tram rails were black and tarnished. No-one had thought to burnish them.

We were rattling down an incline, a stop or two away from the Academy, when the driver braked suddenly. I cracked my head on the panel behind him and leapt up, cursing.

'Not my fault,' said the driver. I leaned into his compartment and looked out of the window. Black-clad women were building a barricade across the street.

The driver wrestled with his gears.

'What are you going to do?'

'Put it into reverse.' He got off his seat and climbed down among the nest of levers and wheels beside him. 'As quick as I can!'

'You can ram that,' I said.

'Not likely!'

'It's only a few old trestles.'

'I'm taking us back,' he insisted; but his harsh braking had dislodged the gear lever.

Out of the window, I saw the black-clad women approach. 'Let me help.'

'Nothing you can do,' the driver muttered, 'damn thing's sprung.' He got back into his seat. 'Oh my—'

A stone clanged against the side of the tram. The driver let down his window and shouted at the women. 'Clear off!' he yelled. The women charged him. He swung up his window again. The women rushed up and smashed it with their sticks. Behind me, the children started wailing. When I turned back, the women had hold of the driver and were dragging him out of his seat. I grabbed hold of his legs but the women were too strong for me: they pulled the driver, wailing, out into the street.

I clambered into the cabin and grappled with the lever. It wobbled about in its socket, dislocated and useless.

Outside, the women were yelling at the driver. They had his arms pinned behind his back. He kicked out blindly at the women in front of him. They laughed at him, just out of range, and baited him with their sticks. I waited till they drifted in front of the tram, then I released the brake. The tram trundled forward down the slope. The women scattered, letting the driver go. I tugged at the brake. The tram stopped inches from the wide-eyed driver. He leapt round the side of the cab. But before he could climb in, one of the women pulled him aside and scaled the side of the tram herself. I scrambled out of the compartment. She caught hold of a trailing edge of my father's cloak and pulled. I fell back. She grabbed me by the hair. I got hold of her arm and twisted it. She used her other hand to pull herself further into the cab. We were face to face.

'Lilith?'

'Let go of me!'

'Lilith?'

'Let go!'

She let go my hair and swung out at me. I let go her other arm and she fell from the window. I leant out. She lay sprawled in the street. 'Lilith!'

She sat up, rubbing the back of her head. She squinted up at me. 'It's me: Tom. Thomas. You stayed at my parents's house!'

The desert had aged her, dried out her face and turned her hair a dirty yellow. She looked like a bedraggled eagle.

I tried again. '*Kemp*. My father's name was *Kemp*.'

'You're his son?'

'Yes!' I opened the driver's door and climbed out of the cab. I offered Lilith my hand, but she refused it. She staggered to her feet. Her fellows ran up, dragging the hapless tram driver along the street by the collar of his jacket. I glimpsed blood in his hair. He was conscious, still; he cursed his captors. The women dropped him and started towards me. Lilith raised her hand, holding them back.

'Lilith,' I said, 'what's going on?'

She laughed, bitterly. 'You must know by now.'

'But you're not one of them,' I said.

'I'm a gypsy.'

'But that doesn't make you—' As I said it, I awoke to the truth.

'Who did you think we were?' said Lilith. 'Where did you think we came from?'

I stared at the women gathered round me, sneering, twirling their sticks. The black-clad women – *gypsies*.

'But – but,' I gabbled. My lethal brush with Mrs Cowie had inured me to danger: only now did I realize the risk I was in, by addressing Lilith and her fellows. 'But you wanted to find a door,' I said. 'A door, into the given world!'

'There is no door.'

I felt my face grow hot. 'I know that.'

'Turn back,' Lilith commanded me. 'Don't go to the Ceremonies. Don't recycle the City.'

'Lilith,' I said, 'you don't understand—'

'Tom,' she hissed, 'it's over. I've spent my life searching for something new, some explanation. *There's nothing there*. It's time we ended the charade.'

I could not answer her. Had I not had the same thoughts myself? How could I presume to contradict her philosophy, distilled from a lifetime's disappointments?

At the same time, I could not stand idly by while the women – the *gypsies* – threw the City onto the pyre of their despair. I needed to attend the Ceremonies. I needed to play my part.

I racked my brain for some ruse. 'We can't turn back,' I said. 'The gear lever's stuck.'

Lilith stepped up close to me, hissed: 'I'm doing you a favour, you fool.'

'I know that! It doesn't alter the fact the tram's broken.'

'Then walk away.'

Behind Lilith, the women were growing restless. The driver, ignored by them, staggered to his feet and, unseen, limped off towards the tram.

'We can't do that,' I said.

The women muttered and stirred.

'Tom.' Lilith's sun-creased eyes flashed a warning.

'There are children here,' I begged her.

'Better the world ends for them now. Better they never know the misery we have known!'

'What would you do then?' I demanded. 'Put them out of their misery?' I had to keep them talking. The driver was climbing stiffly into his cab. If I could only keep them talking for a few more seconds, and try not to inflame them—

The driver slipped and fell into the road. The women heard. They turned and rushed upon him.

'All right!' I screamed. 'We'll go back! We'll go back. Right?' I shot an urgent look at the driver. He blinked back at me, stupidly. He was barely conscious. 'Right?' I yelled. '*We go back.*'

The driver made to contradict me: I snarled at him. He got the message at last. 'Right,' he said, in a weak voice. 'Right, we go back.'

The women cheered, lifted him up and threw him into his cab. There was a moment's pause, then he released the brake and the tram began sliding down the street towards the barricade.

The women gave a shout and scattered out of the way. The tram picked up speed.

'Tom!' Lilith cried. 'Tom, you cheated!'

I flung myself at her and snatched the stick from her hand. 'One problem with despair,' I snarled at her, 'it makes you stupid!' I pushed her to the ground and flung her stick away. She scrambled up and ran after it. The tram was seconds away from the barricade: the gypsy women were on the other side of the street: for a second the tram hid me from them. I waited my chance. The tram came level. I rushed for the open doors. They slammed in my face. I screamed and beat on the glass. As the tram shot by, the driver gave me a look of the purest hatred.

231

'You ungrateful little prick!' I screamed, as the tram careered into the barricade. The trestles gave way, knocked aside by the vehicle's skirts. I scampered after.

The driver did not stop for me: I was not to be forgiven for fraternizing with the women.

I glanced back. The women, with Lilith at their head, were charging towards me. I ran through the gap in the barricade; glimpsed handle-bars. I seized them and pulled. From a pile of kitchen rubbish I drew a child's scooter. It would have to do.

Behind me, the gypsies screamed abuse: I was recycling a piece of their junk! A spiked stick flew past my ear and landed in the road ahead of me. I pushed off and wobbled precipitately down the slope towards the road bridge. Another stick flew over my head. I swerved: The scooter's wheels slipped into the ruts of a tram track. I picked up speed. The scooter's wheels ran faster and faster in their metal channel. I hung on for dear life as the street sped past me. The wind picked up. It screamed past my head. I felt as though I was falling. Where the road met the bridge, orphans were crossing the road in twos. I screamed: they scattered. I flew past. Ahead of me, in the middle of the bridge, the tram had drawn to a halt. I had no brakes. I leaned forward over the handle-bars and dragged my feet along the road. I yelled in fear. The tram moved off. I wanted to throw myself clear, but I was stiff with fright. I closed my eyes.

The front forks of the scooter tapped the rear of the tram and I fell sideways into the road. I heard cheers and clapping. Still in shock, I thought the gypsies had caught up with me: but I had left them far behind. It was the orphan children who were applauding me, laughing and pointing. I dusted myself off and took my bow, amazed to be still alive.

I continued my search for Blythe. The telegram I had received must have been a ruse of some sort. Perhaps Mrs Cowie had sent it. If Mrs Cowie was in league with the black-clad women, then Blythe was in danger. Was this why I had been lured away from the Fishmaker's cabin? So Blythe would be there alone, and un-protected? I jogged back to the southern end of the bridge and headed up Academy Avenue, past Blythe's old digs and the alley where I had rescued her. Climbing the hill was hot work. The chill of the morning had passed. I stopped a moment and shed my father's heavy, enveloping gown. It was grey with dust, specked with mud from the allotments, and torn in several places. I hid it beneath a privet hedge, by the chapel garden; if I had the chance, I would retrieve it before the Ceremonies. For now, speed was of the essence. Unencumbered at last, I ran lightly up to the main entrance and dashed inside.

'Hoi!'

I glanced behind me. An ancient man in a bottle green morning suit was running after me, waving a clip-board above his head.

'Closed!' he panted, 'can't you … can't you *read*?'

I stopped and waited for him to catch up.

'We're closed!' he hissed out. His face was purple and he laboured for air.

How many years had it been since I had first encountered this fussy little man? 'Why aren't you dead yet?' I wondered aloud. 'Have you seen the Fishmaker?'

'Where's – where's your permit?'

I grabbed hold of his clip-board and examined it for clues. The top sheet was blank. The ones beneath were torn from a popular book of pornographic drawings. 'You *useless* little man,' I snapped, and rammed the clip-board into his stomach. He keeled over, winded. I ran through the formal gardens and into the woods. Between the trees, I glimpsed movement. I hurried down the ash path, rounded a corner and rushed headlong into a party of women.

They were not gypsies: they were dressed in white aprons and starched headgear. They looked at me askance, then turned away, averting their faces from me. They were the women of the secretive College of Makers. I'd not seen them in their garb since the last Ceremonies. I wondered how to address them. I remembered their vows of silence. I weaved through them towards the cabin; then I halted, appalled.

A black-clad woman stood guard before the cabin door. This was no sun-blackened gypsy, but one of the City's own women, fallen in league with them. Her face was fat, her pallor deathly, her eyes invisible in the black shadows cast by her protuberant eyelids. In her pudgy right hand she wielded the usual rod of office – red and silver tassels concealed the barbed teeth of rusty nails.

Other women – elderly and emaciated, true sisters of the desert – came out of the cabin, laden with portfolios and plaster casts: Blythe's workings. They bore them across the gravel drive and threw them like so much rubbish into the back of a waiting wagon. I edged into the front row of the silent white-aproned women. I caught the eyes of one or two: saw tight lips, tear-sparked eyes.

'Please,' I begged one next to me, 'where's Miss Maravell, is she safe?'

The woman turned her back on me.

I turned to her neighbour. 'I'm her friend,' I explained, 'she wanted me to meet her.' Again I found myself shunned.

I lost my patience: 'Will one of you tell me what's going on?' I shouted. The women gazed at me. Distrust was written on every face.

'Is she all right? Do you know? It's all I want to know.'

One of the Makers at last relented: 'If we knew where she was, she'd be with us.'

A black-clad woman crossed the drive towards us. Her boots snapped and slipped on the gravel. 'Move along,' she ordered us.

The Makers held their ground.

'You've no business here,' said the black-clad woman. 'Piss off.'

'They've every right,' I said.

More black-clad women descended the cabin steps, their arms full of Blythe's roughs and proofs. They stopped and stared at us.

'What are you?' the virago demanded of me. 'Their matron?' Her fellows cackled at this.

I looked round at the women of the College of Makers. I was not the Makers's spokesman, and I had no right to assume the role. My reason for being here was not the same as theirs. They were making silent witness to the sacking of their temple: I was simply looking for Blythe. There was nothing for me here. I weaved through the silent sorority, away from the cabin, back the way I had come. The Makers said nothing: the black-clad women jeered.

Forlornly, I retrieved my father's gown and donned it, thinking of Blythe.

2

A lone bugler – a thin shivering boy in blue pantaloons – squawked. We followed him down Green Monkey Street to the Circus of Birds.

There was no lewdness this time, no laughter, and too few of us to make a real procession. Fear of the black-clad women had kept many away.

Above us, mobiles swung and creaked in the wind: rats, locusts, cockroaches, shark skulls; dog-headed giants. Some of the older children pointed up at them in black delight. The younger ones shivered and averted their eyes and clung to their mothers's skirts. Black flags snapped above our heads. We sipped wine from blessed dishes. It was not the raw, heady stuff my parents had enjoyed; special herbs were steeped in it, making it thin and bitter.

Every few yards or so, one of Stock's pale young men stood atop a firkin, naked but for a loincloth and a blue wig, dispensing the day's poetry. They were marked about the breast and thighs, smeared with corrosive paints and nicked here and there so that their bodies were striped with little trails of blood. I had been inclined to lampoon these young men before, but their dedication now was undeniable: Binns had prepared them and set them upon their tubs in accordance with ancient and disturbing advices.

There was no music. Instead, Binns had strung wind-chimes along the wires supporting the mobiles. The chimes were fashioned to an old design: resonating tubes were hollowed from the bones of gulls; the leaves that struck them were copper lozenges, each cut to the shape of a miniature skeleton. The sound these chimes made was soft and dull, more like insect talk than human music.

We came to the Circus of Birds.

A dais had been built around the three great legs of the scaffold. Around the dais, with its praying posts and paper altars, the City's flags waved in the air: shadows scudded across us, sharp-edged, as though they had been etched into the light.

I walked around the dais, noted the inscriptions chiselled into its wooden sides, the posts with their paper streamers and blood-stained bases, the ritual knives hung from them on black twine. I looked out for Dr Binns, but no-one seemed sure where he was. I spoke to two or three of Boris Stock's young men, but only one of them knew Blythe by sight, and he had not seen her all day.

I thanked him and continued my search.

Through crowds I glimpsed an old friend.

'Boris!'

'Welcome to the wake!' he greeted me; disgusted, he gestured at the sparse numbers gathered around us. He was wearing a cloak of foil and red silk. Beside him stood Edwin Gross: He had left off his poncho and had bound his pony tail in the traditional black ribbon; but otherwise he looked as he looked every day.

'Have you seen Blythe?'

'Should I have?'

'I can't find her.'

'She'll be with her college sorority.'

'She isn't; I asked them.'

Boris was surprised: 'You spoke to them?'

'They didn't know where she was.'

'They were lying,' said Gross. 'They're famous for it.'

An old woman came over to us and offered us the silver scrap-bucket. I remembered it from my childhood. We each dropped in a scrap of paper; I tore mine from my father's booklist.

'Mr Kemp!'

I wheeled round.

Mr May scooted up to us, wobbling dangerously on cherry-red Tacking skates. He had assembled his costume from the wardrobe of his theatre: calf-length knickerbockers stitched over with peacock feathers, a lace shirt open to the navel, and a woman's fur jacket. He stood up on his points and offered me his hands. 'And to think,' he said, 'that you had never choreographed a show before! Mr Kemp, I am made! There's never been so successful a season in the history of erotic theatre. Now I want to make you a small business proposition ...'

Once the bucket had done its rounds, the shivering bugler squawked twice. We came to attention.

On cue, out from behind the dais came Dr Binns. He was barefoot, his head encased in a mask massed over with wild flowers and artificial feathers. His gangling body was swathed in brightly dyed silk scarves; they fluttered pennant-like in the breeze so that he resembled some great, gaudy, flightless bird. He had saved the day's rudest and most barbaric role for himself. In the authenticity of his gestures depended the success of the day, and he had been rigorous in his researches and preparations.

He ascended the dais and prepared for his dance, standing before us on one leg, his arms outstretched for balance.

He hopped once. Twice. Then he crouched on one leg, the other extended before him to balance his protruding rump – and hopped again. Some of us laughed; others winced. This ugly, comical dance seemed strange to us: the product of some faery realm. It was hard to believe our ancestors had invested these poor, ungainly gestures with such magical significance.

Binns balanced on his other foot and repeated the operation. We stared in silence, aghast at his painful progress about the stage. One by one, Binns shed the fine silk bandannas bound across his chest, tossing them into the audience. A murmur went around the bemused audience as he shed a snowy-white scarf, revealing nipples rouged and pierced through with fine copper wires: Binns had followed the edicts of the ritual to the letter.

'Dear me,' breathed Mr May.

'Shhh!' I hissed (for silence was part of the ritual).

White-aproned Makers climbed up onto the dais, bearing a great wooden frame tied about with a large black flag. They set it before the provost. Another Maker came on, bearing the bucket of paper scraps. She hung it upon Binns's outstretched hand and withdrew, genuflecting as the ancient books demanded. Her sisters untied the black flag and whisked it from the wooden frame. The crowd gasped and stepped back. Suspended from the frame's corners by ropes of cyan velvet, Blythe's fearsome Iron Fish trembled as though it were alive.

Above the Fish, hung upon the cross-piece of the wooden frame, were the ritual utensils used in the preparation of the paper scraps – the fish slice, pepper mill and so on. Binns took them down, one by one, made the required gestures and passes, and restored them to their hooks. He stepped back, raised the bucket and shook its contents into the mouth of the Fish. He put down the bucket, and flung out his arms, pushing out his chest and his hips – an expansive, abandoned gesture – and clapped his hands: his right hand struck the head of the Fish; the left, its jaw. With a rasp of sheathed steel, the needle teeth slid together and locked shut, sealing our scraps inside.

The Maker women ascended the scaffold once more. They loosed the Fish from its frame and bore it over to the scaffold. They fastened the Fish to a thin iron chain by a ring in its snout, then drew back.

With another ugly, painful dance, Binns crept over to the scaffold and turned a handle set into one of the legs. The Fish rose into the air.

An agitated murmur swept over the crowds. Mr May tapped me on the shoulder and pointed behind us.

To the west, where the Folded Rose Hostel squatted like a spider among a web of filthy back streets, a great column of smoke rose up. Another fire? I wondered – then I saw how much more serious the business was.

On the horizon, a black line was forming: line upon line of gypsy women had gathered on the hill. The breeze changed direction, and carried to us the distant snap of their tin drums. The line thickened and spread: they were descending Green Monkey Street towards us.

All around came cries of panic, confused instructions, prayers. The crowd surged forward. I staggered: in front of me, a woman with a baby in her arms fell sprawling before the dais. Mr May and I fought to lift her to her feet, but the pressure of the crowds behind us drove us from her. We listened to her screams.

For a second we held our ground; the next, we were borne

back, sprawling, against the dais. I forced myself around to face the stage. Fists and feet battered my back and thighs. I fought for purchase, punching and tearing my way up onto the dais, but before I could turn and help up Mr May, someone seized me by my trouser belt and dragged me backwards across the stage. I glimpsed the crowds. Seized by sudden panic, they screamed and flailed against the side of the stage. I saw them fall: others, unable to resist the human current, trampled upon them until they too were crushed. Mounting the pile of dead and injured souls, the crowds broke over the top of the dais and rushed over the boards towards me.

My rescuer let go of me and pulled me to my feet. 'Tom!'

It was Henry: he laid hold of me again and shoved me at the scaffold.

'Climb!' he yelled; 'Climb, for God's sake!'

Wailing crowds swept the dais. I fought my way through to the nearest leg of the scaffold and scampered up the frame: Henry followed close behind. Beneath us, the crowds were milling about too fast and too blindly for others to lay hold of the scaffold. Henry and I were on our own.

'Keep going!'

I scrambled up as fast as I dared, past buckets and funnels and jagged spars and spikes. The scaffold narrowed. A few feet above me hung the Fish: it swung about, clanging against the sides of the frame. The press of the crowd beneath was shaking the whole scaffold. I wrapped my arms around the frame and clung there, shaking, till at last Henry came level with me. He was unused to such exertion: pale and trembling, he fought for breath. His pupils were dilated with fright.

'Are you all right?'

Henry took tighter hold of the spars and shut his eyes: 'I feel sick,' he moaned.

'You're safe now.'

'I can't stand heights.'

'Where's Blythe?'

'I thought she was with you.'

'I couldn't find her.'

'She wasn't – down there?'

'Not that I saw.'

Henry shuddered. 'Thank God.'

I did not tell him what else I had seen: her house and workplace ransacked. There was no point in upsetting him. I turned as far as I dared and watched the gypsy women descend through Green Monkey Street.

Their cloaks swished about them as they marched. Some blew kettle whistles; others thumped fish-pans. Still others swung spiked sticks about their heads.

While the front rows beat and bashed at their pots and pans, work parties busied themselves unhooking and demolishing the mobiles, flag-poles, barrels and other ceremonial furniture; they piled it like refuse into carts and wheelbarrows and drew it with them into the Circus, where already the club- and torch-wielding women were embarked upon a hundred atrocities. They threw flaming rags through the windows of the tenements and charged the swarming populace, kicking and trampling the injured where they lay.

The crowds were fleeing from the Circus of Birds, into the maze of quiet alleys leading to the embankment. The general tumult ceased, replaced by the wailing of the gypsy women; a child's screams, brutally cut short; the groans of the dying and the injured.

'We must flee!' Henry cried.

I looked down. The vanguard of the black-clad women was forcing a path towards the dais for their wagons and their barrows.

'There!' Henry cried, 'there's Mr May!'

I glanced where he pointed, and saw Mr May wheeling about the Circus, wobbling wildly on his Tacking skates, arms out-flung, as his wheels caught and slipped about on the shallow cobbles. His tactic seemed to be to move too fast for the women to catch up with him, though many tried, enraged perhaps by his wild costume.

'Let's go after him!' We clambered down off the scaffold and dismounted the dais. Keeping to the lee of the gypsy procession, we picked our way round the outskirts of the Circus, past the piled dead: some had no mark upon them, others were so trampled as to be unrecognizable. There was one girl, so mangled and twisted in the stampede it was hard to recognize her as having been a living thing at all; only her hand moved, fluttering and flapping as though it would have torn itself from her doomed body. Nearby, a young man staggered about, blood spouting from his neck in arcs; he moved slowly and deliberately, gazing all the time upon the splashes he made, as though he were painting some curious design upon the pavement. When it was over, he lay down on the ground, gently, as though he were putting himself to bed, and slipped silently into a final sleep.

The black-clad women had left off their bloody attacks and were converging on the scaffold. We had abandoned our eyrie not a moment too soon: they mounted the dais, howling and swinging their sticks, and beat at the ancient frame. A sonorous clanging filled the air. The Circus trembled in sympathy with the scaffold: it shook like some gelatinous mirage.

'We must stop them,' Henry exclaimed, and started forward.

I went after him: 'Don't be a bloody fool,' I said, pulling him back, 'you'll be cut to ribbons!'

Mr May shot past on his skates, swung around and came to a dead stop before us. 'Mr Kemp! They're pelting the Fish!'

The women were prising cobbles from the square and throwing them at Blythe's magical sculpture. Stones dented the delicate scales. The Fish swung wildly on its line, a clapper in an avant-garde bell.

The women's battering of the scaffold grew more determined. The noise increased. The tenements around us pulsed and slid about us like sun-stroke dreams. Their glassless windows contracted and dilated like sphincters. Doorways clattered and nibbled at the air, mouth parts of a massive crustacean. The ground undulated. Here and there a cobble cracked open. Blooms emerged: bright blue, chrome yellow. Their feathered fronds puffed foul-smelling pollen. Shadows took on solid shape and slid eel-like across the ground, lost-seeming, as though time had abandoned them.

'I'm not feeling very well,' Mr May moaned, rubbing at his eyes.

Suddenly, from the top of Green Monkey Street, there came a great cry. We turned towards it.

'I don't believe this,' Henry said.

I simply stared, open-mouthed. 'Oh dear,' said Mr May.

A party of ancient and terrible warriors, some fifty or sixty strong, barrelled down Green Monkey Street towards us.

Some wielded great battle-axes, swinging them round their heads as they ran. Carried by the momentum of their weapons, they swerved and swept from one side of the street to the other. Others carried broadswords across their backs, loping easily down the cobbled street, as confident and terrible as angels of death. Some swung great hammers; still others long-bows and hunting arrows slung in quivers across their backs. They were dressed in skins and furs, bound with leather and with iron chains. At their head, upon a grey gelding, rode a huge shaven-headed dominatrix. Her head was bound with a gold band, her arms decorated with bronze amulets. In her right hand she hefted a double-headed axe. Its serrated blade glinted wickedly as she rode.

The whoops and wailings of the terrible host echoed across the square; all of us – the innocent and the black-clad alike – froze for a moment, petrified, not knowing what to make of this outlandish scourge.

The host charged into the Circus – and dashed pell-mell at the black-clad women!

'A miracle!' cried Mr May: he jumped up and down; in his excitement he had forgotten he was wearing skates. He slipped and fell to the ground. 'A miracle!' he groaned, half-concussed.

The black-clad women, overpowered by the young Gods come upon them, broke ranks and fled, wailing, to the corners of the square. The warriors gave chase, spurring each other on with gales of scornful laughter. Their weapons were superfluous – their presence was enough to fright their enemies – and so they pulled their blows. With the rough good-nature of ancient heroes, they spared blood-shed, chasing the frighted gypsies merely, and slapping them with the flat of their blades. I watched in amazement as they clouted, tripped and kicked the black-clad women from the square. Their empress, meanwhile, reined in and dismounted before the dais. I ran towards her. Henry called out a warning: I ignored him.

'Great Queen!' I began, and fell to my knees before her, afraid to meet her gaze; if this was some magical power released by our authentic Ceremonies, perhaps it could tell me where the Fishmaker was. 'I beseech thee …'

'Oh hello,' the warrior Queen declaimed, in a familiar tremolo, 'Kemp, isn't it?'

I looked up at her. 'Good God,' I said.

'What's the matter?' Madame Pompadour demanded; without waiting for an answer she turned away and surveyed the square. One by one her charges gathered around her grinning and chuckling and swinging their great weapons about them as if they were mere toys. Madame Pompadour counted them all in like a schoolma'am gathering her class: 'Billy, Eustace, Devlin – *where's Devlin*?'

'He went to take a leak.'

'Who with?'

A chuckle went round the assembled company.

A slender girl ran up and threw her weapon to the ground before me. It clattered woodenly against the cobbles. I picked it up and stared at it. It was a stage prop. Close to, it bore only the crudest resemblance to a broadsword. But from a distance, I supposed, and with the benefit of surprise and terror and a great deal of operatic hallooing and yodelling—

'When those women find out who you really are,' I said, my voice still shaking with shock, 'they will bash your brains out.'

'Oh, don't be such a spoil-sport,' said a man with full moustachios, unbuckling his cardboard helmet. 'We're not going to wear this clobber any longer than we have to. Though between you and me,' he confided, as he shrugged off the belts holding the skins round his waist, 'I'm surprised our ruse paid off at all. But we had to do something.'

I stared about me, astonished by the casual gallantry of the company. What on earth had prompted this highly strung coterie to risk their lives in this way? It was extraordinary; it was admirable.

Someone patted me on the shoulder. I turned. A thin, lined face smiled me a greeting: a woman, wearing a wide silk choker. I swallowed hard. It was Maera LaCouche.

243

'Miss LaCouche—' I mumbled. 'I never expected you – if only Mr Nye were alive to see this!'

Maera opened her mouth and made a sound – a strangled hiss. Her face contorted with pain. She shrugged, and smiled again.

Her larynx was broken; she could not speak.

3

We saw to the injured as best we could. It was some while before I was able to speak to Mme Pompadour again, and ask her about Blythe.

'Certainly I saw her,' she told me, 'last night, at the Opera.'

'The Opera? What business had Blythe there?'

'The provost was with her, I think. Yes, I'm sure it was him.'

'*Binns?*'

'Why yes,' said Mme Pompadour. 'Is there some problem?'

'What were they doing?'

'Talking. Inspecting the building.'

'Had they just arrived, or were they leaving?'

'Arriving, I think.'

'Did you see them leave?'

'*For heaven's sake,*' Mme Pompadour exclaimed, her patience worn away by my interrogation, 'what's this all about?'

'She's been missing since morning.'

'And you suspect Binns?'

'Not until now,' I replied, mysteriously: I went off in search of Henry. It was he, however, who found me first: he waved to me frantically from across the square.

I ran over to him. 'What's up?'

'That friend of yours Edwin Gross is about to get himself lynched, is what.' He led me to the edge of the Circus; a knot of people, yelling and gesticulating, had gathered there. Mr May broke from them and came over to us on stocking feet: he had taken off his skates and had slung them by the laces round his neck. 'Mr Kemp! I've never seen such behaviour! Sickening! Quite sickening!'

244

Henry ignored him and led me through the irate crowds. They had seized Edwin Gross and pinned him, bloody-nosed, against a wall. At Gross's feet lay a body, wrapped up in a cloak of foil and red silk.

'Stock?' I knelt down. 'Boris?' Henry hunkered down beside me and drew an edge of the cloak to one side, revealing his face. One side of it had swelled out of recognition, where it had been crushed.

My heart skipped a beat. Boris, dead? At the sight of his ashen face, a young man in the crowd broke into tears. I glanced up: it was one of Stock's coterie. In the extreme pass we had come to, the youth's brief costume of loincloth and wig appeared cruelly comic: he hid his nakedness as best he could with his hands, and let his tears run unchecked down his face.

Mr May pushed his way through the crowd. 'I saw him!' he yelled. 'I tell you I saw him! With his hands in a dead man's pockets!' An angry murmur went up. Gross's assailants pinned him tighter against the wall and May rummaged through his coat. 'Here!' He drew out a handful of paper bills from Gross's inside pocket and waved them in the air. There were shouts and threats; the crowd began closing upon their hapless captive.

'He owed it to me!' Gross yelled in desperation. 'I knew him. He owed me money!'

Mr May waved the bills under Gross's nose and snarled at him.

'Mr May!' I went over and seized the bills from his hand. I threw them into the air. The crowd grabbed for them. Their grip on Gross relaxed: he wrestled free, but did not run. Affecting disdain, he ignored his captors and dusted himself down where he stood.

'Mr May,' I said, 'I am amazed!'

'Beg pardon?'

'You, the head of a lynch-mob!'

'I saw him!'

'Save your oratory for front-of-house.'

'I did!'

'Look!' I said. 'Your henchmen are even now scrabbling for the money they say Gross should never have touched.' Sure enough, fights had broken out among the crowd. 'At least Mr Gross was owed it.'

'How do you know?' Mr May retorted.

'Boris Stock owed everyone,' I replied. 'And Edwin Gross is – well, Gross is what he is. Now stop these charades and come with me to the Opera: I suspect a kidnap. You too, Edwin, unless you want a rope round your neck: you're safer out of here. Henry?'

Henry, who had all this while stood, arms folded, smiling wryly at the episode, came up and offered his hand. 'Handled like a true moralist,' he congratulated me.

But there was no time for his customary irony. I said, 'It's Blythe.'

At the name of his cousin, Henry's smile vanished. 'You know where she is?'

'She and Dr Binns were seen walking around the Opera last night.'

'You think it's significant?'

'I don't know,' I admitted, 'but I'm not sure I trust Dr Binns. I'm off to the Opera, and you?'

'I'll certainly come with you.'

'I shall gather some men!' Mr May yelped.

'For God's sake, no!' I exclaimed. 'Mr May, what has come over you?'

It is said that we are only ever three meals away from barbarism; but Mr May seemed to have exceeded even this pessimistic prediction, turning from anxious pornographer to vigilante chief in a matter of minutes: it was unnerving.

We ascended Green Monkey Street. Henry and I led the way: Edwin Gross and Mr May followed, locked in fierce, though whispered, argument. It was not until we reached the top of the street that I registered the sounds that had, since we had started our walk, been building in the troubled air. I had thought at first they were the whisperings of Binns's wind-chimes, forgetting of course that the gypsy women had torn them all down. Anyway, the sound was more musical than any the chimes could have produced …

Henry glanced into the air. He caught my eye. He was worried. 'What do you suppose it is?' I asked him. He shook his head.

'Perhaps the Ceremonies are having an effect.'

'Maybe,' he said, unconvinced.

'Oh fuck off!' Edwin Gross screamed.

Mr May blanched.

'Fuck off and shut your mouth. You didn't know him. You have no idea what he was like!'

'Oh for God's sake,' I groaned, 'isn't it enough that Boris is dead?'

'It's no way to treat the deceased,' Mr May declared.

'You weren't his friend,' said Gross.

'And I ain't yours, neither,' said May, with a look of disgust. He paused, head cocked: 'What's that sound?'

We turned and looked down Green Monkey Street towards the Circus of Birds. It was as we had left it. Along the embankment, however, the air had begun to shimmer: odd lines, gradated and regular like the etched circles of a Frennel lens, bled in and out of view. Through this curious disturbance, the road bridge flexed and pulsed, in counterpoint to the unearthly music ...

Henry said, 'It's the bridge.'

'An illusion,' I said, 'surely.'

'No,' he said, dead certain. 'The bridge is, what, half a mile away? Taking into account the time it takes for sound to travel, I'd say what we see and what we hear match perfectly: we're listening to the bridge.'

'A storm?'

'It might explain the odd flux of the air.'

'Then maybe Binns's Ceremonies are having their effect, after all!'

'I don't see why you say that,' Mr May grumbled, 'if the Ceremonies were working, they'd work upon the Circus of Birds first. That's where the Iron Fish is, after all. If it's the bridge making that noise, chances are it's those bloody women, pulling it down.'

This was not a prospect any of us wished to dwell upon. We walked off in silence. I led the way past the Sé and through the open gates of the Goldsmith's gardens, thinking to take my compatriots along the shortcut Boris had shown me, years ago; it would be quicker and safer than the streets.

It brought back too many memories for me: more memories than I could possibly handle.

Mr May and Edwin Gross were arguing again.

'Shut up!' I screamed at them. Henry laid a calming hand on my shoulder. I shook it off. 'Don't you dare bicker here, either of you.' My rage astonished them: even Gross, whose belligerence was legend, seemed awed by it. 'Now – come along!' I said, in the school-masterly manner Boris Stock had sometimes used with me …

Everything seemed calculated to remind me of him.

The Opera was filled with refugees from the Folded Rose Hostel: children, invalids, mothers with babes at the breast, women in shawls and shifts, barefoot boys, impoverished gentry, their stained cravats all askew, with jackets torn and grubby or no jackets at all. They had taken refuge in the Opera's huge basement, among the props of countless shows: old men lay sprawled on antimacassars; around them ran urchin children, waving bits of dentist's apparatus over their heads. A young woman sat with her back against a blood-drenched altar; beside her a young man had made himself a bed from three stuffed ostriches. A fairground booth rocked and wobbled as its occupants turned and shifted in troubled sleep. Tramps had gathered round an ornamental fountain and sat flicking matches at the statue at its centre.

The more resourceful of the refugees were making primitive shelters from whatever came to hand: an igloo, a set of garden furniture, rolls of carpet and canvas, a pile of gates and palings, pallets stacked with turfs and tiles, even sections of wall.

Framing the scene; so tall it nearly touched the vaulted ceiling, stood a triumphal arch: from its shadowy interior came the groans of the injured and the dying.

The smell was excruciating: I fought back my revulsion and stepped between the makeshift pallets. Some of the invalids were horribly burned: the gypsies had torched the whole parish. Others had been trampled in the ensuing riots. A few had bloody heads, struck down by the women's sticks.

I found Miranda bent over the furthest pallet. She had laid her head upon Wilhemina's breast. Her shoulders shook beneath the sheer cream tissue of my mother's dress.

248

I knelt beside her and laid a hand on her back. She shuddered and clung tighter to her mother.

'Miranda,' I said, gently, 'Miranda, look up. Miranda, it's me. It's Tom.'

She did not move.

'Please look at me!'

She lifted her face. She showed no surprise at seeing me: the cruelties she had witnessed had dulled her mind. Her face was a mask of misery, flushed and wet with tears. There was blood over the front of her second-hand dress, where she had Iain across her foster-mother. No sight had ever pained me, or touched me so deeply: not even the sight of my mother on her deathbed. 'Miranda.' There was nothing I could say. I turned to view the corpse.

The women had spiked Wilhemina through her lungs: She had died, slowly drowning on her own blood. Pinkish foam rimmed her lips. I used the edge of my gown to wipe it away. I hesitated – would Miranda resent it, if I kissed her mother, whom I had so badly used? I took my chance, leant down and brushed my lips across her cheek. Her skin was still warm. As I drew away I stroked my fingers down her eyelids, closing them.

'They said we were trash,' Miranda sobbed. She took hold of my arm and tugged at it, feverishly. 'Trash, and fit for burning!'

I took her into my arms and held her tight, letting her tears soak into the folds of my father's gown.

'Mr Kemp?' May came stumbling in among the dying.

'What is it, Mr May?'

'Henry says he can find no trace of Miss Maravell; he wants you to help him.'

At the familiar voice, Miranda loosened her grip on me. 'Uncle!' she gasped, through her tears. She flung herself into his arms.

A pang shot through me: well, let Mr May comfort her. No doubt he had been a better friend to her, and for longer, than I had ever been.

'Good God,' said Mr May, no longer the vigilante chief, but the anxious little man that I remembered. 'Wilhemina?' He looked from her to me.

I shook my head.

He sighed heavily and took tighter hold of the weeping girl.

I threaded my way out from under the shelter of the triumphal arch.

'Tom!' Henry shouted at me, coming out from behind a stuffed elephant, 'stop dawdling!'

I bit back a bitter retort: he did not know what I had just seen. 'Has anyone seen her?'

'No-one, but a stage-hand tells me he saw Binns.'

'Where?'

'Back stage.'

'Doing what?'

'No-one seems to know.'

'Come on,' I said, and led Henry up the stairs and into the wings of the theatre. 'You go that way, I go this. Try every door. If they're locked, break them open.'

'How?'

'Ah.' I had not thought of that. We cast around for some tool to use as a jemmy. 'Perhaps that May person should have gathered us up some help, after all,' Henry said.

'Wait,' I said, 'this is getting us nowhere. The stagehands downstairs should be able to help us. See if you can gather them up. I'll meet you back here in ten minutes. I've a hunch I want to follow up.'

'Well don't be long!'

I set off through the wings and found myself in a large, bare, high-ceilinged room used to store flats during scene changes. I crossed the room: a naked bulb mounted on the wall cast fitful shadows of me over the ceiling and bare plastered walls. Ahead there was another door, larger than the first, and at the end of another corridor, a narrow staircase with an intricate wrought iron handrail. I climbed down and came to a fire door. I shot the bolt back and swung the door open. Beyond lay a corridor bathed in cold electric light; along the walls lay piles of bricks, sacks of sand and plaster, lead piping, old wiring and abandoned tools.

It was as I remembered it: even the clutter appeared familiar. This was the place in which I had last run Dr Binns to ground; and it had occurred to me that he might have brought Blythe here last night.

I walked down the corridor, looking for the ancient arched opening that gave onto Binns's magic room. The doors I passed were new, drab, and all exactly alike. One of them stood open: I looked inside at the mops and rags and tin buckets stacked within. It was the broom cupboard in which I had been incarcerated. Binns's magical bungling—

Dizziness swept over me. I staggered and fetched up against the opposite wall. I had thought at first, the door to the cupboard was ajar. It was not ajar. There was no door.

Of course there was no door.

Now I knew where Binns had hidden Blythe. Cursing my stupidity, I pelted back the way I had come.

There was no sign of Henry back-stage. I took the steps into the cellar four at a time. 'Henry!'

To search him out in all that chaos of prop and refugee, would be a hopeless task.

I shouted blindly into the hall: 'Gross! Mr May!' Strangers's faces turned towards me; no-one responded.

I had no time to waste. Binns had Blythe hidden where no-one but me would ever think to look for her. Only I could get her back.

I ran from the Opera, racking my brains for details of the cruel rite Binns had mentioned: the Fishmaker, immolated on a pyre of ceremonial junk. That much I remembered. I remembered, too, that the pyre was constructed in the Circus of Birds, opposite the dais. But I knew little else: not the time of the torching, nor the precise rites that accompanied it. There was little I could do but reach the Circus as fast as I could and look for opportunities as they arose.

4

Urchins scampered back and forth across the Circus of Birds, picking over the dead. There was no trace of a pyre: I was in time.

251

When the moment arrived, who would build the pyre? Not Binns on his own, surely. And if he had helpers, they were likely to be hostile. I needed a place to hide. I crossed to the window Of a nearby tenement. The interior was obscured by swirls of green paint applied with a rag like whitewash. The sill was rotten. I took off my right shoe and used it to smash the window. I looked around. The urchins weren't interested in me. I swept the shoe along the edge of the sill, knocking the final shards free, and climbed in.

Most of the floorboards were torn up, and the walls between the rooms were knocked through: part of some long-abandoned renovation. To hide here was to invite a twisted ankle, or a nail in the foot. I stepped from joist to joist towards the staircase and climbed carefully: some of the treads were missing, and there were no banisters. The next floor was more comfortable. I chose my lair – it had been a child's bedroom – and gazed out at the Circus of Birds.

The urchins, laden with coats and boots, retreated from the Circus, melting into the alleyways and secret places of the City. Little by little, the black-clad gypsies returned – in dribs and drabs at first, and then, when no ancient warriors emerged to challenge them – in greater numbers. They went about the Circus, retrieving their carts and barrows. They drew them into a circle opposite the scaffold and tipped their cargo – ceremonial lumber, bunting, festive cloth – into its centre. From it they built a tall bonfire. Up one side of the pyre they laid a crude ramp, with panels torn from shattered mobiles.

Last, they formed a human chain leading from the last full wagon to the top of the pyre, passed up the final load from hand to hand: bundles of paper and canvas, with here and there a plaster cast, a wooden frame, some ironmonger's tools: debris stripped from the Fishmaker's cabin.

Around the edge of the pyre other women had collected; they were dressing the skirt of the pyre with bunting and flags. They were not gypsies: they wore white habits—

White habits? It took me a moment to accept the evidence of my eyes. They were Makers. The Makers were in league with the gypsy women!

Binns must have converted them to his plan: now they were helping him perform this cruel rite.

In a sense, their complicity made more sense than the gypsies's. What could have induced the gypsies to work with Binns? A mere love of bonfires?

The Makers walked around the pyre with buckets and tossed what looked like water over the cloths, soaking them.

Water? I shivered. No: spirits, most likely.

When they were done, the Makers lit pitch torches and took up their places round the pyre, waiting for a signal. The gypsy women climbed off the pyre and moved to a safe distance, towards the scaffold, behind the pyre.

I watched closely. They were nearly out of sight. Now if only the Maker women would join them ...

From the shadow of a tenement on the opposite side of the Circus a figure emerged wearing the distinctive ermines of the Academy provost: Dr Binns, come to sacrifice the Fishmaker, as in olden times.

Behind him came two women in white, bearing between them a door, its handle and hinges still affixed.

Dr Binns climbed up the ramp to the top of the pyre;

the Makers followed close behind him. They set the door upright on the pyre's summit. I squinted: on the door was stencilled the legend:

STRICTLY OUT OF BOUNDS TO CONTRACTORS

AND LOW PERSONS GENERALLY

The Makers held the door by its hinges: Binns walked round to the other edge, where the handle was, and swung the door open.

Where the door had been, there floated a disembodied black rectangle: a magical window into a vast, ill-lit interior.

There was movement in the darkness; a figure stumbled blindly towards the light.

I hammered on the glass: 'Stay back!' I screamed, forgetting my danger, 'stay in there!'

But she could not hear my warning.

Released at last from the prison Binns had conjured for her, Blythe stepped into the light.

253

Binns swung the door shut behind her, and the disembodied black rectangle disappeared. The Makers took up the door again and dropped it carelessly down the side of the pyre. Blythe squinted into the smoky daylight, stunned and confused. But before she could defend herself, or even realize her danger, the Makers flung themselves upon her. Whipping off their white aprons, they bound her hands and feet. Blythe seemed so overawed by the scene around her, she made hardly a move to defend herself.

Binns stood by, watching greedily, rubbing his nervous, snake-like hands. His skull-like face and horse's teeth glowed in the etched light of the Circus. When Blythe was bound, he drew the belt from round his provost's gown and strung it between Blythe's bonds, tying it so tight that Blythe was bent back upon herself, her hands and feet nearly touching; unable to move.

Their tasks complete, Binns and his two assistants descended the pyre.

At the same time, the rest of the Makers set their torches against the pennants at the pyre's base, and a curtain of flame rose up.

There had been no opportunity.

Not one.

Cursing, I stumbled to my feet and flung myself out of the room, down the stairs, and over the bare joists to the ground-floor window. I clambered onto the sill and paused, waiting for my moment. Could I get to the ramp without the Makers seeing me?

Just then the rotten sill gave way, tipping me onto the pavement.

I froze where I fell, watchful, frantic, wishing myself out of sight. But the women were retreating from the flames, too taken up with the pyre to have noticed me.

Now Binns stepped clear from the pyre; a handkerchief pressed over his mouth, he emerged from the encircling smoke. His assistants followed close behind him.

I tensed, waiting my moment. If only Binns and the Makers would follow the rest of the women, and step directly away from the pyre, towards the centre of the Circus ...

But even as I thought it, Binns chose to walk the other way – towards me; the two Makers followed in his train.

Any second now they would spot me, sprawled across the cobbles. I had to make the first move. I glanced from Binns, to the pyre, to the retreating Makers. There was still an opportunity: in a moment, the fire would hide Binns and his companions from the rest of the women: it would be my only chance.

Seconds dragged by. Binns turned his head towards me, turned away, turned back again, quickly, surprised—

'Binns!' I screamed, and flung myself towards him.

Binns stared at me, astounded.

I struck him full on the mouth. His teeth split and sank into my flesh. My knuckles sang. He went tumbling. I sprang at the Makers. They had plump, comfortable-looking faces: I struck out at them. They were not used to brawling: they screamed, bloody-nosed, and scampered.

I had only a minute, maybe less, before they returned with black-clad reinforcements.

Binns was feeling inside his mouth with his handkerchief. I snatched it out of his hand. It was blood-stained. I covered my mouth and nose with it and ran towards the ramp. But Binns, with an energy I had not suspected, leapt to his feet and bolted after me. Just as I attained the ramp, he grabbed my legs. I went down. He tried to pin me to the ground. I fought him off. I grabbed him and hauled him upright. 'Binns, you sickening little man, stop this farce!'

He tried to reason with me. 'My dear Kemp!' he wailed through bloodied lips, 'can you not detect my craft?'

'Butcher!' I shouted, and struck him in the mouth once more, to finish him off.

Binns ducked and bobbed up again like a puppet on a spring, grinning through broken teeth. 'I told those black-clad bitches we're betraying the Ceremonies!' he screamed, 'but you and I know the truth, don't we, Tom!'

I stared at him. 'You murderous, obsessive old bugger,' I yelled. I took hold of the collar of his jacket and propelled him up the ramp. A coil of black smoke enveloped us. I staggered, choking and retching: I had dropped the handkerchief. Binns pulled free, turned and shouted something I didn't hear, his form silhouetted against the spreading flames. I came after him. He kicked my shin out from under me. I was too frantic to feel pain: I got up and charged at him again. He staggered back and fell into the fire. I climbed past him, past the ring of flame and onto the centre of the pyre. Through streaming eyes, I looked about for Blythe – but I had fatally misjudged the speed of the fire: but newly lit, already it had become well-established. The smoke grew blacker, the flames higher; the fumes were suffocating.

Dr Binns howled and clambered about in smoking surf. He sprang up, his gown aflame, and reached out to me, a supplicant; his hands scorched and black with soot. 'For God's sake, Kemp!' he howled. 'I was only following the instructions!'

'You're worse than they are,' I shouted. I pushed past him. A roiling bank of smoke drove me back up the ramp. I swallowed a lungful of the acrid stuff. I went dizzy. I fell to my knees.

Binns, his gown still aflame, attained the ramp. He rushed at me and started kicking me repeatedly in the backside. 'Stupid brat,' he screamed, 'leave her be! It's a necessary thing.'

The wind changed direction, the smoke cleared for a moment and I caught my breath. I crawled away from Binns's boot and got to my feet. He tried kicking me again. I caught his foot and twisted it. He grabbed me as he fell: we plummeted off the ramp together, onto the cobbles. Here the air was a little clearer. Binns was sprawled beside me, wailing, nursing his ankle. 'Kemp!' he screamed. I got up and stamped on his knee. 'It's necessary!' he screamed at me. 'We have to burn the Fishmaker. We're making the world anew!'

'I don't want the fucking world.' I leaned over him and I bawled: 'If this is what we have to do, I don't fucking want it.'

Just then, someone in black shoved past me, bent down and struck at Binns's head with a spiked stick. Binns's eyes burst. He shuddered once, and lay still.

The black-clad women had arrived to save their atrocity.

The gypsy put her booted foot on Binns's forehead and levered her stick free. The nails in her stick scraped against his eye-sockets.

She turned to me. 'Right,' she said, and swung.

Blood ran like syrup into my eyes. I bellowed and charged

blindly at her. I heard her curse and fall – over Binns perhaps. I rushed on, too frightened to stop, tripped up at last and rolled to a stop. I lay winded for a moment, then sat up, stunned, and tried to clear my eyes. The soot on my hands stung fiercely: painful tears washed the blood away. I had fallen only yards away from a deep and sheltered portico: I crawled inside and watched from the shadows.

The pyre, well alight by now, and unapproachable, cast its smoke to heaven.

I burst into tears. There were not words to express my loneliness, or my self-hatred.

I had failed my friend. I had not saved her. I had made mistake after mistake. I had not taken Binns seriously enough. I had let myself be fooled by the telegram. I had rushed precipitously from the Opera, when I should have called for help. I had arrived early at the scene and done nothing to prepare a rescue. I had hesitated, minute after minute, until it was too late. I had dropped Binns's handkerchief and swallowed smoke. I had allowed Binns to distract me: I had wasted precious seconds beating him – or not beaten him enough—

The list was as futile as it was endless. It took me so long to enumerate my many, mostly illusory mistakes, when at last I came to my senses, the fire had gone out.

All wood and paper, it had consumed itself with appalling appetite. Only a few structures were remotely recognizable. The charred wooden skeleton of a giant, a flag-pole, a door—

It swung open.

A figure emerged.

I looked about the Circus.

The gypsies were gathered on the other side of the Circus, upon the dais. They were gathering underneath the scaffold.

I scampered from my hiding place to the edge of the pyre. From out a slanting black abyss, an ashen body crawled. It hesitated at the smoky edge of the magical portal, blinking tears.

'Blythe!' I hissed.

The figure looked at me. She was still gagged.

I struggled out of my father's gown and pulled at it, tearing free the stitching around the folds. When the gown was unravelled, I gathered it up and, holding tight to one edge, I threw the bundle up towards her. The gown unravelled like a rug. I used it to protect my hands as I clambered over the steaming wreckage.

Blythe struggled further from her magical sanctuary. I saw that, while her hands and feet were still bound, she had somehow freed them from Binns's belt: more than that, she had slipped her legs through the circle of her bound arms, so that now her hands were in front of her. She chewed at the apron bound round her wrists.

'Blythe!'

She glanced up at me, smiling with her eyes. I reached the end of the gown. I gathered it up and threw it again, and clambered up to her.

Her hands came free. She clambered up onto the magic door, bent down and untied the bonds round her feet.

I grabbed hold of the edge of the black pit and pulled myself up beside her.

She had not bothered to remove her gag. I untied it for her. 'Tom.' She kissed me.

'Behind us,' I panted. 'The gypsies are at the scaffold.'

'Gypsies?'

'Black-clad women. There's no time to explain. Careful as you climb down.' I gathered up the gown again and tossed it over the spent wreckage of the pyre. 'Let me help you.'

She hardly needed my assistance. We ran cowering into the shelter of the portico and peered out. No-one had seen us.

The gypsy women's attention was all on the scaffold. One of their number was turning an iron handle set into one of the tripod's legs—

'How did you free yourself?'

'I'm more supple than they gave me credit for.'

'Your years of Tacking.'

'That and panic. Finding the door still worked was pure luck. Tom, where are the Makers?'

Among the dead strewn around the square lay women robed in white. In my shocked reverie, I had missed their slaughter. Like

Binns, they had outlived their usefulness to the gypsy women; like him, they had paid the ultimate price for their collaboration.

Blythe shuddered. 'That's the last time I accept a public commission.'

'Look: the scaffold!'

The handle turned, the chain rattled; the Iron Fish descended from its eyrie.

5

D r Binns had thought he could make a deal with the gypsies. He had thought that the execution of the Fishmaker would satisfy their lust for destruction. He could not have been more wrong. The Iron Fish – and with it all hope of the City's rejuvenation – was the women's ultimate target. No pretty distraction Binns threw in their way could distract them from their first purpose. It was better, perhaps, that Binns was dead – he would never have to know how misguided he had been, nor how bitter a failure his bloody ruse had proved.

The Iron Fish swung on its line, tapping the sides of the scaffold.

The Circus trembled in sympathy. But these were dying shudders; magic's death rattle. By the time the women laid hold of the Fish, the Circus had ceased to tremble.

It stood: still, grey and ordinary. A square, like any other in the City.

A dry and dusty wind swept the enclosure, bearing sand from far away. Once the City had been protected from desert blasts: it was protected no longer. Now its magic was destroyed, how would it survive the relentless winds, the furnace-like days, the bitter, freezing midnights?

I imagined the City a hundred years hence, bereft of all its sustaining enchantments. Salt breezes no longer played among the harbours. The gulls had disappeared from the Quiet Lake, and the Lake itself had dried to a muddy puddle. Desert traders squatted in the doorways of abandoned coffee houses, genuflecting hourly towards the cracked dome of the Opera in barbaric prayer. On the other side of the City, their children were brutally employed, carving great cisterns from the rock where there had once been allotments. Goatherds drove their flocks to market through the colonnades of the Baixa ...

Dysentery and starvation ravage the populace annually. Winter storms and summer fires whittle away the carved fronts of the City's municipal palaces, sweep through the Folded Rose Hostel and lay whole tracts waste. Adobe and dry stone replace lost porticoes and trellises ...

The gypsy women unfastened the Fish from its line and laid it on the boards of the dais, at the bottom of the scaffold. Some of them climbed off the dais and went down a side-street; a few minutes later they returned with buckets, brimful with some black, tarry stuff. They poured it in a broad circle around the edges of the dais, then clustered once more underneath the scaffold. A lone woman walked to the edge of the platform, struck a match and dropped it onto the sticky ring they had poured round themselves.

A bank of pale flame leapt up over her. Her costume caught and burned furiously in the blustery, desert wind. Sheathed in flame, the woman staggered back to her brethren.

She sat before them, an example, a model for them to emulate – giving herself up to immolation.

The air filled with the stench of creosote. The fire spread round the black ring. The women stayed watching their blazing sister. They did not try to save themselves.

Not content with destroying the City, the Fish, and the future, they were destroying themselves: true to their desert-sprung, millennial beliefs, they had thrown themselves upon the fire.

The dais burned and smoked and died. The wind curled round the tenements once more and disappeared. The pitiless desert sun burned down upon the Circus: grey, drab, undone, unmagicked. Its loss of vital power was palpable; in spite of the heat Blythe and I found ourselves shivering.

'What happens now?' Blythe asked, as we walked up Green Monkey Street, away from the Circus.

'I don't know,' I said.

'What did your father's books say?'

'They spoke of what ceremonies to perform: not what would happen if they were forgotten.'

'Maybe it'll be all right,' Blythe offered, seeking comfort. 'I mean, the Iron Fish was stuffed and hung, wasn't it? Isn't that enough?'

I shook my head. 'The Fish is supposed to corrode. We are supposed to eat the paper scraps as the wind carries them away.'

'That's part of the original ceremony?'

'Every book said so.'

'And now?'

We were arguing in circles. I offered Blythe my only other thought: 'My father knew, I think, what would happen.'

'What did he say?'

I thought back to the day he had walked with me down Green Monkey Street. 'He didn't say anything,' I replied. 'He just went white.'

There was music in the air – the same music Henry and Gross and Mr May and I had noticed, hours before. Too much had happened since for me to take much notice of it, but—

Too much.

Too much had happened.

I took my watch out of my pocket. It was still working.

'Blythe.'

'What?'

I swallowed. 'It's night.'

'I don't understand.'

Of course she didn't. She had spent hour upon hour incarcerated in Binns's lightless prison. She was bound not to have any idea of the time.

But for the rest of us—

I wondered numbly if anyone else, shaken by the day's events, and newly warmed by this incontinent desert weather, had bothered to look at the time. And if they had, what had they made of it?

I tried to keep the panic out of my voice. I failed. 'It's nearly eleven.'

'At night?'

'Yes.'

'Your watch—'

'Is running perfectly.'

'Your watch—'

'It's not my watch,' I insisted. 'It's the sun. The sun's stopped.'

Blythe stared at the sky. 'Tom,' she said, 'what's that noise?'

We turned.

The bridge was yawning, stretching its great arms as it leaned into the warming sun.

It was not a man, but it had learned to move like a man. It dropped its arms to its sides and peered at us over the tops of the houses.

'Tom!' Blythe cried, 'it's your doll!'

I nodded, numbly. I did not know what she was talking about.

'Tom! Don't you recognize it?'

I turned to Blythe, distracted. 'What was that?'

'Your doll. The one you showed me. The one you made as a boy. It's buried in the bridge's heart!'

'Yes,' I said, 'it is the bridge. I think.'

'Tom, you're not listening.'

I wasn't listening: the bridge was moving towards us.

It did not step, or slide, or flow: it moved. And as it moved, it changed. It somehow ceased to be the bridge. It towered above us, higher than the hills of the City itself, higher than any structure, than any thing in our little world. Higher than mountains – and made of dressed stone.

It moved again. I blinked. It was no longer stone. It was brick: a gigantic human tenement, with windows for eyes, a door for a mouth – it moved.

At last my eyes began to grasp what they were seeing: the giant, almost-human form approaching us was not something discrete: it was a wave. Nothing moved, but, like the individual droplets of a sea, it bobbed and bounced as the wave passed it. The metal bridge had bobbed and bounced, and then the stone embankment, and then the brick tenements, and then—

The man-like wave reached the Circus, and stopped. The giant was not metal now, or stone, or brick. It was cloth. Bright button eyes – one green button, one blue, were sewn with bright yellow thread into a face of bright pink panty-hose. Thick clumps of horse-hair framed its head, spherical as a football and as smooth.

'It's my doll,' I said, as slow on the up-take now as I had always been.

'Tom, what does it mean?' Blythe demanded. 'What does it do? Tom, you must remember!'

I blinked at her. The words came to me, unbidden: ' "Through this the sufficiency of the world – "'

'What? What? What's it supposed to mean?'

'Of the world – of the world – is made manifest.'

Blythe cried out in jubilation. 'Tom! It works! Don't you see? It's working!'

I shook my head. My doll? It couldn't be. 'I laid it in the bridge before the last Ceremonies,' I said. 'If the ritual worked at all, it would have worked then.' But even as I spoke, I knew I was wrong.

'Tom,' Blythe laughed, 'don't you remember? *You put it in the wrong place*! Only when we climbed the bridge together, years later, did you put it where it belonged. It's been waiting there, all these years, for this day! Tom? What's the matter?'

Something horrible had occurred to me.

'Tom!'

I said, 'I'm a damnable fool.'

'Why?'

'Binns discovered the doll ritual for himself. I told him I'd tried it, that it didn't work. That's why Binns went on looking for other rituals. If I'd only thought what I was saying, he might never have thought of torching you ...'

But Blythe was not listening. She was gazing at the doll. 'Tom,' she said, 'it's turning real.'

I looked up.

Its lips were of some dry, reddish fibre. Its skin had taken on the smooth pallor of connective tissue. Its eyes glistened, fibrillating painfully about the yellow tendons sewn through them. Waxy tissue oozed round the edges of each socket, setting brown and resinous, making for each orb a set of makeshift lids. Great spines broke through the resinous skin; lashes for huge, increasingly realistic eyes.

The giant opened its mouth: sunlight caught row upon row of needle teeth, not much different from the teeth of Blythe's Iron Fish, but smaller and more sparse.

It gaped at us, mouth open: a shocked, mutilated 'O'. Inside the mouth, which was at least as wide as the Circus itself, and behind the needle teeth, each high as a house, pulsed a blackness so intense, it was more the negation of light than its mere absence. The blackness was compelling – magnetic – irresistible—

'Tom!' Blythe cried, 'the shadows! *It's eating the shadows*!'

Time itself, and light, and distance, seemed to fracture and coalesce. Great snakes of dark weaved through the Circus and the street like solid things. They sprang into the air, wiggling and spiralling – then vanished, drawn down into the monster's black gullet.

For a moment the sky was a mass of black squiggles, as though a frustrated artist had splattered the City with ink from a paintbrush. The next moment, there was no black, anywhere. Where there had been blackness, there was a hazy grey, like paper smudged with pencil, or an old tram ticket.

'Tom.'

The world shook.

We looked around us.

The street was empty. So was the Circus.

Blythe blinked. 'It swallowed itself.'

'And the shadows.'

'Itself. And the shadows. And …

'What?' I asked her. 'What else did it swallow?'

Blythe shrugged.

I studied the street, the Circus below. Blythe was right. It had swallowed – something else.

The sun beat hot upon me. I wiped my forehead with my hand.

I took my hand away.

I stared at it.

I flexed it. The pins in my fingers squeaked.

'Blythe.' I did not dare look at her. 'I'm plastic'

'Meaning,' said Blythe. Her jaw snapped and creaked like a mannequin's. 'It's swallowed meaning.'

The Circus pulsed and trembled, became a living thing again. The guttering of the tenements shivered and pulsed: blood vessels, webbing an intestine. All down Green Monkey Street, the doors clacked and trembled, splintering and reforming until they resembled the hungry beaks of octopi. Around us, the windows bloomed and contracted: a hundred polyps, feeding on invisible food. Street lamps waved in the wind like the dismembered feelers and mouth parts of marine insects. The roofs of the tenements buckled and slid against each other, till they resembled fins, spines, scales: the brittle insignia of warlike creatures of the sea. Lichenous, wind-weathered mouldings decorating the walls of the tenements slipped and fell, became green carapaces, the shells of horseshoe crabs.

The cobbled street disgorged black juice: it steamed wickedly in a light grown timeless and diffuse.

I looked up. There was no sun any more – just a yellow bleed on the sky, and not a bright bleed, either; far from being a source of illumination, it looked as if it were a painted thing, some pigment, or sac of pale fluids. As I looked, the sky shrivelled and gradated, a skein of honeycomb tissues, between which a soft blue cream was smeared, as if for lubrication.

If ever my childhood suspicions needed confirmation, they had it now. This city was no city; nor was the world the world, but rather some great whale, and we were but the self-deceiving flotsam in its belly.

'Look!' Blythe cried, and pointed at the sky. Two birds were mating on the wing above serrated, nibbling roof-tops.

'And there!' Oblivious to the metamorphosis gathering pace around them, a gathering of rustics stood about the street, applauding a smiling, heavily built boy: he was holding a fiddle, it dangled like a toy from his massive paw.

'There!' Behind us, over the tops of the gutted tenements, a great face rose up, framed in a kerchief made of chimney smoke: a woman's face in brick, with pools of stagnant water for its eyes. Two great hands swam into view over the horizon, with

265

apartments for knuckles and bridges for bones and tram lines for tendons, running taut under a skin grey and wrinkled like old newspaper. In one hand the woman held a box of matches, in the other a match. She struck the match and disappeared in a flash of pale fire.

'Blythe!' Satyrs scampered across the street, shooting arrows into each other's hearts.

'Blythe, we've seen all this before!' Barely five feet from where we stood, two silhouettes – one black, one white – folded themselves out of the air: they scampered off in opposite directions.

The City was replaying itself.

In eidetic glimpses, it remembered the maritime fantasies of its bargees, the pictures of its artists, the violent nihilisms of its gypsies, the fancies of its children—

It was dying, and its life was flashing before its eyes: ours with it.

A thousand different scents filled the air: distinct, sharp and pungent, as though sprung fresh from a chemist's bottle: boiled cabbage, dead chrysanthemums, semen, charred insulation, patchouli, bird dirt, chalk dust, soil, sun-dried tomatoes, ink, linseed oil, cut grass, blood; the taste of my own skin flooded my mouth, and for a moment I had the nauseous impression that I had swallowed myself whole.

Suddenly, without any warning, the whole pulsing structure of the City-whale skewed, faltered, glowed with an inner light, rebuilt itself in golds and greens – no more now than a romantic geometry, a cream and yellow dream, it evaporated even as it registered upon the eye.

Colours bled to white, and left behind a charcoal sketch. The charcoal bled, grew smeared and simple—

Stick-figure towers, scrawled in crayon by a child!

The City's great game was over.

Free of itself at last, and empty of all meaning, it screwed itself into a ball and threw itself away.

EPILOGUE

There is an island, set in the midst of a great ocean. Down the centre of the island, running north to south, there is a railway.

All night the goods trains creak into the railway station at the island's capital, and out again, on an unpredictable course over a maze of tracks sprawling uncertainly between the wharves and derelict loading bays of the old harbour.

The station is a draughty eggshell of steel and glass, a bubble of crude modernity. Passengers do not linger there; they prefer to cross the street and wait for their trains in the Café Terminal. The Café is a much older building. It is huge; the old ceilings have been torn away so that the walls are over twenty feet high. Massive fans of polished wood hang from the ceiling: they turn sluggishly in the smoke and steam-laden air.

The dead come here sometimes. They like this place: it reminds them of the old city. Some of them remember the Café Persil. Others are reminded of the Bar Terminal; they shy the metal eagle on the bar with pretzels until asked to leave by a frosty *maitre d'*.

I had an appointment here last night with two old friends. I arrived to find them already seated. The first was an old man with a ruddy and distended face. His eyes did not focus properly, but he was aware of everything: a characteristic of the dead. Beside him sat a dapper, petit young man in a vanilla suit; his blond hair had been quaffed back with hot tongs. He turned to me and I stared into the bloody pit where his left eye had been. 'Hello, Tom,' he said. His smile was mischievous – he meant to frighten me.

We drank coffee and talked about the past. I said, 'Did you really love me?'

'Yes,' said Allingham, 'but it was a long time ago.'

Blythe arrived not long after. 'Allingham!' She smiled: 'how are you?'

'Dead,' Allingham teased her, sweeping back the hair from his empty socket.

The sufficiency of the world had been made manifest. Everything our city was, had been and could ever be, existed now at one and the same moment. The dead had returned; the street maps were unreliable; actions and their consequences eddied about each other in dream-like patterns.

'They say that eventually things will achieve a stable state. Then, perhaps, we will be an island people, dreaming of the desert!' Only Allingham found the notion entertaining. For C.L.S. and Blythe and me it was a reminder that, while our little world might once more seem sufficient, it was not, nor could it ever be, the Greater Realm we had dreamt of as children; that given world of snows and deserts and foreign places – and space, endless space.

Blythe and I had decided to leave the island.

'It seems a shame,' said C.L.S., 'that you must go so soon.'

'We have always sought the Greater Realm, Tom and I,' said Blythe. 'Now we have a chance to find it. Our world is soft and pliable. It is like a new-born thing – its shell is soft. Perhaps we can break through.' C.L.S. sighed and shook his head. 'Such optimism! The longer I consider the matter, the more likely it seems that this little place is all there is.'

I felt my blood rise. 'Such thoughts lead to despair,' I retorted, 'as you well know!'

C.L.S. turned blood-shot eyes to me and smiled, sardonically. 'So?' he said. 'Perhaps, in the end, despair is all we have. Perhaps, after all, we really are only puppets on a trivial stage.'

I shook my head, not because what he said was impossible, but because I could not be both puppet and human. I said, 'You expect me to be content with this lot; but if I am human, I cannot be content. Such discontent can never be said to be fruitless, because my being human depends upon it. A moth that is unwilling to burn itself in a candle flame is not a moth.'

C.L.S. and Allingham Nye exchanged glances and burst out laughing. C.L.S. reached over and clapped me on the shoulder. 'You were a worthy pupil, Tom, after all.'

I smiled blankly, not understanding him. 'What an aphorism!' Allingham chuckled. 'I must write that down.'

But I was out of temper. 'If you had been content to be a puppet, C——, you would not have put that rope around your neck.'

C.L.S. stared at me; we both knew the part my past mistakes had played in his demise. Anger blackened his already distended face.

Allingham patted his old teacher gently on the arm. 'Calm yourself,' he soothed, 'don't be upset. He is alive, remember. The living must make their own choices.'

C.L.S. screwed up his face in disgust. 'And aren't you sick of it? It's that same ridiculous cycle, over and over again: remake the world, get bored with it, knock it down, build it up again, over and over and over. Will it never end?'

But Blythe, who had been quiet all this time, came to my defence: 'It can end in one of two ways,' she said. 'In escape, or in death.'

Allingham and C.L.S. exchanged uneasy glances. 'Death's not so bad,' said Allingham, but his tone did not convince.

'Fucking heck!' With a bellow of coarse laughter, Stock stumbled up to our table and sat down between C.L.S. and Blythe. Broken bones slithered and snapped inside him.

Blood leaked from his ears. 'Listening to you lot does my head in sometimes,' (an unfortunate metaphor that, since it was indeed half-crushed). 'You tangle yourself up in the daftest knots.'

'Oh God,' said Edwin Gross, falling into a chair at a neighbouring table, 'what pearls of nil-rhetoric'

'All I meant,' said Stock, with a hurt glance at his companion, 'is, well, look around you! The world's sufficient again. So why can't we all be happy and content? Let's eat, and sleep, and swive, and be done with it!'

'A philosopher speaks,' Gross sneered.

'Who's getting the drinks?' asked Stock. Gross scowled and slunk away to the bar. He did not ask us what we wanted: it was bad enough that he was still paying for Stock. Death was no barrier to the burdens their friendship placed on his pocket.

Evelyn Christ approached the table. His throat had been torn out with a spiked stick on the day of the Ceremonies. With his usual humility, Christ had tried to conceal the injury with a plain grey cravat, but the lips of the tear poked above the material, a gaudy addition to his otherwise nondescript appearance. 'I do believe, Mr Gross, that Mr Stock's words, if I caught them rightly, have a deeper import than you allow. If I may presume to catechize, it seems to me that, thanks to the astonishing chance occurrences that have befallen us, we now have a chance to embroil ourselves in a whole new life; let us then find the meaning we seek in the round of our daily lives. Let us embrace all these changes to our world, and make ourselves at home here.'

Stock reached over the table and punched me on the shoulder, crunching the bones in his wrist. 'You see, lad? Everything's working out okay. Don't think so much. *Oubliez les anges!*'

A party of workmen at a nearby table looked up from their Calzone and grinned, vacantly; '*Oubliez les bossues!*' they bellowed in unison.

> Oubliez les anges,
> Oubliez les bossues,
> et partout,
> Oubliez les Professeurs!

C.L.S. and Allingham prepared to leave. The dead dislike rowdiness. But before he left, C.L.S. came and stood between Blythe and me and put his cold hands upon our shoulders. 'My friends,' he said, 'if you truly mean to embark on this mad errand, it is possible I will not see you again. By the time you return – if you return – things will be more settled. The dead and the living may no longer share a table, the way they do now. So let me give you some parting advice. Look for a door, by all means. Look for a Greater Realm, a better life. But do not look for explanations. I can say these things to you because I am dead; dead people know a thing or two, believe me.

'There is, at the heart of things, no meaning. Meaning is a quality, not a thing in itself. It cannot be held in the palm of your hand. It cannot be distilled. It cannot be mapped. Meaning is, if you like, a half-opened door, through which one cannot enter. There is nothing of use behind that door, but it is the nature of living things to prise and pull and lever at that door, in the hope of finding – what? Another room, perhaps, and at the end of it, another door, teasingly ajar? Would we ever be satisfied? Would we ever cease to tug at those doors? Of course not! The meaning of our lives is that we lead them. The rest – my friends, my children – is ashes in the wind.'

With these words he left us, and Allingham followed close behind. They did not look back.

Not every part of the City had been transformed. Some parts – the duller, more ordinary parts – had returned unchanged. The wide, empty, wind-blown streets around the canal looked as they had always looked. Dead leaves circled about piles of builder's rubble. There were still no children in the playground Blythe had sketched so many years ago.

Once I'd thought this was a haunted place – but I'd been wrong. Its eeriness sprang purely from its emptiness: there were not even ghosts here. We turned up the street to Blythe's grey, box-like apartment building. It looked much as it had always looked; the cracks in the walls were wider, perhaps, but that was all. Her rooms were crammed with easels and paintings, catalogues and sketchbooks, paints, pigments, thinners and oils – every tool of the trade imaginable. It had not taken her long to restore to chaos rooms Mrs Cowie had so memorably cleared out.

There was so much here that pertained to Blythe's work, I wondered that she had had time for a life. But that, of course, was the point: Blythe had applied her life to her work, totally and without compromise, the way C.L.S. had done, at least when I first knew him. It seemed ironic to me now, that I had left off my friendship with Blythe, whose life as an artist was just beginning, to be the plaything of an artist in decline. I felt instantly at home in this place. Here, shaped and defined by Blythe's personality, was the rigorous environment I needed – but, as so often, I had missed my opportunity.

'Come on through,' said Blythe, stepping into the small room which was her bedroom and private gallery.

Her pictures of beggar women were still hung on the walls – prints: Mrs Cowie had burned the originals. They were not so startling as they had been. The mutation of the City had softened their composition, reinterpreting Blythe's originals with a charitable eye. Around them hung other subjects, from other projects. Each reflected some facet of Blythe's private world.

'What is it, Tom?' Blythe said, shouldering her bag of paints and paper, her notebooks and her rags.

I realized I was crying. 'I've missed this place,' I said. I looked at her. 'I've missed you.'

She put the bag down, came over to me and put her arms around me. I squeezed her tight. This time she did not pull away. She whispered, 'Oh Tom! It is so good to start a new adventure!'

I did not know what she meant: whether the journey, or our friendship, or something more – and I realized, as I held her tight against me, that it did not matter. We were connected, she and I: by intellect, by knowledge, by human sympathy; yes, and by chance. It was by chance, after all, that she and I had saved the City.

As a consequence, some alchemical bond had been forged between us. We had no name for it. We could not call it love; not yet. But it seemed to herald love.

'It's time to go,' she said, and letting go of me, and taking up her pack, she led me out the apartment and into the mellow evening.

It took us several hours to negotiate the harbour, with its complex network of channels and dry docks. Blythe insisted that we stop now and again so that she could sketch the cranes. Huge container gantries on rubber wheels taller than a man dominated the skyline; but it was the old cranes that interested her more.

They had been botched and refitted so many times for heavier and heavier loads, they resembled gigantic dustbins with pipe cleaners sticking out of them. Then there were the abandoned things: lengths of pipe, rusted pumps, signs so eaten away we could only guess what they once said. For a while it seemed that we would never get away, that Blythe would after all find this reconfigured city enough for her needs.

But I misjudged her: by dusk, we had reached the coast. A chill breeze blew in from the sea. I unstrapped my rucksack and from it I took the blanket my mother had made me for the journey. Even beyond the grave, she gave: I took.

We unfolded the blanket and wrapped it around us, so that it shrouded us from the wind. We walked in silence for a while. The tide was coming in. We walked to the water's edge. Behind us the sand grew silvery in patches, and purple and turquoise where it reflected the sunset. The sun had sunk below the level of the dunes. The sky there was an uncertain shade, part green, part pink, hard and delicate like porcelain.

Silhouetted on the skyline, among the dunes, were two low roofed buildings; against the wall of one, in red neon, a sign flashed: AMUSEMENTS. We turned our back on it.

There was no sound but the surf.

I said, 'Is that the moon?'

There were a few small clouds out to sea, creamy with reflected light. One of them was almost circular. As we watched, it grew brighter, as if lit from the inside: then the moon burned through.

The cloud was like a halo, the white of an eye, and the moon was its glistening pupil. Beneath the eye, there was a sailing ship, and its sail was the same creamy colour as the cloud. It was heading inland.

We walked along the beach to meet it.

We knew it was for us.